DONE DIRT CHEAP

AMULET BOOKS
NEW YORK

DONE
DIRT
CHEAP

SARAH NICOLE LEMON

Dedicated to Sabrina, for sharing a dream.
And to J, for bringing coffee without me having to ask.

PUBLISHER'S NOTE: This is a work of fiction.
Names, characters, places, and incidents are either the product of the author's imagination
or are used fictitiously, and any resemblance to actual persons, living or dead, business
establishments, events, or locales is entirely coincidental.

Library of Congress Cataloging-in-Publication Data

Names: Lemon, Sarah Nicole, author.
Title: Done dirt cheap / Sarah Nicole Lemon.
Description: New York : Amulet Books, 2017. | Summary: Tourmaline Harris and
Virginia Campbell, two teenagers from opposite sides of the track, join forces
to overthrow the people in their southern Virginia town who exploit them.
Identifiers: LCCN 2016042024 | ISBN 9781419723681 (hardback)
Subjects: | CYAC: Self-actualization (Psychology)—Fiction. | Family
problems—Fiction. | Criminals—Fiction. | BISAC: FICTION / Thrillers. |
FICTION / Crime. | FICTION / Contemporary Women.
Classification: LCC PZ7.1.L4446 Do 2017 | DDC [Fic]—dc23
LC record available at https://lccn.loc.gov/2016042024

Text copyright © 2017 Sarah Nicole Lemon
Book design by Alyssa Nassner

Published in 2017 by Amulet Books, an imprint of ABRAMS.

Printed and bound in U.S.A.
10 9 8 7 6 5 4 3 2 1

Amulet Books are available at special discounts when purchased in quantity for premiums
and promotions as well as fundraising or educational use. Special editions can also be created
to specification. For details, contact specialsales@abramsbooks.com or the address below.

ABRAMS The Art of Books
115 West 18th Street, New York, NY 10011
abramsbooks.com

"*Where you come from is gone,*
where you thought you were going to never was there,
and where you are is no good unless you can get away
from it. Where is there a place for you to be? No place . . .
Nothing outside you can give you any place . . .
In yourself right now is all the place you've got."

—Flannery O'Connor, *Wise Blood*

FEDERAL *Bureau of Prisons Institution Supplement, U.S. Penitentiary Hazelton: Visitors are not allowed to bring property, packages, food, cash money, checks, money orders, lottery tickets, negotiable items, or any other items through visitation. Visitors who attempt to give such items to offenders will have their visit terminated and lose their visiting privileges.*

Underneath the hem of Tourmaline Harris's pink gingham button-up, a pair of wool socks were hidden—one in each back pocket. Coils of silver barbed wire glinted in the sun, and the flags heralding the gates of U.S. Penitentiary Hazelton clanged against their poles.

This was a test.

A dry run. An effort to push back against the guilt shackled to her for pushing a fallen queen into hell—when she'd called the police instead of her father, and they'd taken her mother away. Here the guilt always felt like a thing. A living thing. Like a slick, leaden thing stretched flabby and amphibious across her shoulders, with bitter-tasting fingers hooked into her cheek, leaching sour down her throat.

And on the first day of summer break—while Anna May and all her other friends were sleeping in after graduation, escaping sentimental mothers, and meeting for brunch—Tourmaline walked into a federal prison with socks hidden in her pockets and the taste of guilt on her tongue.

The windowless prison door slapped shut, sealing her inside a small holding room. A corrections officer—CO—sat behind a Plexiglas wall. "ID," he said without turning, voice hollowed and distorted by the speaker.

Tourmaline dropped her driver's license into the silver tray, blinking as her eyes adjusted to the elaborately locked wire gate in front of her.

This had seemed like such a solid plan at home—put the socks in her pockets, walk through security, and hand them to her mother when the guards weren't looking. Now that she could no longer go back, her stomach twisted. This could go so wrong. What had she been thinking? If it were only socks, this would be easy. She'd turn right around.

But it wasn't socks. It was supposed to be, eventually, the methadone prescription they wouldn't let Mom have in prison. It was Granny's corn mint and palmarosa salve for that rattling cough Mom always seemed to have. And Mom wasn't in a maximum-security federal prison because she was an addict. She was there because of *Tourmaline's* mistake.

A buzzer shrilled. The gate unlocked. The wire door opened, silencing the buzzer, and a bored-looking CO waved her forward.

Too late. Tourmaline shook her head and shoved her license into her pocket. Her fingers trembled, but she tucked her long blond hair behind her ears and followed the CO into the abyss, keeping her gaze on the middle distance as she passed the wall.

The wall—a trophy wall, covered in cheap printer ink, copier paper, and clear tape. Grainy mug shots were plastered on the concrete, right inside the gates, greeting each visitor with a pyramid of sullen faces belonging to those banned for smuggling something inside.

Somehow what she was doing seemed different. She was different.

The wall did not differentiate between honor roll teenage girls who hid socks in their jeans with nothing but good intentions and people who stuffed little beige balls of heroin in saran wrap up their asses.

Having her picture taped up right alongside the bad and the actual worst would be almost as terrible a consequence as not being allowed back to see her mother. Tourmaline did not want to bring any record or reminders of where she came from along to the University of Virginia in the fall. She did not want to see her student ID and think of *that* picture on *this* wall, as if she existed here first.

The guard turned down the hall.

Tourmaline followed.

Everything was quiet, save for the wild heartbeat slamming in her ears. The floors were freshly mopped, and the odor of bleach was in every breath. The hall led away in both directions, alternately dark and light with the kind of fluorescence that was supposed to resemble daylight.

The CO waited behind the metal detector. Lauren Hayes was her name, not that Tourmaline would ever call her that. It was hard to get used to the guards, the gossip, and the feeling of a small, suffocating town crammed inside the concrete.

Tourmaline fought the urge to nervously swallow, stepping through the gates as Hayes waved her forward.

The alarm stayed silent. Only a few more steps to go. Tourmaline held out her hands.

Hayes grasped her fingers—blue gloves powdery on Tourmaline's skin as she swiped the cloth across her palm and down her trigger finger. The chemical checking for gunpowder didn't trigger, and the CO tossed the gloves in an empty trash can.

This was it. All Tourmaline needed to do was stay calm and sign in, and she would have the safety of standing with her back to the concrete wall. The first major hurdle would be over. She waited, fighting to look as if she weren't fighting at all.

Hayes tugged on new gloves. "What's in your pockets?"

At first the question didn't register. But the creature on her shoulders whispered and Tourmaline heard. *She knows.*

Tourmaline tried to breathe, but there was no air. Her cheeks grew hot and she opened her mouth, shaking her head because no words came out. Why hadn't she thought of this? Why hadn't she thought about what to say if she was caught?

Hayes's boots thumped a heavy step closer; leaning in so close Tourmaline could see sparkles in her purple eyeliner and taste the hint of onion from the bagel Mom said Hayes always ate for breakfast. "This is a serious offense," she said, so low it might have been a whisper.

"I—" Tourmaline took a step back, drawing in a deep breath. "I couldn't get hold of anyone. I called fifteen times last month, and no one would even talk to me. I tried to ask."

Hayes's features remained hard.

"I'm sorry. I'm so sorry. I didn't know. I didn't mean to." Tourmaline pulled the socks out of her pockets and shoved them away.

Hayes pinched them between her gloved fingers and tossed them into the garbage.

Thirty-dollar no-itch merino wool socks with reinforced toes and heels dropped into the plastic liner.

"Per the guidelines, your visit today is now terminated." Hayes peeled off the gloves and tossed them into the can on top of the socks. "You will be receiving an incident report detailing this event, at which point you can appeal to restore your visiting privileges."

What? Just like that? Tourmaline looked wildly to the doors beyond the gates. Mom was expecting her. Expecting the graduation pictures and the change to buy snacks and a Diet Coke while sharing prison gossip she'd stored. "I'm *banned*?"

"You must leave the premises, immediately." Hayes pointed down the hall.

"No. No, this can't. I just graduated. She's—" Tourmaline's breath caught.

"Generally, minor violations will result in a banned period of three to six months." Hayes clamped fingers around Tourmaline's upper arm, guiding her toward the exit.

Tourmaline wrenched away automatically, not thinking she was resisting, though she realized too late that was exactly the word they would use for it.

"*Please.*"

Hayes stopped, her voice lowered. "Honey, if you do not allow me to escort you out of the building right now, I'm going to have to arrest you for trespassing on government property."

The creature cinched its webbed fingers around Tourmaline's throat, choking her. How could she have done something so stupid? So stupid. And now she wouldn't see her mom before college.

Her body followed her thoughts, and Tourmaline didn't realize she was moving backward, toward the gates, until Hayes reached behind her back.

The world slowed to a stop.

"Interlace your fingers behind your head."

A sob hitched in Tourmaline's throat and her hair fell over her shoulders, sticking to the sweat on her forehead as she obeyed. The handcuffs clinked cold, but loose, on her wrists.

"I'm not arresting you, but if you don't walk out like a lady, I'll have no choice," Hayes said. Knuckles dug into the middle of Tourmaline's back and they began a slow, awkward walk down the same quiet and bleach-tinged hall.

"I can't be banned," Tourmaline whispered. "I'm leaving for school."

"Your visiting privileges are terminated for attempting to smuggle contraband into the facility."

"It was just—" Tourmaline started.

Hayes's mouth twisted into something almost sad, and she talked over Tourmaline crisply, avoiding her eyes. "The Facility Unit Head will provide a written explanation to you and a copy to your mom, including notice of the length of the ban. If you desire, you may submit a written request for reconsideration to the Facility Unit Head within thirty days, providing additional information of extenuating circumstances. They'll schedule a hearing."

That would take *weeks*. Everything to do with prison went slowly. She wasn't going to get to see Mom until Thanksgiving break, unless she made a special trip and missed school. And how was she going to help now? If she got caught again, she'd be banned for life. Tourmaline tightened her jaw and tossed her hair out of her face, trying to keep from crying.

"You can't claim you didn't know and expect to get by," Hayes said. "If I were you, I'd start paying attention to what's around you."

Tourmaline froze.

Hayes leaned close to Tourmaline's ear, whispering onion into each word. "I hear Wayne Thompson is looking for you."

Wayne had gotten *here*? Heart racing, Tourmaline twisted in the cuffs.

They stood at the end of the empty hall. Alone. Facing a closed door cut out of the concrete block.

What did Hayes know? Was it something Mom needed to tell her and couldn't, now that Tourmaline wouldn't be there? The guards seemed to know everything that went on—except when it had anything to do with administration. "He's locked up," Tourmaline choked out, trying to catch her breath as Hayes unlocked the cuffs. "In Virginia."

Hayes swiped her badge and pushed open the door. The breeze gusted inside, thick and smelling of hot asphalt, ruffling her short ponytail. She gave Tourmaline a pitying smile. "Careful."

SOMETHING told Virginia Campbell that Tourmaline Harris was the type of girl to arrive even to *prison* exactly on time, which meant Virginia was late.

Keeping a hawk eye turned to the thin streams of people flowing into the prison, Virginia sat on the truck bumper, thighs perched off the broiling chrome. If she had to wait until visiting time was over, she might as well get breakfast. Frowning, she glanced at her phone, looking up just in time to catch Tourmaline huffing against the flow of people in the parking lot.

The moment was so perfect it was as if Virginia *hadn't* planned it. "Tourmaline?"

Tourmaline—pretty, blond, blue-eyed Wonder Bread–with–margarine girl, despite her father's reputation—turned and gulped like a goldfish wearing Lilly Pulitzer. "*Virginia?*"

Virginia smiled and pushed off the truck.

In all her years working for Hazard, Virginia hadn't once crossed paths with the Wardens of Iron Gate, but she *knew* plenty.

When motorcycles roared past her on the road, she'd seen the empty-eyed stare of the horned and crowned skull sewn on the backs of the riders' leather vests. She'd heard their stories told like ghost stories—cloaked in fog, late into the drinking hour. She'd heard of their appetites. How their tires ate up the road and spools of darkness tangled in their spokes, sucking up damned souls and women alike, like air for the engines.

Thanks to Hazard, the secretive motorcycle gang was now her secret to gather. *Make friends* was the order. For what, Virginia didn't know. She'd been too focused on the how. Hazard hadn't said outright, but he'd sucked his lip and looked her over in a way that was plenty clear enough. It was a testament to Hazard that he'd waited this long to use her to her best advantage.

Maybe he'd waited too long. A year ago, she wouldn't have balked, and she wouldn't have ended up six hours from home, trying to lie her way into Tourmaline Harris's life.

Virginia tossed her waist-length dark hair behind one shoulder and drew herself up to her full five feet ten inches. "Well, you're the last person I expected to see. What're you doing? Some church thing?" As if she and the rest of their small high school *hadn't* followed along on that whole fiasco Tourmaline went through with her mom.

"No. I— What are *you* doing here?"

"What else? Visiting unsavory relations." Virginia pulled a cigarette out of a pack and squinted in the bright sun. She lit the smoke, giving the moment spacc to breathe as she looked Tourmaline up and down. "You're Tourmaline *Harris,* right? As in, the Wardens?"

If asked outright, *everyone* in Alleghany High could say who Tourmaline was, but Tourmaline seemed to do her best to make everyone forget it in the day-to-day—where all Virginia had ever seen was a studious, preppy blonde passing by in a clump of church kids in the hall. Whatever might have been dangerous in Tourmaline's prettiness was always fast asleep underneath prim day dresses, or jeans and *blouses.* Her hair was the only thing that seemed to fit—long and languidly unstyled, where the Lilly crowd would have a shiny blowout. "I always forget. You're not what I would expect," Virginia said over a long exhale.

"The leather bikini top and assless fringed chaps aren't really dress code approved," Tourmaline said. "*What* are you doing here, again?"

Virginia turned to the prison complex as her hair whipped across her face. Hooking a finger, she dragged the hair back behind her ear.

Everyone in her class would be shitting around at boring jobs all summer, hoping to get laid and wasted before they went off to school. Except her. She would be doing the Wardens. Suddenly, she wanted to run. Instead, Virginia exhaled a long breath of smoke and glanced at Tourmaline. "Can I trust you to keep a secret?"

"About as far as I can trust you."

Virginia bit down on the smile. "My brother is here," she lied.

"You have a brother?"

"Half."

"You have a half brother no one knows about?" Tourmaline put her hands on her hips. "Did you just discover him?"

"He lived in Tennessee. Made it easier."

"I need your skills," Tourmaline said, stuffing her hands into her pockets and scuffing her pristine white slip-ons against the asphalt. "I mean, do you really not know why I'm here?"

Virginia pulled the cigarette from her mouth, a sudden and real smile stretching across her face. "I know."

"Exactly." Tourmaline sighed.

"What are you doing out here already? I was just on my way in," Virginia said.

Tourmaline lifted her chin. "I got caught attempting to smuggle in socks. I was escorted out in cuffs, so you can take a wild guess how that went for me."

That was the most basic, dumbest shit Virginia had ever heard. She put the smoke to her mouth to hide the lurking laughter. *This could work.* "Why socks?"

"I figured if I got caught with socks, I could explain my way out of it easier than say . . . methadone. It probably would have been fine if I'd made it past the CO. But . . ." Tourmaline shrugged, cheeks sucked in like she was biting them.

Pure kitten. "Why didn't you just give it off to someone?" Virginia asked.

"What?"

"Give it to someone . . . ," Virginia trailed off. She'd heard rumors about the Wardens beating a man nearly to a pulp in state prison, but on the off chance it was solely a rumor, Virginia wanted to tread carefully. If Tourmaline couldn't get to her mom—or get *things* to her mom—she would need Virginia.

Tourmaline narrowed her eyes, staring at Virginia as if trying to figure out what language was being spoken. Suddenly, her eyes widened and she gave a bitter laugh. "Shit, you think because of my *dad*? Oh, no. No, honey. You been watching too much television."

"What? No, that's not what I meant. Your dad?" Virginia frowned, shifting and crossing her arms. *Don't blush. Don't blush.* Her face stayed clear, but her chest burned hot and panicky. "What are *you* talking about? Oh my God, did you think I was talking about your dad's motorcycle gang?"

"Yeah, um." Tourmaline rubbed her forehead. "First of all, it's not a gang. It's a club."

"Oh. Sorry. Club." Like there was a difference.

"Second, my dad's *club* is not a one-percenter. They don't do prison shit."

Virginia blinked. "Huh?"

"They're not criminals."

Virginia snorted. "Yeah, *okay*." She grinned and put the cigarette to her mouth.

"I'm serious."

"I mean, I get it if this is the party line. But how dumb do I look?"

"It's a club with criminals, maybe, yes. But not a criminal club." Tourmaline said it in this infuriating, deliberate way—as if explaining something to a child. "They're a club because they really like motorcycles, and brotherhood, and riding together. They support local charities. The Network for Abused Children. That's their whole thing."

Did Tourmaline really believe this? Virginia couldn't tell. "Oh." She tried to make it not seem sarcastic.

"This is all public knowledge. You can tell because they don't have the diamond patch on the front of their cut, and anything they really do is charity runs." Tourmaline tapped her left shoulder with a manicured nail.

Half a second later Virginia realized that by *cut,* Tourmaline meant the patch-covered leather vest and jacket they all wore. The one with the monster staring back at her as they disappeared around the mountain curves. "So, that's just you with the smuggling, then, huh?" Virginia winked.

"Just me," Tourmaline said flatly.

If they weren't criminals, what on earth did Hazard want on them? He didn't concern himself with civilians except when they were paying fifteen hundred an hour plus a three-thousand-buck retainer. Virginia clawed her hair away from her face, stomach sinking. None of this made sense. "So, you're saying they're a bunch of motorcycle grandmas?"

"I'm saying whatever you've heard is bullshit. They aren't criminals." The side of Tourmaline's cheek worked as if she were clenching and unclenching her jaw. "How's everything going? Still doing the pageant thing?"

Virginia exhaled. This wasn't going well. "Yep."

"You won Miss Virginia last year, right?"

"Miss *Teen* Virginia last year. I quit, though." *Retired* was the more accurate word. Hazard had found a younger girl who could still travel around to the out-of-state pageants that brought in the money.

It was unclear whether Virginia was being promoted or demoted. A shudder rolled deep in her stomach.

"Where are you going to school, again?"

"Not going."

Tourmaline looked surprised, but she hid it quickly and nodded. "Oh . . ."

"So your dry run failed. And now you're banned. That blows. How long?" She sucked a deep breath of the cigarette. *Come on, Margarine Girl.*

"Six months? I don't know." Tourmaline's eyes narrowed. "Your question about the Wardens . . . Do *you* have someone who can get things to your brother?"

"I mean. Not socks." Because who risked that much over socks? "But yeah. And I have help speeding up the process."

"If there's. Um." Tourmaline shifted. "Anything I can do. Maybe we could help each other out. If there was something I"—she paused—"could help you with."

"I am a little curious about the whole biker club-not-gang thing," Virginia said lightly; like the idea was a lark she'd always wanted to try.

Tourmaline's expression was suddenly tight. The tail of her pink gingham shirt flapped in the breeze, but she still didn't respond.

"Give me your number, and if I have some time, I'll give you a call," Virginia said, pretending not to notice. "We'll hang out."

"Do you have your phone? Or a pen?"

"You can just tell me. I'll remember."

Tourmaline's eyebrow rose.

No one believed Virginia could remember, which was half the reason Virginia never wrote anyone's number down. Hazard assumed it was a trick. That she had a record of numbers hidden away and regularly consulted it. But she didn't—once a number was in her head, it was there forever.

"I'm good with numbers. I'll remember," Virginia said.

"Don't you have a phone?"

Virginia shrugged. "For work."

Tourmaline sighed and relented. She gave the number and gathered her hair off her neck. "I work during the week, but I'm off in the evenings and weekends."

"Where do you work?" Virginia asked.

"With my dad. He owns a landscaping and construction business. Waterfalls and ponds are his specialty. I mostly do the lawns."

"Is that where all the Wardens work?"

Tourmaline looked at her like she was stupid. "No, most of them have regular jobs."

"Your nails are pretty nice for a person who works landscaping," Virginia said dubiously.

"You don't believe me?"

Virginia smiled. "Not saying that. Just wondering how much shit you're made of."

A grin finally crossed Tourmaline's face and she took a step back toward her truck. "Less shit than you, I'm sure. And I wear gloves." Two steps away, she called back, "Call me."

Flower gardens? Not a gang? What the *hell* did Hazard want with them?

TOURMALINE wasn't usually home from her visits to Hazelton until late, and the long line of motorcycles stretching under the leafy oaks bordering her driveway stood as silent testimony to Dad banking on her not being around. She climbed out of the truck and used the door to crack her back, taking deep breaths of the heavy valley humidity to work out the six hours of interstate stiffness and emotional spiraling.

They were all here. Their bikes tipped on kickstands, one after another in a languid line of chrome. The amber porch lights and blue tint of moonshine slipped from one bike to the next. Country rock blared under the deeply shadowed trees, mingling with the smells of smoked meat and wood fire. All hidden behind a row of sweet bay magnolia, red cedar, and sweet summer darkness.

All hidden, except for Big Mac stationed at the end of the driveway to watch the road, and Sauls standing under the eaves of the garage in his vest and tucked-in T-shirt, nursing a cigarette in the hazy purple shadows as he kept watch over the bikes.

He met her eye, nodded, and looked back to his phone.

Sighing, she slung her bag over her shoulder and texted Anna May. *Party at my house. Save me. Movie?* What she really wanted was to shower, cry, and inhale a package of Oreos. But there was no space for that here. She'd dump her stuff, sit in a dark movie theater with Anna May, and try not to tell her best friend and youth group student leader she'd just tried to smuggle contraband into a federal prison.

Me and Dalton were just heading out. Pick you up?

Ugh. It'd be easy to keep the stuff about her mom to herself with Dalton around, but if he was in the car with Anna May, she'd have to hear about how Dalton found motorcycles an unsafe, ridiculous expression of poorly formed masculinity. *Please,* she texted anyway. Pocketing her phone, she opened the front door of the house with an ache in her chest she couldn't begin to unpack.

A strange woman looked up, blinking in surprise.

It shouldn't have bothered her—Tourmaline had known the second she'd seen those bikes what kind of crowd would be here—but it seemed as if the universe had put the woman there—behind the kitchen counter, having the nerve to be all domestic and shit, putting chips into a goddamn *bowl*—just to dig farther into her skin.

Tourmaline let the door slam behind her.

"Heeyyy." Her father yanked his feet off the table and his boots thumped to the floor. "I thought you weren't going to be back till late."

"I see that," Tourmaline said, dropping her bag into a chair. The kitchen and dining room were one room, divided by a wide counter covered in picked-over food. The table stood overflowing with half-empty trays of chicken and an array of liquor. Her stomach growled. The food smelled amazing. Was it from Moe's? Moe's food didn't usually smell like this. Maybe she was just really hungry.

"How did it go?" Dad asked.

He hadn't told the woman to leave. Who *was* she? Tourmaline bit the inside of her cheek.

The woman stood with her hands folded on the counter. Long nails. Sleek blond hair skimming her shoulders. Big silver earrings jingled softly with even the slightest of her movements, and she wore a tight Harley-Davidson T-shirt, cut deep, with rhinestones on the front. She was young. Not in her twenties, *thank God*. But young thirties maybe.

Tourmaline's stomach turned. She grabbed a chip out of a bowl and looked back to her father with a brow raised. "Can't leave you alone for a second, huh?"

"Thought we'd change it up for a Saturday night. I didn't know you'd be back so soon. We'll get outta your hair in a little bit, don't worry." Dad's gaze kept steady, but in a way that screamed how much he was working to keep it there.

She wanted to tell him she was going out. That she wanted to get away. Judging by the sheer amount of alcohol stacked in the dining room, there were probably close to fifty people outside. Twenty-five Wardens and the rest a mix of party girls and hang-arounds.

Exactly the sort of thing Virginia wanted to see.

"Hey, T!" Jim, a thin black man with graying hair, said as he crossed through the kitchen. He'd been the Wardens' vice president for a long time and should have been the president after Tourmaline's grandfather died, but he'd had to step down after a stroke. Everyone still called him the VP and treated him that way, even though he couldn't ride anymore. "Congrats on graduating. Your daddy says you're off to UVA." He plucked up a roll and didn't really wait for an answer before sailing out the door to the garden. "It's a good school. Don't get into trouble. Be a good girl."

Tourmaline waved. What Virginia and other curious outsiders didn't get was that, in reality, this was boring. It was super weird. It was old men, motorcycle spec talk, and the strong possibility of a hairy, sweaty drunk dude doing something terrifically embarrassing, and only laughing louder about it because Tourmaline was watching. She wanted to hide in her room and turn up her music until Anna May came, not join in the fray.

But it was her house, not the blonde's. So Tourmaline stood there and took a slow bite of her chip. Waiting. Refusing to completely hand over the space her mother used to occupy as queen.

"Don't fuck with my food, Jason," someone she didn't know yelled over his shoulder as he came through the door. He balked at the three of them and ducked his head. "Sorry." His boots clomped hollow on the creaking wooden floor as he skirted around them for the hall.

"That's the new conscript," Dad said, pushing up his worn denim shirtsleeves.

Tourmaline shrugged. "Can't be that new." Conscripts weren't brought around families until the very end; probably no less than a year had passed since he started wearing the bottom rocker, decorated with the word *conscript,* on his vest. Which was after at least a year or two of being a hang-around.

Dad rolled his eyes. He'd meant *new to her.* As if she'd missed the last eighteen years and didn't know how this worked. "Do you remember Old Hawk?"

The woman began rearranging the dip bowls, earrings tinkling and catching the light as she moved. It was impossible not to look in her direction. Which Tourmaline guessed was the point. But for Tourmaline, it was impossible to not remember her mother there instead, presiding over the food and the men alike.

"He was an original Warden," her dad continued. "More your grandpa's time than mine. He would be president if he'd stayed around."

"Who?"

"I just said. Old Hawk." Dad reached for a beer, a little too casually. "They went to Sturgis together, and he bailed your grandpa out of jail. Virginia boys stick together, I guess. He was around when you were young, but you might not remember him. They moved up to northern Virginia when there was a big construction boom up there. Made good money with all those houses. Don't you remember him? He babysat you a few times."

"Kinda."

The woman began rustling the chip bags.

Dad kept talking, louder. "He passed away from cancer a while back. That's his kid."

Tourmaline frowned. "Who? What?"

"The new conscript."

"Oh." Her father never told her this kind of thing. This smelled like avoidance.

The silence drifted back in.

Finally, the woman sighed. "I'm going to take these out to the boys." Her voice was small and feminine. The way Tourmaline's mother's had been before her spirit had drained out and just left the edges. She picked up the bowl and walked out.

"I'll catch up in a second," Tourmaline's father called.

The music had turned up. Jason yelled from somewhere outside.

Tourmaline didn't even want to think about what they would do with this house come August when she left for UVA. She checked her phone and tucked back the wisps of hair falling out of her ponytail. "I'm going out with Anna May. She's on her way."

"You got a minute?" Her father stood and headed toward the hall. "I got something I need to talk to you about."

Something dark and heavy trailed a slow circling beat into the pit of her stomach.

Wayne.

Without a word, she followed him into his office. It couldn't be Wayne. Fourteen years. He'd gotten fourteen years. It had to be something else. Anything else.

Her father shut the door and went around the polished oak desk. The dim evening light filled the room with soft shadows. The sounds of the party were muffled. One of the framed posters on the wall yelled in bold letters over a motorcycle, KICK HER. SHE'LL KICK YOU BACK IN ALL THE RIGHT PLACES. After years of looking at it, Tourmaline still didn't get it.

She plopped into one of the chairs before his desk and tucked her leg nervously underneath her. "What's up?" she asked, voice quivering despite her best intentions. If it was anything good he'd have been able to say it in the kitchen.

Her father stretched his hands out and inspected the horned-skull ring on his index finger, the tattooed lines circling his wrists like bonds, and *Semper Fi* inked on his forearm. Frowning, he rubbed at some invisible spot on the ring. "I just wanted to let you know Wayne came home today."

Tourmaline went cold.

"I wanted you to hear it from me and know this isn't going to affect your life. We'll keep you safe."

"How is he home already?" Tourmaline asked.

"His sentence was only—"

"It was fourteen years." She didn't need reminding. "It's only been three."

"State prison. He was eligible for parole."

"No." She didn't know what else to say. Mom had at least eight more years before she was eligible for parole. *Eight.* Tourmaline could have a Ph.D. by then. She pulled a length of her hair through her fingers and stared unseeing at the ceiling. "What kind of shit justice is that?"

"If you go through life expecting justice to be handed to you, you'll always be disappointed. It's not about right. Never is. It's about the demands of the system."

Tourmaline bit her lips tight, meeting the easy, clear blue of her father's eyes. *Who delivered justice, then?* she wanted to ask, but the question stayed stuck in a ball in her throat.

"I just wanted to let you know," he said. "In case you see him around. I didn't want you to be surprised."

"Maybe he doesn't care."

A look of deep pity crossed her father's face. "Maybe. But if you see him, call me. Right away. We'll take care of him."

Tourmaline stared at her sneakers. There was a tiny bit of dirt on the edge of the rubber and she licked her finger and rubbed at it. What if Dad did something and got sent to jail? She'd lose two parents over the same shit. The same mistake. That couldn't happen.

"It will be fine," her father said confidently. "Wayne probably has better things to do with his time now that he's free. People fixate on one thing inside and forget about it once they get out. Just be cautious. We'll keep you safe."

Tourmaline frowned at the floor, disgusted. Wayne was back. After three stupid years in state prison.

Her phone buzzed and the screen lit in her hand with the text from Anna May.

Almost there. Had to get gas and then Katy LimbaUGHHHH wanted to "chat." Aka pump me for inside info about making varsity. Shoot me now.

Autocorrect is a genius. Katy LimbaUGGGGHHH.

She was wearing navy and black and it really got on my nerves. I don't care who says you can wear them together, you can't. You just can't.

"You okay, T?" her father asked softly.

"I'm going out with Anna May," she repeated absently.

"You don't have to go. We can get out of your hair."

"She's already on her way."

"Oh. Just her?"

"Her and Dalton."

"No one else?" He always sniffed around the topic of boys but never approached it head on.

"No one else." Allen was out of town with his older brother until the following day. Not that she'd ever tell her father.

He pushed out of the chair. "I'll keep my phone on," he said, heading out.

Tourmaline followed aimlessly. The smell of the food hit her as soon as she stepped into the hall, and she remembered she hadn't eaten all day. Anna May still wasn't there, so Tourmaline grabbed a paper plate off the stack, putting the ruffled edge to her mouth and looking over the food. Roasted chicken. Mashed potatoes with flecked things in them. She dug out a spoonful and inspected it with a frown. She should have told Dad about what Hayes had said. *Wayne Thompson is looking for you.* She should go right now. Find him. Tell him.

She stared at the potatoes. What if it was just a rumor? Of course the guard could know if Wayne was released—they'd probably alerted everyone involved in the trial. Mom included. And Mom only knew via the guards. What could Dad do about it, anyhow?

"I think it's rosemary," Jason said from her right. "It's pretty good, but don't tell him I said that."

She blinked. "Better question: Is it edible? I'm still scarred from your charred hot dogs and unfried French fries. Oh God, and the peanut butter and bologna sandwich you made for my school lunch. Remember that?"

"Yeah, I was a nightmare as a conscript," Jason agreed. "I think they rushed to patch me out just to stop me from having to do any more cooking."

Tourmaline snorted, plopping a spoonful onto her plate, half covering the chicken. "I know *I* was grateful when Dad went back to school-lunch duty."

Jason's eyes and the diamond stud in his ear winked at her, but that was just him. He was beautiful and baby-faced; and playing the charming boy soldier was a routine he'd been running long past boy-hood. And his clear hazel eyes always looked bright and sober, no matter how drunk he was.

It was strange to think of him from Virginia's perspective. Most of the things people talked about centered on Jason.

At Mom's trial, Tourmaline had heard all the rumors. There under fluorescent lights, with the stenographer tacking away and the judge leaning forward on his elbows. The federal prosecutor seemed as if he'd spent a week in Moe's just jotting notes on whatever shit people would say. People always have shit to say about things they don't understand.

If Virginia was looking for cheap thrills, what could Tourmaline give her that the rumors hadn't?

Jason put a roll on her plate.

"Eh," she said, adding a spoonful of corn.

"What?"

"One more. Come on now." She pushed the plate toward him, and he shook his head and added another. "So, your new conscript cooks, huh?"

Shrugging, Jason walked his fingers through the line of bottles and plucked one out. "He's all right." He popped the top off.

"Who sponsored him?"

"I did." Jason gave her a smirking rolled-eyes face. "Anyway."

She smothered her chicken in gravy.

"How's your mom?"

She didn't answer.

He took a long drink. "Your dad's talking about selling the Shovelhead."

Tourmaline glanced at him. "Okay?"

He gave her a look and walked off without another word.

Tourmaline watched him go—out the back door, disappearing into the softly lit garden, where everyone gathered underneath the strung lights. On the hazy edges of the dark garden, the woman from the kitchen stood with two others just like her. Tourmaline blinked at the ground and let out a long breath before turning for her room.

She picked a piece of chicken off the bone and stuffed it in her mouth. It was amazing—moist, with an herbed saltiness in each bite; so good she stopped right there, in the hall, and swooped up a bite of potatoes on her finger to try. *Rosemary.* Holy shit, the conscript was actually a good cook for once.

A tall young man in jeans and a T-shirt appeared in the hall, startling her before she remembered he was the cook. The guy who came through the kitchen. *The conscript.*

Tourmaline wiped her fingers on her jeans and moved so he could pass, but he moved the same way. She stepped again, but she was already half a step behind him. "Here. I'll go—" But they nearly ran into each other again.

"This isn't rocket science, conscript."

"I'll go left. You go right," he said.

She stepped right and nearly ran into his chest. Clenching her jaw, she tipped her chin to meet his eyes. A current of something sparked and turned the marrow of her bones to liquid. When had the conscripts gotten so young? And hot?

"How's the chicken?" he asked.

"Fine," she said coolly. He was a conscript, after all. Her dad's friend. Her memories of Old Hawk were a thin collection consisting of a booming laugh and a big black man always wearing a black Carhartt T-shirt— not enough to remember whether this man, his son, looked like him.

"My name's Cash." He smiled. "There's an herbed butter for the rolls."

"Oh." She turned back toward the kitchen.

"I got it." He put his hand on her back, gently moving her aside as he slid past.

She stopped, holding her plate. Music pulsed outside, but they were alone in the kitchen. No one to notice what had just happened, thankfully—his hand on her back, so casual. Didn't he know the rules? He had to.

The conscript dug through extra rolls and bags of chips on the counter, turning with a bowl of butter. "Here."

The heat of his hand still rested between her shoulder blades. She shrugged it off and grabbed a knife out of the drawer. "You know it's not a guarantee."

"What's not?"

She smothered her roll in a thick layer of butter and dropped the knife in the sink before answering. "You have to follow the rules. Just because your dad was an original member, doesn't mean it's a guarantee."

"I didn't know I broke a rule," he said, putting the butter on the counter and pulling out a stretch of plastic wrap.

It wasn't like a rule that was spelled out—none of them were. It was a truth he had to know by this point. *Thou shalt not touch or look at your brothers' daughters.* If he was here, allowed into this home, he was close to patching out. He wore the curved conscript patch in blue-green, black and white, sewn onto the bottom of his leather vest—the rest a broad expanse of empty leather waiting for confirmation. By now, he'd know: breaking those unspoken rules would get him kicked out.

"Good?" He glanced toward the roll as she chewed.

Starting, she frowned. "You made *all* this?"

He nodded.

Ah. Being a good cook gave him an advantage—it meant they

couldn't treat him too badly, because they'd always want something only he could give them. "It's all right."

He tilted his head, raising an eyebrow. "All right?"

She swallowed her bite and narrowed her eyes at him. This wasn't normal conscript behavior. They didn't usually argue if you said their *herbed fucking butter* was just all right. "Do you *like* cooking?"

He put his finger to his lips. "Don't tell, they think they're making it hard on me."

Tourmaline's gaze flickered over him—taking in the polished boots, crisp jeans, and black T-shirt wrinkling across his chest as he smoothed down the plastic wrap. His black hair was buzzed close. Dark taupe skin—pulled tight over thick muscle like a matte finish on a bike. A well-trimmed ducktail-shaped beard. No hint of boy left in the tall, strong-looking body. How old was he? She felt like she needed to know just to orient herself to where she was in life, as if his age were a missing coordinate. "You're not really supposed to talk to me." Or touch her, but she didn't say it. It had been a meaningless, thoughtless touch, she knew—but a conscript couldn't afford to be either of those things.

He laughed. "Oh, that's right. The Princess."

Her phone buzzed in her pocket—Anna May texting she was outside, probably. She ignored it, forcing herself to keep her gaze locked to the conscript's, as if she didn't feel a thing. She lifted her chin. "You won't patch out."

"For what?"

What did he mean, *For what?* Hadn't he been listening?

The conscript crossed his arms and leaned against the counter, looking wholly unapologetic.

"Do you like hanging out with your dad's friends?" He asked it a little mockingly. A little teasingly.

Flirting?

It pulled her up short and left her unsure. How old was he? She swished her hair back like Virginia and lifted her chin. "It's *my* house."

The conscript just looked at her. Deadpan.

"Do you like hanging out with a bunch of rednecks whose only intent is to abuse you until you break?" It left her mouth before she realized what she was truly saying—that this wasn't a regular conscript—and terrible subtext pervaded her words. The Wardens had a few black members, but that didn't mean anything for a conscript. There was no brotherhood until he became a brother. She'd only meant to needle him back in the way he'd done with her, and instead she'd walked right into dumbass white girl territory.

"I'm sorry," she gasped. "Oh my God, I am *so* sorry. I didn't mean it like that."

"I know what you meant." He heaved off the counter, grabbed a napkin, and stepped close.

Her pulse throbbed in her neck, but she refused to back down to a conscript.

He reached around her shoulder.

"What are you doing?" she asked, horrified that her words came out sort of breathless.

"You got gravy in your hair," he said, the corners of his mouth tensing as if he were trying not to smile.

Her heartbeat thumped a deep, throbbing refrain in her chest, and she stared at the ends of her hair slipping through his hands.

"It's *my* club," he said.

"Not yet," she said. And not ever, if he was going to be like this with her. Nothing was innocent when it came to the eighteen-year-old daughter of your president. Not even a conversation.

He laughed. "That's what you think." He winked, balled the napkin, and tossed it into the trash. Turning, he went outside.

Tourmaline stood alone, until her heartbeat dropped back to normal and the damp ends of her hair dried.

That was what she needed. A way to make Virginia feel as if she were standing alongside a tall Warden with her heartbeat in her throat and her fingers shaky. A show. That's what Tourmaline could exchange. Not the truth, but what Virginia wanted the truth to be.

ROBERT M. HAZARD wasn't the big crime boss of anything, least of all Roanoke, Virginia. He dealt on the side of his law practice in pills, a little cocaine, and some prostitutes, and walked around as if he only ever saw himself on a television screen—as a complex, interesting hero in a retro-vibed, critical-darling cable series. The American work ethic lived in bankruptcies, barters, and flamboyant suits by day; powder, women, and the same suit, sans jacket, at night. In the same vein, he frequently danced on the line of inappropriate with Virginia, but after four years she felt safe enough.

Accustomed though she was to the peculiar whims of Hazard's plotlines, when Virginia knocked at the door of the dusty law office in downtown Roanoke and a man declaring himself a bodyguard opened the door, she laughed.

Bodyguard?

He smoothed his braids and plucked at his wrinkled dress shirt. "I'm new."

"Hazard!" Virginia hollered. "Call off the puppy."

Radio silence.

Virginia took a step toward the back.

The man slid easily, blocking the way with an apologetic smile. He reached for the backpack on her shoulders.

Virginia handed it over.

"Thanks," he said, unzipping and riffling through the contents. Dumbass didn't think to look in her boots. He handed the backpack to her, gaze flitting between somewhere around her neck and the floor.

Virginia smiled and turned it up to Supreme Queen—satisfied

when he blushed, fumbled with his magazine, and stumbled down into the high-backed calico-covered chair of the waiting room as the newest member of Team Virginia.

She still had it.

The front offices were dark, but Virginia followed the dim pathway of fluorescent light spilling past stacks of files, mail, warped paneling, and shelves lined with ancient law books. Her backpack slipped off her shoulder and she hoisted it up, stepping through the seventies-style mustard kitchen behind the offices to the back file room.

Hazard—Robert Hazard, *Esquire*—sat in a ripped red leather office chair, pawing through a file box propped on his knees. Boxes full of files were lined up on folding tables, on the linoleum floor underneath, and on mismatched aluminum shelves through the room. Out the barred window, sunset filtered through patchy woods.

He looked up and beamed. "There's the Queen."

"You wish." Virginia sank into an empty rolling chair and kicked her feet up on the edge of the table. The backpack was still on her shoulder.

He leaned back. "What are the Wardens up to this fine summer night?"

Shit. "Stuff." It'd been a week since she'd talked to Tourmaline. She'd called once but Tourmaline hadn't called back.

The master of the dramatic pause, Hazard simply stared at her until it became too uncomfortable to keep facing him.

She dropped her eyes to the files in his lap. "Don't worry. I'm working something."

He looked unimpressed and went back to the box, pulling out a ragged file and paging through it with thick fingers. "Are you wearing *that*?"

He had been her pageant coach for the first year. In the years following, he still had a lot to say about what she wore and where she wore it. This was not how he envisioned her for the role of Pageant Queen

Gone Motorcycle Club. This wasn't even how he envisioned Shady Small-Town Lawyer's Minion, but he didn't have much say in her wardrobe these days, try as he might.

"Dirty deeds, done dirt cheap." She grinned, deliberately running one long finger along the frays in a hole in the thigh of her jeans.

Hazard's gaze flickered to the patch of visible skin.

When he came back to her face, she smiled. Score two for Team Virginia.

He didn't argue.

"What's with the bodyguard?" Virginia asked.

"Restructuring."

"Is there something I should know?"

"Weren't you at the staff meeting?"

Sometimes she thought he ran his side business a little too much like a law practice, and his law practice a little too much like his side business. "When the hell did we have a staff meeting?"

He laughed. "I'm just playing."

Virginia grimaced and looked up at the yellow water stains on the drop ceiling. "If you're restructuring, why don't you let me come work for you as a paralegal or something?"

"Jackie does a fine job, thank you."

"But does she get you coffee? I'll get you coffee. And that cornbread you like for lunch. And wear tight skirts. I'll smile real pretty for the clients. And I—"

"Do you have a résumé?"

Wait, was he serious? She stopped rocking. "I can . . . I can make one."

"Give me an oral."

She put her feet down. "What?"

"An oral *overview*." He smoothed over his hair and propped his chin in his hand, in a way Virginia could see framed in tight by the camera. Scene: eccentric lawyer, sitting behind the gleaming mahogany desk in his front office, finagling his way around the law with cunning and darkly comic moments. "Of your résumé. What's on it? What kind of jobs have you had? Who are your references?"

Virginia couldn't tell whether he was serious or simply messing with her. "Well, you're my reference." She pressed her lips tight. This had to be a game. "And . . . ," she started slowly. "I've had several years' experience as an independent contractor for a large company."

He snorted. "Doing what?"

She blinked.

"Have you ever held a job other than with me?"

Virginia tightened her jaw. He knew the answer. "No."

"Well, then, I'm sorry to say, you have no work history."

"What do you mean? I've been working for you for—"

He tossed the file on top of the file boxes. "You haven't had a job. J-O-B, job. You haven't had to show up on time every day. Or work eight or ten hours a day, five days a week. Have you paid payroll taxes? Social Security? You've damn sure never worked in an office. Do you know how to work a copier? Use Excel?"

It was a sharp zinger in his dialogue. Written for himself. Played for himself. A game meant to mortify her twice over. Once for failing for his test again. Twice for not having the wisdom to see herself realistically in the first place.

". . . dictate a letter? Do you even know how to put things in alphabetical—?"

She leaned forward. "Fuck you," she snarled.

A hand caught her under the chin and yanked her back into the chair.

She gulped. *Shit.* The bodyguard. She'd forgotten.

Hazard laughed and waved his hand. "Let her go, D."

Virginia jerked away and the hand released her.

"Like I was saying," Hazard continued, smirking. "You can't mouth off to a judge. Or another lawyer. Or a client. Or me. It's not just me. Any place you try and go for employment is going to say the same thing." Scooting forward on the chair, he pushed the box back into its place. "Sorry about the . . ." He waved across his neck.

She glared, rubbing the spot under her chin, where she could still feel the bodyguard's fingers. It used to be none of his guys would touch her. It unnerved her to find that that had changed. She bit her lip and didn't say anything else, pulling the backpack off her shoulder and tossing it at him.

Hazard didn't blink, just caught it and quietly pushed off the floor, wheeling himself deeper into the shelves of filing boxes so he was hidden from view of the door. Unzipping the bag, he started pulling out the stacks of bills she'd carefully smoothed out and tied together with hair ties—laying out stacks of twenties and fives and tens. "Any problems?" he asked.

"Nope."

"You aren't with the Wardens tonight," he said matter-of-factly. "What *have* you been doing?" He yanked a hair tie off the bills and began counting under his breath, mouth moving silently.

She turned her eyes to the ceiling. Her count was never off. Not even by a penny. He insisted on counting it three times, every time. But she'd always been good with the numbers.

She'd walked into Hazard's office as payment against the $1,822.15 legal bill her mother had accrued during a DUI. No one thought her worth much at that point—she was a scrawny, tall girl-child who could barely stand to look anyone in the eye.

But Hazard had looked her up and down, sucked on his teeth, and agreed to the deal. He'd put her to work with his last pageant girl and, somehow, magic happened. Scrawny became lithe. Tall became fierce. Girl-child skipped straight to woman. Her mother had simply been desperate, but Hazard had known Virginia was worth more than a petty legal bill. In return for his faith, she'd worked hard and stayed loyal.

And she never forgot the eighteen hundred twenty-two dollars and fifteen cents, *or* messed up her count.

"I met Tourmaline Harris," she said.

"Who?"

"Calvin Harris's daughter."

He paused for a moment. Frozen with a stack of twenties fluttering in the air-conditioning. Numbers dropped off his mouth. He blinked at the pile.

Virginia smiled. "Eleven sixty."

He gathered up the pile, licked his finger, and started over. "Oh, I see." He *tsk*ed softly.

"She was in my class at school." Virginia watched carefully under her eyelashes.

He finished counting out the stack and picked it up, shuffling the bills into his palm and carefully rubbing the edges to unstick them. "Is this girl hanging out with her dad's club or something?"

"Uh . . ."

"Seems odd."

"*Well . . .*," Virginia hedged.

He looked at her over the edge of the bills. "Does this girl know *anything*?"

"She's the president's daughter," Virginia snapped. Tourmaline had to know something. "She said they're not one-percenters."

He shook his head, annoyed. "None of that bullshit motorcycle club law applies to what they are."

"What are they?"

"Dangerous." He went back to counting. "They don't like people like you and me. I told you to befriend *them*, not their goddamn family."

"People like *us*? She said they weren't criminals. It was very clearly explained."

He smirked. "And every teenage girl knows everything always."

She clenched her jaw tight and began scanning the boxes in the filing room to calm down. Roughly a year ago, she'd caught a glimpse of a gun hidden in one of the file boxes, and every time she had to sit there and suffer through his counts or his condescending dialogue zingers from whatever dull episode she was stuck inside, she would recite the number in tiny beige print at the left-hand corner back to herself, looking for it. 7602XF-1842066.

"Virginia." His sharp command brought her eyes to his. Gaze unflinching. "Make friends. You're a friendly girl. This is simple." That same heavy gaze dropped slowly. Sizing her up the way he did everything else—though he never found fault with her body. "That's why I sent you."

There was no question what she was supposed to do.

Virginia's throat tightened and she didn't say anything. Easy and simple, probably. But it felt like a boundary marking the end of something. A place she'd known she'd come to, someday.

"Are they outlaws?"

"Absolutely."

"What exactly do they do?"

He cocked an eyebrow at the stack—counting to a whole number before glancing over. "They are predatory."

"Yeah?" Virginia ran her fingers through her hair, shaking out some of the tangles. "In what way?"

"They own too much of southern Virginia. It's constricting with them around."

Virginia rolled her eyes. Sometimes it seemed as if half of her problems were simply due to posturing.

"Nothing goes on here without the Wardens knowing. I don't want them to know what I'm doing. And the way you sell shit to someone is with a pretty woman." He waved a stack of fives in her direction. "We're moving on to bigger things, Virginia Campbell."

"Restructuring," she said flatly.

"Get the Wardens to pay more attention to you than to me, and both of us are going to get out of this shithole of peddling the same pills over and over again. Find a way into their parties, into their homes, into their lives, and make them love you. Make them bow down and worship at the altar of a beautiful woman."

The same shudder rolled deep in Virginia's stomach.

"Stop jerking around with this child." He waved his hand into the air as if brushing Tourmaline out of the way. "And when they're in love with you, come back and tell me who they are, who they're loyal to, who they hate. I didn't pick you just because you're gorgeous. You're smart. You can hold your own there."

The flattery was true—she hoped—and Virginia softened to it. "And when I finish courting your wolves?"

"I'ma take care of you," he answered.

"You've said that before, you know."

He eyed her. Licked his thumb.

A chill ran down her arms.

"I won't have your usual stuff here tomorrow," he said. "You'll need to come by the house. Nine sharp."

She nodded.

Turning, he started in on a third count. "Go get me supper while I finish counting this. Three-piece meal from Joe's. White meat. Biscuit. Greens. Get extra butter." He pulled out his wallet and took out a fifty. "Keep the change for gas. A bonus. My prettiest employee. And one of my best." He gripped her hand as he handed over the bill.

Virginia stood with her throat thick, allowing her hand to be held until he released both her and the money. She pulled out her phone and headed out, texting Tourmaline. *You busy?*

Virginia waited with the phone in her palm. It stayed silent. *Come on,* she urged the screen. Laughter shrilled outside her truck windows and she lifted her head to two women on the corner just past Hazard's office.

Danylynn and Wave. They tugged down their tank tops and yanked up their shorts, long trails of cigarette smoke hanging like wispy clouds around them in the sultry streetlight. They were Hazard's, but never came close to his door. He'd made complaints about them to the police, even. Which was smart. The light changed. The cars sped through the intersection, not slowing. Danylynn leaned against the telephone pole. A train whistled and the railroad crossing began dinging. Virginia's stomach rolled. If Hazard thought himself the hero of some country crime show, there was no question what role she played. She tossed the phone and started the truck. Hazard was waiting for his dinner.

At the drive-thru, the text lit on her screen. *Come and get me.*

5

"MY, you look dressed up tonight," Anna May said when Tourmaline came up the church sidewalk.

Tourmaline's stomach twisted and she stopped and looked down at her dress. She hadn't realized until just then she'd dressed for the double date with Allen and Anna May and Dalton afterward, not for Saturday night youth group.

"Your boobs look great," Anna May continued from the steps, where she stood greeting everyone; she was in jeans and a simple cotton top the color of freshly mowed grass.

"I just wanted a reason to wear it. Look, it's got pockets." Tourmaline demonstrated the pockets in the skirt of the gathered and flared cotton voile dress. At least she'd worn her boots instead of wedges. "It's not too low, right?"

"It's a little low."

Tourmaline frowned and yanked up the front.

"Hang out?" Anna May nodded at the church steps, brown curls stirring in the breeze. "Hardly anyone's here tonight."

"That's because they're all doing better things on a gorgeous Saturday night." Tourmaline sat on the edge of the step and tucked her hands under her skirt.

Anna May rolled her eyes.

Beulah Baptist Church was one of those pretty, white-steepled country churches in the rolling valley outside of Iron Gate. Neither the church nor the sprawling view of the valley and mountains had changed since Tourmaline used to come in tights and patent dress shoes, holding Mom's hand.

"Did you get your financial aid forms sent in?" Anna May asked.

"Last week."

There was a long pause.

"Did you pick a roommate?" Tourmaline finally asked.

Anna May ran the delicate silver necklace Dalton had given her when they were fifteen over her fingers. "Not until July."

Tourmaline nodded.

The sparrows nesting in the dogwoods in the flower beds chirped in their silence.

Tourmaline stared at her feet. She hadn't told Anna May about being banned. She couldn't. She searched for something to share that would be personal enough to buy back their usual intimacy. "Wayne's home."

Anna May kept circling the chain around her fingers. Staring expectantly.

"So . . . fuck my life," Tourmaline prompted.

Anna May tilted her head toward the open doors. "Really? The language? Pastor JD could hear you, you know."

Tourmaline frowned.

"So, he's out," Anna May said. "Does that mean your mom will be out soon?"

"No."

Anna May looked confused, but she just nodded. "Well, that stinks. Did she like the photos?"

Tourmaline nodded automatically.

"Is Allen coming tonight or just meeting us afterward?"

Tourmaline cleared her throat. "He said he might be a little late because of training." He was set to play ball at the University of Florida, and he trained after he finished working on his family's farm.

"Mm-hm." Anna May raised an eyebrow.

Tourmaline didn't hear her to argue, lost tracing the path that kept her mother in prison—along ruptured discs, to failed surgeries and more and more pain meds, and . . . somehow, somewhere . . . into heroin. Ending with the shell of her mother sitting across the bolted-down table, chewing her fingernails under thin fluorescents. Her terrible prison dye job showing six inches of black roots. Her eyes sharp and unseeing, sometimes clear, but tinged with ever-present pain.

Tourmaline had shown her pictures of Allen in an effort to grasp for a sense of normal by sharing a boy who was not special. They both knew this boy was not a boy who would come visit. Who would put his hands on the concrete, and spread his legs, and bend his head in submission. Mom had liked the pictures anyway. When they said good-bye, Tourmaline had headed back to Virginia to face the boy alone. To face Anna May alone. To face her life with only the ghost of a mother.

"Are you guys dating yet?"

Tourmaline blinked at Anna May's waiting expression. She pushed away her sadness with practiced ease. "Anna May, you ask me the same damn questions these days."

Anna May sighed. "You don't date. Yeah. Okay."

"It's low-key. Not all of us have to be you and Dalton."

"If you didn't lie to your—"

"It's not as much about Dad as you think." Tourmaline narrowed her eyes. "Do you think Allen wants to meet him like a boyfriend? After everything?"

"I think Allen should man up."

Tourmaline rolled her eyes. "He's going to UF. I'm going to UVA. There's no reason for him to go through that nonsense. *I* don't want to go through that."

"Then why are y'all wasting your time?"

Tourmaline didn't answer.

"Are you hooking up?" Anna May asked, with her judgment only thinly veiled.

"Okay," Tourmaline said, standing up. "I'll see you downstairs."

"Tourmaline."

"Great talk. Can't wait," Tourmaline called behind her, only feeling a little guilty.

Pastor JD caught her coming down the steps, putting his hand on her arm to stop her. He made such a big fuss over how she was doing that pressure built in her chest as if she were being suffocated.

The interaction had been like that for a while—she remembered that now. Between visits, it'd slipped her mind, only to surprise her again.

After he moved on, Tourmaline hid behind the church, wishing she had a cigarette, until Allen texted, looking for her.

Conversation was easier with Anna May once they began again at putt-putt and ice cream after youth group ended. But nothing relieved the sense of weight in her bones. The feeling that she might suddenly lift up her putt-putt club and whack someone over the head simply for enjoying themselves.

The wind came down the mountains and wandered through the stalks of the hayfield beside the putt-putt course, drowning out the bugs with a gentle rushing sound. She leaned on her club and watched Allen as he swung his club back and forth under the lights like a bat. The shadows flickered across his long arms, and the intensity of her frustration billowed under and out into something else entirely.

"I like your dress," he whispered as they walked back to get ice cream. His breath stirred the loose strands of her ponytail, curling in the humid night, and he smelled faintly of sweet feed and aquatic cologne.

41

She looked over her shoulder, caught his eye, and grinned. It suddenly felt as if the night itself were her path and her power was nearly bursting her skin.

Anna May slid to Tourmaline's side as the boys went to deliver the clubs; Tourmaline hugged her tight in silent agreement that the tension earlier was already forgiven.

"I can't believe this is our last summer like this. We have to hang out more often, while we still can." Anna May rested her head on Tourmaline's shoulder. "This is the end. We're leaving. Finally, right?" She laughed.

Tourmaline's gaze flickered to the crisp edge of the mountains—they stood midnight against the lingering deep ocher leftovers of sunset, as if the night came from them and not from the sky. "Yeah," she agreed softly. "I'm excited."

"We'll have to do our school shopping together, okay?"

"Oh my God, yes." Tourmaline squeezed her tight. "I wish we were going to the same school."

"We can visit, though."

Tourmaline nodded, refusing to believe it would happen until it did. Anna May was going to school with Dalton. Sometimes it seemed certain they would continue always just as they had, and other times it was impossible to ignore that their paths were diverging even while they stayed in the same place. "I'm going to use the bathroom real quick," she said, pulling away.

"I'm getting your ice cream. Teaberry—"

"—in a pretzel cone," Tourmaline said at the same time as Anna May.

They laughed.

"I got you." Anna May waved her off as Dalton and Allen came back.

Tourmaline headed toward the parking lot for the bathrooms. Her phone vibrated in her pocket. *You busy?* From Virginia.

And in that second, it all flooded back.

She'd been fourteen and lying—saying she was spending the night with Anna May when sneaking off to stay with her mom. She'd been angry with her dad. Missing a boyfriend. Missing a mother and not quite comprehending what had taken her.

Mom had been staying at her dealer-slash-boyfriend's house in Roanoke. Wayne's house.

One night, Tourmaline woke and couldn't find her. That wasn't unusual, but she'd pulled up her dad's number and gripped her phone tight as she searched the run-down house, knowing she would someday confess her lies in order to protect her mom. Knowing Dad'd come save them both. "Call me," he'd always told her. "I'll take care of her."

The night had been hot. Eighties. Wayne was passed out on the couch, but Tourmaline's mom wasn't in the house. Not on the porch where she sometimes liked to sit. It was so hot the sidewalk was still warm under Tourmaline's bare feet.

Tourmaline found her mother in the passenger seat of Wayne's burgundy Oldsmobile, her tangled hair splayed out against the velvet seat. Tourmaline's trembling fingers couldn't find a pulse. A passing train drowned out the sound of her heartbeat in her ears.

It was the first time she'd ever called 911. Not her dad. It'd seemed obvious in the moment.

The cops showed up before the ambulance. She watched as her mother startled awake and freaked out. More cops came. They pulled her mother out of the car. Then a gun. Then a laundry basket's worth of heroin.

Tourmaline stood on her bare feet in the patchy grass of the vacant lot and watched it all happen. Her actions in motion. How many times had Dad told her, "Call me if your mom is in trouble. Call me, so no one can take your mom. We will take care of her."

She'd brought the cops there and then they were all beyond her father's reach. And because of that, Tourmaline knew she needed Virginia's help. It had been her responsibility to make the right call and she had failed. She couldn't afford to fail again.

The screen dimmed. Her fingers hovered over the keys, but she didn't type a reply. The dark humidity was heavy on her skin, as if breathing tight against her.

Tourmaline knew what Virginia needed. *A show.* But how could she offer one? It wasn't as if she could just arrive at the Wardens' clubhouse with a friend and ask to hang out. Was there any place in her father's world she could go?

Shoving the phone back into her pocket, she turned the corner for the women's bathroom. The fluorescent lights over the concrete building hummed in a way that reminded her of Hazelton and made her shiver to hear the girls' voices echoing from inside the winding concrete hallway.

A man's voice called from the shadows at the edge of the lot. It was familiar. As if he were calling for her. Tourmaline turned, half expecting a Warden.

"I *said*, 'Well, aren't you having fun?'"

She froze. The world fell away.

Wayne.

His untied boots crunched the gravel, footsteps falling silent as he stepped onto the concrete walk in the light. He looked older than she remembered, though his eyes were the same—unearthly and sharp. As if he were part nocturnal creature with a gift of evasion. He wore a clean shirt and too-big shorts, but it was impossible not to remember, immediately, the sight of him belly-down in the street in Roanoke, hands cuffed, in his underwear and socks.

Yelling.

Drooling.

The flashing lights of the ambulance taking her mother away reflected in his glittering eyes. The way they'd looked, fixed on her. Finding her at fault.

"Is that your boyfriend?" Wayne lifted his chin toward the ice cream stand. "He doesn't look like a Warden."

She swallowed. Everything inside her held tight.

"I just stopped to say hi to my favorite daughter."

"I *have* a dad."

He clutched his heart in mock hurt. "And here I thought all that cereal of mine you used to inhale meant something." He laughed. "I'm just teasing."

Was Dad here? Were any of the Wardens? Probably not, if she was still standing here talking to him. She backed up a step.

He didn't follow. "Has your mom said anything about me? I sent her a message. I was thinking about her."

Wayne's looking for you. She could almost taste the guard's onion bagel.

"Was that Anna May with you?" Wayne called lightly—as if he were a friend or a relative, inquiring about someone he knew. "What a lovely young woman she's grown into."

Shit. Tourmaline stopped, tongue pressed to her teeth.

She spun, slowly. The silence buzzed.

"What are we going to do about you, T?"

Healthy decisions? Things that won't violate your parole? But she swallowed her thoughts and stayed silent. Playing dead seemed the only reasonable thing to do in front of a man like Wayne.

He nodded. Then tilted his head as if listening to something Tourmaline couldn't hear. His glittering eyes met hers. He smiled and spoke softly. "I'ma make y'all pay."

Tourmaline's head buzzed. Or the lights? She swallowed and kept still. So still, she hoped she had folded up into thin air and disappeared on the wind.

But Wayne looked over toward the putt-putt—the people—and smiled. "Bye, now," he said cheerily, with a wave. Like a shadow, he slipped into nothing.

A group of girls came toward the bathroom and their voices—high and urgent—filled in the dark chill that rooted Tourmaline to the concrete.

What now?

She touched the phone in her dress pocket. *Dad.* It was the only answer.

But as quickly as she planned her own rescue, she saw the aftermath. Wayne would watch her call. He would follow—waiting behind the headlights until she walked to her car or Allen's truck. Worse, her father's truck. Wayne would reappear from the shadows, ready. He'd intended to walk away from this moment, in furtherance of another.

And there went her life.

What was she going to do about it?

The girls' laughter echoed against the concrete block.

Tourmaline pulled her phone from her pocket and sent a text.

Come get me.

6

VIRGINIA could barely keep up with the swish of Tourmaline's dress, despite having a good four inches of leg on her. They had parked in a gravel-and-weed-covered clearing behind a rectangular building plopped along the road. Tourmaline had immediately spilled out of the truck, striding into the night with convincing confidence. Virginia's only choice was to follow.

Tourmaline stopped at the edge of the low-slung brow of a rickety porch and smoothed the flyaways in her hair. "Do you have cash?"

Over the years with Hazard, Virginia had acquired an intimate knowledge of shithole country bars, but she'd never been sent to this one. There was no sign. No light but a lone streetlight along the bend in the road. Neon red and green glowed liquid through glass-block windows. Was this the Wardens' clubhouse?

"A little," Virginia said, looking around for some indication of the Wardens, something she'd missed. But all that was beyond them was the night sky. The stars were crisp. The wind roared high in the deep mountains, but didn't touch down on this hidden ridge.

"Do you know how to play pool?" Tourmaline asked.

"I guess."

Tourmaline tugged up her boots. "Be cool, all right?"

Virginia chuckled. *Be cool?*

"Something funny?"

Virginia gestured to Tourmaline's dress. "Are we here for a luncheon?"

Tourmaline rolled her eyes. "I'm here to make some money. It's up to you for anything else. That's our deal, right? I bring you around, you do with that what you want."

"That's the deal." Virginia's pulse fluttered.

Tourmaline turned for the door, hair whipping in the wind.

Virginia glanced up and down the road, making sure she had it all committed to memory. Time to work. Fluffing her hair, letting it pull dramatically around her face, and adjusting her cleavage in the black tank top, she followed Tourmaline inside.

Cigarette smoke hung in thick spools and music throbbed, more bass than twang. The door scraped the gouged wood floor as it swung shut, and the whole bar looked up, as if they'd taken attendance and everyone had already been accounted for.

Virginia's stomach knotted, but she had the drill down pat—chin up, shoulders down, hands relaxed, eyes narrowed, and a tiny smirk on her face. The haze smelled like grilled onions and burnt tar and tobacco. A sticky bar ran along the left. A few tables scattered through the floor, with nearly burnt-out lightbulbs hovering over it all. In the back two pool tables sat supported by cinder blocks.

Tourmaline cut for the dark corner past the pool table, seemingly oblivious to the backward glances of the men she passed. Simultaneously wildly out of place and absolute ruler of all, she pulled a few cue sticks from the wall and handed them to Virginia. "Find the least bent."

Virginia started to eye one, but Tourmaline gave a tiny shake of her head. She laid the cue across the top of the pool table, and sent it rolling toward Virginia.

The bend became obvious.

Tourmaline picked two more and handed her one, gaze cutting sharp. "Just pretend you know what you're doing."

"Oh, hey, my specialty."

Virginia helped Tourmaline rack the balls, glancing to the bar and tables. The men were more than willing to look back at her, turning on their bar stools to watch, but faces wouldn't be enough. She'd need to build some kind of *thing*. Hazard expected this to happen immediately, and he didn't waste time with people who did not follow his instructions; he simply made them pay. It was the worst time to be dicking around.

"I think they like you," Tourmaline said with a sly grin as she pushed a single, delicate bracelet up her arm and sank a striped ball into the pocket right by Virginia.

"Of course they like us."

It was a truth universally accepted—especially in this crowd—that *two* beautiful eighteen-year-olds were better than one. Bonus points for a blonde and a brunette.

Tourmaline rounded the table, eyes narrowed at her shot. She took her turn and narrowly missed.

Virginia went next, but her shot bounced off the wall and spun out haphazardly.

Tourmaline didn't look impressed.

Irritated, Virginia rested on her cue. "You said you make money doing this?"

"I *will*." Tourmaline bent over—lining up a shot, taking her time—and Virginia couldn't quite tell whether Tourmaline was getting her shot right, or letting the bar get a long look. There was a strange duplicity in her steely eyes as she stared down the cue.

Finally, she shot.

The ball just missed.

Virginia arched an eyebrow and waited for Tourmaline to come around the table. Leaning into Tourmaline's neck, she whispered, "You missed on purpose."

Tourmaline paused in her careful brushing of the chalk. She flashed a warning look and moved away.

Tourmaline looked perfect—the church dress, the girlish boots and goddess hair. Perfection was the bracelet catching the light as she lined up her shots and the lingering trails of clean floral perfume. But it didn't run deep. There was something about the whole thing that made it seem like a show.

Like a hustle.

Virginia smiled. Slow. Knowing. Relieved to have one piece figured out.

Tourmaline bent and strung the cue through her fingers, carefully eyeing the ball.

A big guy moved out of the crowd to watch. He crossed his arms over his torn Miller T-shirt and moved the wad of dip in his lip. A Warden?

Tourmaline missed the shot and straightened toward him with a sheepish grin, saying something Virginia couldn't catch. They certainly seemed as if they knew each other.

The guy laughed, and after a moment's pause, motioned for someone across the bar.

Virginia wiped her sweaty palms on her jeans and tried not to look irritated that she didn't know what was going on or whom she should pay attention to. Hazard's games seemed like lessons in retrospect—meant to instruct her so the only thing she suffered was a little embarrassment. She bent and took her shot, somehow managing to sink the right ball into the right pocket.

"Pretty good shot." The big guy smiled and dug in his pocket.

"Thanks," Virginia said with practiced ease. She leaned against the pool table. "Are you going to introduce me?"

"Bill," he said over the chew, gaze flickering over her. "Your old man let you out like that? All pretty without him?"

Virginia wasn't sure whether he meant her dead dad, a boyfriend, or whether he knew she worked for Hazard, so she covered her confusion with a laugh and a wink. The wink worked on Bill, but not on the tightness in her chest.

He pulled a five from his wallet and placed it underneath his sweating beer.

Tourmaline looked at Virginia, hand out.

Ignoring the sick feeling in the pit of her stomach, Virginia leaned the cue against the edge of the table and dug a five out of her pocket.

"Mind if I borrow that?" someone asked behind her.

Virginia spun.

A Warden? With Bill? He was young. Maybe mid-twenties. Rail-like body, but sinewy arms and his face a little baby soft around his cheeks. He pointed to her cue.

Virginia glanced at Tourmaline, and Tourmaline nodded. "Uh. Sure." Virginia handed the cue over.

Tourmaline smiled—this pretty smile Virginia hadn't seen before—as she leaned over and reracked the balls. "Go easy on me, now," she said to the boy.

"I think y'all are the ones who should go easy on me," he said. He swished the chalk over the tip of the cue in a way Virginia found annoying, but mostly because of his unoriginal comments.

Tourmaline walked to the other side of the table, eyes narrowed, as the thin boy broke.

Well, hell, she needed *something*. Virginia leaned against the wall, arranging herself so it looked as if she were watching the game while she scanned the farthest shadows, straining for anything that seemed biker gang. Biker *club*, she corrected herself with an internal eye roll. What did the Wardens look like when they weren't literally wearing a sign?

Tourmaline knocked her elbow.

Virginia startled.

"Bad luck," Tourmaline said with a shrug, holding her hand out.

Virginia's first instinct was to slap her, but she just dug out another five.

The thin boy racked them this time, a little smirk on his face. The same kind of smirk twisted on Bill's mouth as he eyed Tourmaline's ass strut to the other side of the table and break. Virginia went back to searching, looking past the small crowd that had gathered with their beers in hand. In the shadows, she spotted a guy at the bar she hadn't seen before. Huge and tattooed, with ripped shirtsleeves and pointed ears. There was something familiar—a pull in her gut that Virginia always listened to. *There.* Had to be. She straightened off the wall and tightened her jaw, heading through the crowd with singular focus.

"Virginia," Tourmaline called.

But Virginia kept going. This was taking too long. She was losing money and time. Smiling, she leaned over the bar. Before she could even open her mouth, the guy with the ears looked up. But he wasn't looking at her.

Virginia frowned and followed his line of sight.

Two men were just sliding onto stools at the end of the bar. Both men were tall, but not huge. Fit, but not nearly as big as Ear Guy. One was white. One was black.

The white guy—the older one—scanned the room, gaze crossing hers as it passed.

She'd seen him before—the memory popped into her head instantly, one of those memories that was insignificant at face value, but had lingered as a deep impression. He'd been in the cookie aisle at the Covington WalMart. Looking like he'd crawled out of some deep hole that started on the western edge of the Blue Ridge Mountains and went straight into smoldering hellfires. He'd looked like sex. Smelled like alcohol. And lord, he'd attracted a whole lot of attention from all the housewives as he'd flicked through the packages and tucked up a pack of Oreos under his arm. She'd been weak in the knees for the first time in her life. When he turned to leave, his bright hazel eyes had met hers and slid right on past—same as they did this time.

"We have to go," Tourmaline suddenly whispered from Virginia's other side.

Virginia turned away, trying to appear calm. "Did you win back my money?"

"No. I forfeited. Come on."

Forfeited? Virginia froze. Running it over in her head. *Not lost?* It clicked. Virginia straightened, swiveling to get a good look at the two guys at the bar. *At the Wardens.* Tourmaline was hustling, all right. Hustling Virginia with this pool thing and shabby bar, giving Virginia an *experience.* It was good. Until actual Wardens showed up.

Slapping the bar, Virginia jumped up. "Busted," she said to Tourmaline with a wicked smile. She always did find it easier to deal with disaster when it hit, rather than anticipating its arrival.

Now that she knew the players, she knew how to fix the game.

7

BILL was smoothing out the money and carefully folding it, bill by bill when Virginia snatched it back and put it under the mug. "She's not done."

"Hey, now. She quit." He took it back, glaring.

Virginia glanced over her shoulder. The two Wardens leaned over the bar, backs to her.

Theatrically, Virginia ruffled back her hair and pulled the rest of her money out of her pockets—fingers trembling despite her best efforts. "You know what? I'm bored."

Bill fell victim to the show, but he managed to shrug. "So?"

"It's not like that," Tourmaline snapped at her elbow like a circling mosquito. "I swear I didn't mean—"

Virginia twisted her arm out of Tourmaline's grip. "How about we make this more interesting?" She held up the rest of her money, acting as if the entire bar were watching—pageant smile on, pageant wave fanning the bills for the crowd. Elegantly, she placed the money underneath the nearly empty mug. "Winner takes all."

Bill exhaled a low rumbling sigh as he pulled out his wallet. "All right. I'll play." He too held up the money for the crowd, finished the beer in a swallow, and stuck it all underneath.

Now there really was a crowd, keeping a wide berth, but holding their beers with amused grins as they watched.

"You." Virginia found Tourmaline and jabbed a finger at her. "*Socks.*" She wasn't about to let Tourmaline get away with breaking the deal she'd made.

Tourmaline's jaw tightened, but she picked up the cue and put her hand on her hip as the thin boy racked.

Virginia didn't bother looking over toward the bar. It wouldn't be long.

The boy went first, sinking half his balls right away.

The crowd pressed closer, glued to Tourmaline's reaction.

Tourmaline held her chin up, eyeing the table with poise. She didn't look like Margarine Girl at this specific moment, with her eyes calm and her hair brushed behind her. A cold fire was lit in her eyes and she looked ready to spit in someone's face.

Virginia's stomach twisted in knots, but she leaned against the pillar casually, breathing in deep breaths of Bill's Miller T-shirt–scented sweat and stale beer.

"Got plans tonight?" he asked.

"Yeah, watching my girl kick your boy's ass."

He laughed. "I meant after."

Virginia didn't answer.

It was Tourmaline's turn now. Finally. She bent—expression set and hip sunk as she lined up her shot between slim fingers.

The crowd held its breath.

Virginia, too.

Tourmaline tightened her jaw and hit. Three balls flew into the pockets.

The crowd shifted and murmured.

But Tourmaline didn't seem to notice. Immediately, she rounded the table and settled down, as if she'd known all along the place she would go. Lining up the shot, she smacked another ball into the pocket. Then a fourth.

A fifth.

Tourmaline chalked up, eyeing the two remaining balls and the eight ball.

The crowed leaned in.

Bill straightened off the pillar.

Virginia waited with bated breath, but not for the shot. *Three. Two.*

"What in the actual fuck are you doing?" a male voice boomed over the music.

One.

The older man stepped out of the crowd and slapped the cue stick out of Tourmaline's hands with a startling fierceness.

Tourmaline didn't flinch.

"Hey, man," Bill said, taking a step forward, hands up to calm everyone down.

The man turned, expression stone-cold and mean as hell under the dim light.

Virginia's breath lodged tight in her throat.

The look stopped Bill in his tracks. "Hey, sorry. I didn't know she was with you," he said.

"She's not," the man spat out. He turned back to Tourmaline. "Don't make me call. We'll *all* pay for that."

Tourmaline just stood there. Finally, she swallowed, and her eyes flickered between the two men. Suddenly, she pushed off and strutted past, head high.

Straight out the door.

"They're old enough. They knew what they were doing," Bill said to the black guy, as if by way of asking apology.

"They did," he said with a nod, turning to follow. "But you don't."

Shit. Virginia blinked in panic. She'd forgotten about her money, still sitting under the empty beer mug. She tried not to look at it, storming after the two Wardens as they followed Tourmaline. "What did you do? That was my money she was playing with. Wait," she called, pushing out the door after them. The wind snatched her breath away and the three figures walking ahead didn't look back.

Doubling her speed, she caught up to Tourmaline as the two Wardens headed for their bikes on the opposite end of the lot.

"Get on home," the older one yelled.

Tourmaline glared into the dark and flounced toward the truck.

Rage boiled under Virginia's skull, and with two long strides in the slippery gravel, she shoved all her weight into Tourmaline's shoulders. "Some of us fucking work for a living," she yelled as Tourmaline and her frothy dress went sprawling into the dirt.

Tourmaline scrambled up, mouth open. "Why did you do that?"

"Because you *hustled* me."

Tourmaline snarled and shoved back. They grappled for a minute, words lost in pushing and scuffing. Tourmaline twisted Virginia's arm back.

Virginia screeched and kicked at the other girl's shins.

"I didn't mean to. I'm sorry, okay?" Tourmaline yelled, but at the same time she threw a punch.

Virginia ducked. "Oh, yeah, I can really tell."

"No. *Wait.*" Tourmaline skidded backward and tucked her arms into her sides, looking like she was about to cry.

Virginia stopped, chest heaving.

The Wardens still sat across the lot. Close, but not close enough.

"I'm really sorry," Tourmaline said as she dropped her hands to her thighs and bent to catch her breath. "For the whole thing."

"Oh, you think?" Virginia threw back. "Which part? The part where you made a deal and *lied* to me? Or the part where you ditched me when ordered by your little guard dog over there."

"He's not." Tourmaline straightened and wiped her eyes. "Look. I'm sorry. I'll pay you back, okay? I promise."

Virginia clenched her jaw, glaring at her. "Right." Her stomach churned. It was like her first pageant all over again. Where there was so much more on the line than whether or not she did what she was asked.

Where the sum of her worth was back up for consideration. It shouldn't be; she'd proven herself again and again. But in her bones, she felt it. Sensed the change.

The wind gusted, swirling dust into their eyes, and when Virginia bent her head against the sting, she felt tired. Drained.

"His name is Jason," Tourmaline said in a half whimper. "I didn't think it'd be him. Usually it's Pickup who hangs out here. He wouldn't tell my dad—he thinks it's funny. But Jason will tell."

Virginia's gaze flickered up. *Who?*

"He's sergeant at arms, but don't tell a soul I said that."

"What?"

"Jason. Is sergeant at arms."

Virginia raised her eyebrow, a sudden shot of adrenaline rushing up her spine. She wanted to turn and look at him, sitting across the lot on his bike, but she didn't. "Oh."

"We good now?"

"No," Virginia retorted.

"What do you want?"

Virginia took a deep breath. She wanted whatever was so precious it had been hidden behind this elaborate ruse.

Behind her, a bike roared to life and Virginia jumped. A second started; their engines drowned even the wind as they passed by. Virginia dug her keys out of her pocket, heart racing. "Ready? I've got other things to do." She jumped in and turned the key.

Tourmaline got in.

Virginia pulled out of the lot, turning after the rapidly disappearing bikes.

8

TOURMALINE clutched the dashboard as they whipped out of the bar parking lot. "Wrong way."

Virginia ignored her.

"It's the other way, Virginia," Tourmaline snapped. Her phone buzzed from the center console, where she'd dropped it. Probably another text from Anna May or Allen, asking whether she was okay, whether she'd made it home. She'd told them she was sick, but Anna May had already texted asking whether that was Virginia Campbell's truck she'd left in, so there was sure to be a reckoning. It didn't matter, though. Anna May, Dalton, and Allen were all excused from Wayne's game, and at this point Tourmaline didn't care *what* happened to Virginia.

The moon crawled out of the tree line. Virginia kept on behind Jason and the conscript, passing by several places where she could have turned around. As if following them.

"What are we doing?" Tourmaline demanded. "I need to get home. I'll take care of the money tomorrow."

Virginia's jaw tightened and she glanced in the rearview. "I think someone is following us."

Tourmaline's heartbeat dove. *Wayne.* Mouth dry, she twisted in the seat and squinted out the back window. High beams blinded her. "Are you sure?" She tried to sound as skeptical as possible. Not afraid.

"I'm pretty sure they followed us out of the bar. Watch." Virginia went faster.

The headlights behind them sagged for a brief moment before

surging forward. Catching up. Pursuing. Tourmaline's chin hit the back of the seat. *Shit.* What now?

"You're paranoid," she said firmly, turning forward.

Virginia stopped at a four-way intersection and glanced back. "But what if I'm *not* paranoid?"

Frozen there, at a crossroads under a June moon above the Roanoke Valley, Tourmaline pinched the bridge of her nose and tried to think. She just needed to shake Wayne and get home. To safety. *Was Dad even home?* Shit. He wasn't. It was Saturday night. He was at the clubhouse.

A car pulled out of the black from the intersecting road and sped ahead of them, heading in the direction Jason and the conscript had disappeared.

It took a slow second. Tourmaline blinked, Wayne forgotten. Her stomach clenched as she stared at the license plate disappearing into the dark like a roach scuttling out of a tiny hole in a wall she'd long patched. This could not be happening. Was he following Jason and Cash? Following *Wardens?* "Keep up with that car," she seethed.

"What car? Ahead of us?"

Tourmaline waved. "Just go. Come on."

Virginia obeyed.

Tourmaline took a deep breath, steadying the heartbeat throbbing in her head. For a second she could smell the Old Spice and French fries of the interior. She remembered the view from the backseat. The chattering radio she strained to decipher. Virginia was going to get her show, after all.

"Who is that?" Virginia asked tightly.

"No one you'd know."

"I'm not asking to be polite."

"Yeah, well, if you won't know, why does it matter?"

Virginia straightened and looked in the rearview again. Shadows pinched worried lines across her forehead. "Screw you and your bullshit." The truck slowed.

"Don't you fucking dare." Tourmaline yanked Virginia's arm off the steering wheel, making the truck swerve wildly and Virginia slap at her hands. "You want a look into the Wardens? This is it. This is the shit I don't want anyone to know." They had to keep going. Jason wouldn't recognize who was behind him, and the Wardens had to know.

"Who's in the car, Harris?" Virginia yelled.

Tourmaline spoke through clenched teeth. "It was a state detective's car."

Virginia slammed on the brakes, hurtling Tourmaline into the dashboard. "What the hell are we doing following a state detective?" she screeched. "I can't do this."

"He's following Jason," Tourmaline yelled. "And Jason needs to know. *That's* what we're doing."

Virginia twisted over her shoulder, looking away from the road. "I can't. I *can't,*" she said in something startlingly close to a whine.

"Just keep driving," Tourmaline pleaded. "I have to know if it's him. This isn't a coincidence."

State Detective Alvarez had found out she'd been at the scene, met her at school one day before the trial, and told her he could help her mother. She'd gone with him because she hadn't known better. She'd done exactly what he wanted, telling someone she thought cared about her mom—burning down everything and everyone she loved in a wide swath of destruction. And she hadn't realized she'd been played—that it'd been wrong—until it was too late. The creature on Tourmaline's shoulders came sharply into focus, snickering in her ear as its wet, sulfur-tinged smell tickled her memories and delighted in her agony.

She had done this. She had caused this. "My mom is in a maximum-security prison for fifteen years because of . . . him. He's not here to make sure we're all holding up. He wants something."

Virginia looked in the rearview again, for so long that Tourmaline wanted to tell her to look at the road before they wrecked. "Shit," Virginia breathed, gaze finally flicking forward.

The surge that pinned Tourmaline against the seat seemed as good as words.

The road twisted into a series of switchbacks. With no dump points, they were all stuck in a slow, winding descent.

"He's hanging back from the bikes," Virginia said softly as they spun. "Maybe it's just the same car. Not the same person."

"No. He's hanging back because he knows where they're going."

Virginia kept one eye on the rearview as she spun the truck along behind the others—one link in the loose chain of disaster floating down the mountain. "What's the plan here, Harris?"

Tourmaline hit the button for the window and leaned against the door, dragging in deep breaths of the lush night air to combat the tightness in her chest. "Let's pretend there's someone following us. Can you lose them if I tell you where to drive?"

Virginia snorted and sat straighter in the seat. "We'll find out."

"There's an old logging road up here," Tourmaline said. "Get out of sight before you make the turn." She took another deep breath, pulling hair out of her mouth as it thrashed in the wind.

Virginia slammed on the brakes, the tires screeched. She laughed, wild and unearthly, mid-wrestle with the truck as the frame shuddered, eager to spin. "Who knew I'd be doing *this* with *you*?" Virginia hollered, hair whipping in the fierce wind.

"I should have put on my seat belt!" Tourmaline yelled back, bracing herself between the door and dash.

The truck slid nearly to a stop on the road.

"Yes," Virginia said primly. "You should have."

Tourmaline yanked the seat belt across her lap.

Virginia slammed it into second gear and hit the gas, engine roaring. They sped around the curve.

"Right there. Right there." Tourmaline jabbed her finger into the dark. "You're going to miss it. Turn, dammit."

9

THE truck bounced up into the brush with a terrible grinding sound, plowing through pitch-black, branches scraping the paint. The headlights washed over a rocky dirt road and the tires caught in the gravel, pulling them out of the hold of the trees.

"Cut the lights!" Tourmaline yelled just as Virginia killed them.

"Watch behind us!" Virginia leaned out the window, fighting the ruts in the road. "I can't see shit."

Tourmaline twisted. The truck bed kicked. But the only thing behind them was the night. "I think we're good."

The road stayed dim, but Virginia kept the truck moving.

A text from Allen lit on the phone Tourmaline had dumped in the center console when Virginia picked her up. *Want to come over?*

She picked up the phone. The truck bumped and dipped. Her knuckles brushed the wilted cotton of her dress and she closed her eyes, fingers frozen against the weight of her past. Allen was for the girl she could not be right now. Tourmaline dropped the phone and gathered her hair off her shoulders with sticky palms, scanning the woods around them.

"You sure that detective was following them?" Virginia asked, still half outside the window. "I mean. Since they're just law-abiding citizens and all."

Tourmaline ignored the sarcasm and snapped a rubber band over her ponytail. "Pull off up here. We'll cut through the woods to my dad."

Virginia parked, and Tourmaline led them into the woods, clinging tight to a deer path through the tangle of creeper vines and blackberry bushes.

"What else do you do for fun?" Virginia grumbled in a whisper as Tourmaline let another blackberry branch smack behind her.

"Hilarious," Tourmaline hissed.

"Still confused as to why you're wearing a dress."

"You picked me up from a date."

"A date?" Virginia snorted. "With who?"

"Allen Baker."

"A.B.? You had a date with A.B.?"

Tourmaline glared behind her. "Don't do that."

"Do what?"

"Pretend like you're shocked. I'm not one of your little plebeians."

Virginia was silent. Sticks snapped. Then, "He does have a thing for blondes."

"It's not a thing. We're friends. He goes to my church."

Virginia snorted again.

"Sometimes," Tourmaline amended.

"Hey, while we're on the subject: Tim Flemming? True or . . ."

Tourmaline groaned. Her yearlong relationship with Tim Flemming in eighth grade had ended the way all eighth-grade romances end—with a text. Except that Tim had alluded to a long conversation with her dad, and the rumor spread that Tim had *literally* pissed himself when her father threatened to end his life. The actual breakup and the subsequent rumor had left her gun-shy about the whole endeavor of dating, especially when it involved her dad. "Of course it's not true."

Virginia laughed. "Oh, poor Tim."

Tourmaline crouched and half crawled, half waddled as the path dipped under a thicket of mountain laurels. Fuck Tim Flemming. Tim wasn't the one with a dad suddenly faced with the panic of a teenage daughter and the concept of payback. "Well, thanks for your care. I've managed."

Behind her Virginia whisper-yelled, "You aren't helping your credibility, you know. You're full of shit. About your dad. About your life. You've worked really hard to make people think otherwise, but—" Virginia grunted; more sticks broke behind Tourmaline. "But it's just a hustle. Like in the bar back there, where you play all-innocent girl in a pretty dress in order to get by. I don't know what you are, Harris. But I *know* you're not innocent."

Tourmaline stopped and craned her neck against the thicket to stare at the dark mass that was Virginia. "Go piss up a rope," she whispered, furious that Virginia had the nerve to say it and suddenly terrified it might be true. "I know what the Wardens are. What I am. I don't need to prove it to you. Why can't you believe anything but lies?"

Virginia didn't move. Or answer.

Tourmaline bit her cheeks tight and turned back to crawling. They were almost back to the road. She'd have to be careful they didn't get turned around in the dark and come out right above Alvarez's old hiding spot.

Standing again on the path, she wiped the sweat and dirt off her forehead as Virginia crawled out. Too late, she remembered she needed Virginia's help to get things to her mom until she could go back and do it herself. That it had been the whole point of Virginia being there in the first place. "Sorry." *For the truth.*

"Nothing to apologize for," Virginia said, briskly brushing off her jeans. But her voice was tight.

The wind rushed high in the treetops—a dull roar hardly touching them under the deep tangle of vines and canopy as the hillside sloped steeper. After a few more minutes, the lights and the sounds of the clubhouse appeared and the hill fell out from underneath their feet.

Tourmaline paused to catch her breath, leaning against a thick oak. The clubhouse stood in a clearing below, tucked along a rushing, spring-fed mountain brook. Under white pines stood hemlocks, and black cherry trees that bloomed thick and white in the spring. It was an old building, sided with rough-cut planks. A soft stream of bass and guitar slipped through the cracks and carried on the wind.

Tourmaline hadn't seen it like this in so long; she'd forgotten what it used to feel like. Safe. As if there would always be a place she belonged. When she was in middle school and things were falling apart with her mother, she imagined running away to live in its attic, where she had often stretched out on a rag rug and played Candy Land by herself while the rain pattered on the roof. Looking back, she realized she'd only been there when her mother couldn't care for her—first because of the pain, and then because of the drugs—and she was forced underfoot at her dad's, like a puppy in the way. But she hadn't known she was an intruder then. It'd felt like home.

She closed her eyes and listened to the water. To the whisper of the wind. To the music that was always in the background of her life. It was all coming back now. Her throat ached with longing for that home and that mother—even a mother who'd abandoned Tourmaline in places a girl wasn't supposed to be.

A stick snapped as Virginia stepped beside her.

Tourmaline put a hand out. "Careful, there's an edge. It's steep."

Virginia nodded, a mixture of moonlight and the security lights outside the clubhouse casting shadows on her face. "They party here?"

Tourmaline nodded back. The lights swam, liquid and soft. The way you wanted romance to be—a little dark, a little mysterious, enticing you into some kind of lush, hidden world with a bottom rhythm of music and a sky as high as the stars. Unbidden, the conscript appeared in her thoughts. She shook her head to rid herself of the enchantment and lifted her chin. "They're my dad's friends. Do *you* want to hang out with your dad's friends?"

"My old man is dead."

Tourmaline bit her lips. *Shit.* She'd forgotten. "I'm sorry."

"Don't be." The night and shadows and moonlight mixed in Virginia's hair, seeming to pour out of her body as if she were emitting the night itself.

"Let's find a way down and get my dad." Tourmaline hitched her skirt higher on her thighs and started picking her way along the edge of the ridge. Hayes's warning echoed in her head again. Like an alarm, it kept going off. *You have to start paying attention to what's around you. You can't claim you didn't know and expect to get by.*

She knew. She was paying attention. Wayne was looking for her. Alvarez was back. But she found herself scanning the hillside with the wind biting the back of her neck in warning. *You have to start paying attention.*

What wasn't she seeing?

They clung to the ridge, high above the washed-out cut, and deep in what Tourmaline was certain would prove to be poison ivy. When a wash with a slope gentle enough to slide down opened up, she paused.

Virginia stopped at her side, breathing heavily. "What's your dad going to do about a state detective, anyway? Politely ask him to leave?"

"He'll . . ." But Tourmaline couldn't finish. What would he do?

"Mm-hm." Virginia seemed smug.

"It's not that," Tourmaline bit out in a whisper. "Everyone wants to fight the bikers. Even the cops. So it doesn't matter what he does, the story will always be he started a fight. He needs to know."

"Right this second?"

"I mean . . ."

"Why not wait until the morning, and then he has time to plan instead of just react?"

Tourmaline clenched her jaw and turned from the wash. They'd lost Wayne. Alvarez didn't know she'd seen him. There was no telling what kind of state her dad was in right that second. Virginia had a point.

"Ugh, fine. *I'll* deal with it."

"I didn't mean that," Virginia said.

"Go back to the truck. I'll figure a way out." Tourmaline pushed onward, scanning the edges for a car. It was a little spot Alvarez liked to hide in—a hollowed-out place in the hill where he could scan license plates and note bikes or run radar. If that car was there again, it was Alvarez. If the spot sat empty, it might have just been the same model, but not his car.

"I think this is *also* an ill-conceived idea," Virginia muttered, trampling in the brush behind her.

Tourmaline nearly smiled. Who would have thought the ever notorious beauty queen Virginia Campbell was the kind to stick it out? The idea made a tiny knot in her chest, like she had been feeling lonely and hadn't noticed until someone showed up.

A little farther ahead, the ridge pulled away, and there, overlooking the hollowed-out spot where the base of the ridge met the road, a dark car sat in the shadows.

Tourmaline crouched and chewed her lip, stomach sinking. This didn't need to be pretty. Pulling her cell phone out of the pocket of her dress, she turned on the screen. "Find some big rocks."

Virginia dug in her back pocket for her phone, matching Tourmaline's whisper. "We're low-tech tonight, I see."

Tourmaline flipped her off and picked through the dark by the light of their phones, amassing a pile of heavy sticks and rocks at the edge of the ridge. "Head back to the truck," she whispered, tucking the phone away. "It should be straight up that way."

"You have twenty minutes to get rid of him; then I'm picking you up down here," Virginia said. Her footsteps faded quickly, sucked into the summer-growth forest.

Tourmaline crept close to the edge of the ridge. The car sat neatly parked between two tall, shady spruces. Picking up a heavy rock, she tightened her jaw, eyed a spot on the roof, and threw.

The rock landed just where she'd hoped: dead center in the roof, with a terrific crunch.

Rushing, she picked up a stick and heaved it over. A second rock. Pelting the car with debris. Her last rock bounced off the trunk and she dashed behind a tree, watching. Waiting.

A floodlight hit the trees just to the right of her shoulder. As if he'd been waiting for *her*, not anyone on the road.

The tree she stood behind was not wide enough to cover her if the spotlight moved. Tourmaline bolted. The spotlight followed.

The ridgeline dipped toward the road and she fought to clutch at the deepest threads of night. Her boots slipped in the leaves. A pain stabbed into her bottom ribs. Fuck her life, and fuck Virginia, too—she should have just gone straight to Dad the way she'd planned. Or even asked Virginia if she had a better plan. Surely anyone had a better plan than this.

Tourmaline ducked behind a large shadow, discovering it was a lichen-covered boulder as it slapped into her back. Her heartbeat throbbed in her eyes—the moon and the dark sweep of the ridge mixing strangely. She pinched her lips shut tight to keep from panting.

The car passed slowly on the road. Gravel crunching under the tires. Spotlight sweeping the ridge above her.

Then it all fell dark again.

Something tickled her knee and she closed her eyes and forced herself to keep still. Sweat trickled into her eyes. The dress she'd picked out that night, imagining its cool, soft layers brushing against Allen's warm skin, felt dingy and wilted and just as ruined as she did. It was hard to remember she'd even been in that life—at youth group, worrying her top was too low, watching Allen under the lights, ordering teaberry ice cream and talking about college.

The night stayed silent. The tree frogs outpaced her breathing. Her phone buzzed.

Tourmaline stood and watched the road carefully, but Alvarez was gone.

Her phone buzzed again. Yanking up her boots, she walked out to the road, keeping to the edge as she waited for Virginia to pick her up.

Wisps of hair stuck to her forehead, but she didn't bother brushing them back anymore. The adrenaline ebbed. Her phone slapped her thigh as she walked. She was going to go home, shower, and, after a good night's sleep, tell Dad everything that had happened. He would know what to do, and they would do it. End of story. She closed her eyes and took a deep breath. Yes, that was it.

A noise sounded in the distance and Tourmaline turned. A low thrumming. The wind? A growling. *No.* She closed her eyes.

The roar of a Harley.

10

IT wasn't Jason. Or Sauls. Or Big Mac. Or any of the other guys whose bikes she knew and whose shadows she recognized instantly. She could tell by the tip of the night, the rush of her heart, off racing again, but in an entirely different pitch. She could tell by the bike. By the way he stopped in an easy, controlled near slide when she moved into the road. No one she knew stopped like that.

The engine cut. He sat on the road, silent. The soft metallic pricks of the cooling engine filled in the silence like popping sparks. Waiting.

"Fancy meeting you here," she said, blood rushing to her cheeks as the words left her mouth. Between this and having just watched Jason threaten to call her daddy on her, he probably thought she was still in middle school.

But for the first time all night, she felt sure of her safety, and uncertain of everything else. With him, she did not have to face anyone's curiosity or fear. She did not have to worry about what he might know or what he didn't know. He was her father's man, a Warden, and whether he knew it or not, he was already tangled inside her history. In the dark, it was easier to have courage she did not have by day. Though she knew she shouldn't, she threw her shoulders back and stepped over the front fender of the Fat Boy, pulling up her dress to straddle his front tire so he couldn't leave.

"I'm on my way to let Muir's dog out," he said. His voice was deeper than she remembered. "What are you doing out there?"

She crossed her arms over the handlebars, thanking God for low-cut dresses. "Haunting the woods. Didn't realize how close I was."

"Hm. Suspicious."

She shrugged. He was still a conscript. She was still his president's daughter. She didn't need to defend herself.

The conscript straightened and nodded his chin behind him. "Want a ride home?"

Yes. Her longing was instantaneous and emphatic, but she gulped it down. Boys alone were problematic; adding motorcycles to them would be disastrous. "No?" She could tell she didn't sound very convincing.

He put his hand on his knee, leaning his weight to one side as they listened to the wind roar above them.

A wind she could feel in her blood.

"It's going to storm," he said mildly. As if they had run into each other at the grocery store parking lot.

How old was he? She didn't need to ask. She was eighteen, but he was a grown man. Devoid of any gangliness that would hint at boyhood. He could have been twenty-something. He could have been thirty-something. He wouldn't care if she asked his age, but deep down she wanted him to care. She wanted eighteen to be able to reach that far. She licked her lips and forced herself to ask, "How old are you?"

"Twenty-three," he said immediately, like he'd been patiently waiting for her to ask.

Nineteen. Twenty. Twenty-one . . . Five years. Five years between where she stood, in a battered dress, and where he sat, big body edged in shadows. "Is conscript your full-time job?"

"I'm a chemical engineer. I work for a land remediation firm."

She blinked. He was a grown man. With a job. And part of her dad's club. This was hopeless. Her granny was shaking her head in her grave, saying to the cemetery, "That girl's problem is she's way too big for her britches."

"You in school?" he asked.

"UVA in the fall."

"Exciting."

The wind gusted, drowning out their voices with a sudden clattering of branches and upturned leaves.

"You need to be careful," she said softly, dismantling herself from his front tire. "Conscripts aren't supposed to be . . . stopping on the way to take care of Muir's dog."

"That old bastard's just fine."

Tourmaline frowned. "Muir or Peanut?"

The conscript laughed. "Peanut."

"He's mean. Bit me three times, and Muir of course made it all my fault."

"Who can blame him?"

"For making it my fault or biting me?" she almost asked, and then realized that was a bad idea because what she really wanted to know was *Do you mean you want to bite me?* and she couldn't even think in that general direction without blushing. "You're really not getting the very obvious and explicit hints I'm trying to get across, are you?"

"I need to go take care of the dog, got it."

Ugh, he wasn't dumb. He knew exactly what she meant. "Stop."

"Stop what?"

She crossed her arms and glared, confident it was communicated well even in the dark.

"Am I not supposed to talk to you because you're going to take advantage of me once you get me alone and in the dark?"

He was teasing, but she was deadly serious.

"If so—"

"You're not respecting the rules," she interrupted him with a snap. As if it hadn't been clear the first time they spoke.

The dark figure stayed still. Silent.

Her words came fast. "I'm not the club's. I'm my father's daughter. Not a party girl. Not available for . . . conversations," she explained, mortified suddenly to say these things out loud. Her fingers trembled at her sides. "It's disrespectful."

"Am I disrespecting you?" He sounded alarmed.

"Not me. The way things . . . ," she trailed off.

"Do you think I'm interested in the way things are done?"

She opened her mouth and then realized she wasn't sure what he was talking about. "Your dad . . ."

"Was an Original Member."

"Bill—" she started.

"OM," he said curtly. "All the people in this club who look like me are original members. *I'm* a conscript. The first black conscript. I'm the definition of 'not the way things are done.' And yet . . . here we are. Doing them."

She clenched her fists. This wasn't the conversation she meant to be having. "I don't mean because you're black, *idiot*. I mean because I'm your president's daughter."

"Are we fighting?" he asked, teasing still.

"We aren't doing anything. Stop pretending you have no idea what I'm talking about." He needed to comprehend that he couldn't play this game without risking everything he most wanted, even though she desperately wanted him to play.

Shifting the bike between his legs, he looked up and down the road and put the kickstand down. He got off the bike—the outline of his long body clearly visible in the dark as he took off the helmet and came toward her.

She wasn't breathing. Hadn't moved. That liquid heat spilled hot and furious through her body again, as if she'd put her hips snug to the front forks and it'd melted all her insides.

He stopped right in front of her. Legs spread wide. Close enough to see his eyes in the moonlight as he looked down at her. "You don't have to tell me how the Wardens work, all right? I'm not running off and telling anyone I found you on some dark road and we talked about Peanut's feeding schedule." He looked away. "But I feel like, all this reminding me of it, might be because you're trying to remind yourself?"

The blood throbbed in her head and she couldn't make heads or tails of the right thing to say. "I don't . . . I don't know." It came out breathless and she didn't even care.

He tilted his head, as if to kiss her, but he only looked at her mouth. "I like your dress . . ." His lips parted in a tiny smile.

Her body hung right on the edge, waiting. Her pulse shot through her skull.

"What if you asked me . . ." He said it softly. Not hesitant, but light, like the wind roaring high above her, but barely brushing the ends of her hair. "To respect *you*. Not the club."

And she did so want to ask. To demand. To just see what he was, other than her father's man. But she couldn't do that.

"We could say hi when we passed each other without you worrying about my patch," he said.

She pulled up. Blinked. What a little shit. "I see why you get along with Jason."

But he still had that small smile on his face that made her hope he was thinking about her dress, or biting her, or kissing, or *something*.

The road shifted and the stars drew closer and she was nothing but the wind roaring in her ears, roaring in her fingers. And she felt, maybe only wished, that it moved the same way for him.

He turned away, cracked asphalt grinding underneath his boots. "Get home safe, will you? I've got a dog to feed." He slung over the bike, started it up, and roared off.

Tourmaline stood in the dark. Alone. With the conscript's taillights disappearing into the shadows. The winds high and threatening. The trees watching. Her frozen at fourteen.

There was no chance she could find her way into that. Not while she wandered in the no-man's-land between the past and the future. Between childhood and the life she'd thought she'd have by now. It was only two and a half months until she left for UVA. Until she left all this behind and became the person she'd intended to be all along.

Her phone buzzed again and she pulled it out.

Another text from Allen. *Someone was asking for you. I told him I didn't know you just to be safe. It seemed kinda weird. Is this something with your dad? I'm freaked out now. I can't get hurt. Haha. But really tho.*

Her heart stuttered out its beat.

It was impossible to tell from the text who the man was, and she wasn't about to grill Allen for details to determine whether it was Wayne or Alvarez or a suspicious-uncle Warden who'd seen them together. But it didn't matter. She suddenly understood what Hayes had been trying to tell her all along. *You need to start paying attention to what's around you.*

She heard her father again, sitting across the desk talking.

We'll keep you safe.

She could not, eventually, evade Wayne. Not without intervention. He wouldn't grow tired of the game, no matter how far from this town she moved. It didn't work like that. There would be an end. Someone was going to pay for her actions. *Again.* So she'd tell her father—but how was Dad going to take care of Wayne? *Really?* Just talk to him? Command him? Would Wayne obey? Whatever he did, he would do with Alvarez waiting in secret spots, and Tourmaline had the sudden and sickening feeling that the law could be twisted into traps no matter what.

She stuffed the phone back and lifted her chin to the trees and the stars beyond.

The hairs on her arms crawled straight and rigid. The wind was high with warning as it knocked the branches together. Her eyes snapped to the rustling canopy, and she exhaled. Where *the hell* was Virginia?

She was going to need Virginia if she wanted to stop Wayne. Without her father.

A BUNCH of roses sat on the steps of the yellow rural Gothic house turned run-down duplex.

Virginia stopped in her tracks, in one abrupt scratch of her sneakers on the concrete sidewalk. The roses were wrapped in pink paper—full, a thick two dozen with their petals just beginning to open. They were of a red so deep they almost seemed black in the shadows of the porch light. She frowned and stepped over them, heading to the seventies plaid couch beside the door.

Her mother cradled a beer between her knees and a cigarette in her fingers. It was early and she smiled dopily as Virginia sank into the damp cushions.

"How was the pageant?"

"I wasn't at a pageant."

"Oh. Where were you?"

Virginia shrugged and stretched her legs onto the sagging porch rail. "Doing shit." She should have felt hopeful, after the night with Tourmaline. But she mostly only felt just as bone-tired as she had in the parking lot behind the bar. That was usually how she felt around her mother. How else were you supposed to feel about a woman who couldn't take care of herself, let alone you? It was a waste of time to have feelings about it at all.

"Pete brought me roses."

"That was nice of him." Virginia lit a cigarette, her stomach twisting. Where had Pete gotten such beautiful roses?

"He's a really good guy."

"Mm-hm," Virginia said absently, dropping her head to the back of the couch. She stared at the bugs circling the porch light. A cop car gunned past, lights circling. No siren. Another followed.

"Rob was an asshole."

"Rob *was* an asshole," Virginia agreed. Though she was sure Pete was, too.

"Did you win?" Mom asked. "Where's your crown?"

"I'm done with pageants, remember?"

"Right. I knew that." Her mother took a long drink of the beer.

"V! You're home." Her mother's roommate came out of the apartment. Landon had moved in with them two months ago, when he'd broken up with his violent ass-hat of a boyfriend. Mom had offered because she didn't like to be lonely, and Virginia had agreed because she didn't like shouldering all the rent. Landon's job as a bartender at a strip club in Lexington kept him out most nights, and he never seemed to mind coming home to find Mom sleeping on the porch. "I feel like you're never home these days."

"I'm not." She put the cigarette to her mouth and tried not to look at Landon and encourage him to keep talking.

"Virginia needs a job." Her mother slurred it out in a way that made perfect sense. "Got an opening?"

"I don't need a job. I have one," Virginia corrected her mother just as Landon's eyes perked up.

"Raven's about to go on maternity leave. I can talk to—"

"Stop being so precious, Virginia," her mother interrupted. "It's just waitressing."

"I don't need a job. Remember? I still work for Hazard. You got me that job."

Her mom frowned. "But you're not doing pageants anymore?"

Virginia yanked her legs off the railing. It'd been a waste of a knife, blunted by the armor that was her mom's spaced-out drunkenness.

Now it was only Virginia who felt raw and annoyed by the conversation. She stood. "I need to get to bed. It's an early morning." But instead of going inside, she held the cigarette up and crouched over the steps to get a closer look at the roses.

"V."

She swung around.

"Aren't they nice?" Mom said.

"So nice." Virginia kept the card she'd pulled out of the roses in her palm. "Night."

Inside their upstairs apartment, Virginia didn't look at the card until she was sitting on the toilet lid, waiting for the hot water to make it to the third-floor shower.

V—I know you're going to miss the crowns. I'll make it up to you.

R.H., Esq.

The dew lay thick on the roses the next morning, still undisturbed as Virginia stepped over them and threw her bags into the truck. She'd left the card in the bathroom trash, ripped into shreds so her mother or Landon wouldn't accidentally find it. Thick currents of clouds drifted across the mountains as she drove into the cultivated Roanoke suburbs to perform her duties as a low-level drug dealer.

Hazard lived in one of those housing developments with "Plantation" somewhere in the name—with their manicured and land-scaped yards and their expansive Jeffersonian-style houses set back from the road with baby trees planted along the driveway. She'd been there before—to drop things off or pick things up—but she usually broke down shipments at his office or warehouse. Not at his house. It was hard not to slow and look at the houses as she drove through the subdivision.

Thunder rumbled ominously behind the trees by the time she parked the truck on the damp asphalt driveway and knocked on the back entrance.

"The Queen. Your kingdom." Hazard bowed affably as he opened the patio door and let her inside. He was wearing sweatpants and a Georgetown T-shirt (though she was pretty sure he'd *not* gone to Georgetown). "Some coffee?"

She slid the door shut behind her and plopped her bags onto one of the bar chairs. "Yes, please." Tumi—another one of his dealers—usually handled this chore with her, but there didn't seem to be any sign of her in the house. This wasn't something that made Virginia immediately uncomfortable so much as it was something she was immediately aware of.

"And I got apple fritters. I know they're your favorite." He placed a plate and napkin on the marble island, following it up with a mug full of steaming black coffee.

She swallowed, hungry for both the food and whatever unnamed thing tightened in her chest at the sight of pristine white stoneware on a veined marble countertop.

Hazard pulled out her chair, but she didn't sit—just perched lightly against the chair so it looked as if she were sitting. The battered backpacks she used for work looked even dingier and more torn up than usual.

"Did you get the flowers?" Hazard put a fork down beside her and leaned against the counter. "I never know if things make it to you."

Virginia nodded, carefully cutting through the fritter with the edge of the heavy silver fork. "I got them. You didn't have to do that."

He waved his hand. "I know you're worried about what's going to happen next. I just wanted to show you I appreciate all the work

you've done and how hard you hustle. Everything's going to be fine."
His hand dropped to her shoulder, rubbing it casually, as if an after-
thought or a punctuation on his assurances.

The touch didn't bother her. Not technically. Just intensified her
awareness. The smell of the house—empty and clean. The gentle sound
of the central air. The way the ridges of his hand caught on the back of
her arm. Why wasn't she at the office? Had he just wanted to get her
out of the office to show her his appreciation? The food and coffee and
flowers? Virginia stayed relaxed, putting another bite of the fritter into
her mouth and pretending she did not even notice his touch.

After a few more seconds, his fingers brushed her neck as he moved
away. It seemed like an accident and she bit down on her shiver.

The house seemed quieter.

"Tumi coming today?" she asked casually.

"Nope. She called in sick. It's all you."

Her stomach twisted and she hid behind a swallow of coffee.

"If you want to hang out afterward, there won't be anyone here. You
can watch TV. I have some new movies; my daughter dropped them off
last time." He shrugged. "I don't have time."

"Oh . . . ," Virginia said softly, poking at the apple fritter. She wasn't
hungry anymore, but felt she should eat it.

He topped off her coffee. "I have a golfing appointment, so I'll be
out all afternoon. You're free to make yourself at home. Fridge is full."

She ducked her head and forced another bite. "Thanks," she said
over the fritter. It gummed up in her throat and she swallowed great
gulps of the bitter coffee to pull it down.

This time Hazard patted-slash-rubbed the middle of her back. As if
she were his daughter. He did have a daughter a little older than Virginia.
In law school. She gripped hard to the idea that this was the episode in

which the story line focused on his relationship with his daughter and how paternal he felt in the emptiness of the big suburban house. He'd never truly given her a reason to believe it was something else.

"No problem at all. I got your back, V." He moved away, swallowed the rest of his cup, and placed it in the sink. "I'm just going to go shower. Everything's set up in the office. Upstairs and to your left. You'll see it."

She waited until he'd left and dumped the rest of the fritter in the trash. Maybe she'd just gotten so used to men reacting to her in a certain way that she didn't know what normal interaction was anymore. Hazard had been her boss for four years, and while he'd always appreciated her looks, it was never in a way that crossed a line. This was just a transition from pageant appreciation of new dress and good hair to appreciating her "hustle." There was no need to panic. She grabbed her bags and went upstairs.

The shower was running. The master bedroom door was open, but not all the way. It wasn't weird. It wasn't weird. It wasn't weird. She repeated this over and over, trying to tell her pulse and the stiffness in her spine what was true.

She shook it off and walked through the open double doors into Hazard's home office. He'd cleared the desk and set up her stuff there. The room was bright even though the clouds outside had only thickened. It smelled of books and coffee, and when she sank into the leather chair, her toes hit the heavy bag he'd left underneath the desk.

Relief flooded her. This was normal. Nice, even. Everything was fine. She unzipped the black bag and began pulling out the pills, the taped-up pound of weed, and her things for repackaging. Hazard kept the scales, and bags, and even the marker she used to mark the bags just in case someone needed help remembering the difference between Oxy and Vicodin. *Never underestimate stupid* had been one of Virginia's first lessons. *Never trust your employees* had been one of Hazard's.

She got it all laid out and began to work. It would take an hour or so—dumping out the pills and separating them. Pulling apart the weed and weighing it out. She did her own clients first. Then moved on to Tumi's and Danylynn's lists. She knew them all by memory; starting the ritual in the quiet house, insulated from the storm, melted away the last of her tension. There were extras this time and after double-checking, she pulled them to the side and began packaging the rest. Maybe Hazard would let her do this here every time. She'd always choose coffee and fritters and a nice study over a law office on the weekend and gas station coffee.

Hazard came rushing in, only half dressed.

She jerked straight in her chair and quickly looked back to her work.

"Sorry. I'm running late and left my watch in here." He started looking through a drawer at her elbow. He smelled like the shower and it was hard to avoid the intimacy of the moment.

She shifted on one arm of the chair, trying to put distance between them without making him aware of it. "I've got extras?"

"Right. Smart girl," he said affectionately, still sorting through the drawer.

Had it been a test? She frowned and the tension in her spine ratcheted higher. She'd passed, though. It was fine.

He pulled out the watch and closed the drawer, looping it around his wrist to latch it. "Package them up all together. I've got a new staff member."

"Restructuring?"

"That's right." His big hand went to her hair, patting through it. "So sharp."

She held very still, stifling the urge to jump.

His fingers dropped to the side of her face, gently pulling her toward him.

Her stomach dropped.

This wasn't his paternal longing. This was something else. She still sat in the chair, motionless, as he presided over her.

The room shimmered with dropping pressure. The edges fell away. She forced herself to keep breathing. This was simple and yet it was the same as the Wardens. *Stop being so precious, Virginia.* But she didn't move.

He looked at her impassively. He didn't need to force her. The fact was, they both knew he could, alone in this big house with its marble countertops and her long-standing reputation as wild and wandering. With her fritter, half eaten in the trash. There was no way for her to win. And if she said no now, it wouldn't mean anything. He was the one who would decide.

She swallowed. Tried not to flinch. Or close her eyes. Stiffening, she arched her back and neck just a fraction, to tug against the pull of his fingers. To pull away in this silent and immobile stalemate.

His eyes narrowed.

She forced herself not to cower.

A car door slammed.

They jerked apart, turning to the window.

A middle-aged man in a polo shirt and khakis got out of a sedan and opened the door to the backseat, pulling out golf clubs even as he looked to the churning sky.

"Shit, I'm late," Hazard said, fumbling with the watch again.

Was he pretending to redo his watch? She couldn't tell. He seemed suddenly awkward. Confusing.

She sat frozen in the office chair. Barely breathing.

"Finish and lock up when you leave. If I find it unlocked, I'm docking your pay," he said curtly as he turned away. "And I better hear something about your new friends this afternoon. Text me. I'll be waiting."

Virginia stared out the window. Watching the man in the driveway. The black Impala. It was a cop car, she realized a full ten seconds later than she would normally have. This was the home of Robert Hazard, Esquire. This was the ruse. She narrowed her eyes as the man checked his cell phone, smoothed his hair, and jingled his keys while he waited. It looked like it was about to pour. Were they actually going golfing? Suddenly, she thought of her mother, sleeping at home. Happy. Warm. Drunk. Mom had nothing but good things to say about the lawyer who'd helped her out of a tough spot. The charming lawyer who understood these situations. Whatever the situation might be.

What if she opened the window and rained weed and pills onto the cop's head? Would he care? Probably not. Probably Hazard had done the cop's bankruptcy, and the cop felt Hazard had taken care of him through a vulnerable time. Probably the cop would have sold *his* daughter for this security if they didn't take Hazard's fee straight out of the bankruptcy settlement. Hazard would continue to foster that feeling of benevolence—golfing, dinners, legal advice that seemed to be free.

Hazard came out, apologetic and charming, shaking hands and laughing. They looked at the sky and shrugged. Beer in the clubhouse was always an option.

She didn't turn away from the window until she watched Hazard load their clubs and drive away. Texting Tourmaline, she rushed to finish her work.

It was unquestionable now. If she didn't find a way to distract the Wardens, *her way*, she would ultimately have to do it *his way* or face the consequences. And she wasn't sure she could survive his revenge.

She triple-checked the locks before getting in the truck and speeding out of the neighborhood of mini plantations.

12

TOURMALINE woke, leaving behind hazy dreams of the conscript to blink in the face of a stone-cold-sober reality and a shrilly ringing phone.

Anna May.

"What?" she croaked.

"I thought you were coming to church. We were going to do lunch afterward," Anna May said, sounding disgustingly chipper and faintly irritated.

Tourmaline dropped back into her pillow.

"Remember, we made plans last night?"

She tried to think, but couldn't remember anything except that Alvarez was back, Wayne was after her, and she liked a man her dad was going to kill. She might as well have woken up without a driver's license and with her algebra homework undone for all the ways she felt fourteen again. "I have a migraine," she managed. At least it was true.

"Oh-*kay*," Anna May said.

"I'll call you tomorrow?"

"Fine."

"I'm sorry," Tourmaline said, but Anna May had already hung up.

Rain fell in sheets outside the window. She crawled out of bed and went into the hall, calling through the house as she stumbled toward the kitchen. But all stayed silent. Shadowed. Had Dad even come home? When did he start considering her old enough to be left alone?

Putting her hand over her face, she tried to think beyond the building waves of pain in her head. She was eighteen. He trusted her to be at home and be okay with it. He was probably at Jason's. She was eighteen.

She was in control. The sound of the rain pricked her as if it were hitting under her skin, and she dropped her hand, squinting in the dim light to start a pot of coffee and retrieve her phone.

She found her father's text. He hadn't come home. He said he was at Jason's. She tried to believe him, not to think of the blonde.

Rain drummed a steady beat on the roof, dripping thin rivulets down the glass door. She didn't wait for the coffee to finish brewing before pouring herself a mug and popping a Tylenol. Sitting cross-legged at the table, she dropped her face into the steam coming off her coffee, basking in the warmth as she looked at the texts from Anna May asking where she'd gone the night before and whether she needed anything.

Erasing all the messages, she closed her eyes. Wayne. Alvarez. Mom. The conscript. All of it too big and too much to contain as it drilled out through her temple.

A low rumble of thunder echoed in the empty kitchen, and the sound sent a new wave of pain cutting through her brain so profoundly that she didn't hear the knock on the door until it had faded. Frowning, Tourmaline looked up from the blinking cursor and stared at the door.

Whoever it was knocked again.

A wild hope that it was the conscript shot through her body. That he'd be standing outside on her step in the rain in that black T-shirt, looking down on her, gaze flickering between her mouth and her eyes. For a moment the thought almost expunged the pain of her headache. But it couldn't be him. That would be insane.

Drawing a deep breath to calm her skittering heartbeat and quell the hope, Tourmaline dropped the phone and ran for the door.

A man stood on the step, tucking himself under the eaves to stay out of the rain. His shirtsleeves were rolled up and his face was slick with a thin sheen of rain. He wasn't familiar.

She had wanted it to be the conscript, but she hadn't known just how much until he wasn't there. Frowning, she spoke behind the mostly closed door. "Sorry, my dad's not home right now."

"Tourmaline Harris?"

She narrowed her eyes. The only people who came looking for her made her want to never be found.

"Do you have a minute?"

"What do you want?"

He looked surprised at her tone, but his expression smoothed instantly. "We can talk out here. It'll just take a second."

She opened the screen door and slid outside. Wary. The throbbing in her head faded behind razor-edge alertness. Who was this? What did he want?

The concrete step was damp under her bare feet, and she kept one hand resting on the edge of the doorframe, prepared at a moment's notice to hop back into the house and lock the door.

"I'm Special Agent Tom Mitchell, FBI." He held out his hand. She noticed the badge on his belt.

Her blood went to ice. A federal agent? She swallowed. Stared. The air had been all sucked out of the rainy summer morning. After Mom, it was hard enough to see the security guard at school. And with Alvarez back . . . This couldn't be a coincidence. Could it?

Tourmaline blinked, searching his face for anything to trigger her memory. It wasn't there, but countless memories she'd wanted to put away forever waited in its place. "Are you here about Wayne?"

He dropped his hand and tilted his head. "Who?"

"Wayne Thompson. The guy whose heroin my mom got busted for? Just released? Any of this ringing any bells?"

"I'm not familiar with your mom's case beyond the basics. That's not really why I'm here."

Of course not. She tightened her jaw and looked away. Even though she'd known better, disappointment pitched deep in her stomach. As if she'd expected something different after everything that had happened.

"I'm sure you're aware this area has been going through some difficulties with heroin. Your mom." He dipped his head in acknowledgment of the ribbon of sticky black highway that had claimed her mom. "With the interstates right here, it's becoming more and more of a problem. I'm here—" He paused, and then corrected. "The FBI is here, as part of a special task force combating the trafficking and distribution of heroin."

"What does that have to do with me?"

He paused again, as if weighing his answer. "It doesn't. Per se."

She gave him a cold look, putting her hand on the screen door to threaten going back inside.

"Maybe it does. Does it?" he asked.

That her mother was an addict did not mean she'd know all about heroin use in southwestern Virginia. "What are you saying?" But it clicked as the words left her mouth.

He was here for the Wardens. *For Dad.* Because he thought they were doing something with heroin.

Hayes's warning bell tripped again. *You have to start paying attention to the things around you.*

He looked past her, as if scanning the house and barn and committing it all to memory. "Maybe your dad's club needed a way to make money, and your mom got caught up in a wave a lot of folks are finding themselves in? A casualty of war. I spent eight years with the Pagans. Similar kind of thing."

She swallowed. "The Wardens aren't that kind of club. You think my dad would have anything to do with that after watching my mother?"

He looked into her eyes then, a sad smile pulling on his mouth, as if he were watching something he'd seen before and he knew how it would go. "I've seen a lot of girls like you. Saying that same thing. Wives. Girlfriends. Daughters. It's not even that you're lying, either . . ." He shrugged, a terrible kind of sadness still creased on his face.

Heat bloomed in her cheeks—anger and embarrassment mixing as the thought occurred to her that maybe, *maybe,* she was a fool here as well. That she didn't really know. That the warnings she should have been listening to were these. But the thought was so sickening and terrible she immediately shook her head.

She wasn't. She knew. This was all just a game to make her do what they wanted. She wasn't about to fall for it again. "Outsider's misconception," she said coldly, jumping back inside. "Have a good day, now."

The man shoved his boot into the door before she could close it.

Her heart quickened, but she glared at him as if he didn't outweigh her by a hundred pounds and a shiny brass badge.

"I can help you," he said. "We can talk about your mom. Talk about her sentence."

"That's what they always say," she snapped, struggling to smash his foot in the door. "Until you're sitting in a courtroom finding out they lied. I've had help before. I'm good for a lifetime."

"I'm not *accusing* your dad of anything. I'm just trying to sort out what's true and what's not. Let me just . . ." He dug in his pocket and produced a business card. "Here. In case there's anything you think might help. Or even if you need something. Anything."

She clenched her jaw and ignored the card, pressing the door harder on his wedged foot.

He grimaced. "Just in case." Picking up her wrist, he shoved the card into her limp hand, and with a quick tug, pulled out of the door.

Tourmaline flipped the dead bolt and watched him leave from the window, only turning away when his black Suburban disappeared down the driveway.

The card was still in her hand. Thick paper with his name and number on it. A tiny FBI seal in raised ink. She thumbed over the seal, the edges on her skin turning to pain inside her head. The truth was not what he wanted. No one wanted the truth.

Maybe not even her.

You can't claim you didn't know.

No. She couldn't think like this.

In her room, she shoved the card deep in her nightstand and burrowed back under the covers. The ceiling stared back at her.

That guy—the agent—he was wrong. The CO was wrong. Virginia was wrong.

She'd know.

Tourmaline kept repeating it to herself, staring at the ceiling, head throbbing. But the more she repeated it, the less she believed. It slipped out from her fingers like a flower-painted porcelain teacup she'd taken from her granny's hutch, something she wanted so desperately to return untouched to its shelf; but she felt it slip through her fingers as she stumbled on the way back. Belief. Shattering.

Maybe she didn't know.

Tourmaline closed her eyes, falling into the depths of the pain in her head, and somewhere inside her circling thoughts she landed, half dreaming and half remembering her sixteenth birthday.

Mom had called from prison, Dad had gotten her a cake, and they ate it alone. No Wardens. No Mom.

That afternoon, Dad had been outside with a few Wardens, and she went out the way she normally would—seeking out warmth like a stray kitten, content to curl up in some cozy corner of the garage and be around people she knew when the rest of her life was foreign.

Dad had turned when they saw her coming.

She'd given a tiny wave-shrug and ducked her head.

He'd not smiled as deeply. But she only saw that now.

Turning his shoulder, he'd stepped in front of her and not acknowledged her.

She had been in her own world, not his, so it wasn't something to take much note of, and she'd pulled her hands out of her jacket pockets to sit on his bike.

It was the same thing she'd done since he first put her there as a baby. Propping her up in his lap for Mom to take a picture. Lifting her up on her own when she was older, and telling her not to get fingerprints on the gas tank. Taking her for rides as she clutched the middle of the handlebars and laughed at the wind in her face. She sat quietly. Pretending to ride. Pulling the bike off the kickstand to test the heavy weight while Dad wasn't watching. The conversation had been boring—just the soothing backing track to a life she remembered having before her mother had left. The sun was setting. The dogwood was losing its blooms.

The wind had gusted. She remembered because it took her hair and pulled it out behind her in the spring sunshine, and she'd opened her mouth to taste the hints of melting ice and mountain snow still left as the wind poured off the ridge.

And she remembered because that was when Dad's hand had fallen gently on her shoulder.

She blinked and looked up. They all stood there quiet. Serious. No one really looking at her.

"Go inside, Tourmaline," Dad had said softly. "And stay there."

Her face had burned with the kind of embarrassment that she could still feel now, half asleep in an empty house with a summer rain on the roof. It was the kind of embarrassment everyone seemed to understand except her, which made it all the more embarrassing. She'd wanted to cry, right there, right then, but she'd gotten good at holding back tears.

Biting the inside of her cheek hard enough to draw blood, she'd stood off the bike, lifted her chin, and walked inside. Searching: trying and failing to see what she'd done. She'd never been sent away like that . . . not by her father. And the thought consumed her, choking her, that she'd done something horribly wrong and hadn't known, while everyone else did.

Inside the house, she'd slammed her bedroom door and screamed. A scream she half hoped they'd all hear, standing out in the driveway in a place she couldn't be.

But if they heard, Dad never mentioned it.

She'd caught sight of herself then, in the dark. In the single beam of pale spring sunshine that clung to her room when the sun had dipped beyond the window. In that pale silver light, her eyes were angry and heavy with unshed tears, and her cheeks flushed. Her body had gathered a woman's sway to meet the road in front of it. And she'd looked . . .

Like her mother. Her mother, the Queen. Not her mother, the fallen. Like the wild woman who had both laughed and kissed with abandon. The one who had danced on the borders of everything. Where Dad and the rest of the Wardens were lesser gods, crawling on their knees to pay tribute to her hold on the fates. But that woman didn't exist anymore, just the space she'd once occupied. That Queen had faded away to sit in United States Penitentiary, Hazelton, while Tourmaline screamed because she was alone and cut off from all she'd ever known of love and family, trying to hold the echoing space her mother had once inhabited without having any understanding of what that role entailed.

Tourmaline could see now what had happened.

She began to see it soon after that day—laid bare in the strange men she passed. But then, slowly, she saw it even in the Wardens—even the ones who understood, without Dad to remind them, that she was still a child. It was in their eyes. It was in the way they smiled—finding some joy she didn't understand when they looked at her. A joy sometimes complex. Sometimes simple enough to make her sick.

And she knew that they knew.

Thou shalt not . . . That was when she discovered that law: when it applied to her. That was when she discovered it wasn't her world; she just lived in it.

The rain drummed harder. Tourmaline blinked at the ceiling, reaching for sleep but fighting it all the same. She should text Dad and tell him about Wayne. Her hand pushed out, groping for the phone, but the movement sent a heavy wave of drumming pain behind her eyes. She tried to lift her head, but the white walls seemed so bright and searing that she quickly gave up.

What if she *was* wrong?

About everything.

Virginia would know. Virginia was the kind of girl who would know the answer to these questions.

Finding the phone, she forced her eyes open, texting Virginia to ask whether she was busy. But the pain in her head twisted and sharpened, as if there really stood a creature on her chest, gleefully poking its razored fingers in and out of her skull. And the only way to get out from under the creature was to give in to the darkness.

13

"YOU okay, honey?" A soft voice reached down into the pain.

Mom?

Tourmaline pushed away the covers and forced her eyes open. The dull light from the windows sent a sickening wave of nausea over her, and a hot knife continuously impaled her temple.

"You look like hell." It wasn't Tourmaline's mother sitting on the edge of the bed, but Virginia. Long wavy dark hair. One eyebrow ever arched over suspicious blue eyes.

Not Mom.

The disappointment hurt more than the migraine. How could she still be expecting her mother to be there, after all that had happened?

"Migraine," Tourmaline muttered, throwing her arm over her eyes. Hot tears collected underneath her eyes. Spilling over. Down her cheeks.

"Did you take medicine?"

"No." Tourmaline moaned. If *Virginia Campbell* was here, the horrible things inside her head were probably all real as well. "I don't want them. I just need to sleep," she croaked through a dry mouth. It wasn't until the bed sagged, rolling her into a body, that she realized Virginia had left and come back.

"Come on. Let's get you fixed." Virginia shoved tablets into Tourmaline's palm and pulled her upright at the same time.

She didn't want to sit up. Or take medicine. The emptiness of sleep beckoned her, and she let her body fall back.

Virginia hooked an arm around her ribs and pulled her forward. "Come on. Just sit on the floor."

There was no fix for this hurt. But Tourmaline closed her eyes and slid off the bed, slumping to a heap on the floor. Carpet under her thighs. The humidity heavy on her arms and legs despite the air-conditioning. The smell of food cooking. With Mom.

Mom cooking. Mom rubbing her back. Mom sitting on the floor of her bedroom, playing cards. Mom everywhere.

Tourmaline rarely cried about it anymore, but the loneliness exploded in her chest, leaving her aching and raw on her bedroom floor. She sobbed as if everything in her head that hurt was simply built up of tears that needed to be let out.

"Here." An ice pack pressed to the back of Tourmaline's neck. Cool hands lowered Tourmaline's feet into scalding water. "Tell me if this is too hot," Virginia said.

Tourmaline gingerly dropped her wet face into her knees, pressing the tender eye sockets against her kneecaps to relieve the pressure. "What are you doing here?" she mumbled.

"Came to collect on that money you owe me."

Tourmaline's mouth watered, but she swallowed it down. She would *not* be sick. "What time is it?" she asked, trying to orient herself a little.

"Nearly supper."

Dad had to be home by now. She needed to tell him.

Slowly, more things came into focus, pulling her out of the past. Eventually, she lifted her head off her knees. Her cheeks were tight from dried tears. Her knees were still wet. The ice pack slid down her back. The water had cooled.

She looked through her window: They were out in the driveway. As they had once been. As they always would be. Jason. Dad. The conscript. Standing around a bike and talking.

She sniffed and met Virginia's calm gaze. "Let's sit outside."

Tourmaline flicked water off the lawn chair and sat, tilting her head to the clearing skies and the thick beams of light filtering through the wet trees.

"Real pretty back here," Virginia said, plopping into a chair next to her. "I might almost believe your dad knows something about gardens."

The garden was a hodgepodge of experiments intended to screen the back garages from view of the driveway, but like most things, Dad had managed to pull it together.

Staggered cedars, magnolias, and festuca grass broke down to an unfinished flagstone path winding through the rosebushes, zinnias, and pink coneflowers. There were three waterfalls, all different—products of Dad trying out new techniques. A well-worn path cut between two lilac bushes to the garage.

Virginia pulled her leg up and lit a smoke.

Tourmaline erased a voicemail from Anna May and slouched in her chair, staring into the garage. The doors were open, the lights on. Inside, Jason, Dad, and the conscript picked their way to the back.

Part of her had hoped the migraine had intensified everything, even reality. But now it was clear: Her faith was faltering. She could feel doubt there, a growing shadow over everything. And inside that doubt, Wayne became more and more her responsibility. She took a deep breath of the smoke from Virginia's cigarette.

If there was ever a guide for those shadowed and twisting paths, Virginia Campbell would be it. "All right, let's try this again. What do you want with the Wardens? No bullshit."

"No bullshit?"

"Not even a little."

Virginia sighed and slumped in her chair, playing with the lid of the cigarette box. After a minute, she answered, "I'm not sure. I want to know."

"You mentioned. What about?"

"About men who are more than men. About why you say they aren't criminals, and yet everyone around them acts as though they are. I want to know whether they're good men who do bad things, or bad men who do . . ." She shrugged. "Bad things."

"This seems like pretty cheap shit, if you're asking me."

"It's always valuable to know what kind of men your world is made of."

Tourmaline rolled her eyes. "They aren't *your* world."

"The same kind of men are everywhere."

Tourmaline's eyes followed the conscript as he helped her father roll out the bike. What kind of man was he? A younger Jason? Something else? "Is everything they say about *you* true?"

"Oh, absolutely."

Tourmaline tore her gaze away from the conscript. "So, the drug dealing?"

"I'm actually a member of a cartel," Virginia said primly.

"Oh, the *Full of Bullshit* one?"

"Oh, this is fun," Virginia said. "Try some more."

"You slept with the assistant principal to graduate with honors?"

"Much easier than working, don't you agree?"

"You had four abortions?"

"Fourteen," Virginia said coolly over a rush of smoke.

Tourmaline clenched her jaw. "You were born nine months after your mother slept with the devil, and that's why your eyes are so blue and your hair is so dark?"

"Absolutely." Virginia winked.

"Is there anything about you that isn't bullshit?"

"Nope. That's how come I know it when I see it." Virginia stabbed the cigarette in Tourmaline's direction and grinned.

"What's the worst thing you've done?" Tourmaline challenged.

Virginia didn't answer right away, eyes narrowing as she took a long drag. She exhaled and looked down. "Being young and naive was the worst thing I've ever done."

They were the same age. They'd been in the same grade in school their whole lives. But in that moment, Virginia seemed a much older type of eighteen, with a much different level of thinking.

Tourmaline picked at the edge of the lawn chair. Through the dripping lilacs, the conscript adjusted something on the engine. The sun hit his neck, finding some thin layer of bronze to light in his dark skin.

Was *she* being naive? What if there was more truth in that courtroom than Dad had let on? There *had* been times he'd lied. Softly. Gently. To protect her from things she didn't want to know. He'd told her the starlings on Jason's cut were for different accidents. And she'd thought, *Boy, he sure is terrible at riding a motorcycle.*

She'd forgiven her father, though he didn't ask for forgiveness, simply because she understood his intention. When she was fourteen, what those starlings in the wind had stood for was something she had not ever wanted to know.

But now?

Maybe all she needed to know was buried beneath well-meaning men who whispered soft lies in order to protect her from things that already had her by the throat.

The creases of sadness on the FBI agent's forehead haunted her. Maybe, deep down, she might not be the one who would know. Maybe she'd be the last to know.

The conscript stood and moved away with a surge of force coiled tight in his muscles, making her stomach jump.

Her father got on the bike and started it, then nodded.

The conscript turned for the house.

Taking a deep breath of the heady scent of dripping lilacs, Tourmaline tried not to watch him the whole way to the door. "Why exactly do you think they're criminals?" she asked carefully.

"It's just one of those things everyone knows. Collective knowledge and all that shit."

"Give me an example."

"Someone is in prison for murder."

Tourmaline thought for a moment. Murder? She crossed her arms and legs and shifted to face Virginia. "Dre." She nodded. "Otherwise known as Drunk Off His Ass Half the Time and in Recovery the Other Half. He's been doing that for twenty years just fine. I mean. Fine enough. One day, he was driving home after two drinks. The other driver ran a light at high speed, flipped the car, and died. Dre was shaken but walked away. Or would have. The cop knew Dre, knew he was a Warden, and did a Breathalyzer at the scene. He was just over the legal limit. Now he's serving a ten-year sentence for vehicular manslaughter on a DUI."

The Wardens had attended the funeral of the other driver—a single man who cared for his elderly mother. They were still caring for the mother he'd left behind. Jason cut her grass every Tuesday himself. But none of that made Dre any less of a Warden, or the situation any less screwed up for everyone involved.

Virginia flicked the cigarette and shifted. "I see." Her gaze stayed fixed through the lilacs. "How about that guy they put in the hospital in a coma?"

"What guy?"

"The bar fight one."

Tourmaline repeated something she'd heard. "Allegedly."

"Well, is it true, or not?"

"They were at the bar. And there was a fight. That happens." Even she knew there was a certain type of man who was always looking for a fight, and to that kind of man, the Wardens were always a sure bet.

Virginia smashed the smoking stub underneath her flip-flop and pulled out the box for another. "How did your parents meet?"

Tourmaline frowned and cut her eyes at Virginia. Dre's story was public knowledge for anyone who wanted to wade through court records. Bar fights, ubiquitous and simple to explain. Her family's stories were something different. Valuable. Private. "Um." Tourmaline picked at the frayed thread in her cutoffs. "My dad broke down. She gave him a ride."

"I heard she was in high school."

"She was our age."

"And dating someone else."

Tourmaline stretched in the chair. The story had been told often. Mom used to snuggle on the couch, Tourmaline beside her, with one of the club scrapbooks opened between them. On the first page was a photo of the entire club—the Wardens of Iron Gate—straddling their Harleys and ready to make the long trip down the coast to Florida.

Mom had taken the photo. That fact was always part of the story. That Mom had been there, behind it all. Always.

The page would turn. Tourmaline would sit up and lean over the picture. And they'd stare at a picture of Mom, curvy legs bared on either side of Dad as she straddled the motorcycle and they mugged it up for the camera. *Margaret Garrett and Calvin Harris, Daytona 1994* was written carefully underneath in Mom's handwriting.

Dad had been twenty-six, but Mom only eighteen. She wore a crown and a thong bikini.

Now it was a little weird. Embarrassing. Certainly not a picture she was about to drag out and show Virginia. But back then, it was different. Tourmaline remembered the crown more than anything. Mom had been a princess.

No, ma'am, Mom had answered with a soft laugh. *Queen.*

Now, all anyone thought about Mom was *Burnout,* and all

Tourmaline's good memories were shaded with tragedy. There was no way to divide the two, to explain how the *Queen* and the *Burnout* were different people, one inside the other. But for once, someone was asking about the Queen rather than the Burnout. "Dad was riding this half-dead Bagger when he broke down outside her school. She was outside, after cheerleading practice or something. I don't know. She gave him a ride."

Eight years older, wearing a ridiculous mustache and working construction, the version of her dad that had struck up a conversation with barely eighteen-year-old Mom was the kind of guy who now gave Dad nightmares. *It was a different time,* Dad said when Tourmaline teased him about it once.

It might have been a different time, but Mom had always been the kind of person to forge ahead first and dance quick with whatever happened. The Daytona trip was the first thing they'd done together as a couple. Where it was serious. The Queen coming to take her future throne.

And now the throne sat empty. The woman in the silver earrings and others like her were aiming for the empty space Mom had left behind. Not in her family, but in the club.

"Are there any others as hot as Jason?" Virginia asked.

Tourmaline snorted. "You're asking the wrong girl."

"Now who's full of bullshit." Virginia laughed and the chair squeaked. "You're lying out your teeth if you tell me that man isn't the most gorgeous thing you've seen." She waved the wafting cigarette into the air toward Jason.

"Oh God, no. It's like putting britches on a pig."

Virginia smiled like she hadn't quite planned on smiling and tapped the cigarette on the edge of the chair.

Smoke trails twisted lazily between them and the men, and the flock of starlings flew across her mind, and it all became serious again. "He's not the nicest . . . with women," Tourmaline said.

"You have my attention."

"Have you seen his vest?"

Virginia shook her head.

"Not that you would really know this, but vests are really personal. All of them have, like, shit to say, some are . . ." She made a face. "Things I wish I didn't know."

Virginia's expression steadied and Tourmaline suddenly realized it meant she was hiding a reaction. "I'm a big girl, Harris," Virginia said. "That doesn't do anything but make him more appealing."

Virginia would never understand what Tourmaline had heard in that courtroom. How everything had been laid out in confusing, revolting detail. "How? How does that make him more appealing?" Jason did not make it difficult to sleep with him. For a split second she wondered if he would even sleep with *her,* and when the answer was not an immediate no, she closed her eyes in panic and wished she could bleach the thought right out of her mind.

Virginia didn't look at her. "Because he's fucked up and doesn't hide it. Or maybe that's all he wants you to see."

Tourmaline twisted to look again at Jason. "It's just weird," she forced herself to say through a dry mouth. "He's my dad's friend. And he's old." Dad cut the engine, and she suddenly realized how loudly she was talking.

"What's happening over there?" Virginia asked quietly, quirking a brow and nodding in the direction of the garage. "They been standing there for a while. Are they going somewhere?"

Tourmaline held her hand out for Virginia's smoke. "That's the Shovelhead. I think he's trying to sell it. It's supposed to be a project bike, but Dad never works on it."

"Oh."

Tourmaline took a deep breath of the tobacco and menthol, and studied the bike. "I'm not big into bikes, but I like that one. It's all original, classic Harley iron—"

Virginia gave her a *WTF* face.

"Shut up. I know. It's the least girly bike ever." She passed the smoke back to Virginia's outstretched hand. "But it just sits behind the lawn mower, and occasionally they get it out and stand around looking at it, and nothing ever happens. It's so irritating. To see something so cool be so useless. At least if he sells it, someone might use it."

Virginia gave a tight, smoke-filled laugh. "They should name it Tourmaline."

Hilarious. Tourmaline rolled her eyes. "I rebuilt the forks."

"The what?"

Tourmaline leaned forward. "See those two rods that come down from the handlebars and attach to the outside of the wheel? Those are the forks. The front suspension is built into them. Often you get these old bikes with, like, dried-up suspension. I tore the forks down and rebuilt the suspension."

Dad had brought the Shovelhead home one winter day in the middle of Mom's trial. It was clearly an emotional impulse purchase. Tourmaline understood: She still had several pairs of boots from those days. The Shovelhead had been the first and only bike Dad had let her do anything on. She still remembered the cool, slick feel of the metal as she eased the rods back into the greased outer shell. And how satisfied she'd felt when the project was finished.

"Damn, girl. Look at you," Virginia said. "Why'd you stop there?"

"I don't think he wanted anyone else around when he let me do that. But that moment passed." When Tourmaline's father worked on bikes, he wanted Jason or someone with real experience to help him. Not Tourmaline.

"You should keep going."

"It's not my bike."

"Yeah, but. I mean, would your dad really care?"

"Probably. I don't know." Her mom had never done anything with the bikes. And since that day in the driveway, Tourmaline did not go places she wasn't welcome. "I once heard my mom say, 'Why bother having your own bike when you could get your own biker?'"

"I appreciate that lovely thought," Virginia said. "But, like, you could have both."

Tourmaline tipped her chin to the leaves and smiled. "I miss her."

They were silent for a few minutes, the only sounds the whisper of wind and the raindrops, and every so often Virginia taking a deep drag on the cigarette.

"What is it you really need?" Virginia flicked the smoke; ash shook free into the breeze. "Is it just to get a pair of socks into prison?"

If only. If only she were still sitting here, trying to find a way to restore the things broken in the past instead of having to fight a consuming present. Who knew the banishment was only the *start* of her problems?

Our fate cannot be taken, it is a gift. It was something the Wardens always said. But Virginia made it seem as if fate were something she had by the throat and forced to her will. And maybe in that, there would be an answer that would allow Tourmaline to move beyond the day her life had finished falling apart.

She swallowed and forced the fear into words. "I need to do something about Wayne. Without my dad."

14

"WHO'S Wayne?" Virginia muttered over the cigarette, hoping against all hope it wasn't the state detective. Any situation involving a state detective might be the one thing worse than doing this Hazard's way.

"My mom's ex-boyfriend. He just got out of state prison and is after some kinda revenge." A strangled look twisted Tourmaline's face. Jaw tight. Eyes hard. Not even a little margarine as she sat there without the makeup or preppy clothes to dull a history of danger now evident in all her limbs. "She went to prison for a federal drug and weapons charge. They were his drugs. His weapon. And my panic."

Virginia put the smoke back to her mouth and narrowed her eyes at the lilac bushes, trying to catch a glimpse of Jason through the branches again.

Wayne. The guy Tourmaline had put in prison. This was serious. They'd jumped from socks to people. Tourmaline probably didn't have any idea what she would want to do about that. Or what she might *have* to do. Virginia stared at Jason's back, cigarette to her mouth. If she kept on this way—bartering only for time around the club via Tourmaline— she would have no guarantee of getting what she needed.

Jason glanced behind him, eyes bright even over the distance as his gaze connected with hers.

Virginia's heartbeat surged ahead, but she forced herself to stare back until he looked away, expression unchanged. She released a tightly held breath and glanced at Tourmaline. "What's this Wayne like?"

"Exactly what you would expect of a low-level drug dealer in Roanoke, Virginia. Always on a concoction of something. When he was with my mom they were playing with Oxy and meth." Tourmaline blinked at the ground and slumped a little deeper in the chair. "He's not smart. Or clever. He's got a weasel quality that keeps him alive, I think. Like every time death will have him, he *just* manages to wiggle loose. But I haven't really seen him in four years."

"How do you know he's after revenge?"

Tourmaline hesitated. "A guard told me."

Virginia relaxed a little. "That's probably shit. Prison gossip."

"He found me last night." Tourmaline shifted and the chair legs scraped against the stones. "Before I had you pick me up. He'd followed me there."

Shit. Virginia stared at the cigarette. Her phone buzzed and she knew without looking that it was Hazard checking in. Part of her felt as if she were still sitting in that office chair, with hardly any air and the sudden jerk of reality tugging on her face. It made her stomach heave, but she wasn't sure if it was from the memory or because she was letting him down by not giving in. None of this was just a job—it was the rest of her life. Her no wasn't worth much when she kept trying to spend it everywhere. And she heard her mother, squawking over the cigarette, *Stop being so precious, Virginia.*

The breeze gusted, warm and wet. A smattering of drops plunked on the mostly dried stone. Jason shifted back into the space between the lilac bushes, and instead of addressing Tourmaline or thinking any more about Hazard, Virginia focused on him.

He wasn't wearing a vest, just a ratty black T-shirt with short sleeves that showed a nasty smear of scars on his left arm. Not scars. More like his skin *was* the scar. It made her uneasy. Virginia wanted to know what had happened, but she didn't want to ask Tourmaline. The evening light bathed him in melted-butter warmth, picking up the blond in his dark hair and deepening the gold in his tanned skin. He laughed at something Tourmaline's father said, a hint of dimples under his beard, the boyish charm in stark contrast to the hardness of his body. A deep ache opened up inside Virginia's chest, threatening to pull her inside out. An ache she didn't understand at all, except to know she did not want Jason to be work, no matter how easy the job would be.

Virginia shifted in her chair, turning back to Tourmaline. "How serious is this?" *And how serious are you?*

Tourmaline shrugged. "I don't know." But her voice seemed small and tight, as if she did know. "I just need to keep him from bothering me ever again. Without my dad or anyone getting involved."

Just. Virginia rolled her eyes and flicked the smoke. "Oh, you think me and you can beat him up or something?"

"Well. I was . . . I mean. He's only threatened me. So maybe I can get him to move on. I just need him to move on."

"You want to reason with him? With the guy who you just said was mixing Oxy and meth?"

"No, that won't . . ." Tourmaline looked stricken.

"He sure sounds reasonable."

"My dad would be able to fix this," Tourmaline snapped.

"Maybe. But you don't have nearly the same reach." Virginia crossed her legs. "I'll help. But it might be messy. If he violates his probation, they'll send him back. How you want to go about that will depend on how long you want him back inside."

Tourmaline didn't meet Virginia's eyes. "I should just let my dad take care of it."

And the fact that she could do that, if she chose, made Virginia's mouth tighten and any sympathy she might have had drain away.

"Listen here." Virginia leaned forward on her knees, forcing Tourmaline's skittery gaze to hers. "I'm not going to sit here and tell you what you should do. I'm here to tell you what no one else is going to say. If you want to handle this, without hiding behind them"—she stabbed the cigarette toward the garage—"you have two options. You can do what I just told you. Or you can go find yourself a lawyer, and a judge who will issue a piece of paper, and a cop who will come out to this address I'm sure he's familiar with, to a last name he knows means bad shit, and enforce that piece of paper. Believe me when I say that rarely goes well for women on the *right* side of the law. And you, Tourmaline, are on the wrong side of the law."

"I haven't done anything."

"Doesn't matter. You're a Harris. Of the Wardens."

Tourmaline mashed her lips together and looked away. "But if *they* do anything, Alvarez will be watching. If they even, like, fuck Wayne up. There's State Detective Alvarez just, like, whistling on his way to work, ready to turn simple assault into murder two or something. I have to be the one to do it, or they will."

"Only those of us who have any expectations of safety ever speak up. *Especially* in a goddamn court." Virginia flicked the cigarette with vehemence, half irritated she had to sit here and explain, and half relieved to make the truth into words and lay them around someone else's neck for a change. "You can't end this until you end him, basically. I don't know what that might mean for you. I'm just telling you what it usually means. There's not much that'll work on a not-clever, beat-down, strung-out man looking for revenge."

Tourmaline shook her head, looking vaguely sick. "I've got three months until I leave. I can't let any of my family go to prison for this. I can't tell my dad or Jason or anyone. I'll just have to . . . survive until then."

Virginia's phone buzzed, and the words she'd so vehemently pushed out of her throat seemed to sink back into her stomach. She dug her phone out and glanced at the unread message.

I'm starting to get impatient. From Hazard. *I thought I left instructions.*

I'm here. In the middle of it. We'll talk later, she replied. Her heart skipped a beat, but she tightened her eyes and lifted her chin. "So, what is it they actually do together? Just party?"

"No," Tourmaline retorted, as if she were offended. "They have church every week, and rides and—"

"Church?"

"Not like church church. Their club meeting. They do events. Like most clubs. You know, none of this is anything special. I mean, the one thing they do special is their court runs, I guess." Tourmaline shrugged as if she'd only just thought of it. "Sometimes caseworkers will call the Wardens for a kid to be escorted to court when their abuser is going on trial and the kid is feeling anxious."

Virginia blinked. "They go to court with kids?"

"Not like *go* with them, just escort the car and sit in the parking lot. Occasionally, one or two will sit in the back of the courtroom, but only if the caseworker requests. It can make the right kid feel a lot better to face their evil with twenty tough-looking bikers behind them."

"Oh." Virginia frowned and put the cigarette back to her mouth.

It was starting to make sense that Tourmaline insisted they were good. That Tourmaline seemed so naive. It wasn't innocence so much as a worldview. To her, the Wardens were righteous.

Virginia couldn't help but be jealous—both of the way Tourmaline saw the world, and also of the idea that for some special children out there, there had been men to stand up when they could not. What would it have felt like for someone like Tourmaline's dad to be sitting in the back of the room while the judge evaluated whether or not there were any grounds for CPS to keep Virginia away from her dad? It felt as if that could have made all the difference. The judge would have seen the Wardens and not sent her home. She could have, for a moment, shared in the safety Tourmaline had enjoyed her whole life and not ended up here. Virginia's gaze flickered to a new message from Hazard, cigarette burning away in her fingers.

If the Wardens had sat in the back of the courtroom for her then, would she even be sitting here today?

The question seemed too big and full of tangled decisions to think far on. And there was no answer for *this* day, except to keep going forward.

She looked up just in time to see Tourmaline's dad duck through the lilacs. "You goin' to be staying for dinner, Tourmaline's friend?"

"It's Virginia." She held the cigarette off to the side and turned on a bright smile. He was a worn and wild sort of handsome, with a nice smile and something innately fatherly. Like a rough sort of mother bird. "And hell yes, I'll take dinner."

She knew she'd opened strong when he dropped his eyes and chuckled. "All right, girls, why don't you wash up? We'll see how this food does. Mexican." He made a face and headed toward the house. "I don't know. If it's bad, you can blame the conscript. I'll see that he's adequately punished." He went inside.

Tourmaline straightened—a crisp, gathered expression on her face. "Forget about Wayne. Forget everything I said. I'm leaving in less than three months. I'll ride it out."

Something twisted in Virginia's stomach. She'd forgotten somehow that they'd graduated. That everyone else was going on to some kind of college, or school, or jobs they intended to grow in.

Except me.

"Mexican." Virginia brightened and took one last deep breath of the smoke, leaving behind questions about fate to face the earthly things she could manage. "I'm starved."

15

TOURMALINE left Virginia in the bathroom to wash up for dinner and sent Anna May an emergency *The ridiculous is too strong please make an excuse to need me* text.

She'd have to cross her fingers and look over her shoulder for the rest of the summer. Maybe spend a lot of nights in or something. It didn't matter. She just had to make it to August.

When she stepped into the kitchen, the scent of rich meat simmering in its own juice and fresh-cut tomatoes and peppers drowned Tourmaline in a hunger so intense she thought she'd faint before she ever took a bite. But she wasn't entirely sure it was all the food's fault, so she avoided looking anywhere near the conscript's turned back.

Her father sat at the head of the table, legs propped on the edge and hands folded over his lap while he talked with Jason.

Tourmaline pulled her chair out and slumped, checking her phone, but there was no reply from Anna May, which was the way it'd been trending all day. Tourmaline mindlessly scrolled through her phone and tried not to feel annoyed.

"Church after dinner. It won't be a late night, T," Dad said to her, patting the table as if her hand were on it. "We're mulching tomorrow."

"Oh, joy," Tourmaline drawled.

"Mulch." Jason shuddered. "I remember those days." For a long time he'd worked with Tourmaline's father, but these days he was gone more and more.

"Always so much whining about mulch," Dad said.

A sizzling sound came from the kitchen and Tourmaline couldn't help but glance over.

The conscript stood at the counter, chopping onions, as if there were no one in the room. He gathered the onions into his cupped hand with the flat edge of the knife and dumped them into the pan.

It was weird to have him in the kitchen like this, even though all the conscripts did the menial tasks—cooking, cleaning bikes with a toothbrush, cleaning *bathrooms* with a toothbrush. (The bathrooms in the house had never been cleaner, and every time there was an event families attended Tourmaline heard all about the clean-bathrooms conscript again. And the conscript who'd done science fair projects. And the Girl Scout cookies . . .) There was a rule about not making a conscript do anything the member wouldn't do himself. She knew, he knew, they all knew that doing work like this was just what it was to be a conscript. But knowing didn't make it less weird or the subtext less meaningful.

Cash bit his lip and tossed in more onions, looking relaxed and at ease in a way conscripts usually didn't.

God almighty, she wanted to close her eyes and die naked in his arms. There it was. *Thou shalt not,* and she damn well wanted to.

She slid farther down in her chair and looked back at her phone. She couldn't see a way to make anything happen, let alone a relationship, even if he wasn't a conscript. Patching in would make his position in the club less tenuous, but the consequences of getting involved with Tourmaline more severe. The betrayal would be bigger. She was certain she could live with how pissed off her dad would be, but she couldn't expect the conscript to make that choice. That was a boots-on, plunge-into-the-icy-depths, not-going-back thing. She blushed. What was she even thinking? *Dreaming.* That's what she was doing.

16

VIRGINIA met her gaze in Tourmaline's bathroom mirror and took a deep breath. *What now, Virginia Campbell?* She'd come this far on her own. She'd held on this long. Now she would make something of the situation. Her way.

Reaching under her shirt, she pulled off her bra and stuffed it into her pocket. It was cheap, and not until she'd had it tucked away did she realize all roads might lead her to the same place. That maybe this was all she truly had to use. Fluffing her hair and fixing the long dark strands carefully around her face, she avoided looking at herself in the mirror.

Now wasn't the time to hold back. If there was one thing she should be good at by this point, it was working a room full of grown-ass men. Slipping into the hall, she lingered in the shadows and studied the pictures hanging in the hallway.

Here on this family wall, Tourmaline was depicted sitting in a lawn chair in the summer, holding an American flag. She was probably ten. Smiling that sweet margarine smile in a white T-shirt, with her hair in two braids. A younger, more crumpled Jason sat in a chair beside her, half out of the photo, a dazed look on his face despite the tight smile for the camera.

And though he did take a girl's breath away, she preferred him now. With the weight of existence age had given him. With more sun and more beard. His presence in the photo was noteworthy—either he'd earned a weird spot in the family, or they didn't know how to crop him out. It had been Jason speaking just then, back in the kitchen. Jason who'd asked Tourmaline whether she was all right. Jason who kept glancing past Virginia.

To Tourmaline?

Virginia tightened her mouth and moved on.

A woman who looked like Tourmaline laughed over her shoulder. Her blond hair was pulled to one side. The leather jacket across her shoulders was embroidered with crimson roses and green leaves, and strung with black fringe and silver medallions. On her lower back, the words *Property of Harris* embroidered in white among the leaves. She was the kind of woman who made even Virginia want to linger and stare, and not on account of what she looked like, but because of the look of wild spaces and freedom in her whole being.

This was the woman who was once married to the Wardens' president, had his baby, and now resided as a number in USP Hazelton, doing time—at least, according to Tourmaline—for a boyfriend's transgressions.

The woman in the picture was what Virginia always thought she'd become. What she'd grow into. And suddenly, it seemed as if she might not become that woman at all, but skip immediately to the woman residing in federal prison, doing time for a darkness she couldn't escape. Or she might become the woman her mother had always been. The one always too wrapped up in grief to realize she was wasting it on a terrible man.

A tired longing flared deep in Virginia's bones.

She didn't want to do this. Any of it. She wanted to get off this road that seemed to have no end. She wanted to know that in less than three months, she, too, would be leaving this all behind for a better, safer place. And it choked her to stand here, in Tourmaline's house, and see just how far from that she truly was.

It was quiet. A lull. Time to make an entrance.

Virginia shook her body awake, hardening each limb, look, and thought as she stepped out of the hall. In order to survive, she couldn't get caught here, longing for someone else's life.

She scanned quickly, taking in Tourmaline's dad at the head of the table, Tourmaline at the end, and Jason leaning on his elbow between them. The black guy who'd been with Jason at the bar stood in the kitchen, cooking. The tiredness she'd felt in the hall was pushed deep beneath the exhilaration of doing what she did well.

They all turned to look at her.

They were only three men, in jeans and T-shirts, the air conditioner in the window and the ceiling fan overhead fluttering their sleeves. But despite the clear age differences, together they all seemed alike— brothers bred in the mating of gnarled oaks and springs gurgling under ancient boulders. It seemed as if none of them had been born, but had walked out of the darkness, full grown, on the back of a harsh mountain wind. They were myths, for certain. Centuries dressed in days. They were tall tales that already outrageous men told of things wilder and crazier than they.

They were dangerous, she could sense that. The awareness brushed her skin with cold and tingled the hairs on the back of her neck. At the same time, the nature of the danger evaded her—it was wrapped inside average, warm bodies, contained in the smell of old carpet and dry seventies wood paneling mixed with rich food and burnt tobacco. Earthy and warm and close all around, filling a deep hollow in her belly. Comforting in its baseness.

And really, they weren't *very* different from regular men, these Wardens.

Jason stiffened without moving—a satisfying reaction after he had twice looked right past her. The guy cooking looked up. Tourmaline's father yanked his legs off the table and sat up, tension around his eyes as he avoided looking in her direction.

None of this was new.

Tourmaline sat at the head of the table like a dogwood in the bare branches of wild April. She was relaxed, her hair held back by a headband but loose and wild to her waist. Her *blouse* half tucked into cutoffs. She sat impervious to the men coming down from the woods. Gone was the quiet, forgettable girl Virginia barely remembered from school. This girl made sense. This girl was in context. This girl was someone Virginia could almost like.

WHEN Virginia walked in, no one would have noticed if Tourmaline had gotten on her knees and crawled to beg at the feet of the conscript. Tourmaline's stomach pitched steep and fast.

Virginia's tanned legs stretched for miles out of the untied sneakers, and her slightly oversized T-shirt draped just so as to catch the languid curves of her body. Virginia's gaze flashed around the room. The intense blue of her eyes, framed with long black lashes and what looked like yesterday's eyeliner, lit bright with deeply retained mystery. And the wild beauty contained in Virginia's body—the thing Tourmaline had always recognized in tiny stabs of jealousy—called now to be pursued.

"Where should I sit?" Virginia asked, gaze lighting on Tourmaline hardly long enough to ask the question.

Tourmaline bit her cheek and shoved out the edge of a long bench running down the empty side of the table. "We were just about to get started."

Virginia sat without looking. "What're we eating?"

It was an alternative world. A mind-boggling tear in the fabric of the universe. Tourmaline didn't even try to hide how aghast she was. *What. The. Hell?* She'd expected Virginia to be as bored as she was satisfied to finally meet these small-town-notorious old men. But Virginia had marched into the room like a woman in a den of lions, unveiling a slithery black whip and swinging it right around to crack through the air—making the rest of the room remember their mouths were full of teeth, their bellies with fire, and they lived to do her will.

It made Tourmaline think of her mother.

It made her stomach tighten.

Panic descended.

The world was all wrong.

There was distance between Tourmaline and the woman with the silver earrings. Distance between *family* and the girls and women who tried to latch on to the club. But in this moment, the distance was smashed pancake flat. They were the *same*.

18

VIRGINIA sauntered to the battered wood table, back straight, careful not to show all that moved under her skin. She wrote the lines she wanted them to read—not simply that she was beautiful, but that she was in control of her beauty. In control of all things. "Where should I sit?" she asked.

Tourmaline shoved out the edge of a long bench running down the empty side of the table. "We were just about to get started."

Virginia sat. "What're we eating? It smells amazing."

"Marinated skirt steak fajitas with fresh guacamole, Spanish rice, cheese, sour cream, and homemade tortillas," the guy cooking replied.

"T, why haven't you ever introduced us to your friend? Virginia, wasn't it?" Jason asked. His gaze wandered lazily from the edge of the table to her eyes, mouth curled into a mischievous smile.

For one split second Virginia careened wildly out of control, heart pumping so hard she thought it might crack open and stop altogether.

His mouth curved deeper. Eyes brighter. And in the sharp black nothing fixed straight on her soul, she felt caught in something unexpected.

"How could I be so thoughtless as to not introduce you to all my high school friends?" Tourmaline snapped, pulling Jason's gaze.

The interval was long enough for Virginia to resume breathing and gather back the use of her body.

"What happened to your arm?" Virginia motioned to the scars. "I know the ladies treat you like a piece of meat, but did someone try to make sausage out of you?"

He looked away dismissively, as if he hadn't heard.

Tourmaline's dad cleared his throat. "Any summer plans, Virginia?"

"Wreaking havoc and causing mayhem throughout southern Virginia," she said with a smile, not looking in Jason's direction. He was nothing but temptation and she needed to focus. "How about you?"

"The same." Tourmaline's father laughed. "The same."

The guy cooking set down a colorful platter of softly charred and tender strips of steak, and peppers and onions. "Let me get the tortillas, one second," he said. "And a plate for you, Virginia. I didn't forget."

"I wasn't worried," she sang. If she wasn't going to use Jason, maybe this one? She glanced over her shoulder, and as he came back, she smiled. "Do you have a seat? I can make some room." She slid down on the bench.

"The conscript isn't eating, " Jason cut in dismissively.

"The what?"

"No one," Tourmaline's dad said, using the tongs to gather up a thick helping of dripping slices of charred beef.

The man went back to the kitchen without saying a word.

"It's like pledging. He's pledging," Tourmaline said. "So he doesn't get a seat at the table until he's earned it." She flicked her fork at the table. "They've all done it. Except my dad."

"It's not like pledging. At all," Jason said to Tourmaline. "This isn't a fucking fraternity."

"Well, how else do you want me to describe it?"

Jason shook his head and reached for the platter. "I want you to . . ." He snapped his hand together, *Shut up.*

Tourmaline raised an eyebrow and took a bite, managing to look completely unimpressed.

"Well, you're sassy tonight," Tourmaline's dad said.

Tourmaline didn't respond. Her gaze flickered to the kitchen and back to her plate.

Oh. Virginia straightened. It wasn't Jason who Tourmaline wanted. Jason sat in the picture with her as a little kid. He'd be like a brother. And even if Tourmaline saw what he looked like, she'd seen him as old for too long.

But *the guy in the kitchen.*

He was both old enough and young enough for Tourmaline. He was a big guy—tall and muscular—with a nice smile and a solid presence, holding his own space, even in a room with two others who each could fill it.

Understanding did not deflect Virginia from her own survival for one second. She twisted to find him in the kitchen. "I didn't catch your name?" She smiled, suddenly appalled at the hesitation pulling her mouth tight. It should not matter that the girl in the frothy dress wanted him. Virginia needed someone. Tourmaline bothered with love, Virginia dealt in life, and there could be no first without the second.

"Just the conscript," Jason answered instead.

"Cash," Tourmaline said.

The entire table froze.

Virginia turned back. Instantly, her stomach twisted.

It wasn't anything new—the look on Tourmaline's face—but for some reason it stung. This should have been clean and painless. Instead, Virginia wanted to fix it. To take it back. To apologize and somehow keep Tourmaline from hating her.

And with no prospects, no plan, and the only reason she was allowed at that table hating her, Virginia's future looked dim.

19

TOURMALINE lifted her chin, jaw jutting forward, and heartbeat pounding in her head. Why had she been calling him the conscript? He wasn't *her* conscript. He wasn't anything but a man who'd lost his dad and who had stood on a dark road asking what she might want for herself. And that man's name was . . .

"Cash Hawkins," Tourmaline repeated, meeting Virginia's eyes only because she didn't have the nerve to meet her father's.

The food was served. The conversation flowed.

Virginia started talking with Tourmaline's father about someone they both knew whom Tourmaline didn't.

Jason openly stared. Or glared. It was always hard to tell.

Tourmaline's stomach churned. She needed to get out. Get some air. A lot of air. "Excuse me." She pushed away from the table, eager to leave.

No one noticed. Her father's phone started ringing and he got up to answer. Jason kept his gaze fixed on Virginia. Virginia winked back. Cash put pots in the sink. No one was following. No one cared.

Tourmaline left the house dizzy. One minute she held all the keys and all the doors and the world was all hers, as long as she stayed in her place, and the next moment she'd been tossed out with nothing of her own. Neither felt like what she wanted.

She pulled on her boots instead of flip-flops. Her stomach was alive and trembling as she dug through her father's truck for a smoke, and tried to decide whether to give in to the urge to scream. Shuddering, she lit it and took a deep breath.

Why ride a biker when there was a bike she'd already put some work into?

She flicked the smoke into a puddle and stalked toward the garage.
Hello, Shovelhead.

Her heart beat wildly at the thought of someone seeing her. As if they were catching her with one leg in her pants and her head stuck inside her shirt.

But no one did.

The evening light spilled into the shadowed garage. The stretch of concrete between her and the outside was clear. Tourmaline put her head down and pushed, legs straining to roll the Shovelhead outside and hauling back to keep the long, low monster of iron from rolling away.

Taking a deep breath, Tourmaline turned the bike on, pulled out the choke cable, and twisted the throttle a few times to open up the lines. *Come on,* she prayed with a furtive glance toward the house, and threw her whole body into a vicious kick.

The engine barked to life—a deep, ripping bellow that unzipped a rush of blushing fear and excitement through her body. She threw her leg over, torn between embarrassment at doing this and embarrassment at being embarrassed.

They'd seen her now—Dad and Jason. They shouted over the engine. Coming to drag her back while Virginia and Cash looked on.

Tourmaline bit her cheek and pretended they weren't there. If she got held up here, she'd be held here forever—always afraid of the spaces where she wasn't allowed to go. She eased the choke cable back to the sweet spot in the engine and began to feather the clutch.

The road materialized from the raindrops left on the leaves. The shimmer of evening sun. The heat rising off the drying asphalt. Her heartbeat rocketed along with the RPMs. The bike moved forward, putting the noise, the confusion of people, and the whole world behind her.

◆20◆

IT DIDN'T seem as if the three men Tourmaline left behind should have been as shocked as they were that the little dogwood flower on the branch had unfolded into some deadly wood sprite and roared off on their old bike.

Tourmaline's father stood in the driveway staring at the road where Tourmaline had gone. "Should I go after her?" But he didn't look as if he were asking either Jason or Cash. "She's not wearing a helmet." He frowned and turned to the garage. "She doesn't fucking know how to ride!" he yelled to no one in particular.

Virginia stayed silent. Still. Fading into the trees and the side of the house. If she caught his attention in the wrong way, in the wrong moment, she'd be gone. Especially without Tourmaline here. Better to wait for an opening rather than try to force something. Her phone buzzed and she twisted away from the men to check it.

From Hazard. *Come by the office tomorrow. 9am.*

Virginia shoved the phone back into her pocket and took a deep breath. It was okay. She'd make what she had work for him. She could handle this.

"You don't think she'll run into anyone," Tourmaline's father said. "Right?"

"We can go out after her," Jason said.

Cash's gaze flickered between the road and Tourmaline's dad, and his mouth looked as if it wanted to smile but knew what was best for itself.

They'd all finish dinner though, right? Virginia's mouth watered, and without thinking, she shifted toward the house.

Jason spun.

Virginia ducked. And immediately realized her mistake.

Their eyes locked, and she could see—*see*—the recognition interrupt his entire body as he flinched and stepped back.

Virginia slowly stood, refusing to drop her gaze and make the moment worse. But it was terrible. She'd given up an awful sort of revelation about herself: You had to be trained, down to your bones, to duck the second someone turned. It always showed up in the worst possible moment.

There was a horrific pause during which neither of them knew what to do but both of them knew something had happened. A slow tide of heat drew into Virginia's cheeks—back prickling like she'd been pressed into spikes, and only Jason stood between her and freeing herself.

He blinked and seemed to shake it off. "What do you think you're doing?" he asked sharply.

"Me?"

"You," he said firmly, as if she'd told Tourmaline to do all this.

"I was here for dinner."

Jason put his hands on his waist and took a step closer, towering over her. "What else have you been doing with her?"

"You really think this is my fault?" Virginia laughed and crossed her arms, refusing to back away as he advanced.

"I know you." He pointed his finger. "I know exactly who you are."

"You don't know shit," she snarled, hoping with everything she was made of that she was right.

"Jason!" Tourmaline's dad barked.

Virginia pressed her lips tight.

Jason turned.

Tourmaline's dad glowered at both of them. "Sauls just called. You have to go." He was speaking to Jason. "You too, conscript."

Cash went inside.

Virginia turned to follow, still thinking of her mostly full plate, but ran straight into Jason's immovable chest.

He stood in the doorway. Silent. Eyes narrowed.

"Excuse me," she huffed.

He didn't move. The bright hazel eyes snapped just as they had when she thought he was flirting. Now though, Virginia saw that they were a purposeful distraction—that their look could always be seen as flirting when the whole time he was just being an asshole, glaring down at her as if she had leaned over Tourmaline's shoulder and whispered for her to bite some poisoned apple.

"Tourmaline isn't home right now," he said, putting his arms up in the doorway, broad chest pushing toward her in a declaration of space.

"So, what, I'm just supposed to leave?"

"Yeah. You are."

"I didn't finish my food."

"Don't care."

"I was invited."

"Don't care."

She narrowed her eyes.

He tilted his head and narrowed his eyes back, mocking her.

Virginia turned to see if Tourmaline's dad was hearing this ridiculous shit. But he was frowning into his phone, and if he'd overheard he didn't seem to care.

"Go on now," Jason whispered in her ear, close enough for her to feel his breath, warm and soft on her neck. A small shiver of something equally good and bad ran down her body as he moved behind her. "And if I catch your ass around Tourmaline again, we are going to have a problem."

Virginia would have turned and kept arguing. Certainly she wasn't going to get pushed out by this asshole breathing down her neck. But the small moment of hesitation brought some clarity into her thinking. If she fought back, she might not have another chance at getting further. And right now, she didn't have much to bring to Hazard except the tail end of his patience.

This wasn't over. "Fine," she snapped over her shoulder. With as much dignity as she could muster, she walked to her truck and left.

RIDING into McKinley Hollow on that growling Shovelhead made Tourmaline feel something she hadn't quite felt before. She did not need to be told where to go, or how to get there. There was no steel frame to hold her encased in its comfortable grasp. No laminated glass to protect her from the elements. Vines tangled into emerald trees, hanging arched and low over the twisting mountain road. The road bent up and away, and the old bike seemed as happy to be out of the garage as Tourmaline was to be swallowing great lungfuls of the sweet mint and wild onion air.

She loosened her death grip on the handlebars and took a deep breath. And as she put the house farther and farther behind her, she felt more at ease. More sure.

Until she came up over a hill and noticed the familiar Impala, drifting the hill behind her.

Alvarez.

The honeysuckle breeze turned sour. *Shit.* Without even thinking, Tourmaline shifted forward and yanked open the throttle.

The bike responded immediately.

Mistake.

The bike lunged straight for a wall of thick tree roots and leafy bramble. Panicking, she clamped down on the brakes. The engine dove. The back fishtailed.

She slithered around the bend, losing it, feeling the massive weight slip out from underneath her. Not breathing. Not blinking. Just praying that the bank was dirt and not stone.

It was neither. She slid around the corner to face the back end of the sheriff's parked cruiser.

The bike stopped, wedged underneath the back bumper of the car. Everything went mute.

The cop appeared over her, looking as scared as she was. "Are you all right?"

She gasped.

He blinked.

Tires slowed by her head. Panicking, she twisted and scrambled out from under the bike, gritting her teeth at the burning sensation running down her leg and arm.

"He was—" she started. But she frowned and just stared, the rest of the words unsaid as the Impala disappeared down the hill.

"Aren't you . . . ?" the cop trailed off, peering at her thoughtfully.

Tourmaline shook her head without even realizing he hadn't finished. And there on that road, she suddenly realized that Virginia might be right—at least about this. Tourmaline *was* on the wrong side without ever having done anything.

"Don't move—I'm calling an ambulance," the cop said.

"No!" she screeched. "No. I'm fine. Look." She twisted her leg to show him. "Just scrapes. I wasn't going fast."

He looked at her leg and cringed, fingers still on the radio.

She refused to look. It already burned like hell. If she looked, she might get scared, and fear was to pain what gasoline was to fire. "I just need help picking up the bike. I don't need an ambulance."

"Did you hit your head?"

She touched her hair. Had she? "No." Her fingers slid down the tangles. "Look, it's fine. I'm fine. I'm totally fine." She took a step toward him and her knee buckled, skin screaming along raw, scraped edges.

Putting her hands on her waist, she straightened and forced a perky smile. "See?"

He said something into the radio and then looked at the bike. "Aren't you Calvin Harris's daughter? What were you doing? Is this his bike?"

"No," she retorted. "Who is that? I just . . ." She frowned. *Shit.* She had no license. No helmet. Couldn't call Dad. But how was she going to get out of this? She bit her lip and stared at the bike at her feet.

"Are you okay?"

Now he was going to go back to the ambulance nonsense. *Think, Harris.* She closed her eyes and tried to be more Virginia. "What were *you* doing is the better question."

"Me?" He sounded shocked.

"Parked on a blind curve. On the wrong side?" She opened her eyes and huffed. "Help me get this up. I'm sure it's already flooded. You're going to have to block traffic for me until I can get it started. This is a dangerous curve. Do you know how many people die from this shit? Can't. Even. Believe." She kept talking as they dragged the bike out from under the back of his cruiser. Tourmaline squatted while the cop pulled, and together they heaved it up on its kickstand. "You're a cop," she gasped, heart pumping furiously in her ears, dizzy from adrenaline and exertion. "Don't they teach you this stuff in cop school?"

He stood there, panting in deep breaths, looking between her and the bike and the road.

"Well, do you want this to happen again? Get out there. Block some traffic!" She waved him into the road.

He frowned. "I should set a flare."

She limped out of his way. Was this actually working?

He fished a flare out of the trunk and lit it in a sudden burst. "Don't go anywhere. I'll be right back," he said, belt shifting as he headed up the road.

"Oh, don't worry." Tourmaline floundered, saying whatever came into her head first. "I'll be here to discuss this whole bike situation. This is an antique. Original frame. You better hope to God it's not bent."

He disappeared around the bend, the trail of sulfur and smoke hanging in the heavy air.

Oh dear lord. She shoved her fist into her mouth and bit hard. *Please don't be bent.* The engine was probably flooded, but *maybe* since it had cut off before she went down, it would start.

The cop was still gone. It was worth a shot. Jumping on the bike, she stood over the seat and drove every bit of bone, fat, and strength in her body into a kick.

Thank the lord, it started.

Tourmaline roared away, spitting gravel and feeling as if she didn't know who she was *at all.* The cop was a diminishing figure waving wildly in her mirror.

The chase was on.

She scooted up. Hugged the gas tank with her thighs. Lowered her elbows.

The first right that opened in the hillside was a tight, cracked road leading away from the river. She turned, careful not to open the throttle until the bike had straightened out.

It dug in deep and hauled her up out of the hollow with a growl.

A flicker of blue flashed in her mirrors.

The *one damn time* she did something, she fell headfirst into trouble—or rather, rear-ended it. Tourmaline gripped the handlebars tighter, palms sweaty. She couldn't get caught now. This was it. Like it or not, she'd brought herself here and there was nothing to gain by holding back. She opened the throttle wide, the bike screaming and rattling so loud the whole valley could hear.

She spun the bike in another left, circling back over the hills. Her hair whipped across her face, but she kept the throttle hungry and gnawing at the road. She did not know herself at all, but she knew this was going to work only if she beat him to the river. The cop was a curve behind. Maybe more.

Hopefully more.

Another turn. Another slip in the gravel. More of her heart choking her throat. But she was back on the main road, and she opened the throttle wide, centering the front tire on the double yellow and speeding past a Westvaco truck hauling timber.

Next to the truck, the tires stood taller than her head, and the iron beast beneath her suddenly felt like a toy. A split second of the trucker looking down, and she'd be nothing but a bump under his tires. But then, she'd spent most of her life feeling exactly like that, only without the ability to go faster. Swallowing back the fear, she opened the throttle wider. Pinned back. Hell-raising fast. The wind whipped through her hair, and if she could have forced her jaw to unclench and her mouth to open, she could have swallowed it all whole.

The trucker laid on the horn.

But Tourmaline kept her eyes trained to that sliver of the James River just visible through the trees. The logging truck slipped behind her with its jaws of steel and that deep drone in the tires.

She slowed, then veered off the road and popped over the edge down the gravel bank. Her teeth shook—body tight. She braked desperately and cut the engine. The back tire skidded, but she'd learned her lesson and kept it loose. All she needed was to get under the bridge before the cop caught sight of her.

The bike clanked and squeaked, and she slowed to a stop at the bottom with her heart pounding. Pain washed up her side, made worse by the still heat coming off the river, and she grimaced against the tears pricking her eyes, boots slipping in the dirt as she walked the bike alongside the concrete pillars and twisted to look back up the road. Where was the cop?

Two men stood fishing farther down the bank, casting lines into the river and sending curious glances in her direction. "Five-oh," one of them said, focused on the far bank and reeling it in.

It took her a second to realize he meant the cop.

She twisted farther, catching sight of boots at the top of the embankment. *Shit.* Gritting her teeth, she shoved her boots into the gravel, pushing the bike deeper toward the brush on the other side of the pillar. It wasn't even the prospect of jail that bothered her; it was the idea that she'd fail so spectacularly at taking the bike in the first place. That her face would be put up on another kind of wall—one of shame. Dad would tell the story to everyone, and they'd all laugh. Her face turned fiercely hot just to think of it.

Why ride a bike when you will just end up in jail, mortified and needing a biker to bail you out?

"How's the fishing, gentlemen?" the officer yelled.

Tourmaline closed her eyes, cringing.

"Been better." One of the men tossed his line. "Loud tonight. Dumbass bikers acting like they always racing somewhere."

"Ahhh...," the cop said. Gravel tumbled, as if he were sliding down the embankment.

No. No. No. She held her breath.

"Just so happens, I'm after a bike. Looking for a girl on a motorcycle." He was just around the corner now. Three more steps, and she'd be caught.

She tried to keep from breathing, but then her heart felt as if it were going to explode in her chest, and she sucked in a deep breath of the heavy river air.

The guy fishing shrugged. "Well. I don't know about a girl, but I seen a motorcycle pass by here no more than a minute or two ago. What was it?" He looked at his buddy. "Harley. What year, do you think?"

The other guy readjusted his hat. "Oh. Hm. I'd say a 'sixty-nine, 'seventy?"

"So it went over the bridge? North on this road?" the cop asked.

"Yes, sir. Headed right into Iron Gate. Didn't know you were looking for it."

"Thank you for your time." His boots thumped away.

Tourmaline eased a long breath out, but didn't move.

After a few minutes, the guy fishing cast again. "He's gone," he said.

She slumped over the handlebars. Relief flooding through her.

He snorted and shook his head.

His buddy outright laughed, and hollered, "Hey, man, you gotta see what this cop was after."

Someone else was hiding from the cop, apparently. He cut out of the bushes no more than five feet in front of Tourmaline in a blur of brush and sticks.

She shot straight up, eyes wide.

Wayne.

IN THE light of day, he looked older than Tourmaline remembered. Balding. Camo T-shirt sticking to his concave chest. He looked terrible, really—as if a crow shit him on a fence and the sun hatched him out. His expression clamped down tight and he started toward her with a steady look in his eye.

So much for avoiding him until she left town.

Blindly, she scrambled for the kick start. She would not cry. Or stop. Or be scared.

She was just going to fly. Standing over the handlebars, she kicked. The engine coughed and didn't turn over. In the moment she needed it most, it wasn't going to start. She dropped her eyes, panicking.

Mistake.

A scabbed, dirty hand clotheslined her, crushing her windpipe and snapping the back of her head against the concrete pillar.

"Hey there, T," Wayne sneered. "Long time no see."

He squeezed and she was choked down to the past.

The clock said six a.m. She could taste the sugary cereal she poured herself while watching This Old House. *She could taste the warm milk. The feel of the scratchy carpet under her legs because the couch was too disgusting to sit on. The way a younger, less haggard-looking Wayne had kicked through the living room in his boxers, sat on the broken couch above her, and silently poured cereal into a cup. How his leg had hit her arm and not moved, and the milk in her stomach had soured. How she pulled herself tighter into a ball and realized, with her mother still sleeping in the bedroom, why Dad forbade her to come over here. Why she had to lie and say she was at Anna May's if she wanted to spend time with her mom.*

It wasn't because he hated Mom. It wasn't even really the drugs. Wayne had chewed and stared bleary and red-eyed at the television, and even though she'd moved, his leg had found her arm again. He could hurt her. There was no one here to stop him.

He finished his cereal and Mom woke up. Tourmaline left when the sun hit the cardboard on the windows and the air was filled with the deathly fumes that smelled like dead cats rolled into burning carpet. And for that day, she was safe. On her way home, she promised herself she'd never come back again.

But she had.

Just once.

And now she was here, pinned under his hands, with no one to stop him.

She clawed at his hands. Tried to kick out his knees with her one free leg. *She* was going to stop him. Snarling, she got her hand up and shoved her fingers into his eyes.

"*Bitch,*" he exclaimed, twisting away, hand slipping.

She pushed him off and righted the bike, heaving all she had down on the kick start.

Still. Didn't. Start.

Wildly, she looked for Wayne, trying to see him before he caught her unawares again.

His friends had him by the arms, dragging him away. "Cut it out!" one of them yelled. "Don't you know who that is?"

"Oh, I know." He shook them off and started right back for her.

She kicked. The engine choked and died. Her pulse seemed to slam out the curses. *Shit. Shit. Shit.*

"Her daddy will kill you, man. That's Harris's kid. Remember Ray?"

Somewhere in her panic, deep inside, she froze and looked at the men, all tangled up like wildcats on the bank as they tried to hold

Wayne back. *Who's Ray?* Her leg was already coming down hard on the kick start, and underneath her, the engine exploded.

Wayne paused. He remembered Ray.

The question still hung in the air—horrifically unanswered—but Tourmaline popped the clutch and hung on. Without even realizing she knew what to do, she slipped the clutch and sank back.

It was *just* enough.

23

TOURMALINE'S throat ached with the worst sore throat she'd ever had, and her fingers trembled from the pain throbbing in her right arm and leg. But she was committed.

She stashed the bike in Alvarez's empty spot and slipped into the woods on foot. Hunkering in the brush where she and Virginia had stood just the night before, she now watched. The clubhouse sat inside a burst of liquid heat that had broken off the sun to linger under the pines. In this world, where it was just her and all that seemed pitted against her, she wanted to see this place apart from its enchantments.

They came for church. To pay respect and worship at the altar of brotherhood. To become–together–more than one man in a great big world. To drink beer, smoke like a chimney, and laugh loudly about not-*that*-funny things.

The ghost of Wayne's fingers lingered on her throat as she counted off each man and each bike, studying them as if seeing it all for the first time. There was nothing between her and the world as it truly was. No one to stop Wayne. No filter or veneer. No safety. This was the world she had inherited. A world she had, in part, made. What other things had she not seen? Who was Ray?

The sun dipped behind the edge of the mountains, spilling emeralds licked in flames and trails of molten fire across the valley. All she had become was because of rules being made about her and applied to her. Rules she had no say in but was complicit in affirming. Things she called fate to avoid confronting them. Wayne. Alvarez. Her mom.

And, absolutely, the tall shadow standing watch in the yard while everyone else collected inside.

Shaking out the tangled blond lengths of her hair, she stood and headed for the clubhouse, keeping to the darkness—afraid that in the weak shafts of crimson light spilling through the branches, her already flaming edges would burst into all-consuming fire. At the edge of the trees, she pursed her lips and whistled a shaky version of the long trill of the whip-poor-will—the bird that sang only at sunset and dawn. A herald of change.

Cash twisted, scanning.

She took one step out into the purpling shadows.

He found her, eyes wide.

The full, unadulterated shock of seeing him, in this world, without being afraid to look him full in the face rushed straight to her head, dizzying, and stunning, and pumping from her ears to her fingertips. Without hesitating, she plunged forward into the open, striding for the night that had collected under the eaves of the clubhouse.

Cash looked panicked. The chains on his belt jingled softly and his boots thumped in the grass as he rushed to catch her.

They met in the shadows.

"Jason has Sauls out looking for you," he whispered, putting his arm up against the side of the building to shield her from sight of the entrance.

"Ask and you shall receive."

"What happened?" He looked at her arm.

"Oh. Shit." She glanced at the shallow, bleeding scrapes all down her arm and leg in the faint light. Bits of black asphalt were stuck in the edges. It looked rough. "Learning curve. I'm good now."

He looked over his shoulder at the door.

It was a simple steel door, battered with black boot kicks and smudges under a floodlight. But the whole club lay on the other side—save Sauls and Cash, and Cash wasn't allowed to attend church as a conscript. There would not be laughter if they all caught her here, in the shadows, with him. The shame would be public and it would be brutal. The thought spurned her on, some bitterness cementing her body in determination.

"What are you doing?" Cash asked, moving closer.

It was the first time she'd seen him act like a conscript—namely, slightly terrified and on edge. "I'm . . ." And then she stopped, mouth half open and the question hanging, because really, she didn't know what she was doing except that she'd begun to look her fears in the face and couldn't stop until she'd placed them all.

"You've got to get out of here. Go home and wait for your dad there."

"I didn't come to see my dad."

He met her gaze then—something unspoken surging in argument between them in the twilight. "You can't be here."

"Don't quote the rules to me, Cash Hawkins. I was born on those rules."

"We both were," he reminded sharply.

He was right. And she fell half in love with him right then for that reason alone. She crossed her arms and leaned against the rough-cut boards, the smell of pine and motor oil in every breath. "Been up to much this summer?" she asked with a smile, as if they weren't hiding in the shadows and she wasn't talking in a whisper.

"What the hell, Tourmaline?"

She ignored him, looking off into the woods. "I've been kind of busy, too. Thinking about maybe starting a project, though. I got this bike thing. I don't know."

He sighed. Looked toward the door. Back to her. Hesitation and panic caught in his body, though he wore them well enough. Lowering his head, he stepped forward, a breath of space between them now.

She gulped and straightened. Nothing nonchalant or low-key about *this*.

"I don't want to see it go this way."

"How did you expect it go?" she asked through clenched teeth, annoyed that he thought he could avoid this. Like she hadn't been the one to warn *him*.

"Slower, for one thing," he snapped, leaning even closer. "Patched in, for another."

She swallowed. She'd forgotten he was trying to smash through worlds of his own. She looked to his eyes in the shadows.

The tree frogs sang.

And in the middle of nothing but fear and anger, she was consumed with the idea that he might . . . *just might* . . . kiss her. And as soon as she thought it, she saw he was thinking it, too, and it was all very confusing what exactly they should be doing.

He swallowed, the thick movement in his throat nearly undoing her. "We both know it's not the time or the place. For this."

For kissing or for making a scene? She nodded, but her body didn't seem to know, either.

"I want to do it all the right way," he continued. "For my dad."

She pulled back; satisfied to see he stayed where he was, tight and hanging on the edge. "You can do the club the right way. But anything . . . between us . . . is always going to be wrong."

He shrugged.

"I miss my mom," she whispered desperately. "She would know how to navigate this." She knew how to get what she wanted. "It feels like she died, but I know she's still there, at least. I'm sorry that your dad won't ever come home. I'm sorry you're here without him."

He nodded, rubbing the back of his neck and looking back to the door again. "Okay. Thanks."

She was screwing this up. What should she have said? What did he need her to say?

"I'm—" She looked around. "I'm going to go. I'm sorry."

He nodded again, still looking at the door.

She was on a roll with disaster. Throat thick, she rushed for the woods. The feeling of being caught prickled against her back, spurring her onward until she slipped into the darkness of the forest.

Shit. She swiped at her cheeks with both palms, forgetting how she'd even gotten there until she smelled the exhaust and rubber on her hands. Her life jumbled together, crossed and crisscrossed in a flurry of roads in her head that she couldn't untangle. And all she wanted, at that moment, was to be home in bed, safe. She sniffed and stumbled up into the woods, not hearing anyone behind her until he grabbed her wrist.

Cash pulled her back. She was still crying, still caught in the tangles of her head.

She fell into his chest and forgot everything but his abrupt solidity and his warm hand gently coming to rest on the back of her neck.

His breath flooded her ear, making her knees quiver, and he whispered the numbers, hurriedly. "Text me," he finished, squeezing her neck and releasing her back to the woods.

She stood frozen, heart slamming wildly as he jogged back out into the dark yard toward the floodlight reflecting on the long row of motorcycles.

He stopped, spread his legs, and crossed his arms over his chest.

The night was still. The birds all nestled down. The frogs continued their chorus and the wind kissed the tops of the pines.

And in the light silhouetting him in the distance, she could just make out the rapid rise and fall of his chest.

24

THE THING about having Wayne choke her was that everything else in Tourmaline's life immediately adjusted to that standard.

Almost arrested? No big deal—the cop wasn't trying to kill her like Wayne was.

Scrapes all down her arms and legs? Hell, they were almost a good thing, simply because they were self-inflicted.

Ray? Was he in pursuit? No? Then she didn't give a shit who Ray was.

So, when she sped away from the clubhouse, cheeks still hot and the heat from Cash's hand still pooled on the skin of her neck, Tourmaline didn't head home. She'd already paid up the suffering required to get the bike and herself out on the road; she was damn well going to make use of it. Somewhere out in the humid darkness, Sauls, Wayne, and at least two cops were all looking for her, but she had a fast bike and the number of the boy she liked safely tucked into her phone with instructions to text him, so really, she was invincible and they'd never find her.

First, she drove back and forth in front of Anna May's house until Anna May came out—her stern-looking father and Dalton close behind.

"Thanks for returning my texts!" Tourmaline yelled as she drove past again. She left, keeping an eye out for cops while she got herself to the drive-thru.

Two men came up to her while she sat eating French fries off the gas tank. They wore T-shirts and unlaced boots, but instead of giving short answers with her eyes down, in the hope that they'd leave, she leaned back and smiled. There was nothing here to fear—and if there was, somehow, she'd face that head-on. The standard wasn't to remain untouched and perfect in her room of white walls and Van Gogh's

Almond Blossoms, the standard was to remain alive. And if she failed, what did she care? She would be dead.

She sat there as a girl freed. A woman released. A woman without fear of men. And she marveled that at her most hunted, this was what she'd feel and where she'd be—sitting in a dim McDonald's parking lot answering two strange men's questions about the bike.

1972 FLH.

Not a Panhead. A Shovelhead. See, the top of the heads here are a little scooped out, look like a shovel?

Yeah, the original came with saddlebags. They're sitting on the garage floor.

There's a wiring issue. Only a kick start for now.

A pain in the ass? Tell me about it.

I laid it down being stupid. I'm fine. These just look bad.

Her arm and leg hurt, but the injuries weren't as bad as they looked, even though her fingers trembled as she ate fries, and when she shifted her weight on her leg, her thigh shook like a sewing-machine needle.

"Is it yours?" one asked skeptically. "Or, like, a boyfriend's or something?"

"It's mine," she said coolly, determined to make it be so. She'd buy it from Dad if he made her.

He looked to his buddy and they both shook their heads and smiled at the ground, as if they didn't know what to do with a girl eating French fries off the gas tank of a mean old Harley.

It was like catching a glimpse of herself in a mirror. She was that girl they thought she was, in part.

She had long known she was the girl who already had too many shoes in her "to college" pile, still wore bows in her ponytails, and kept her nails done even though it made no sense when she worked landscaping.

But now she saw that she was also the girl with deep curves, cutoff shorts, and tangled hair, sitting on a bike, with all the wild and messy history that came with the last name Harris. That she'd been that all along, and no matter what she did, that history would work itself out in her bones. And love would be someone who would understand all of who she was and not be afraid.

Courage bolstered, she picked up her phone and pulled up Cash's number. *I think the engine on this bike is running a little high. I might have made that up, but that's what I'm feeling about it. Any thoughts?*

She sent it. Tucked the phone under the inside of her thigh. Picked up a fry.

"Do you mind starting it for us?" one of the guys asked.

"Sure. When I'm done with my fries," she said, chewing. She tried not to stare at her phone.

"How old are you?"

"Eighteen," she announced brightly.

He just smiled and nodded. "I was eighteen when I got my first Harley."

"Yeah?"

"I had this old Honda when I was eighteen," the other guy said. "Eighteen when I wrecked it, too."

Both men laughed—a nice kind of laugh, filled with old memories and good stories. Tourmaline joined in because she, too, had an old, well, *recent* memory and a good story. Somewhere beyond or above or away from the moment, she looked at herself and wondered how she'd gotten there. But even when she considered herself from a distance she didn't want to be anyone else. Not right now.

Her phone buzzed, and she snatched it up.

Maybe needs the idle adjusted? You make it home or did it break down on you?

She grinned, stupidly and sloppily, and her greasy fingers slipped as she texted back. *I stopped for fries. It's not broke down yet.*

The two men talked between themselves, respectfully quiet as they waited for her to finish and start the bike. The parking lot lights hummed and the tree frogs still sang.

Church over? she typed.

Cash replied, *Not yet, but I'm not going to be your watchman.*

No sir. Never.

You probably have twenty minutes.

Her cheeks were starting to ache from how hard she was smiling.

I liked that you called me Cash. Not the conscript, he said.

The stupid grin felt sloppier and wider and when she shoved a fry into her mouth, staring at the screen, she could barely close her mouth to chew. *Well, you aren't my conscript. So . . .*

That'd be a much different experience, I think.

What do you mean? I make all my boyfriends stand outside the door with a beverage at exactly thirty-five degrees in case I want it.

Only after it sent and she reread it did she cringe. Why did she keep forgetting? Always having a cold drink handy was the usual low-level shit conscripts had to do for their sponsors, but Cash was making her reframe the entire way she interacted with a conscript. She fumbled with the phone, still cringing. *Oh God, WHY DO I KEEP DOING THAT?*

Mm-hm.

Conscript seems like it could be an awkward intersection for you. No? Am I making shit up?

It can be awkward. Everyone's pretty good, though.

She wasn't sure she believed him. Everything that could be tested was. Any weakness would be found. What kind of man you were and where your line was. They'd have easy ammunition with Cash. But Cash would know that it was only for a time, and afterward those same persistent assholes would have his back without question. Would take up his burdens alongside him.

You'll always have Joe, she texted back, thinking Joe, another black Original Member, would be extra protective of Old Hawk's kid.

Joe just tells me how much of a pussy I am, but yeah, I'll always have him. Then: *Erase that last text, please. I wasn't thinking.*

She rolled her eyes. If Dad was reading her texts, that one text about Joe wasn't going to be the problem. But she did as Cash asked and told him it was done. She shifted her weight on the bike. Her back was starting to hurt, being slouched like she was. She straightened into her usual posture and immediately relaxed. Princess, fine. But Princess who did as she pleased.

Her phone buzzed again and she smiled until she read it. It wasn't from Cash.

The neighbors called the cops about the noise. My dad had to spend twenty minutes calming them down. What's wrong with you? From Anna May.

Tourmaline's face flushed hot and she stared at the text, uncertain how to answer. Finally she put it down unanswered.

Cash texted. *Sounds like they're almost done. If you're still eating fries . . .*

Oh shit thanks. She crumpled the bag and tossed it into the trash can on the sidewalk.

The two men looked up, but Cash sent another text. *You going to be around later to talk?*

She thought she might as well have driven to McDonald's in the pink Hot Wheels Jeep she'd had as a kid, given how ridiculous her face felt, but she ignored the men and texted right back. *If I got someone interesting to talk to.*

Ha. Okay. I'll let you know if I see anyone.

She stood and shoved the phone deep into her pocket. Then slammed back down on the kick start. The one time she didn't much care what it did, it of course woke right up.

The two men nodded, grinning at her and each other.

"Sounds amazing!" one of them yelled.

"Thanks!" she hollered back, putting the bike in neutral and carefully inching her way back out of the parking spot.

"Nice meeting you." The other one waved.

Not knowing what to do, she put it in first and gave them a salute. Which ended up awkward as hell.

But then, it didn't matter what she did, because she was gone.

She should have left sooner.

In the driveway, the headlight washed over her father sitting in a lawn chair in the driveway.

But where there had been fear inside her chest, now there was a still space. While her throat ached and her leg was bleeding and she'd talked freely with Cash and with strange men at McDonald's, Dad's disapproval could not touch her.

She puttered into the garage and cut the bike, the roar still in her ears and hands.

Her father didn't say a word, didn't even move out of the firmly planted lawn chair as she covered the bike.

Tourmaline closed the garage door and headed for the house.

"What were you thinking?" he asked as she passed.

She stopped, hands slack in her pockets. *What was she thinking?*

Too much. She was thinking of the weight of Cash's hand on her neck. The moment where they shouldn't have been thinking of kissing each other and were. She was wondering whether the cop had given up looking for her. Whether Anna May was still angry. Whether Wayne still ate cereal on that disgusting couch. Who the hell Ray was and why his name had held so much power. She was missing her mother, while trying *not* to actually think of her so she wouldn't be overwhelmed inside that ache. But mostly, she was thinking Virginia had been right about everything.

Except, Dad wasn't asking her about any of those things, but about why she went on a *joy ride*.

And for that shard of spun-sugar childishness now crushed under the concrete pillar of the McKinley Hollow Bridge, there wasn't really a reason she could offer. It was as simple as this: It had bothered her to watch them all stare at that damn bike so many times and never take it out. It was as complicated as taking the counterfeit crown and shattering it across her knee. Neither reason was something she wanted to talk about.

She stared at the garage door and stayed quiet.

He flicked ash into the dark, the end of his cigarette a red ember in the dark. "That was incredibly dangerous."

"You do things that are dangerous," she said softly.

"Honey, it's different."

How so? But she didn't ask. He wouldn't know the answer, either.

"Not even a helmet." He said it with nearly infinite disappointment.

She held her ground, swallowing the urge to defend herself. What would she say, anyway? Without even closing her eyes, she saw Wayne's face. Felt his hands clamp on her throat. Smelled the sickening blend of foul memories and present woe.

"Your mom called while you were gone."

Her stomach pitched. She'd missed a call from her mother.

"She said you should come visit. She misses you."

Tourmaline felt as if she'd fall apart right there, break into countless pieces and drift away. At least she wouldn't have to be there when Mom got the letter saying she'd been banned.

"I've been meaning to talk to you about something, Tourmaline," her father said. *Not Dad.* He was using his president's voice.

She lifted her chin and cleared her throat. "Yes, sir?"

"I was thinking about everything that's been going on, and I just wanted to tell you how much I respect your strength and the decisions you've made to stay committed to doing the right things. You've pressed on through the chaos involving your mother. You haven't let any of the usual teenager things pull you away from your studies or your future. You've grown into a very respectable, sophisticated young woman. That's—that's something really incredible to watch. I never thought I could raise a daughter like you. Especially on my own."

She had to admit he was compelling. Telling her the things she most desperately wanted to hear. The gravitas in his voice held her right there, as if his words didn't completely contradict the way he made her feel. Even in the moonlight, she could see everything that made him president. The way his hands folded to catch a glint of light on the massive silver ring. The way he sat, at ease, confident in his power. The lack of movement when he spoke. Even the way he smoked—she could see it was *part* of him. Part of the president.

It was power.

Power to build his own world. Power to be who he wanted inside that world. Power to never let anyone clamp a hand on his throat and to bring consequences upon anyone who dared try.

She wanted to scream. To reach out and rip it off him and find her way into it.

He kept talking as if to someone in the club who had stepped out of line; his cigarette smoke trailed into the dark. "I just want to encourage you to stay committed to the path you began. I want you to remember who you are going forward. There's a lot of things out there"—he waved the cigarette gently toward the road—"that aren't going to seem like bad decisions, but are going to distract you from what you want to become. Or take you places you don't mean to go. I know it felt like not a big deal to take that bike out there tonight, but people who want to hurt me will not even hesitate to take advantage of you. You're a good girl, with a bright future. I don't want to see even a bit of that slip away." He stood and ground the smoke under his boot. "I'm proud of you, T." He tucked her hair behind her ear, patted her cheek, and smiled in the moonlight. The unspoken *Don't let me down* tacking its weight onto her mind.

Tourmaline's shoulders sagged.

He turned for the house.

"Dad?"

He paused, hand on the door. Waiting.

She had to tell him. To hang her head and weep in defeat. For she didn't have what she needed to save herself from Wayne. Swallowing, she focused on the pain cinching her throat, as if Wayne's hands were still there. She was about to tell him, but when she opened her mouth, she asked, "Do you know a Ray?"

"Ray?" her father repeated. "What about a Ray? Ray Longwell?"

"A Ray someone would be afraid of you for. A Ray everyone would remember."

"What? No." Her dad snorted. "The only Ray I know is a buddy. He's a supervisor at Westvaco. I play pool with him occasionally. Why?"

It was a terrible moment. A sudden shift where she watched her father—the president—*lie*. A lie she would have believed an hour ago. "I don't know. I just heard someone . . . Never mind." Suddenly, it was *all* in question. Everything he'd ever told her.

He *was* going to kill Wayne. He or Jason or even, God forbid, Cash. But the order would come from him. And he'd do it whether Alvarez was watching or not. She could leave for school, but it would not be with the burden of the past lightened.

"Are you okay?" her father asked quietly. "Are you *doing* okay?"

"Yeah," she answered automatically. "I mean, I'm fine."

"I'm worried about you. Hanging out with this Virginia girl. She's not from church."

"Nope. She's not." The breeze gusted, sending a fresh rush of tingling stabs into her leg. She touched her throat, wondering if it would bruise.

"Be careful. You'll make it through." His voice was low and calm. Soothing. "I'm not going to let you get hurt. Don't worry."

She should tell him about Wayne.

"Come here, honey." He pulled her into his chest and hugged her tight.

She took a deep breath of his T-shirt, throat taut as he stroked her hair, as if she were still a little girl—before the little girl had died one summer night on a red velvet Oldsmobile seat with panic in her hands.

"It'll be okay."

It would be okay, because *she* was going to take care of Wayne.

25

VIRGINIA arrived at Hazard's office promptly at nine Monday morning, waiting outside the locked back entrance for someone to let her inside. CSX trains clattered through the trees. The wind was already hot and it snapped the skirt of her old pageant interview dress against her thighs. The dress made her feel younger, as if she could stand next to Tourmaline in it and even she could be that spritely dogwood blowing in the breeze. White petals defiant. Too late, she realized she did not want to be wearing a dress for this meeting.

Hazard let her inside, wearing his bloodred power suit, a crisp white shirt, and cowboy hat. He didn't say hello, just beckoned with his hand for her to follow him into the office. She didn't get to know the script ahead of time. She was watching the opening credits, and all she could hope for was that she hadn't been written out.

Virginia straightened her shoulders and walked in as if she were walking onstage, following Hazard as he subtly ducked under the door frames on the way to his office.

A phone rang and there was a faint smell of fresh coffee that made Virginia's stomach rumble.

"Close the door," Hazard said, putting his hat on the desk.

She did. As soon as the latch clicked, he started in about the extra pills he'd told her to put to the side.

Why weren't they individually repackaged, Ms. Campbell? Are you trying to be sloppy? You're succeeding. You can't be sloppy and worn-out and tired for this. This is not how I run things and I don't care how long you've worked for me, I'll fire you. I'll fire you and I'll make sure you don't work for anyone in this state. And if you end up on the street, turning tricks like the whore you are, I'll have every cop in the county arresting you. If you're a stripper, I'll have the health department in there measuring your thong. If you're a waitress, no one in this town will leave you a tip. If you're a grave digger, no one will fucking die. That is how much you will want for work. I will not tolerate this. Sloppy work puts you in prison. You are not allowed to fuck up if you want to stay employed.

At first, she tried to explain. She'd asked about the extras and he'd said to put them all together. He hadn't given her a breakdown. She hadn't been given a list. She had packaged them. How was that sloppy?

But he just talked over her until she fell silent.

Finally, his voice dropped and he straightened his tie. "Tell me about the Wardens."

She told him all she knew in a flat voice, looking toward him, but not at him.

The yelling started again.

Again, she tried to explain. "This is what you asked for. To distract them. To know what they care about."

Again, he talked over her, drowning out any defense.

Someone knocked on the door and cracked it open. "Your nine fifteen is here." The secretary ignored Virginia.

Virginia automatically turned for the door, assuming it was over.

"Sit down," Hazard snapped.

The 9:15 walked in, looking like shit on a stick. He wore a ball cap pulled low and his fingers were dirty, but he plopped into the seat beside Virginia like he owned the room.

"Give him your bags," Hazard said curtly.

Her jaw dropped. "Why?"

He just looked at her, expression dead, until she pulled the backpack off her shoulder and handed it over.

"They're color-coded," she told Nine Fifteen.

"Write down the code," Hazard said.

"But—" Virginia started.

Hazard held up his hand. "Just do it, Virginia."

She shouldn't have gotten upset, no matter what he said. It meant he was in control. And handing over her stuff didn't just mean she was losing her work—her codes, and her clients, and presumably her paycheck—it meant she had lost his trust and his faith. But she steeled her face and did as she was told.

"You're done with this. I want you to focus on the Wardens. You keep showing up in this cheap, girlish shit." He gestured to her dress. "You're not taking this seriously. Maybe you don't have enough time to focus on it. This shouldn't be hard."

Nine Fifteen took the bags and leaned back, watching easily, not at all embarrassed to be witnessing her mortification.

"Go back and do it right this time," Hazard snapped.

Virginia's fist clenched at the unfairness. This wasn't what he'd told her to do. She had been doing it right until he changed the rules.

"Go through Harris's home office and take pictures of anything that hints at income, or payouts, or anything illegal. Do it, or you'll beg me to fire you. Change your clothes and get to work," Hazard said. "I've got stuff to do."

Virginia stood and left without a word.

Outside, when she opened her mouth to cry it came out as a scream. Her fists curled and her body pulled apart. What had happened? She hadn't done anything wrong—had she? Jerking open the truck door, she jumped inside.

There was only one thing to do.

In a squeal of hot asphalt and gravel, she headed into the mountains.

26

DANYLYNN and Wave stood in front of the vacant and boarded corner store, flip-flops in their purses and heels strapped to lotioned legs in the purple twilight. While she waited and gathered herself, Virginia brought them iced teas and cigarettes from the gas station down the street. The women knew why she was doing it, knew Virginia had thought herself better than this and was now trying to make repayment . . . as if it would deflect her fate. And maybe she'd never stand *there*, at the light, listening to the trains and the cars and waiting for a truck to stop. But she'd be with them all the same, and they knew it.

When Hazard left, she said her good-byes and walked up the street.

He waited for her by his SUV. The wind whipped the bloodred pants against his boots. The streetlight cast a long shadow on his face in the night.

She walked straight and sure. She had dressed carefully—a skintight, sleeveless black jersey dress with strappy, flat sandals, good hair, fresh makeup, and a single (fake) diamond necklace, one Hazard had given her for winning Miss Teen Virginia. Sleek silver hoops hung from her ears and she'd dabbed her mother's old perfume on her wrists even though it made her gag and feel the ghost of her father's hands.

"Good evening, Miss V," he said, tone neutral.

"I've got what you asked for," she said, pulling out her phone and shaking it. "I emailed you the pictures." She'd staged them to buy herself some time—some receipts he'd have to zoom in on, court papers, and personal correspondence her mother's roommate had in his room. Just enough time to find out for certain what was happening.

His smile emerged from the shadows. "My girl."

She leaned languidly against the hood, hating that the streetlight illuminated her every flicker and curve, but kept him in the dark. "As always," she sang cheerily, pageant smile fixed to her face.

"Want some dinner?" He opened the passenger door. "I was just about to grab some food."

"Only if you're buying."

"Some steak? Wine?" He held the door wider and swept his hand for invitation. "Is that good enough for a queen?"

"It'll do." Virginia straightened, fussing with her dress as she climbed inside.

Her heartbeat quickened and the smell of new car made her head hurt, but as Hazard walked around the front of the car the light caught his self-satisfied smile. Virginia's stomach twisted, but she kept her body in perfect submission to her will.

"It's been a good day. We can celebrate. I got something for you," he said, starting up the SUV and pulling out of the parking lot. "A gift, if you will. Take a look below."

"Below? As in . . . ?" He had a secret compartment under the center console, but she wasn't sure she was even supposed to know about it.

"I know you're sharp. That's the kind of woman I like. Go on, look."

Virginia took a deep, silent breath and scooted over in her seat to pull up the center console and the floorboard below. It was just a dark space where the flickers of passing streetlights didn't reach. She pulled out her phone and leaned over, half afraid it was a trap of some kind. As if she might lean over and fall into nothing, an empty prison she would never escape from in the center console of his SUV.

But all that rested below were several paper-wrapped and taped rectangles. She frowned.

"Like that?" Hazard asked.

Like what? Weed? She poked at one and it was firm. Dense. Not weed. Not . . . "Holy shit," she breathed.

"Fifty bricks of heroin," he said. "Welcome to the future, V."

She stared a moment longer. Counting. She could only see twelve. How had he fit fifty into this truck? Worried she was looking too long, she forced herself to replace the floor and move the console back. "Yeah, all right. That's not what I expected."

He chuckled. "That's why I needed you to do this with the Wardens. I don't worry about the police, okay? I worry about the Wardens. Police have to work within the law. I can play that game. The Wardens move outside of it. It's important they don't know anything about this until it's already happening. If they know about it, they'll stop it. And you are such a lovely distraction and spy." He reached over, gripping the back of her neck in his big hand, thumb sliding over her skin. "I told you I'ma take care of you."

She tried not to panic. This was it, then—this was what had changed. She was not a child, and her body was still what held the most value. This was just a new way to use her body. A new way to use her ability to think fast and toss her hair. And what she'd always thought was hers and hers alone, he'd always used for his benefit.

"You smell like an old woman," he said with a soft laugh. "Is that yours?"

"No," she managed. "My mom's."

Hazard's thumb rubbed a hole in her skin and she focused on the fence posts rushing past in the headlights. "I'll buy you something better," he said. "Not roses. You're too fresh. Nothing floral, that's too sweet for you. You're too different. Something with orange and sandalwood, I think," he continued, thumb still sliding back and forth along the curve of her neck.

Her throat was too tight to answer. She didn't know where she was or where she was going. But she knew one, definite, absolute truth.

Virginia Campbell, Hazard's pageant queen, was finished.

27

VIRGINIA found Tourmaline in her empty kitchen, crying as she scrubbed gravel out of long, angry-looking scrapes on her legs and arms. Her phone lay on the floor across the room with a cracked screen, as if she'd thrown it.

There was no need to say that everything had changed and the world had gone to shit. They both knew it without talking, somehow. Virginia sank beside her on the kitchen floor and began organizing the first aid scattered on the linoleum. "You're falling apart on me, Harris."

"My mom was high." Tourmaline's chin quivered. "She called me and I could just tell."

Virginia didn't say anything. There wasn't anything to say. The only thing she could offer was to exist in the same world and look it all in the face beside her.

Tourmaline scrubbed her arm harder, sobbing.

"You're going to rip off any skin that's left," Virginia said, swatting Tourmaline's hand away.

Tourmaline dropped the rag and looked at it. Tears still streaming down her face. "I'm not banned."

"I thought they banned you for the socks?"

"I called because I hadn't gotten any paperwork. They didn't have any record of it. When I asked, my mom said she hadn't gotten anything, either. She said Hayes just told her I'd forgotten something and had to leave. That'd I'd be back soon." She sobbed again. "Hayes didn't file anything on it. She was *nice* to me. I can try again, with your help."

Virginia looked at her hands. "We'll make a plan."

The seconds ticked by loudly in the thick silence of the warm kitchen.

"How's the landscaping business?" Virginia asked quietly.

Tourmaline dipped her rag back into the iodine water and her eyes flickered over the length of Virginia, as if looking for Virginia's wounds. But she didn't ask why or what had happened; she just sniffed and wrung out the rag. "You have to mow in a straight line, Campbell."

Virginia held up the box of Band-Aids. "You're going to have to use like one hundred and thirty-five of these, you know that, right?"

Tourmaline hiccuped a laugh and threw the Neosporin at Virginia's forehead. "Fuck you."

They clung to each other like cats stuffed into one skin. Virginia pulled weeds and pushed a mower in brutal sunshine, crisscrossing her lines with Tourmaline's. They fell into an easy rhythm—Tourmaline as much adrift as Virginia, keeping her own trajectory, parallel, and hardly intersecting with her dad's life. After a few days, Virginia stopped worrying about running into Jason, though she wasn't dumb enough to assume he didn't know she was working with Tourmaline.

A week into it, she stopped going home—afraid she'd just find one of Hazard's guys waiting and her mom subdued with a fresh bottle of tequila. Or worse. She slept in her truck deep in the woods and spent the days wandering around finishing deals she'd already had set up. Along the way, the whispers started churning. A low rumble in the ground, warning of an oncoming disaster.

Hazard was looking for her.

The threat hung in the heat. Lurid in the shimmering waves on blacktop at full sun. Grim in the darkness as she fell asleep listening for the sounds of sticks breaking outside her truck.

A week turned into two. Two stretched toward three. One day of mowing turned into a few more days. She hung on, caught in a world made of hazy, droning summer afternoons and nothing else. Virginia kept telling herself that she was going to be fine. She could just walk away. She didn't really owe Hazard anything. He didn't need her; she was just a girl. He could find those anywhere. But deep down she waited for whatever had begun to just hurry up and finish with her. It didn't matter that she escape her fate; it mattered that she had a say in it.

A languid haze settled over the mountains for the Fourth of July. Even the shade was so thick with humidity it created its own atmosphere, brewing purple thunderstorms deep in the malachite forest. Virginia parked at Tourmaline's, relieved to have arrived safely for another day, and headed for the open garage door.

As usual, there was no sign of anyone else. Just Tourmaline sitting inside the garage, her back to the driveway as if she had no need to be looking behind her.

Virginia put her sunglasses on her head and stepped inside. "'Sup, Girl Scout?"

Tourmaline didn't look up from the video playing on her lap. Her white sundress was tucked around her thighs, wedges hung up in the rungs of the shop stool, and she had her chin inside her hand, staring. "Trying to figure out what the hell I'm doing."

"With what?"

Tourmaline held up the screen. An old guy with a giant mustache held up a piece of something—a car part or something—and said things Virginia didn't understand. "Um."

Tourmaline paused the video and swished her long ponytail over her shoulder. "I was looking for how to fix the start on this bike."

Virginia climbed into the seat of a mower and put her legs up. They were supposed to be heading to some Fourth of July thing the Wardens were doing. Family Day, Tourmaline had said. Virginia hadn't known it would be as fancy as Tourmaline's white dress implied; and Virginia now frowned at her shorts and airy blue tank top.

"Anyway. I couldn't find how to do that, so that was pointless. But then I got distracted by videos about other shit I didn't know about. Like, I'm watching this one about taking off the header—"

"What's a header?"

"Uhhh . . ." Tourmaline lifted her head, a chagrined expression on her face. "I don't know."

She was, as usual, in way over her head. Virginia slid down on the seat. "Girl, I don't know how to tell you this but . . ."

"No. Okay. I sort of know. I know this . . . Look." Tourmaline clambered over another mower to the bike in the back of the garage, carefully keeping her dress out of reach of any of the equipment. "This part here." She waved her hands in demonstration over the exhaust pipes shooting out along the side toward the back, looking more like a showroom model than someone talking about fixing up the bike. "These are the pipes, but they don't always say pipes so I think it's, like, the whole exhaust system? Maybe?" She sighed and stepped back, hands on her hips. "Or maybe where the pipes meet the muffler? Do they meet? And, like, that's maybe more up into the engine. Here? More?" She pointed to where the exhaust pipes disappeared into the side of the bike. "Maybe?"

Virginia shook her head and took a deep breath of the smell of the heat on the tar paper under the metal roof.

"Honestly, though, how does anyone learn this shit? I mean . . . ," Tourmaline muttered, sitting back down on the stool and pushing start on the video again.

"Where is everyone?" Virginia asked casually.

"Oh, they're at the dealership already. I'm dragging my feet. Can't do this stuff when my dad's around."

"You don't want the old man knowing you're fixing his bike?"

"Not until I can make it my bike."

"Aren't you going *away* to school?"

"UVA is close enough for weekends. I could come home." Her cheeks pinked and she tucked her head to study the screen.

Virginia frowned, feeling something was off. "So, you're going to rebuild it?"

Setting the screen on the workbench, Tourmaline picked up her purse and stood, looking at the bike stuffed into a dark corner. "I don't know." She looked to Virginia, smoothing down her ponytail. "I'm scared to say yes."

"Scared of what?" Virginia glanced at the bike. It looked dusty.

"I'm afraid I won't be able to do it. That if I say I'm going to do it, I'll just face-plant in front of fifty men waiting to laugh."

"What are you going to school for, again?"

"Early childhood education."

Virginia barked a laugh. That did not dovetail into motorcycles. "That's right. You want to be a kindergarten teacher."

"I never said kindergarten. I'd really like third grade. Third grade is perfect. You're young enough to do crafts and old enough to really get into cool books and science."

And suddenly, Virginia felt like she could see Tourmaline's whole life ahead of her—this easy, interesting little life tucked into southern summers and back to school in the warm fall and her little collection of motorcycles and motorcycle babies. "God, I can see that. Like. Yeah. You've got your sweet little teacher job and then you come home and are, like, *Oh I need a bigger head.*" Virginia laughed and moved her legs out of the way of Tourmaline's swatting. But inside, her chest ached so much she had to put her fist into her breastbone to try and ease off the pressure.

"Let's go. I made us late." Tourmaline huffed. "You want to drive?"

Virginia rubbed the bone harder, but it didn't erase the ache. She swung off the tractor. "Sounds good."

Apparently the broiling heat was just the sort of weather in which a large percentage of men wore leather vests, revved hot engines over hotter asphalt, and ate barbecued pit beef.

Sighing, Virginia put her hands on her waist and spread her elbows wide. The grass cowered dead and shimmering pale in the stretch between the edge of the asphalt and the fenced ribbon of interstate concrete. A semi blasted past, but the grass barely moved. Each car that passed made her feel more exposed. More certain that Hazard would spot her. But she pressed her lips tighter and refused to falter.

"That's a Screaming Eagle mod kit thing," Tourmaline said beside her as if Virginia were listening.

Tourmaline managed to look like unmelted margarine in her aviators and swinging ponytail. She ate pit beef on a sweet roll while talking about the difference in busting out the baffle in your pipes versus different custom pipes versus made-in-your-genius-cousin's-garage pipes—apparently one thing she *did* know about.

Jason probably did have some secret deep love for her. Any one of these men might, with her talking that shit in between big bites of her sandwich in that white dress. She could be as dumb as a box of rocks with a wrench trying to fix up that old bike and they'd all forgive her and kiss her on the forehead when they tucked her into bed.

Where were the drinks? Virginia needed to be drunk. Instead, she swallowed and eyed the bike Tourmaline pointed out behind her sunglasses.

It wasn't chrome, but flat black. Low-slung and thick. Mean. It made her think of Jason, but Jason was standing next to some blindingly shiny thing she assumed was his.

Tourmaline didn't say anything right away, and when Virginia glanced at her, she was just standing there with this shit-eating grin plastered on her face.

Oh. *Cash's bike.* "Cash got your tongue?"

"Stop," Tourmaline hissed.

"Someone's got a crush," Virginia sang teasingly.

"This isn't—it'd be . . ." Tourmaline stopped her huffing and stepped close to Virginia's ear, suddenly sharp and cold. "No one can know; otherwise he'll be kicked out. So quit your little teasing-Tourmaline game and shut the hell up."

Virginia adjusted her sunglasses as she scanned the crowd, smiling despite herself, because she did *so* like to be reminded that Tourmaline wasn't as butter on bread as she seemed. "*Fiiine.* But I'm offended you haven't told me about this."

"There's nothing to tell."

"Mm-hm."

"Just let me go at my own pace."

"I didn't know you even *had* a pace." Another semi blasted a puff of hot air. Virginia scanned the crowd, watching so it wouldn't take her by surprise. "Come on," she said, hooking her arm into Tourmaline's. "While you're pining away for a full-course meal in secret, let's go find me something that comes in a to-go box."

"Are you talking food or guys?"

"Both, honey," Virginia said.

Tourmaline smiled as Virginia pulled her along, all effervescent and girlish giddiness in her step. She was thinking of Cash. Dreaming. *Her* day stretched ahead hot and damp in all the right ways. In that pretty white dress and the dreamy sense of distraction. Virginia hated her and envied her and loved her all in one terrible crush of annoying aching, while she couldn't stop herself from scanning the crowd for anyone who might be waiting with ready hands.

"Oh, here, you have to see Jason's bike," Tourmaline said, making a hard right and tugging Virginia along.

No, she did not. Pulling out of Tourmaline's grip, Virginia stopped.

But Tourmaline was already there.

Virginia followed, slowly.

With Jason having his vest and T-shirt on, it was easy to forget the horrible scars and just see the pretty face. Frowning, she glanced his way, curious to finally see the patches Tourmaline had talked about.

On the front of Jason's leather vest, the array of patches came into focus. Colorful, small birds in flight. An ace of spades right over his heart. Skull and crossbones on the side of his scars. But at the top, two small rectangles in black and white caught her eye.

DISABLED VETERAN on the left. COMBAT VETERAN on the right.

Virginia froze. If that wasn't clear enough, there was a crimson-and-orange globe and eagle on the hem. Beside it, a round, tan patch with a blocky country map circled in words: BEEN TO IRAQ, AIN'T GOING BACK.

Jason smiled at Tourmaline. "Staying out of trouble?"

"For the moment," Tourmaline said loftily. "Virginia wanted to see your bike."

"No, I—" What an *asshole* she was. Virginia's face burned—the first time she'd blushed in years. She swallowed and shook her head, taking another step back. The blush deepened. *God.* She put her hands to her cheeks.

Tourmaline gaped. "What's—?"

"What kind of bike is it?" Virginia cut in over her, dropping her hands and trying hard to ignore the burn still in her face.

"Fully customized Softail Springer."

The bike dripped in chrome—it would glow in the moonlight, a slipstream winding around the mountains. Virginia wondered whether it felt like everything she imagined. Gripping the waist of the shadow, her chin on his shoulder as the night swallowed them. No one could touch her inside that darkness.

Behind the glare, she noticed the whitewall tires and the slick cerulean-and-sapphire-painted gas tank—which color it was depending on the tilt of her head. She stepped closer and crouched to look at the engine. Her warped reflection peered back at her. "Are these custom, too?" Virginia asked, pointing to the pipes in an effort to ask any question that sounded even a little like she knew what she was talking about.

"Yes, ma'am." He sounded actually nice.

She sat back on her heels. "It's gorgeous."

"Sounds even better."

She glanced at him, and he almost seemed to smile. It caught her off guard. Made her insides open up and rush awake with no mind to the fact that she knew he wasn't truly smiling. Standing, Virginia stuffed her hands in her pockets and shrugged. "I'd need a ride to make a full determination."

He barked a laugh. "Keep dreaming, little girl."

Just like that, she felt less like an asshole. But with his sparkling eyes held tight to hers, she found herself smiling sweet sugar, cocking her hip, and vomiting out whatever sprawl of words came into her head first. "Didn't we cover this 'little girl' thing already? Don't pretend you don't like them young."

His face tightened immediately.

She wanted to grab after her words in a desperate attempt to stuff them back inside. He'd probably not meant to hurt her. Not really. And where he'd thrown a jab, even she knew she'd returned with a grenade.

Jason looked away, and it was hard to keep breathing, so—dummy her—Virginia kept on talking. "I mean. I guess I'm young. But not inexperienced. It's hard to tell which is more valuable." She cringed as the words left; hearing them sounded so horrible. "A full life in a short amount of time is what I mean. Not the other . . ." She gulped, awkward. God, when had she *ever* been awkward? "How much of a mess do I have to be right now before you shut me up with a ride?" She laughed, but it fell flat.

Jason still ignored her.

Virginia would have gladly been buried under the asphalt at that moment.

"A hot mess?" another Warden asked, coming up behind Jason. "Are we talking about a girlfriend of yours, Jason?" He wore a vest and boots, the same as the others. About as old—though Virginia would probably remember his age instead of forgetting it the way she did with Jason. Sharp, beady eyes echoed a narrow, pointed beard. His bald head made him look a little satanic, echoing the undercurrent of danger present in all the others.

"I like a hot Southern mess," Jason said to the man with a grin.

"He does like pageant girls," Virginia replied, half horrified to hear herself talking again.

Jason was still ignoring her. He smacked the man on the chest. "Have you seen Aubrey?"

"Naw, brother," the man said, sharp eyes looking Virginia up and down in appreciation. "Why you looking for her?" He offered Virginia his hand. "Flying Ace, but friends call me Ace. And you are?"

Virginia smiled. Finally, something familiar. "Virginia. I'm Tourmaline's friend."

"She's eighteen," Jason said, as if she were ten.

Ace smiled. "Perfect."

Virginia laughed. "See, you know." She winked. It seemed silly, standing there, to think she'd avoided this direction. *Making friends*, as Hazard put it, could have been easy. A close-her-eyes-and-gotten-it-over with sort of thing. She was much less valuable than she'd considered herself, in the end. But now there was no point.

Ace jerked his thumb at Jason. "Don't worry about him. He's a lost cause."

"Conscript. What could you possibly have to say to her?" Jason said.

Cash looked up, mid-word it seemed, as he stood next to Tourmaline.

Virginia hoped Jason wasn't watching Tourmaline's cheeks, because they turned dead-giveaway red.

"Oh, nothing. I just came over to listen to you tell the girls how you picked out the paint to match the shade of blue in their eyes."

"Oh, but it does match," Virginia cut in, pulling Jason's chin back toward her and away from blushing Tourmaline. She bent and put her sunglasses on her head, opening her eyes wide along the gas tank. "Look," she said, meeting Jason's eyes.

"Gorgeous," Ace said.

Jason grunted and looked away.

"It *is* pretty damn close. Look," Cash said, his arm brushing Tourmaline's as he spoke.

Tourmaline blushed harder—like the pretty young thing Jason guarded. If only they could've seen her five minutes ago, telling Virginia to shut up about how she was going behind everybody's back with Cash.

"Tourmaline, here, take my picture," Virginia said, digging her phone out of her pocket and holding it out.

Tourmaline held up the phone, and Virginia smiled.

Jason frowned.

"Thanks," Virginia said, straightening. "So when you going to take me for a ride?" she asked Jason.

"Never," he said.

Virginia laughed. "We'll see."

"You're going to be waiting a long time."

Ace cleared his throat. "Uh. Jason."

"I bet you I won't wait that long," Virginia purred, finally feeling that she was on steady ground and determined to keep his hazel eyes right on hers, even if they were bright with irritation.

"I wouldn't be betting on those odds if I were—"

"Jason," a woman squealed, bounding through the semicircle and into his chest, arms around his neck.

He staggered back a step, looking surprised, and his gaze flickered from Ace to Virginia to the woman at his chest. Then his hand went to her waist, and he smiled. "Hey, I was looking for you."

"Well, here I am!" She pulled away and settled under his arm.

Virginia snorted. "You weren't kidding," she said to Ace. "He does like them crazy."

Because, of course, the bouncing blonde was Miss Teen Virginia from four years ago, Aubrey Winthrop.

"Virginia," Aubrey said, smiling. "It's so good to see you."

"Thanks, Aubrey. Good to see you." The polite words and smile came out of habit, but then she wondered why she'd bothered.

"We competed for Miss Teen together the year I won," Aubrey said, flashing her dimples at Jason. "Virginia was just a little thing then."

"I wasn't that little." Saying it made her feel like she was in middle school. But it had been her first year working for Hazard, and she could have snapped Aubrey's neck and taken the crown without a peep if she'd been told to.

Virginia's stomach churned, and she felt all out of breath. This was all such bullshit anyhow. Bullshit, when she had Hazard trawling for her. Did she really want to say she'd spent her last days standing on sticky asphalt bickering with a man she didn't give two shits about?

"You want to go for a ride, Aubrey?" Jason asked.

Virginia spun and walked away.

TOURMALINE'S mother faded back into a ghost. Her wounds turned into fresh pink scars. And Wayne stayed a man with a vise grip—a threat in every shadow.

Her world continued on, good and bad, without even a pause of respect for the tumult it was in. That's how life always went. She texted Cash every night on her broken phone. She laughed and whined along with Virginia while mowing. She passed the garage and ached to ride again. She stood there, staring at Jason's bike, with a hot asphalt breeze puffing in her face, closing the fractions of centimeters separating her arm from Cash's, and the world zipped into nothing when his arm brushed hers.

Don't smile. Don't smile. It would be a dead-giveaway type smile and she couldn't afford any more of those.

Cash shifted, boots scraping the ground. The scent of laundry soap and cologne and leather pushed its weight against the wind. His forearm, tight and muscled, drifted back against hers.

Tourmaline couldn't help glancing down. God, mens' arms were the best thing in existence. The muscles. The tendons. The sleeve of Cash's white T-shirt fluttered in the breeze. Without looking straight at him, she could see his profile and feel the heavy stance of his body. She swallowed, everything feeling thick and aching and as if she couldn't even move her body except to fall into him.

"Tour-muh-line."

Jason.

She snapped up, the spell broken. "Yeah?" Did she look guilty? She thought she might look guilty.

Jason frowned and waggled his fingers like he was brushing her away. "Your friend might need you."

"What?" She suddenly realized Virginia wasn't standing there anymore. "What did you do?"

Jason tightened his grip on Aubrey and made a face as if Tourmaline had said something absurd. "I didn't do anything."

"Why does she need me?"

He rolled his eyes and shifted away from her, turning to talk to Ace, bringing Aubrey along with him.

Beside her, Cash turned to answer the question of a girl who hadn't been there a second ago. Tourmaline felt him leave and couldn't say a word.

Jason looked over his shoulder as if to say, *Why are you still here?* Without thinking, she dropped her gaze again to the starlings on his vest.

The girl talking to Cash laughed, and he along with her.

The blood pounded into Tourmaline's face, reminding her with each throb that she was barely out of high school, not yet into college, and altogether more child than woman. So what she'd been texting Cash the last few weeks? He had other girls, probably. Probably the one talking to him right now, standing close with her hand coming to his arm as she laughed. Because that girl *could*. If she wanted.

And Tourmaline wasn't supposed to.

Tourmaline hid her hands in the folds of her skirt and tried to stand there as if she belonged. But the group she'd been with a few minutes ago had become altogether different, now that Virginia wasn't there.

"I'm going to find Virginia," she said to no one in particular, trying not to scurry away.

Virginia was nowhere to be seen, and Tourmaline began wandering among the booths, alone and lost in the crowd. This part of the day was more a public event, with bikes and food and raffles that went to the charities the Wardens supported. Her phone buzzed.

Doing anything tomorrow night? I'm actually free.

Ugh. Allen. Tourmaline sighed. *Sorry, I won't be around much anymore.*

Oh hey. Look at you. Who is he?

Nope. That was not happening.

Okay. Well. Call me if you need me. 🙂 😂 🥒 Allen replied.

Subtle, she replied, rolling her eyes.

She stopped in front of a food vendor, distracted by trying to decide whether she wanted to risk eating chili cheese fries while wearing this dress.

A laugh rose above the crowd, and Tourmaline turned.

The woman with the silver earrings—her father's new girlfriend, she supposed, though it pained her to admit the fact—stood in a booth running a raffle for the Network for Abused Children. Same cute blond hair. Cute shirt. Cute sunglasses. Beside the woman stood Tourmaline's dad with sunglasses and a grin, and his hand on the small of the woman's back. Neither of them saw her.

Tourmaline lost her appetite. Her phone buzzed and she looked at it.

Where did you go? From Cash.

The fries stuck in her throat. Listening to the sound of a woman who was not her mother laughing, half terrified of running into her mother's ex-boyfriend, knowing Cash stood there with a girl she did not know and Jason who fucked anything that moved. Thinking of those things made alarm bells ring that Cash hadn't even tripped. She started to type back that Jason had shooed her away, but she erased it and just sent *Wandering.*

Come back, Cash texted.

The sun beat down, the crowd moved around her, the woman with the earrings laughed, and Tourmaline stared at her phone and felt more alone than she had when she *was* alone. Part of her wanted to go stand beside Cash and talk with him just the same as the woman—to laugh and put her hand on his arm. For all the party girls to see, so they knew they'd have to go through her in order to get to him. But that was the last thing she could do.

I have to find V, she texted, and forced herself to move farther away from Cash.

Tempting fate with the chili cheese fries, she ate at the edges of a crowd that she couldn't help but feel at once separated from and a part of.

Cash found her a few minutes later. Stopping a good distance from her, he gave her a restrained smile. "Hey."

"Hey," she mumbled over her fries and chili.

"I came looking for you."

She picked at the fries, wishing interacting with him wasn't all so complicated. "You found me."

"You okay? You just left."

She gave him a flat look. How could he not understand they couldn't be caught even talking?

He frowned. "You're around for the whole day, right?"

"I had planned on it."

He smiled. "Good."

She couldn't help but give him a wry grin. "Yeah? What is it good for?" And maybe talk like that came out of her mouth just because the ache and heavy-limbed feeling she got when touching him still lingered, and she knew she couldn't do a goddamn thing about it.

"Well, it's just nice to have you around, I guess. Even if it's a little torturous."

"Too bad you can't go anywhere," she said quickly, shoving food into her mouth because she didn't know what else to do with herself. There was an awkward pause as she chewed and tried not to look at him. "There're waterfalls up in the mountains above the lake. It's cooler up there. No crowds, either." She held his gaze.

He laughed, cheeks flooding deep red as he twisted away some. "Evil." His gaze flickered to hers and she was pleased to find him half teasing, his eyes bright with something intense that sent her pulse fluttering in her neck. "That's what that just was."

Torture was what it was to hear his thick voice late at night and not have access to him. Torture was what happened when touching herself wasn't enough. She stuffed another fry into her mouth, annoyed and exhilarated all at once. "Jason's probably looking for you."

Cash groaned. Stuffing his hands in his pockets, he gave her a look that sent a rush up her whole body, then turned and left.

She continued to eat chili fries without tasting them. When she went to dump the rest in the trash, she found Virginia, surrounded by the evidence of chain-smoking. "There you are."

"Still here," Virginia breathed weakly.

"You all right?"

Virginia didn't answer, just took another deep breath. She hadn't ever explained why, suddenly, she'd needed a job, or what had her walking around as if a little distanced from the rest of the world, but Tourmaline hadn't pressed the question. Now that they were working together, she'd started to see that Virginia was a shell for another Virginia and another, like nesting dolls or boxes inside of boxes. Sometimes Virginia said things that she seemed to think were completely normal and Tourmaline had to quickly arrange her face to agree, while silently making a note to bring it up again some time when it seemed Virginia might answer.

Pulling out her phone, Tourmaline stared at the text she'd sent Anna May that morning. *Hope you're having fun today. Miss you!* She'd forgotten to check for an answer until now, but it didn't matter. The text had been read. And ignored. Wordlessly, she held her hand out for Virginia's smoke.

Virginia handed it over.

Tourmaline took a deep drag and closed her eyes. "I have to find Wayne."

"And do what?"

Tourmaline flicked the ash, suddenly realizing someone might see her and tell her father. "I don't think he's living under that bridge." She passed the cigarette back.

"His old house?" Virginia asked over a deep breath.

Tourmaline nodded, her stomach turning. "I'm half afraid to find him."

"I would be."

They stood there, surrounded by flies buzzing over the trash cans and the mixed smells of fried food and asphalt and garbage. Tourmaline crossed her arms, frowning at nothing.

"You could always just get him to violate his probation. Get him sent back to prison," Virginia said.

Tourmaline nodded again. "If I can find him." What she really needed to know was the truth about Ray—the one thing Wayne and his friends had all seemed to fear. If she knew what the Wardens were feared for, she might know what to do about Wayne without having to ask. Alvarez was watching the Wardens. Not her. Jason's face drifted across her thoughts.

Tourmaline straightened.

Who would know better than Jason?

All this time Jason had stayed the same guard in the shadows, acting the steady soldier while the empire moved around him. Jason was sergeant at arms. Jason was *exactly* who would know about Ray.

When she lifted her head to take the cigarette back from Virginia, a car parked on the edge of the lot, tucked into the shade, caught her eye. Alvarez's car, with no one inside.

Tourmaline went cold, but she bent her head and put the smoke to her mouth, coming up casually. "V, look to your left, but be chill about it."

Virginia did. "What?"

"It's Alvarez."

"Where?" A beat passed and Virginia's voice went cold. "The black Impala?"

"It's that state detective's."

Virginia was quiet. She put the smoke back to her mouth, fingers trembling. "What do you want to do?"

Tourmaline stared at the car. "Nothing."

But it was a reminder of the consequences if Dad, or any other Warden, got to Wayne first.

29

DOUTHAT LAKE was sunk into a bowl in the lush green Alleghany highlands. It lay electric blue and shimmering white in the brutal sunshine, the late-afternoon air draped over the beach like a heavy, white-hot veil.

All Tourmaline really wanted was to be down with everyone swimming and grilling, stretched on a towel, creepily staring at shirtless Cash from behind her sunglasses. But she waited in the shade of the oaks and sassafras bordering the parking lot for Jason. Determined to find out the truth about Ray.

Virginia waited with her for a while, then took a long drink from her water bottle and turned for the beach. "Tell Jason to see if Aubrey can reach the stick stuck up his ass," Virginia said, ice cubes clinking against the aluminum as she left.

Tourmaline blinked. "Um. I'll leave that gem for you."

Jason came over the hill in a glare of light, and by the time he parked his bike alongside the others and cut the engine, half the beach was looking into the wooded parking lot with frowns.

"Hey," Jason said as she walked up, sounding uncertain.

Tourmaline tugged at her dress and adjusted the strap of the bag on her shoulder.

"Where's that girl you were with?" she asked.

"I dropped that *woman* off at her car."

Tourmaline nodded, confused by his annoyance. "I was thinking of something."

He didn't look at her, frowning at the gas tank and then carefully wiping a section with the edge of his T-shirt. "Shoot."

Tourmaline crossed her arms behind her back and clenched her fists. "Do you know a Ray?"

"Ray who?"

"A Ray who would make people scared."

He looked at the gas tank, hesitating a fraction of a second. "No, ma'am." He tilted his chin at her and blinked. "I know a Ray Longwell."

She rolled her eyes. "Yeah, yeah. I know him, too." Clearly there was a Ray everybody knew about, except her.

"Why do you ask?"

Tourmaline shrugged.

"Is that all you wanted?"

She frowned and studied him for a moment. Jason had always been around, always in front of her. Now she tried to *see* him. She knew his history. He'd spent time in the military, and when he came home he'd turned up at the clubhouse so drunk he couldn't have hit the floor with his hat. Dad had sobered him up and given him a landscaping job until he was ready to move on. Except Jason never did move on. "How did you find the Wardens, anyway?"

"Just knew 'em."

"Like how?"

"Everyone knows 'em."

"Knows what?"

"I don't know, T. It's a tight area. Everyone just knows. Why?"

She narrowed her eyes. "Why did you want to join when you got back?"

"Well, I didn't have a bike when I left. And I was just a kid. And I didn't know anyone."

That wasn't her question. "No, I want—"

"Is everyone down at the water?" Jason interrupted. Setting the bike carefully on the kickstand, he dismounted.

"Yeah. But I—"

He started walking away.

Did everyone just get to dismiss her when they were finished? He hadn't even answered her question.

Tourmaline chewed her lip, thinking of the cop with the lit flare disappearing behind her. She had done that. She had done that and she'd driven that Harley like a bat out of hell. She'd driven like a bat out of hell and put her fingers into Wayne's eyes. She'd escaped, talked to men at McDonald's, and limped around for days, not crying even when she had to scrub the sweat and grass and dirt out of her open wounds when she got home from work. Pulling her shoulders back, she remembered she was that girl, and she called out: "I remember you."

Jason stopped and half turned, a look on his face she couldn't figure out.

"I remember when you first came," she repeated firmly, meeting his gaze straight on.

A breeze must have moved in the trees above, because the dapples of light through the branches wavered across his shoulders. Across his wildly blown and choppy hair. It caught that glint in his eye that was always there, but her heart suddenly sped up as something shifted in the changing light.

Suddenly, she looked at him and knew what Virginia saw. What she felt. He was gorgeous, absolutely. Heart-wrenchingly beautiful. But more than that—Jason had all the confidence of a man who knew what to do, at any time, combined with all the fragility of a man who did not quite know how to live. And whether Tourmaline liked it or not, even though she cringed against the feeling, there was the urge to strike out after him. To bring him back to life. She wondered whether Virginia had the same urge, or whether, for Virginia, that look was just recognition someone was out there with her.

Tourmaline ducked her head as Jason came back, nearly afraid to look at him now. "The first time you came over. We had hot dogs. You looked more scared than any conscript before or after. It took me a long time to realize it wasn't that you were scared—you were in pain."

The asphalt crunched, and when she looked up, the glint had softened into familiar Jason. "I'd just gotten to the point where I could ride. Everything was still healing. I was in physical therapy for a long time. But you were really little. What—like, second grade?"

"Try fifth grade. I was eleven."

He nodded.

"How old were you when you left?" she asked.

"Younger than you." Jason laughed softly and shook his head, as if he couldn't believe it, now that he thought about it. Sighing then, he dragged his hand through his hair and looked at the ground. "I was seventeen. I signed up in October and it was next stop, Baghdad, in March."

"Oh."

His face seemed to fight to stay still and his eyes avoided hers.

What did he see, when he saw her? Tourmaline tried to stop the blush that poured into her face, but it was useless and she had to press on and pretend it wasn't there. "What did you do in the Marines?"

"Why are you asking?"

"I've never asked. Sometimes it takes a while to see the things right in front of you."

His gaze flickered to hers, alarmed.

"Sorry. I didn't mean to pry." She crossed her arms and searched his eyes for any indication of the answer anyway. "I hadn't meant to ask about this. I was just . . . thinking. About everything. All the things I don't know."

He looked away and gave a short, flat sigh.

Tourmaline chewed the inside of her cheek.

"You've seen the scars. Do you think I got that doing paperwork?" Jason straightened and widened his stance. "I served. I'm proud of my service. I survived."

She could see the pride, but it didn't look the way she had expected it to look. She didn't really know how to define what patriotism was on him. Or what to say in return. For a minute, they just stood there, listening to the faraway laughs of people down at the lake and the sizzle of the sun hitting the canopy above them.

"So you came home and just knocked on our door?"

Jason roused, eyes blinking back into focus. "The conscript's dad, he was a Vietnam vet—about the same age as me when he served. I met him at Walter Reed. He helped me get involved. The transition is hard. The Wardens made it easier."

"Cash's dad?"

He frowned and cut his gaze in her direction. "Why do you keep calling him that?"

"I don't." A wave of horror crashed over her. *She had.* "I just . . ." *Shit.*

"You should be careful. It's going to sound like something it isn't."

"I don't. I mean. It isn't."

"I'm just saying. He's too old for you, number one. The rest of the reasons aren't even . . . Your dad would—"

"My dad could get over it," she snapped. "But it was just a mistake."

Jason eyed her. "You're gonna make trouble for him if you're not careful."

Tourmaline winced, her stomach sinking deeper and deeper. What had she been doing with Cash? Thinking they could get away with this somehow. Jason was his sponsor. Jason held his fate. Jason was suspicious.

Shit.

She couldn't keep texting. Flirting. Wanting. She couldn't do any of that without ruining his life. She wanted to cry, but she just closed her eyes and growled. "I *don't*. Virginia just uses his first name, so it's in my head."

"Virginia." He bit out the name as if spitting nails.

"What's wrong with you?"

"What?"

"And her? I don't get what your thing is." It wasn't like Jason to be annoyed by a girl. Let alone one of Tourmaline's friends. She frowned and moved to the side as a car pulled past them.

Virginia was solidly a girl you could envision on the arm of an older man, but one richer and older than Jason. "She's eighteen," Tourmaline said.

His eyes met hers, some hardness in them she hadn't expected. "I know."

"How old are you?"

"I'm an old man."

"Trust me, I know. But how old is that?"

"Twenty-eight."

The car circled back, slowly easing past them. Tourmaline kept her face turned away from Jason so he couldn't read her expression. On the one hand he was younger than she'd thought. On the other hand, he was still a lot older than they were.

"I don't want anything to do with your friend, T. Don't worry."

"Oh."

She looked at her feet and found herself remembering Virginia putting ice on her neck and giving her medicine and rubbing her back until she felt better. She thought of Virginia's fierceness. "She's a strange eighteen. It's different from mine."

Jason rolled his eyes. "Eighteen is the same. You're babies."

"Your eighteen was different from mine." She lifted her head. "Where were you for your eighteenth birthday?"

His mouth twisted. After a long pause, he answered. "Iraq."

She opened her hand and pretended to drop the mic.

He smiled grudgingly. But genuinely.

And she knew everything was changed again, because his smile made her own heart race, whether she wanted it to or not. She swallowed and hoped he couldn't see it. "Virginia's eighteen is not my eighteen. We aren't friends because we're the same age or having the same experience. We don't have anything in common."

"Why are y'all friends, then?"

They weren't really friends at all, not in the way Tourmaline had always had friends. But she looked up, trying to figure out how to explain. "We're friends because when girls—women—are alone in this world, they're easier to pick off."

Jason's mouth opened to respond.

But brakes squeaked, and both Tourmaline and Jason turned.

A sheriff's SUV had stopped beside them and rolled down its window. "Y'all are going to have to leave," the deputy said, pointing at Jason.

He dropped his hands open at his sides and moved in front of Tourmaline. "What?"

"You and all your buddies down there." The deputy jerked his thumb. "Out."

Sauls was suddenly there, and he stepped beside Jason.

Tourmaline took a step to the side to watch.

"This is a family beach," the deputy said.

"We're here with our families, officer," Jason said.

The deputy shook his head. "I just don't need any trouble today."

"There isn't any." Jason started walking toward the SUV. "I mean, unless you're going to start it."

"Don't take another step." The deputy fumbled, jumping out with his gun drawn at his side.

Jason stood still.

Sauls twisted and met Tourmaline's eyes—seeing she'd moved, he shifted between her and the deputy.

"We're not going to have any trouble today," the deputy said.

"When do we make trouble? We're a family club."

The deputy didn't answer. His gun was still at his side. She couldn't see the deputy's face, but she saw how white his knuckles were on the gun.

"Fine." Jason spat in the dirt by the deputy's boots. "Happy Independence Day." He stalked away to the lake. "Get in Virginia's truck, Tourmaline," he hollered over his shoulder. "And don't get out."

Tourmaline looked at the deputy.

But the deputy nodded to Sauls.

She clenched her fists and went to sit in the sweltering truck, half-born and feeling stuck in the effort.

Two months, she reminded herself. In two months she could leave this whole insular world behind. Except now she didn't know whether that was a comfort or a heartache.

30

THE FLASH of a Buick lurking behind the trees in the parking lot brought Virginia into complete and utter sobriety, despite the water bottle of vodka between her knees in the sharp, rocky sand. The sun blistered her shoulders, but her blood turned to ice at the sight of one of Hazard's hired men, Burley, in that stupid car he insisted was not tan, but *champagne*.

Hazard was on to her, waiting for the break in the screen.

Virginia pushed her sunglasses tighter to her face and stared at the lake. She was safe for the moment. If Burley had seen her, he'd also seen the fifty other people on the beach, half of them Wardens. But there was no getting out of this. Her time was up. She had to run. Leave the state. It was time, anyway. There was nothing for her here. Her stomach—empty of food and full of watered-down vodka—churned.

When the sheriff kicked them all out five minutes later, she wasn't sure whether to be relieved or afraid, especially when she found herself following a long line of cars and bikes kicking dust deep into the woods, heading for Jason's house.

And as everyone bowed their heads to pray over the meal—women, and babies, and grown-up children, and sweaty little kids flanking the sides of the Wardens—Virginia kept her chin up and her eyes open, scanning the crowd.

It seemed obvious now. If you were to have the right to be here, someone had to speak for you. Tourmaline stood beside her dad. Virginia beside Tourmaline. Aubrey beside Jason. Tourmaline had spoken for her. Said she was trustworthy. And for the first time ever, Virginia wished she were worth Tourmaline's trust.

Jason turned his head and caught her eye. Staring her down. *Which one of these things is not like the others?*

Virginia let her eyes drop. She wouldn't have been able to hide behind Tourmaline and the Wardens much longer anyway.

They ate. Virginia hungrily. She'd been living on cheap hamburgers all week, and the spread was amazing. Ribs and coleslaw and cake. A last meal actually worthy of being called a last meal.

But it ended up being a waste. Like everything the last few weeks.

She barely made it to the woods behind the house before throwing it all back up. One bag of pilfered chips mixed with a little more watered-down vodka later, and everything managed to stay down. Even her body knew. The only good thing in her life wasn't hers, never would be, and she'd never even had a chance at being part of it.

Virginia settled in a darkening corner of the porch, sipping at the water bottle and feeling as if every point and line in her body were going in the wrong direction, at odds with itself.

Tourmaline sat on the swing, bathed in sweet summer light with a baby perched on her thighs while she talked to the wife of one of the Wardens about going to UVA in the fall. Jason stood in a tight circle of Wardens, laughing. The brutal sun dipped low behind the trees, and they lit a bonfire and gave the babies sparklers before the moms snatched them away.

It seemed lovely, everything warm and glowing from sparklers and firelight. The tree frogs sang in the darkened woods, and a slight, though muggy, breeze had picked up. But Virginia watched from the shadows as if she had her face to a window—where she was, she could only watch other people's lives instead of having one of her own. Forced to feel the sense of family and brotherhood surrounding her as she stood outside of it all.

Virginia's eyes burned. Her body ached from sitting.

The babies were taken home. Tourmaline joined a group of older kids playing with the fireworks. Aubrey was glued into the crook of Jason's arm, laughing at something someone said.

Virginia pressed her face harder against that window, drowning under waves of longing. *Fuck this shit.* She pushed up and went inside, past the kitchen and the little living room. Past the bathroom, to the end of the dark hallway, far from the party.

The door wasn't open, but Virginia went in anyway, flicking on the light with the kind of nerve reserved for one's last days. The quiet eased her chest, and she took a deep breath, blinking as her eyes adjusted.

Jason's room was sparse. Empty, except for a mattress on the floor and a gouged and beaten wooden dresser with a fan on top. Leaving the door cracked, she flipped on the fan and went to inspect the few pictures tacked above the dresser.

Picture One: Jason sandwiched between six topless women at some country-looking thing. His cheeks were red, whether from the serious bottle in his hand or because the women made him blush, she wasn't sure. Picture Two: Jason with Tourmaline's dad; Jason looked like a kid in the photo. Tourmaline's dad, younger. They looked like father and son. Smiling with their arms over each other's shoulders and their nearly identical Wardens vests. She lifted her fingers, cocked them, and quietly blew off both heads in the photo.

It didn't make her feel better.

How long would it take Hazard to find her if she left southern Virginia? He didn't seem like the type to go after her, but then she didn't know for sure. Hugging herself, Virginia turned and stared at the rest of the room.

The mattress was empty but for a sheet. A blanket was tidily folded on top of a pillow that lay on the floor to the side. That was it. The entire room.

Her chest was held in an invisible vise, choking the air slowly out of her body. Maybe she needed to rest or something.

Plopping on the mattress, she stretched out and stared at the ceiling, at the porch light casting shadows into the trees outside. The fan swept back and forth. Back and forth. She closed her eyes, and the sounds of normally breathing people drifted away.

"What the hell are you doing?" Jason said, sounding like someone who'd just walked into the house to discover his dog had shat over everything.

Virginia didn't move. "I just can't catch my breath. It's so hot I can't breathe."

"Go not breathe somewhere else." He pointed with the bottle in his hand. "Get out."

She ignored him. "Do you sleep on the floor?"

Silence.

"That's kind of weird," she said.

"Get out," he repeated sullenly.

"No, thank you."

"It wasn't a request."

She stared at the ceiling. Her throat thickened. "I just need ... I just need a minute, okay?"

"Definitely not here. Now." Jason swung his whole body in the movement this time. "Out."

"I know." She paused and dragged a deep breath in, vision swimming. "I know. But where? Where do I go ... ?" She had to breathe, suddenly realizing she sounded frantic. "To just get a goddamn minute to breathe?" She tried to breathe more deeply, but there wasn't enough air.

Jason was quiet, jaw tight.

She shook her head and closed her eyes, sucking down deep

breaths. Why hadn't she just done it Hazard's way? Smiled and faked it. Silken treachery and untouched heart. Grown into what she'd been heading for—a hard girl come into a cold woman. What gave her the right to want anything else?

Jason cleared his throat. "Hazard?"

She froze. "You knew," she stated flatly. He wasn't an asshole at all. He had only been protecting his people, his family. And rightfully so. Virginia's throat tightened and she gripped the sheet, expecting him to snap. Finally. It would be a relief.

The fan clicked and swept across the room.

Jason did not drop his gaze. "You'll pass out, and in the dark you'll start breathing again," Jason said. "That's what happens."

"Are you sure?" she croaked.

"I'm standing here, aren't I?" And he *was* standing there. Shoulders dropped. Limbs loose. Eyes darkened in the dim room and the long day.

It was quiet for a long time, except for the whirr of the fan sweeping back and forth. Finally, he sighed and closed the door.

Her breath caught in her throat, but in a good way. Most of the misery drowned in a sudden plunge of anticipation she hadn't known she was capable of.

He didn't say a word, but put his beer on the dresser and sat down on the other side of the mattress, turning to stretch out beside her. Feet crossed at the ankles. Boots on. He folded his hands over his stomach.

The fan swept over them. Back and forth.

"How did you know?" she whispered to the ceiling.

"It's my job to know."

"I'm out of time. I don't know where to go. Where should I go?"

"I don't want to know."

"Where would you go?"

"To hell. And I'd take whoever pursued me." He laughed, an undercurrent of strange bitterness mixed into the softness. It was not the same laugh he'd had with Aubrey, and she was glad.

Virginia closed her eyes, feeling the weight of his body pulling in the mattress. "Why do you sleep on the floor?"

"It feels safer."

"Why do you have a mattress?"

"So I don't look like a serial killer when I bring a woman back."

"Pretty sure serial killers have mattresses," she said.

"But if they didn't, you'd definitely think serial killer."

"Mm . . . maybe."

Jason sighed. "Where can you go that lets you leave the anger behind? That's where you should go."

She frowned at the ceiling. "I'm not angry."

"You're angry."

"No. I'm not."

"The kind you have . . ." He reached over, slowly, tapping his finger into the soft part of her upper chest. "Deep in there. The kind that is keeping you in the same places, with all the same people, doing all the same things. The kind that's poisoning every other feeling."

She wasn't angry. All she needed to do was recover some control. The fan clicked, paused, and went back the other way. The air touched her face, and she breathed deeper. "How did you get the scars?"

"IED."

"Do they hurt?"

"No. But sometimes they make it hard to breathe," he said.

"Breathing is hard."

"It's easy to hate yourself for breathing. Not as easy to stop as you'd hope."

Virginia turned her head, letting her gaze trace the outline of his profile in the lamplight. "Are you afraid you might just stop? Like one day it will be too heavy and hard and you'll open your mouth and just not find the will to do it even one more time?"

He watched the ceiling. "No. I long for that."

She felt then—for the first time—the difference in their ages. In their lives.

"You can't run from that feeling. Or your anger, really. No matter where you go. That's what will kill you, long after your enemy is dead. That's the hardest to escape."

She tried to breathe deeply, right where she was.

Jason stayed very still. Quiet. As if he didn't even notice she was there.

"I did this to myself," she said. "This is what I deserve. I'm just afraid of it. I'm being a pussy."

"Hey now, don't knock pussy."

She snorted.

Something like a smile pulled at his mouth. "This is your life." He nodded. "And you can't tell what you deserve or don't deserve, because you're too busy being angry it happened."

What the hell? "I'm really not angry," she said, half laughing and half feeling as if she might cry.

He chuckled.

"I don't have any feelings," she insisted. "Except . . . resignation. That's a feeling, right?"

He raised an eyebrow. "You mean, except the cold, dead grip of anger. Just that one."

She rolled her eyes. "Is this because I tried to slap you that one time?"

"First, you were clawing, not slapping." He picked up her fingers and ran a thumb over her nails. "And no. That's not why."

"I wasn't mad at you."

"I know. You were scared. You felt cornered."

She stared at him, dangerously close to throwing up, or crying, or something. She didn't want to ever move from this bed. She wanted to bring herself to his chest and smell the leather and smoke and beer on his skin. She wanted to drag her hair over his stomach. To taste his fingers and his mouth and his neck. She wanted to trace the lines of his body. Every line. Even the ones stapled into place. She wanted to breathe his breath and have his weight crushing the air out of her so she would keep dragging more in.

He saw it. She didn't realize he could read her mind, until he blinked, and she understood he could see exactly what she was thinking.

She couldn't read his mind. Or his eyes. But he hadn't left.

"I remember you from a long time ago," he said softly.

Did he remember her at Wal-Mart? "When?"

"Your old man's name was Ray."

Virginia didn't move. She did not like to talk about her old man, especially now that he was gone. It felt as if talking about him would resurrect his ghost, and she remained afraid of even that.

"You're eighteen," Jason whispered. "A baby."

"I *wish* I was eighteen." She wished she were a normal eighteen- -year-old girl. She wished—deeply wished—she were blushing Tourmaline, talking about college and her dorm. But Virginia watched "normal" through a window. And she lay there, screwed up enough to hold her breath at the idea he hadn't left, and normal enough to know it was kinda fucked up that he was still lying there. But he was tragic and beautiful, and he moved at her elbow like a fox at dawn. He was all she could have ever hoped to have.

He hadn't moved. "You're like a ghost," he said softly, eyes searching her face for something she didn't understand. "And I don't know what to do about that."

She pushed off the bed, slinging past him to lock the door.

That moved him. He bolted upright, shaking his head and rubbing his face. But no words came out of his mouth, and before he had more time to protest, she wrapped her hands around his waist and rolled her body slowly into his.

The stiffness in his back softened. She could feel his heartbeat through his ribs against her chest.

His hand came to her chin and grasped it firmly, tipping her to meet his eyes. "You're not going to do this." His breath came short. "We're not."

But she wanted to. She didn't feel like there was a single bone in her body that could be girlish until her chin was in Jason's hand. And now that he was holding her, she felt the way Tourmaline looked when Cash brushed her elbow. Giddy and girlish and full of potential for good things. Things that smacked of feelings and that wouldn't be there if she was truly a dead woman walking.

Smiling, Virginia closed her eyes and slid her hands under his T-shirt. Not a tremble in her hands as she skimmed her fingers around his waist and up his back. The ridges and wrinkles of the scars slipped under her skin the same as the rest of him.

He still grasped her chin, holding her there. Heartbeat hitting hers.

The fan swept back and forth.

She opened her eyes.

His eyes were darkened. Dipping his head, he softly kissed her. Once. Twice. Three times. The third time he lingered.

Letting go, he got up walked away, and left the door wide open in his wake.

31

WHEN IT got quiet. When all the men who had been Tourmaline's family when her family had fractured went down to the fire—their forms looming as distorted onyx shadows against the trees. When the woman with the tinkling earrings showed up and Dad held court with her by his side. When Cash gave up texting her because she wasn't texting back. When he stopped shooting her confused glances. When he stopped looking at all. When it was only her, with her legs pulled up, gently swinging on Jason's porch in the dark.

There the blossom started falling apart in her hands, a flower long picked and the petals wilting in pieces.

There was more noise. There was more drinking. There were more women she didn't know. Women arrived who were not far from her age. Ray stayed a secret the Wardens all shared that held power she did not have. And it suddenly occurred to her that a flock of starlings would eventually be pinned to Cash's as-yet-undecorated vest. The starlings, which all the men had in some manner, stood for—as the state's attorney had put it—"sexual feats and conquests."

Desperately, she tried to tack the petals back on—to remember these nights as they had been. To bring back the feeling of life and power and magic. She'd fall asleep on her mother's lap with bits of marshmallow still stuck to her fingers. Her father would carry her to bed smelling of wood smoke and gunpowder. The hollow but not vacant eyes of the horned skull on his jacket would be the last thing she saw before he turned out the light and her eyes weighed shut.

But it was too late.

The dogwoods had fallen. Crushed beneath heavy boots.

Virginia came out of the house and plopped down beside her on the swing, startling Tourmaline away from watching the men in the dark.

"How is . . . you know . . . going?" Virginia asked.

"It's complicated," Tourmaline muttered.

"Oh." Virginia took a deep breath and withered into the hard-backed swing. "Well, that makes two of us." She leaned into Tourmaline's shoulder and said nothing else.

The swing creaked, back and forth. The air mixed with honeysuckle and wood smoke.

Tourmaline whispered, "All this time, I thought I had the life I'd intended to have. Until someone told me it was just a toy'd they made me to keep me quiet."

"I envy your toys," Virginia muttered.

"There's no place for a grown girl here."

Virginia snorted. "You're right. No girls. Only women."

Tourmaline's throat choked tight. Mom had done all this. Mom, who'd picked up a strange man eight years older than she was. Mom, who wore a damn *thong* on the back of a Harley in a huge crowd. Mom, who kept the books in Dad's office detailing the club's history. Mom, who had taken her crown on her own, before putting it down for the black tar highway.

And again, there was an empty space where Tourmaline had hoped for the gentle, older hands of a wise woman.

A burst of laughter erupted from the woods.

Both girls looked out over the railing.

Someone—*Jason?*—was dancing with a girl . . . or rather the girl was dancing on him . . . one of those who had drifted in since the families had gone home.

Tourmaline had the distinct impression it was past her bedtime.

"Aubrey," Virginia spat. "I'd recognize that stupid hands-on-her-knees move anywhere. It's her signature." She stretched out a long leg out and pushed off the railing.

The swing groaned and whined as it swung back.

Tourmaline kept watching Aubrey, transfixed. How had Mom done this? If Tourmaline wanted Cash, she'd have to do the same. Somehow. Her way. There wasn't anything wrong or right in that. If she didn't want to stand and take her place, she didn't have to. But if she wanted him, this was the world she'd have to master. "You once said the worst thing you ever did was be naive." Someone turned up the music, but Tourmaline didn't look. "We have that in common."

"It's the worst."

"The worst," Tourmaline echoed, but her words felt lost inside the pulsating beat.

Our fate cannot be taken.

The night breeze caressed her face. She'd never appropriated those words for herself—they were always her parents'. The Wardens'. But now she wondered. What was her fate?

"There you are, girls." Her father's voice boomed in the dark.

Tourmaline jumped. Virginia sat upright.

Tourmaline's father came up the steps, stepping into the light with a smile. "Time for you girls to get going. I'm staying out here tonight. Make sure you lock the doors when you get home, okay?"

Tourmaline swallowed. "Can we stay?"

"*Here?*" Her father blinked, mouth open, looking outright horrified.

Tourmaline blushed. "Yeah. I mean. Until we're tired." And, because neither she nor he actually wanted her to stay in the least, she smiled sweetly. "Why not?"

"No, honey. It's not . . ." He shook his head and looked away. "You don't want to hang out here. With a bunch of old men. Go home, and you and Virginia have fun. Watch movies or something. The fireworks are over." He patted her cheek and went inside.

"Wow, you really showed him," Virginia said dryly.

"Your commentary is *so* helpful."

"I try." Virginia stood like a rousing panther, bringing all her power back into her limbs.

Dad came back out onto the porch with a bag of chips, giving them a strange look as he passed, boots thumping quickly down the steps. "Get on home, girls," he yelled back when he hit the yard.

"Don't you want to say good-bye?" Virginia asked, giving her a meaningful look.

Yes. She wanted to say hello, too. And answer Cash's texts. And go over to where he was putting ice in a cooler, wrap her arm around his waist, and stand alongside him. But Jason's warning was fresh in her mind. "It's complicated."

"Well, then." Virginia pulled her keys out. "If there's no trouble for us here, let's go find trouble elsewhere."

They drove out the long dirt road and turned onto the highway, switch-backing up the mountain with the radio cranked and the windows rolled down. They took deep breaths of the mountain air, gathering energy for another round.

The truck began to drift toward the edge of the road, but just when Tourmaline looked over to Virginia, expecting her to correct course, Virginia slumped over the wheel.

A massive upheaval stole Tourmaline's scream.

The truck bucked wildly. The road fell away into brush. A tree appeared, and just as fast, the truck folded around it with a terrible crumpling sound.

All went still.

She lifted her head, dazed. What had happened? She blinked, trying to make sense of it.

Virginia was draped forward on the steering wheel, head lolling.

"Oh, shit." Tourmaline smashed at the seat belt release, but it didn't budge. She strained to Virginia's neck, fingers trembling as she felt for a pulse.

"What?" Virginia murmured from underneath her tangled hair.

Relief flooded through her. "Are you o—"

Virginia's door was wrenched open. A man ducked inside.

"Oh, thank God," Tourmaline said, trying to catch her breath. "I don't know what happened—"

But the man just pushed Virginia out of the way—carelessly, roughly, as if she were a bag of groceries tumbled in the back.

Tourmaline froze, heart pounding as she tried to make sense of what was happening.

Virginia's head twisted and thumped against the side of the truck. Her eyes opened halfway, glazed and lost, meeting Tourmaline's in the dark.

"V? Are you all right?" Tourmaline struggled against the seat belt, trying to slip out. "What are you doing?" she yelled at the man.

He ignored her, unbuckling Virginia's seat belt and yanking her out.

"Stop. Wait." Tourmaline stretched and grabbed at Virginia's wrist. This was all wrong. Why wasn't Virginia fighting?

With a grunt, he wrenched Virginia away, dragging her out of the truck.

"Let her go!" Tourmaline screamed.

The man threw Virginia over his shoulder, a dark hulking shadow in the night. He started up the hill, Virginia's head bobbing behind.

Tourmaline smashed the seat belt release over and over, but the belt only tightened down on her. "Bring her back!" she screamed. The memory of what she'd told Jason whispered in her ear, mockingly. *Easier to get picked off apart.*

She screamed again and kicked at the dashboard. The seat belt choked her. Steam hissed out of the engine, billowing haze between her and the dark woods.

"She's my friend!" Tourmaline yelled, crying.

But there was no one to hear.

THE NIGHT was dark and the road forsaken. The driver's seat empty. The creature over Tourmaline's shoulders laughed a hissing echo into the dark. Or maybe it was only the truck, hissing steam and spitting fluids. *We're easier to pick off . . .*

Tourmaline startled and wrenched the seat belt again. She had to find Virginia. She had to bring her back.

Wiggling the seat belt release didn't help. The catch refused to budge. She twisted, trying to squirm out of the belt. It only cinched tighter. Hands shaking, she dug out her phone and called Anna May.

No one picked up.

"Why aren't you ever there?" Tourmaline screamed into her voicemail, tears blurring the screen, suddenly finding she'd wanted to scream that for months. She hung up heaving dry sobs and tried to calm down. Tried to think.

She was going to have to call Dad. Or Jason. And they'd *all* been drinking.

She wiped her eyes, her fingers frozen over Cash's name. He hadn't been drinking—he'd been on food, cleanup, and fireworks duty when she left.

Tourmaline hesitated a second longer before smashing her thumb on the send button and pressing the phone to her ear. She squeezed her eyes shut against the sinking feeling in her stomach.

"Hey." Cash sounded as if he were trying to stay quiet.

Loud music flooded through the phone, and she swallowed the urge to scream in frustration. "I need some help. I'm sorry. Virginia was driving, and we went off the road and I'm stuck and . . ." Her voice, which had started out calm, ran out of pitch. She took a breath and started again, slower. "I'm sorry. It's Tourmaline—"

"Are you okay?" He sounded like he was moving. Something rustled and his voice deepened, serious and urgent. Scared. "Tourmaline, *are you okay?*"

He *cared*. Hearing the depth of it, hearing the intensity, was a rush of emotion, and she sobbed out, "I'm not hurt, but I'm stuck in the seat belt. Some guy took Virginia. I have to find her. I have no idea where he came from or where he took her."

"Some guy?"

"He *dragged* her away." Tourmaline stared into the tree still lit with the truck's headlights. *Don't panic. Don't panic.*

The phone rustled again. "I'm coming, honey. I'm coming. Where you at?"

She twisted against the seat belt cutting into her neck, but the road was empty and dark. "I have no idea," she wailed. "Oh, wait." Dummy her. She opened the maps, found her location, and put the phone back to her ear. "I'm on Bear Run Road, halfway between the exit for Buchanan and the turn for the lake. In the brush."

"I'll be there in fifteen minutes. Don't move."

He seemed to have forgotten she was stuck. Keeping her phone clutched in her hand, she waited, afraid that at any second someone else would appear out of the mist, collecting girls from the woods.

Finally, Cash's bike roared up and cut off.

A sob of relief hitched in her throat, and she quickly wiped her eyes. Now wasn't the time to cry. She had to find Virginia.

"Tourmaline!" Cash yelled, crashing through the brush.

"I'm here."

"Arms up." He appeared at the driver's-side door, knife open in hand.

She threw her hands to the roof.

With two quick slashes, he'd cut her free and snaked a thick arm around her waist, pulling her out of the truck and into the grass.

She stumbled forward, stomach clenched. "I have to find Virginia. We have to call someone." But who? The cops? Would they even care?

"What happened?" Cash folded the knife and put it in his pocket.

"I don't know. He just grabbed her and took off." She started up the hill toward the road. "I have to figure out where she is."

Cash caught up to her, pulling out his phone as he walked.

"What are you doing?"

"I'm letting Jason know I got you."

She stopped. "You told Jason?"

"I had to get permission to leave."

She groaned. Now Jason knew she'd been lying and that she had Cash's number. "Why? Why the hell would you do that? Couldn't you have made up an excuse?"

He didn't even look bothered, tucking the phone back into his pocket and looking down the road. "Were you hurt at all?"

"I'm fine. Virginia isn't." Why didn't he seem bothered by this? "That man took her. She was unconscious."

"You didn't hit your head or anything?"

Tourmaline touched her head; there was a sore lump on one side. When did that happen? "Yeah, but it's not . . . It was just a little thing."

"A little thing?"

She pulled her hand away. "I'm fine. I have to find Virginia." It felt like screaming into the wind. Her words weren't going anywhere. "Why aren't you taking me seriously? This is serious."

"I *am* taking you seriously." He turned for the bike, talking over his shoulder. "That's another reason why I told Jason. Jason's taking care of it."

"Wait. Jason's taking care of it?" Suddenly Tourmaline felt as if she *had* hit her head hard, dizzy and nauseated—trying to track all the threads of people in her life and keep them untangled when they were just snarled into tight knots. "How does Jason know where she is?"

Cash handed her his helmet. "I don't have an extra."

She crossed her arms tight around her chest, rage rattling inside her bones. Her voice sounded high and strangled. "How is *Jason* going to take care of it? He wasn't there. He doesn't even know which way she went." How did *he* know better?

Cash sighed. "I know this is your friend, but it's also club stuff. Trust me. You don't need to worry. He's got it under control."

"Don't fucking tell me that." Tourmaline shoved away the helmet and clenched her fists. "Don't."

He dropped the helmet back to the seat. "I'm not trying to be an asshole. I'm telling you what I know. Jason knows where she is. He's on his way to get her now. He left the same time as me."

"Where is she?"

"I don't know. He said he's with her boss."

Her boss? "She doesn't really have a job." Or did she?

"Well, I guess not like a job job. But dealing is a job the same as anything else."

"Dealing?" Tourmaline was about to say that Virginia didn't deal drugs, but Cash cleared his throat and Tourmaline realized she did. "How does *Jason* know?"

"It's his job to know." Cash spoke as if it were so stunningly obvious he wasn't sure why he had to say it.

A prickling sensation ran up over her scalp.

She was a fool. She'd brought Virginia in. Trusted her. Thought, even, that Virginia was someone who could understand all the things that made up her life. Even her mom.

What had Virginia been doing at Hazelton that day, anyhow? Was there even a brother? What about the job Virginia had been doing with her? *She* was Virginia's boss.

Virginia had expected the man who'd wrenched her away. She'd known. That's why she hadn't fought. That's why she had seemed so nervous.

Tourmaline had tried to play Virginia, but all along, Tourmaline was the one being hustled. Now they were both screwed.

33

TOURMALINE'S face burned. And then burned more. A sick feeling rose in her throat. The only person she'd thought of as a true ally. A friend.

Complete and utter bullshit.

She rubbed her eyes, wanting to scream.

A screech owl trilled in the dark above them, heralding the sudden gust of a honeyed breeze.

"Where did you go today?" Cash asked in nearly a whisper.

"What?" she snapped, suddenly remembering he was there.

"We were talking and then you and Jason were up in the woods for a while, and . . . ," he trailed off. "Then you weren't there."

She faced him, stomach still churning. "You just don't get it," she said quietly. "I called you by your first name today, by accident, and Jason was up my ass like, *Oh, why are you saying that? Do you have something going on?* Now he knows we've been talking. That I have your number. And that I lied to him. Now the one thing I didn't want to happen is going to happen."

"It's not like we're hooking up."

She ground her teeth. "That's not going to work as a defense."

"No. We're . . . I mean. We're just talking."

She groaned and tucked her hair behind her ears, lifting her face into the warm breeze that carried the watchful owl's ballyhoo. "Either I'm your president's daughter—and that girl can't be talking to you. She can't want you. Or I'm Aubrey Winthrop—and that is a girl I was always told never to be. You don't get to be both—I can't be respected as a daughter and be sleeping"—fuck, she'd said that out loud; she winced—"with a member."

He looked confused. "What am I doing? Who's Aubrey Winthrop?"

Tourmaline shrugged, frowning. Her footing was unsteady and she was only ankle deep. How on earth did she imagine she could go further? And Virginia. Stupid Virginia. She tightened her fists, still smarting from the betrayal. If she couldn't judge her own friends, how on earth did she expect to make her way in her father's world? How could she trust Cash?

"Do I have to pick?" he asked.

"Yes, you have to pick," she snapped. "You're the one who decided there are only two options."

He pulled back and laughed. "Me?"

"You."

"And how in the hell did I do that?" He sounded more annoyed than he'd ever been with her.

"Because you're a Warden." She crossed her arms. "Because I'm someone's daughter, someone's party girl, or someone's ol' lady. That's the system."

"Uh, no."

"Because I don't get to exist in this world apart from you."

"You existed long before I got here."

"But Cash." Her shoulders slumped. "I exist to you. But not anyone else. I'm a . . ." With her hands she shaped the air into nothing, grasping after words. "A thing. A piece of paper with a girl drawn on it that is arranged in the background to look the way it's decided I should look. Even if I don't think of myself that way, I'm afraid it will be that way for the rest of my life."

Cash's mouth settled in a tight line. Muffled fireworks popped in the distance. He looked annoyed. Frustrated with her. It twisted her gut and made her want to fall on his shoulder and take it all back. But she didn't move. She didn't say anything else that might cut away at what she had already said. "You can't have me and the Wardens. And the Wardens are your dream. We have to back off, and I'll fix it with Jason. He won't listen to you about it, but he'll listen to me."

Cash slid an opened hand onto her neck, thumb brushing over her earlobe. "You don't know all I dream of," he said softly.

She didn't breathe. A fierce longing watered in her mouth. She tilted her head just a bit, toward the rough, warm skin of his palm. A sudden urge to find some part of him to taste.

But Cash moved on, slipping her hair back over her shoulder and letting his hand fall to his side. "Remember we were talking about how I went to school in North Carolina?" His voice was low and charged in a way that just encouraged that sweet ache building through her stomach. Stuffing his hands into his pockets, he turned to look over the ridge. "One time, when my dad was nearing the end, I drove the Blue Ridge Parkway back from school. My dad had always talked about it, and we'd moved when I was eight, so my memories of here are pretty vague. It took damn near forever to get from North Carolina to Front Royal—but there was something about it. I never got tired of looking down into those hollows and cirques." He laughed softly, tilting his chin to the moon. "That near-endless stretch of blue hills."

Tourmaline's throat ached to listen to the depth in his voice. The obvious love.

"People hear 'Blue Ridge Mountains' and they think of, like, fucking *John Denver* and toothless hillbillies. If you're a paper girl, I'm invisible. Nonexistent. No one hears 'Appalachians' and thinks of me." He tapped his chest, hand shadowed even under the moon. "But it is *mine*. It was my family working the iron ore furnaces. My father's father in the mines. My history in the unmarked graves along the back roads of

North Mountain. This is where I was born. These are *my* mountains, no matter what anyone thinks. This is where my parents carved out their own story, together, in a time that isn't that far gone and still doesn't like people to step outside whatever box has been assigned to them." His gaze flickered to her, dropping to look at her mouth.

For one heart-stopping moment she was sure Cash was *finally* going to kiss her.

But he swallowed and looked back to her eyes. "I passed these exits on the interstate for years without stopping, but on that trip on the parkway, I promised myself I'd take the exit. I was sitting at a diner eating a ham and cheese. I see a guy pull up on this nearly reflective Seventy-Two, and while I'm sitting there, knowing what the future probably holds and already mourning my dad, and feeling that ham and cheese just wedged into my throat, the man gets off and I see his cut." A smile split his face. "*Wardens.* It was my dad. It was fate. It was who I was and where I belonged, and I'd only needed to take the exit to find it."

Now she really couldn't do this with him. The stakes were too great for two people who were committed to other things. She bit her lips tight and stared at him, taking a step back in agony.

"My story isn't what people think of as the usual story. But then, the people who define who I'm supposed to be are the same people who define what you're supposed to be. I knew what it was to be a black conscript, even in a mixed club. It's fucking southern Virginia, T. My history is here and it's slavery and no one is going to get around that. But I get to own what happens next. I get to make the decisions about who has a say and what story gets told. I knew your dad had a daughter, I was warned well and plenty before I even met you. Honestly, I didn't think anything of it. But you . . ." He ducked his head, laughing as if embarrassed. "You had this giant plate of food. And this sharp look in your eye. And you walked in like you owned the place."

"Well, I do," she snapped. But then she remembered that her dad owned it and it'd been a Wardens party—a moment when he wouldn't have ever expected to see her. It was the space in her life she'd owned— owned simply by showing up and not backing down.

Cash just kept going. "Your hair fell into the gravy. And, I don't know why, but that was all it took. And getting to know you has been like. Like learning to ride here. These roads are curves that always threaten to wind around you, instead of you winding around them. I've been riding since I was old enough to drive, but suddenly I'm turning a bend and positive I'm going to eat concrete. You make me feel like that. And all of that is to say—whatever happens—the only people who matter between me and you are me and you. And I don't care if that's not how it's been done before, that's how it's going to go between me and you."

He said it as if he expected it to be good. As if it meant they had come to terms. Resolved the things they owed service to.

Tourmaline couldn't do anything but stand there and feel her heart breaking over something she had never had but desperately wanted. Because this was what would happen: She would stay a respectable daughter in order to keep her family, and he'd pin starlings to his vest to gain a brotherhood.

The wind pulled her hair back across her face, dragging it out in long white trails under the moonlight. Something inside her chest firmed up. Straightened. Felt calm. "You belong here. It looks good on you. I have . . . so much respect for you. The Wardens are lucky." Tourmaline smiled and nodded toward his vest. "Come on, take me home."

Cash nodded. What looked like disappointment flickered across his face, but it might have been a passing shadow of the trees or an owl in the moonlight. He handed her the helmet and turned away, sliding one leg over the bike and pulling it upright.

The wind caught her hair and tossed it back over her face. And there, in the moonlight, her mother was there, pushing her on. In the whispering mountain air and the dip of the treetops, bending toward Cash.

The motor started in a flooding growl and Cash straddled the bike, waiting for her to climb on behind him. He was a shadow in the darkness, the bike darker than coal.

She lifted her chin into the wind and yanked the helmet strap tight. The paper girl did not need to define her life anymore. She could be the whole person she'd been that night at McDonald's, unafraid and free. It would not be safe. It would not feel sure. But she could do it, if she wanted. Stepping on the foot peg, she planted her hands on his strong, muscled shoulders and swung onto the seat behind him.

He stayed perfectly still, head dipped forward, as she settled behind him without moving. She kept her hands on his shoulders, her stomach scooped in. Every bone in her body wanted to pull close, wrap her arms around his waist, and hold on. But she kept her distance. She hadn't yet decided. Hadn't yet gathered all the required courage. She might lose both the future and the past that way, instead of one or the other.

"I'm good," she called.

Cash lifted his head and put the bike in gear, twisting between her knees as he looked behind them, making sure the road was still empty. Slowly, he pulled out and sped up.

The wild mountain air streamed faster, barreling through her hair and over her limbs. Full of seduction and persuasion. She pressed down on his shoulders, tempted by the wind to abandon her body for the stars, wrap her legs tight around Cash's hard torso, and pull them both down low into the earth and loam. But she just swallowed and tried to mirror the sway in his body as the road wound around the ridge.

She took a deep breath of the wind, dripping with evening primrose and honeysuckle in full bloom. They roared out of the trees, into the open—with the valley bright under a quicksilver moon and the wind howling over the exposed crags and gnarled pines. As Cash leaned into a curve and she followed the roll of his body, she caught a glimpse of the road over his shoulder—winding into the dark as a sinuous silver ribbon. It was beautiful and wild and enthralling. It choked her. Took away her breath. Brought her blood surging and boiling as if it had heard the call of the wind and the open road and needed to be released. And suddenly she remembered.

You're a mountain road. Straightaways, sure, but also curves that come back in on themselves and always threaten to wind around you, instead of you winding around them.

Cash straightened back out, opening the throttle wide.

Carefully, Tourmaline eased herself forward—opening her legs wider and pulling herself snug against his back.

He took one hand off the handlebars and squeezed just behind her knee, encouraging, pulling her tighter.

She slid her hands down his back, wrapping around to rest, palms open on his flat stomach, and held on.

Just in time for the descending curves.

He put his hand back on the handlebars. The wind whistled in her ears and throttled her hair behind them. As Cash leaned, so did she. And the moon tracked them through the trees, throwing their shadows on the road.

33

VIRGINIA woke in the car and stared at the ceiling. It'd only been a few weeks of hiding out and mowing with Tourmaline, but it felt like her whole life. Now it was here—the funeral of Virginia Campbell, whatever she may have been. May she rest in peace.

Virginia's cheek pressed against the soft material of the backseat, and amber streetlights flashed randomly onto the carpeted floor. In that moment, without any veil between her and the truth, she thought of Tourmaline and of Jason. Of those people who did not like her or call her their friend and who were the ones she most desperately wanted to be loved by. The ones she wanted to count as her people. It seemed clear now that she had gone to Tourmaline not to preserve some idea of her own external value, but to preserve this feeling—this horrible, heart-wrenching ability to love and care, even when she wasn't lovable. And in the end, Virginia had taken what she most wanted, used them, lied to them, and driven one of them into a tree.

Virginia's head rocked as the car turned. The dark hum of the road that would end at Hazard's droned in her ear.

What now, Virginia Campbell? A cat with nine lives. Sailing through the starry night with all four paws in the air. How many had she used by now? What life was next?

Sail through and . . . *twist.*

Virginia closed her eyes and would have fallen back into a drunken sleep if not for the firm grip on her arms, hauling her up and out of the backseat. The sweet breeze lifted her hair off her face and she roused, automatically raising her head and opening her eyes to the night. This place was familiar. Too familiar. Her stomach twisted.

Now it did not matter whether Hazard had seen her in the brush, or whether he knew she had his picture hidden in her email in Jason's sock drawer, or whether he simply thought she was shirking his orders. Her fate would be the same no matter the offense.

The man kept her arm bent behind her back, pushing her through the thigh-high grass toward the weathered late Victorian.

Empty and forsaken, the house was set in the brush of the valley below the Blue Ridge. Its peaked corners leered over her in the dark. The man pushed her past the ornately trimmed and sagging porch. Past the plywood-covered windows. Around to a single set of steps into a bare steel door.

This was her last chance to make a run for it, and even though she twisted her head in the direction of the horizon beyond the fields, where the soft amber glow of light from a sleeping town was strung as a beacon, she kept her feet going past the moment. Stupid had never been part of her moves. There was *absolutely* a gun somewhere on the man's body, and if she ran, they'd make whatever followed five times worse because they'd had to go get her.

He pushed her up the creaking steps and, without letting go, rapped his knuckles three times.

The door swung open.

Hazard stood there, backlit by fluorescent work lights. No "Esquire" tonight, just a T-shirt and a pair of old-man khakis. "Well, don't you look prettier than a pat of butter melting on a stack of flapjacks," he said with a smile, pushing the door open wider.

"You should have just invited me. I'd have come to your party," she purred, as if she were walking into this godforsaken house of her own free will and not being dragged out of a backseat like some hog-tied calf.

He smiled. "Your spirit is always so wonderful." Pushing up his sleeves, Hazard stepped back into the shadows of the house.

"I could have brought something. I make a damn good potato salad."

"Oh, no, darlin'. You're the guest of honor tonight."

Keeping her shoulders from dropping, she met his eyes in the astringent light and wrote the lines she wanted to believe, the lines she wanted them all to see—that nothing they could do would touch her where it counted, that she would take what was due on the chin and come out the other side no worse for wear.

Someone shut the door behind her. The air inside the house was suddenly stale and heavy.

"You disappointed me. Hurt me, even," Hazard said, leaning against the skeleton frames of the cabinets behind him. "We had such a nice dinner and I got home expecting that email."

About the Wardens. She'd faked them. Good enough to hold up under a quick look, but not under scrutiny. Virginia swallowed and took a long stride in his direction, gathering as much verve as she could to plant it into the creaking, dirty floors.

A hand clamped onto her elbow and yanked her back.

She twisted into the pain and cried out, shoving and twisting to break free.

Her heartbeat stuttered. She tried to lift her chin, but found it would go no higher.

"You should have known better than to try and trick me like that. I didn't think you were stupid enough to think it would work, but . . . I misjudged you. You aren't what I thought. And to add insult to injury, you tried to avoid me?" He shook his head and sighed. "You betrayed me." He pushed off the counter and nodded to someone in the shadows. "Let's go. I have court in the morning."

Virginia's stomach dropped out from underneath her and her knees weakened. She should have run. Should have been long gone. Why had she stayed?

The man holding her tightened his grip on her arms, and another man unsheathed a buck knife.

This was the point when she should pass out. But everything stayed monotone and dull and real in the most horrible way. The wind rattled the roof. Hazard didn't move from the counter. Watching. He was too smart to do it himself—like he was too smart to rape her, too smart to bribe cops with money, too smart for his own good.

Pass out, she ordered herself. *Go back to sleep. Find the dark and hide there until it's safe to come out.* Her heartbeat slowed, but her eyes stayed open. She twisted her arm, testing the man who held her.

He shoved her to her knees.

Pass out.

But everything stayed as it was.

"Put her on the floor and do it," Hazard said.

She *was* on the floor.

The man holding her arm pushed her down, and she wrenched away. "No." She didn't want to lie down.

A solid thump of dull pain shot up her back, and she only realized the man had kicked her over when her chin hit the floor.

"No. Put her on her back."

She swore she wasn't going to fight. She *knew.* Knew what fighting did. But in that second, her reality became too real and she forgot. Screaming, she kicked right up to her feet and yanked her arms away.

For a second, she was free. Standing on her own, breathing hard as she faced down Hazard and his knife. A cat with nine lives, but a bobcat awake in a hungry spring. She met his eyes and the thrum of her heartbeat twisted.

He was going to pay for this.

He would pay for the smirk he'd given her when he had evaluated the awkward girl-child she had once been, and agreed to take her in the absence of cash; and he'd pay for the smirk now. For standing there as if this were all business, something on the to-do list, and not something he had long ago made deeply personal. And suddenly she was drowning in all that anger Jason had told her was there. She could not be angry at her mother for that moment—even though that was the moment she was truly, deeply, angry over—but she'd be angry at Hazard for all the ones after.

The second lasted less than a second.

They had her again, hauling her backward.

She twisted and kicked—to give them a hell of a time getting this poor rounder down. Something in her middle hurt blunt and thick, knocking the wind out of her. But as the blooms of water stains on the ceiling passed before her eyes, she remembered Jason and the clicking fan and she breathed again in one great gasp.

The back of her head thumped on the dirty wood floor. If she didn't fight, she'd be hurt. If she fought, she'd die.

And she wanted to *fucking live.*

Don't fight.

"Pull her hair out, Warren."

A third set of hands jerked her up by her hair and then ripped it all upward, twisting her neck.

Virginia swallowed the scream, but a noise escaped her throat as she hung, choked.

The man with the buck knife started sawing.

What was he doing? Her heart thumped wildly. *Survive.* It pounded. *Survive. Survive. Survive.*

Hair fell back to her shoulders, chopped short. Little by little the tension abated until the man held her by only a thin rope of uncut hair, sending pain searing through her scalp. She twisted, arching, trying to hold herself up—but the men holding her wrists just yanked her back down.

The knife flicked through and the fire abated.

She smacked the back of her head on the floor. Tiny bursts of light drifted over her vision, but not the darkness she longed for.

"Just taking what's mine," Hazard said with a smile. "What's next? How about those nails?"

She closed her eyes, locking in on the end, on making it through. He could take these petty things, but he could never take her will. Her heart hammered a million miles a minute.

"Well, hell," someone drawled out long and heavy.

Jason. She opened her eyes. The same ceiling was above her, but she'd *heard* him. Had she finally passed out and started dreaming?

"I'm not interrupting, am I?"

Virginia lifted her head.

Jason stood in the doorway. Hands on his waist. T-shirt billowing out gently in the breeze that rushed through the open door.

"Perfect timing," she croaked. "Did you bring the potato salad?"

"Shut up, Virginia," Hazard snarled.

As if punctuating, someone kicked her side.

She forced herself to use the last of her breath to groan. For Jason. Just in case.

"Let her up," Jason said, sounding deadly.

"With all due respect, this really is no business of yours," Hazard said. As if to emphasize his point, two more men appeared out of the shadows, one on either side of the door.

Virginia's throat choked in fear. This wasn't right. Didn't Jason have people with him? Suddenly, she realized he wasn't wearing his vest, and for some reason she couldn't explain, her stomach twisted.

"I'm not looking for a fight. And I won't hold this against you." Jason paused, jaw twitching. "But I want her *now*."

"That's not how this works. You should know." Hazard took another step, knife in hand. "Where're your *brothers*?"

Jason crossed his arms. He didn't look worried, even as the two men moved with him, glancing at Hazard like dogs waiting for their cue. He found her eyes, expression impassive. "Come on, Virginia."

She pulled against the hands that pinned her, but they held firm.

"You may not be looking for a fight, but you'll certainly get one," Hazard said.

Fear prickled her back. She was more scared for Jason than she was for herself. Hazard would kill Jason, no matter what he did. He was here alone. Without protection.

For her.

Her throat tightened, and she yanked and twisted.

"Hold her!" Hazard yelled.

The two men twisted her arms, and a massive boot came down on her chest, sinking so much weight into her ribs the whole world split into pain. She gasped and went limp. The boot eased only a little. Just enough for her to find Jason across the room.

The grip on Virginia's arms loosened, and she tested it slightly, skin slipping underneath the men's sweating palms. Why hadn't Jason brought more people? More *something*? But really she wondered why he had come at all. She was not worth this risk.

"I'm doing you a favor. Coming alone. It's up to you to take the favor."

Something changed, electric and tense in the air.

"Listen," Hazard said, taking a step forward. "There's nothing special here. She'll be fine, I promise. I'll even deliver her to you when I'm finished. There's no need to . . ." But he trailed off as Jason took a step forward.

"There's no negotiation."

Hazard only paused a moment. "Stop," he ordered. "Let her up."

Jason didn't move.

They let her go, and Virginia scrambled away, running for Jason before she was even upright. She didn't drop her eyes from him, just in case it was a dream and she lost him by looking away. Wrapping her arms around his waist, she slung herself behind him.

He didn't disappear. He was warm. And solid.

And real.

She wanted to cry. But she just put her forehead in between his shoulder blades and took a deep breath. Of the wood smoke and sweat and leather and soap that was all Jason. Of something *safe*.

"This is done now," Jason said. He took her hand off his waist and held it tight, turning for outside.

As they hit the ground, he pulled her into a run.

34

HIDDEN in plain sight, a mile from the road, in a rocky cow pasture, Virginia sat on the tailgate of Jason's Ranger, staring into the trees. Beyond the thick oak limbs they sat under, the hills rolled abruptly into a dark wall, separating them from the valley from which they came. Sleeping giants they could not pass until they were not pursued.

All that anger she hadn't believed Jason about had ripped open and engulfed her in its fury. Her head pounded. Her heart ran fast. Her body remained locked to that dirty wood floor even though she sat unfettered, staring at the mountains. She longed to crawl to the rim and stand among the table mountain pines until she was gnarled and bent, and her roots clung deep against the wind, the passing rain, and the clouds drifting rime ice all winter.

"Is Tourmaline okay?" she asked finally.

"She's fine," Jason muttered over the flashlight between his teeth, pawing through a little Rubbermaid bin of first-aid supplies he'd pulled out of the truck.

Her stomach tightened. She had been afraid of his anger, but was now more afraid of his gentleness. More afraid of how to live now. "I didn't mean to hurt her. I didn't feel tired . . . I didn't think."

He took the flashlight out of his mouth. "You're not allergic to latex, right?"

"No." She stared as he started opening gauze pads. "How did you get Hazard to let me go?"

"He's afraid of the consequences of telling me no."

"Which are?"

He didn't respond.

The wind swished smooth patterns through the grass and shook the leafy oaks stretching high into the dark sky. She swallowed and looked down at her hands, remembering the grip of his fingers as he pulled her through the grass.

"You okay?" he asked.

"I'm alive."

"That'll do."

She sniffed and nodded.

"How do you feel?"

"Lucky."

He made a soft chuckling sound. "I mean, what hurts?"

"Everything." The more the adrenaline ebbed, the more pain she found.

Grasping her chin, he gently turned her head to inspect whatever it was that stung on her face. Despite the circumstances, Virginia felt that same feeling in his hands—of girlishness and softness she wouldn't otherwise have known she had. Of peacefulness somehow. She closed her eyes and soaked it in.

The flashlight switched on again, blinding her even with her eyes closed.

"Mmm," he said.

"What?"

Jason didn't say. The light went off, and he tilted something liquid. "How long have you been working for him?"

"Since I was fourteen. My mom got a few DUIs and couldn't pay the legal fees to keep herself out of prison. He took me instead. I was worth eighteen hundred, twenty-two dollars and fifteen cents."

"After your dad died?"

"My daddy didn't die," she whispered, looking up at Jason and into the moonlight. "He was put down." She rarely thought about it, if she could help it. But everything was raw and cut open, oozing in horrible ways. Including his memory. Her father had been murdered—found dead in his recliner in the house, a bullet through his temple, no sign of any other disturbance. The sheriff had done the usual sort of investigation, but nobody much cared to find who'd done it. It was well known what kind of person he was, not that anyone did much about it except blame Virginia's mother for not leaving. No one except her mother had really mourned him, and only God knew why.

Jason didn't move for a second, and then he readjusted the gloves. "This is going to sting," he said softly. He pressed the pad to her chin and it did sting. It stung like hell.

"Take a deep breath."

Virginia tried, but couldn't take much of one. The air cut off in a sharp gasp of pain. She forced several shallow breaths instead.

"I'll check that out next." He dabbed the gauze again. "Where's your mom now?"

"Drinking? I don't know. Hopefully drinking peacefully, I guess. I moved back in with her a couple months ago, but she has a new boyfriend so I mostly stay out of their way."

"Where did you live when you didn't live with her?"

"A boyfriend's. We aren't together anymore."

"What do you do for Hazard?"

"Pills and, when out of state, cigarettes. Or. I used to do that. I don't know what's ahead of me."

"At pageants?" He sounded surprised.

She nodded, wishing it wasn't so dark that she could see his eyes. "And at school."

"Not a bad hustle. Not at all." He put the gauze down and started rustling with another one. "So, what happened?"

"I don't know." She paused, pulling a long burst of night air into her nose. "I realized I wasn't as valuable as I thought. He wasn't going to . . . force me . . . but he . . ." She stared at the mountains shadowed under the moonlight. "He was going to wear me down. Break me and remake me into something I never planned to become."

The wind gusted, catching the shorn and choppy ends of her hair and pushing them into her face. She winced as they brushed the edges of whatever was raw and open on her jaw.

He straightened. Gathering up the loose hair, he twisted the ends. And tucked them into the back of her tank top.

They immediately started slipping out, and shamefully, she wanted to cry that her hair was gone. But she just licked her lips. "Why are you alone?"

He shook his head, peeling off his gloves and pulling out a new pair. "Because I'm a sugar-frosted fucktard of the first order." He sighed and brought another gauze pad to her face, dabbing something cool onto whatever stung. Probably from when she hit the floor, she realized. "I broke a few rules tonight. So we're going to try and keep this quiet."

He'd come for her without the protection of his brothers, without the patch on his back that made him something bigger than one man, and the realization of what he'd risked bloomed wide and expansive in her chest. Swallowing, Virginia stared into the sky and the hazy stardust shining into the valley. "Rules?" she choked out.

"What's a line if you don't cross it now and then?" He put down the gauze. "Take another deep breath."

Virginia started a deep inhale and was cut short by a stab of pain in her ribs.

"Raise your arms."

She did.

He stepped closer. "I'm going to check your ribs; is that all right?"

"Yes."

"Just breathe normally." Jason put his hands on her ribs, pushing gentle pressure through her shirt and the gloves he still wore. The moonlight slanted across his shoulders, shadowing his face.

She clenched her jaw.

"Take a deep breath."

Inhaling as deeply as she could, she moved her hands to his shoulders, gripping tight as the pain hit her ribs. The wind died down and the wood thrushes began a midnight chorus, trilling clear and sharp under the oak limbs threading above their heads.

"Again." He moved. His fingertips closed on her ribs. The weight of his big hands cinched together what felt ripped into shreds.

She clasped her hands behind his neck.

"Again," he whispered, voice thicker.

She wanted to kiss him. To taste him. This shadow under the moon that had come for her. Her breath came faster, shallow against the pain. She swayed closer.

He abruptly pulled away. "Does Tourmaline know?"

Virginia blinked, longing stuffed into her throat and pain stabbing into her ribs with each unsteady breath. "Yes," she croaked, and then remembered all her lies. "Not really."

"She's asking for you." Jason peeled off the gloves. "I think your ribs are just bruised. If you want, I can take you to the emergency room."

Her throat tightened. With Jason, she had a chance—a small chance, but a chance. With Tourmaline, however, there was nothing. Not if Tourmaline knew all Virginia had done.

"I'm okay."

"You sure?"

Virginia nodded, easing herself off the tailgate.

"If it hurts real bad, you can gently wrap them. But don't leave them wrapped long." He stuffed the trash into a grocery bag, head still down.

"They'll heal better if you just leave them alone and take it easy." He put the bag down and started piling things back into the first-aid container.

She reached for his hand, but he kept putting things into the trash. "Jason," she murmured.

The question weighed on her chest, suffocating her worse than the constriction in her ribs. What was she worth to him that he'd taken this risk? "You didn't have to do this." She wanted to say she was sorry, but the words felt flat and dull and like nothing they needed to be.

"I know," he said without turning. Said with control.

Her hand slipped, barely gripping his wrist, but she didn't move, staring beyond him, beyond the moonlit field into the pitch-black horizon. The sun was going to rise soon, but it was hard to imagine what kind of day it would bring. "Please tell me why?" she cried, horrified to hear the breaks in her voice.

Jason took her wrist and gently pulled out of her grasp. "You're someone Tourmaline cares about. She was afraid for your safety."

Because of Tourmaline? "That's all?"

"That's all," he said.

She remembered his mouth. How he tasted of something sweet and sharp and deep. How he'd held her so gently and kissed her so intently. She crossed her arms and looked away, swallowing until her throat felt clear. "How much longer do you think we need to stay here?"

"I don't know. I don't know how badly he wanted to punish you." He shut the truck door and pulled out a smoke. "And how much of a risk he's willing to take by going after me."

The birds called to each other, and the honeysuckle breeze played with the ends of Virginia's hair. "Mind sharing?" she asked.

The moon was on his face now, and his eyes flickered up to her as he dragged in a breath. The sharpness cutting even in the dim, blue light. Pulling the smoke out, he handed it over.

She took as deep a breath she could, grateful for the steadying buzz. "I'll leave some pain meds for you."

She nodded and exhaled, staring at the glowing ember. "Thank you."

He didn't say anything.

If she had more than a yawning black longing in the space of her chest, she'd have thought something like she would love him forever for coming for her. For this one moment—in which she hadn't asked, hadn't deserved, and he'd risked it all for her anyway—meant the world, and the universe, and all she could imagine of goodness being in existence, and if he had whispered that he was God, she would have worshipped him for eternity. Turning, she offered the smoke.

He reached.

She pulled it away.

His gaze came to her. Confused.

Taking a quick step, she pushed into his chest. Into his mouth. Holding the smoke clear of their bodies.

Despite what he'd said a minute ago, his mouth opened, hungrily. That same sharp, sweet taste. That same overpowering headiness. She could get used to its shock.

His warm hands opened on the outside of her thighs, pulling her hips snug against him.

She put her hand to the side of his face, grabbing the scruff of his beard just in case he moved away. When he moved back, she nipped at his bottom lip.

Some noise escaped his chest and his arms wrapped low over her ass, cinching her tighter, higher into his body. He pulled away and buried his face in her neck, wrestling—she could feel it. Not wanting to want her. Even as his warm mouth opened on her throat, his grip was loosening.

She gently bit at his earlobe, his earring cool on her tongue. But she'd slid down just far enough to cut into her ribs. Wincing, she tried to push herself back up.

But the pain had broken the rush between them.

He gripped her hips and set her down. Away from him. Exhaling, he nabbed the still glowing cigarette out of her fingers and dragged in a deep breath. A shaking breath, she saw with satisfaction.

"Too late, Jason," she whispered. "I see you." Just in case he thought she might forget about him when he wasn't there. Just in case he thought she'd forget what he had done.

His eyes flickered up, pinching the cigarette between his fingers and exhaling a long wispy cloud. "Stop looking."

She wouldn't. He'd come for her and now she was his, whether he wanted her or not. She was going to help Tourmaline, if Tourmaline would take her help. Lifting her chin to the dark tide of mountains, she took a deep breath against the pain.

And above all, she was going to make Hazard pay.

35

REALITY stayed suspended in the tumult of summer wind until Cash stopped the bike in her driveway.

Using his shoulders, Tourmaline pushed up and off the bike. Her fingers trembled as she took the helmet off and handed it back.

"Hey." He grabbed at her fingers before they slipped away.

She couldn't help but come back to him, back to the place where it was nothing but him and the road, and the roar of wind and horsepower. A smile tugged across her face. "Yeah?"

"You're going to keep me company tonight, right?"

Yes. But annoyance flashed and she tilted her head. She was tired of this teasing. This looking and acting as if he were going to kiss her, though he never did. "I don't know. I might need a little something. Some *incentive.* It *does* mean I'd be up late."

He laughed.

She stepped closer. Whatever lay ahead could wait while she lingered in this moment. For this moment, she was safe with Cash. For this moment, with him, she could be bold and fearless and free, and the paper girl was just a thought, not a destiny. She pulled her leg up and slid across his lap, managing somehow with magic to do it effortlessly.

He was surprised. He shifted his weight on the bike, his boots scraping the ground. But the surprise lasted half a second. He dropped the helmet to put both hands on her waist, and it bounced off the ground and rolled away in a show of complete disregard for anything else.

She smiled.

She was still smiling when his mouth found hers. Hot and eager. He bunched the skirt of her dress in his fists, wrists sliding up her thighs as he gripped the fabric around her waist, pulling her snug against him. The kiss was nothing but the sweet night and the moonlight. It was an open road and fast wind.

And it was perfect until he pulled away and whispered into her lips, "I have to go."

She bit her lip and waited, breathing.

His hands pulled away, achingly, spread wide to gather up the pieces of her on the way from her waist to her knees.

She leaned back. Breathing hard. Heart fluttering.

He offered his hand.

A second more and she took his hand and crawled off the bike, this time not effortlessly. This time her legs trembled and her body buzzed as if she were a hive and dripping with summer honey. This time she stumbled in the driveway and he put his hand on her hip to steady her. "Got it?"

She took a deep breath and tried not to look at the house. "I'm good."

"You'll be around?" He grinned.

She laughed, big and loud and terribly unfiltered. Putting her hands on her waist, she tried to calm down. "Yep." She nodded. "I'll be around."

But as soon as his taillights disappeared from view her phone lit with a text from an unknown number.

Have V.

Jason? He'd never texted her before.

She texted back. *Bring her to me. She's mine. I don't want the club dealing with her.*

You sure?

Yes. Virginia would pay for her treachery.

◆ ◆ ◆

It was four in the morning by the time Jason showed up with Virginia, hauling Tourmaline out from under the covers where she'd been texting Cash for the last few hours.

"Delivery," Jason drawled, gently pushing Virginia toward the step when Tourmaline opened the door.

Virginia's eyes flickered up to Tourmaline's. Her hair was all whacked off as if someone had gone at it with a weed cutter, and the bugs circled her head in the porch light. She didn't really look *at* Tourmaline, but glared at Tourmaline's chin. Everything about her looked wracked and ruined.

"Where did you find her?" Tourmaline met Jason's eyes in the porch light. She would not be lied to.

"On her back, getting the shit kicked out of her for some manner of ill-doing." He eyed Virginia in a way that pulled Tourmaline up short. Equal parts careful indifference and something Tourmaline could only label as adoration. *Jason liked her.*

Virginia's chin went up in the silence; she didn't see his expression.

Jason's gaze flickered back to Tourmaline. "I haven't told your dad."

"He probably won't know if no one tells him," Tourmaline said, her stomach alive and trembling the way it had that afternoon. It seemed to her that seeing Jason as the man he was to everyone else had changed something between them, balanced the power somehow. Now she knew she could speak to him in a certain way and he would listen. He would listen without ever considering why he was listening.

"I'm not really an advocate for that, but . . ." Jason shrugged.

"This isn't his problem. I'll deal with it." She nodded as if he had already agreed, tucking her hair back behind her ear.

Jason's forehead pinched, but he nodded.

Tourmaline dropped her gaze to Virginia.

Virginia looked at her feet.

"If you want, I'll get her truck out tomorrow and tow it to the conscript's to fix. Just text me. Your decision." Jason spun for his waiting truck, leaving Virginia's fate in her hands.

Tourmaline stood stunned for a split second, marveling at what had just happened. It had worked. She folded her arms and leaned against the door. "You lied to me."

"We made a deal."

"Under false pretenses." Not to mention she'd thought they were beyond a deal. That they were friends.

"I didn't know you would be someone I could trust," Virginia argued.

"It's impossible to trust other people when you aren't trustworthy in the slightest."

Virginia lifted her chin and her tone turned to ice. "What do you want me to tell you? Everyone looks the same. How am I supposed to know the difference between an enemy and a friend when I have nothing but enemies?"

Tourmaline tightened her fists. "And drugs?"

Virginia dropped her head. "I can't apologize for doing what I needed to do. But I am so sorry about your mom."

"Yeah, great," Tourmaline choked out.

Virginia's gaze flickered to hers. Pleading and shadowed in the light. "My mom is an alcoholic. I know what that feels like, but I did it anyway. I'm so sorry." She said it softly. With nothing extra. No excuses or ornamentation. Just the words, quietly spoken.

Tourmaline bit her cheek and looked into the shadowed trees and bushes starting to glow with the heat of the coming day. She'd almost rather Virginia go back to being defensive. She was angry at Virginia's treachery, but also at herself for believing.

But *punishing* Virginia felt too close to punishing herself. Tourmaline thought of Virginia's wrist slipping out of her grip as the man pulled her away. And Tourmaline thought of shaking her mother's shoulders against a burgundy velvet seat. Remembering the desperation. The panic. How nothing could get beyond the guilt of having betrayed a person you loved. And suddenly she remembered her wrists slipping free of the CO's cuffs and the door that had opened in the concrete wall. She remembered that Hayes had, in the end, not filed a report, though she should have. Forgiveness came from places you didn't expect.

The thrushes began their melancholy songs, *eh-oh-lay, eh-oh-lay*, under the leaves in the dark garden behind the house. Tourmaline turned off the outside light and closed the door, settling down on the step in the cool, dewy morning air. The sky was fading from blackest night to pink charcoal. She propped her elbows on her knees and rubbed her eyes. It'd been a long night. She loathed to say the words. But there were no other words to say. "All right. I fucking *forgive* you."

Virginia just stared as if Tourmaline had pulled out a gun; she blinked, looking panicked. There wasn't much relief in her expression, only fear.

The moment Tourmaline recognized the fear, she knew she'd done the right thing. "Did you eat?" she asked in a softer tone.

Virginia's shoulders sagged and she opened her mouth as if to say something, but all that came out was crying.

The funny thing about forgiveness was that it could only be passed along.

36

VIRGINIA couldn't shake the feeling that, at any second, Jason and Tourmaline would turn around seething with fire and brimstone. She told Tourmaline the whole truth, allowed it to pour out in a desperate attempt to bring the final blow upon her instead of waiting for it to surprise her. But the sun rose and the day dawned, and all Tourmaline did was stand, brush off her ass, and hug her/drag her inside.

They ate stretched on the couch, legs stacked across the cushions and plates on their stomachs. All the windows were open, to catch the breezes and air out their panic.

"Do you know what the Wardens do? Like, what they really do?" Virginia asked, sopping up the last bit of syrup with her pancake.

"I don't. Do you?" Tourmaline asked.

Virginia shook her head.

"But they do something. There's something we don't know," Tourmaline said.

Virginia nodded. "Definitely."

"It's not drugs, right?"

Virginia was surprised by the hesitation in Tourmaline's voice. "No. No way. I mean, I'd be shocked by that," Virginia said.

Tourmaline fell silent.

"Is that your mom in the hall? The picture of the woman in the leather jacket with roses on it?" Virginia asked, not looking at Tourmaline.

"Yeah. That's her."

"She looks like you," Virginia said.

"You mean I look like her?" Tourmaline asked.

"No. I meant she looks like you. Do you have any other pictures of her?"

Tourmaline heaved herself up and nodded toward the hall. "Come on, I'll show you."

Tourmaline opened one of the hall doors and Virginia followed her into the dark, cool room. Heavy wooden shutters kept out the sun, and the air felt stale and still. A rudimentary office occupied the shadows. It had the depth of something sacred Virginia didn't know how to explain to herself.

Tourmaline turned on a lamp and the pale light fell across opened photo albums. "I was looking at them last night, before Jason called. Trying to figure out what . . ." She sighed. "What to do, I guess." She flicked quickly through the photos, and Virginia only caught the brief blur of men and motorcycles.

Cash. This wasn't just a boy to Tourmaline, it was a life. At least for as long as she wanted to be with him.

But Tourmaline pulled out a shoe box from the desk drawer and set it on top of the scrapbooks, lifting the lid. "These are my family's. Not as much club. Though you'll see there's a lot of overlap." She started picking through photos, handing certain ones over to Virginia. "Jason when he first got here. He worked for the landscaping business for a while before he even started hanging around the Wardens. They wanted to give him time and he needed to figure out how to build a life."

Virginia took the picture, her heart squeezing tight. Jason looked like a boy in the photo. A terrified boy. A hunted boy. She wanted to find him, right then, and hold him.

"Do you know of a Ray?" Tourmaline asked suddenly.

Virginia handed the photo back. "Like, my old man?"

There was a moment full of silence.

Tourmaline exhaled a long breath. "Never mind." She handed over another photo. "Him and Cash's dad when they all came down one time. Cash's dad sponsored Jason to become a member, but he wasn't local anymore, so he had to find someone who would do the work of being a sponsor. My dad agreed to do it, for Old Hawk."

Virginia looked at the photo. The terrified boy was still terrified, but smiling. He wore a tan Army T-shirt and was being held in a headlock by a big, laughing black man who looked vaguely like Cash.

"And so Jason is doing it for him now," Virginia thought out loud.

Tourmaline nodded. "It's a big deal. Jason and Cash are changing things about the club. But I think that's what they meant to do."

"What's the point of rules if you don't break them now and then?" Virginia said with a smile, still staring at the photo.

Tourmaline chuckled. "You remind me of my mom sometimes. Like, how I imagine my mom was when she was young. Before everything shitty started."

Virginia's heart raced a little.

"She'd have liked you. She would think you would make a good queen. That's not a word anyone uses, by the way, it's what I call it." Tourmaline handed Virginia another photo. "I always thought my dad would get a new girlfriend or something and she'd take that role, but I don't see that happening. It's not working that way. Jason is changing the club. He won't be president for a long time, but he almost doesn't need to be. It's changing and my dad is allowing it to happen." Tourmaline shrugged. "My mom would think you're good for Jason. You won't let him get away with this shit he tries to be."

Virginia smiled. "I'm not sure I have that power, but I like the idea of it."

"You do. You can't see the way he looks at you, but I can." Tourmaline made a face. "My question—which I can't ask anyone—is, what does this mean? Is everything in a moment of change? If I just go along with what's always been, am I betraying myself? If I try to change everything, am I betraying the club? The club has always been family to me. But now, it can't be, unless I decide to make them my family." She gave a heavy sigh and took the photo back, digging deeper into the box. "Oh." Her tone dropped into disgust. "Ugh, look. Wayne and my mom." She handed it over.

Virginia froze. "This is Wayne?"

"Yeah, he looks sort of weasel-like, right?"

Virginia stared at the photo. At the beady eyes and thin shoulders and stained fingers. It was the 9:15. The 9:15 who'd been so amused to watch her demise. The 9:15 who got all her clients, her bags, and Hazard's trust. "Fuck," she breathed.

Tourmaline's head snapped up. "*What?*"

"He's working for Hazard." She dropped the photo and stepped back, finding Tourmaline's eyes. "They're moving in heroin. Together. And the—" The Impala! The cop car with the gold clubs being pulled out of the back was the same car that had been in the parking lot yesterday. The one Tourmaline said was the state detective. Virginia screamed, because the words were so big and the connections were falling like dominoes and the whole world spun with her fear that she'd never escape. *The Impala.* The cop Hazard went golfing with. "Fuck the cop," Virginia sputtered. "Your cop. He's working with them. They're all in on it."

Tourmaline didn't say a word. She stared at Virginia and sank into the chair as if her legs had given out.

37

THE FRONT of her truck stood stripped back to the engine. Pieces of fender and front grill and engine parts littered the floor, arranged in a carefully disordered pattern. The long tubes of fluorescent lights hummed against a turned-down country station and the chorus of bugs and tree frogs outside the open garage door. Oil and gasoline mixed freely with the heavy musk of honeysuckle and warmed pine.

Virginia sat on an upside-down milk carton on the floor, elbows on her knees, as she watched Jason and Cash work on the mangled truck.

Tourmaline perched silently on Cash's motorcycle.

Finding a way to stop Hazard, the cop, *and* Wayne seemed impossible. They didn't even know where Wayne was. Or how to get him to violate parole—though that seemed to be the only thing they could do. It'd been a few days and they were still arguing in between yards and weeds and mulch. Still trying to hash out a plan. But they'd made no great advance.

This wasn't a game.

"He's not in the same house. I went by this afternoon."

Virginia twisted on the crate. "You went alone?"

"I was riding the bike."

"Don't do that shit alone. I'll come next time." Virginia kept her voice just above a whisper so as not to attract attention. Sighing, she flicked a mosquito off her ankle. "He's like a dog. He'll just trot back and forth on the same path until someone kicks him off."

"So where does a dog go when someone kicks him out of his bed?"

Virginia shifted on her crate and shrugged.

They fell silent then.

Virginia's eyes wandered back to the stripped-down truck and Jason's arm buried in the engine. His muted red T-shirt was ripped at the shoulder, and part of a slick perfect biceps twisted out as he worked. It'd be easy to disappear around him. That's what she should do, so as not to remind him of what she'd done. Who she was. Except, she didn't want him to ignore her. She wanted to bite that muscle in his arm until he moaned.

Stretching out her legs, she sighed and spoke in a normal tone. "Are y'all gonna feed us anytime soon?"

Jason didn't look up. "No."

"I can order something. Have them pick it up," Cash said, wiping his hands on a shop rag. "Want Harry's?" he asked Jason.

"Mmm. I want those whiskey-and-molasses wings," Virginia said. "That's Harry's, right?"

Jason rolled his eyes.

She caught his glance and meant to smile, but froze halfway. What if he regretted every thing he'd ever done with her? He had to. She would if she were him.

He went back to working.

"What do you want?" Cash asked.

"Nothing," Jason grunted, angling the can of WD-40 into the engine.

Cash shrugged and dropped the shop rag.

"I'll come help you order. Wings, Virginia?" Tourmaline said, hopping off the bike. All that eagerness simmered right beneath her words, her body strung as tight as a pulled-back bow.

Even Jason looked up and narrowed his eyes as he looked between Tourmaline and Cash.

No way were they going to get away with this for long. You could practically smell the heat.

"Virginia?" Tourmaline asked again.

Virginia looked up. "Yeah. Sorry. That's good. And some fries."

Jason shifted so his back was to her.

Tourmaline practically bounced after Cash into the dark.

Standing, Virginia pushed her hair behind her ears and walked to the side of the truck.

"What's going on with them?" Jason asked.

"Not a clue."

"You lying?" He looked underneath his arm and cocked an eyebrow.

"Probably always." She curled her fingers tight over the opened engine block.

He didn't say anything, but the edges of his mouth tightened as if he were trying not to smile. He strained against the bolt smashed up inside the engine.

"How bad is it?"

He shrugged and kept working. "The conscript is pretty good at fixing shit. I'm relying on his diagnosis once we get it stripped down."

She squeezed her fingers on the sharp edge of the engine cavity and swallowed, wanting to explain in this brief moment alone with him that before him no one would have remembered the truck, let alone gotten a tow, or put this much time into anything of hers. She wanted some way to tell him how much she wanted him to hold her bones in his hands and turn her again into the girl she wanted to be.

But all those things Virginia felt a deep ache to say and do were like everything else in her brain—scattered and fragile and broken. She could only look at them and know they went together *somehow*. It was a terrible feeling. Terrible. Her hands were sweating and she tightened her fingers even more on the sharp edge until bright, rusted pain cut through the choking feeling, and she only heard the humming lights. And this feeling, this moment, was what she'd fought so hard to preserve. It seemed strange. Without smiling, she whispered, "Thanks."

He stilled, his back tightening for a split second. As if the word had caught in his body, snagging in his movement. "Don't think of it."

She loosened her grip and it all came tumbling down—pulling back and forth in her stomach as she watched him work in the silence. "I don't have words," she choked out. "I mean. I have a lot. For this. But I don't often have to use words."

He straightened then, a serious look on his perfect face.

And she was sure feeling would be the thing that, in the end, killed her. But for him it was worth it.

"How're your ribs?" he asked, voice deep and husky.

"All right. My hair managed to survive, too." She touched the shortened strands that had decided to pull up into rough curls in the humidity. "Sort of."

"It's nice. Doesn't drag you down like . . ." But Jason didn't finish the sentence.

"I can't hide behind it, though. I miss that. It was my dark curtain thing."

His gaze briefly slid down her throat and came back up, mouth turned up in a tight, but amused smile. "You weren't ever trying to hide anything that hair covers."

She knew it was there, under his skin. The part of her that wanted to bite his shoulder knew he wanted to feel the sink of her hot teeth while his hands gripped raw and hungry on her hips. The part of her that wanted to spin in his hands and sink back into him knew he wanted to thrust forward and slide a hand up her spine to grasp the back of her neck.

But he just stood there, powerless in his eyes and unyielding in his body.

"You're going to fucking kill me," she whispered. Kill her with shrugged-off kindness. Kill her every time she looked at him and he looked away.

He didn't say anything.

Virginia didn't want to step toward him this time. She wanted him to come to her. She took a deep breath and tightened her jaw, forcing her body to stay put.

He blinked and turned away, picking up where he'd left off with the bolt.

38

THERE was something about walking across the threshold of Cash's that Tourmaline felt very deeply but couldn't identify. Something that made her feel as if she weren't ready. That she hadn't been ready for any of this, but now she had arrived—with new skin, and new edges, and new places in the world, dark though they might be.

The house wasn't anything special. Cheap and clean, Cash had said when walking into the kitchen. She wandered after him, eyeing his stride and the movements of his body as he pulled a menu out of a noisy kitchen drawer.

He leaned against the counter with the menu and tucked the phone into his shoulder, boots braced on pea-green linoleum. But the orange cupboards and yellow countertops were absolutely spotless, looking as if a man lived here and not a young, wild conscript in a motorcycle club. A tea towel hung neatly folded on the stove handle. A cinnamon-scented candle sat in the middle of the small kitchen table.

She wanted to open up his chest and see which parts were tea towels and orderly houses and which parts were wild conscript and weigh them out to see the balance, but she just crossed her arms and headed toward the stairs to explore.

His room was as neat as the kitchen, bed covered in a smoothed-out navy quilt, and the walls a soothing gray. Curtains on the window soaked in the last glow of twilight, and at each side of the bed stood a nightstand and a lamp. A million different things pulled under her skin at the sight of his room and his bed. At the heavy scent of clean sheets and old wood floors. She took a deep breath and walked in only far enough to glance at the dog-eared books on the table. Dante's *Inferno*.

She frowned and moved it aside. Underneath it, a Bible. On the table was a framed picture of a man Tourmaline recognized as Cash's dad and a woman whom she assumed was his mom. They were both on bikes.

Cash's mom rode.

She stared at it. Studied it. Longed for what that photo depicted in a way she'd never expected to long for a future. Suddenly she hoped Cash's mom would like her. More than like her—accept her.

Her father wouldn't be angry about their relationship because of their races—he would think of their ages and Cash's membership in the club long before he got to black and white. But it was hard to know whether a thread of the belief that they simply *shouldn't* be together didn't still exist, maybe so deeply buried that her father wouldn't even recognize it in himself. And she hoped, looking at Cash's mom, that it wouldn't be the same. That his mom wouldn't have a deeply buried belief that they simply *shouldn't* be together.

The second bedroom was an office of sorts, messier than the rest of the house but with a computer open on a desk, rolled papers, and shelves filled with thick books that boasted titles like *Heat and Mass Transfer, Mechanics and Thermodynamics of Propulsion,* and *Mechanical Vibrations.*

She shut the door and turned back down the stairs.

"Done snooping?" he asked when she came back into the kitchen.

"For now."

"Food should be ready in twenty minutes. You and Virginia can take my truck."

Tourmaline nodded, leaning her hip into the counter and looking around. The future seemed to fade and pulse with her heartbeat. It'd seemed perfectly clear on the road under the moon. It was less clear back on earth with everyone else.

"What did you think?"

"I think an old man lives here," she said with a grin.

Cash groaned and shook his head. "Don't say that."

She hoisted herself up to sit on the counter's edge and swung her legs back and forth. "How long do you think it will take them to get suspicious we've been gone too long?"

"Well, Jason knows we've been talking." He shifted off the counter and stepped closer. "Obviously."

Automatically her knees opened, though she wasn't sure how far he'd go. Her heart raced, breath tumbling over itself.

His hands came to her legs, fingers curling around the tendons and softness behind her knee—pulling her just the slightest toward him.

The backs of her thighs stuck to the countertop and he released the tension, but kept his hands where they were.

"Are you in trouble?" she asked. She was on his level. Knees at his waist. Easy to settle her arms on his shoulders. Easy to pull her chest toward him.

But he didn't quite answer.

The space between them shrank.

Cash's hands slowly slid up her legs, just above her knees. His fingertips pushing on the edges of her skirt.

She looked down, wanting to see his hands there, on her legs, against the yellow floral laminate countertop. Blood pumped in her ears. In her fingertips draped on his spine.

His fingertips sank into her skin, as if responding to her look. His breath was on her neck. On her jaw.

All she had to do was lift her head and his mouth was there. Lips parted. Waiting for her.

Her mouth watered.

The door opened. They shot apart.

"It's just me, relax," Virginia said. "The bathroom?"

Cash cleared his throat. "Upstairs and to your left."

"Thanks." She stomped up the steps.

Tourmaline heaved a sigh, fingers trembling.

"Jason's grumpy," Virginia called from upstairs.

Tourmaline glanced at Cash.

"I think we should tell your dad," he said. "I told Jason we're only talking. To go any further, though . . ."

"No." She gulped, still running after her heartbeat. "We're not doing that. You won't patch out."

"It'd be better to tell him sooner rather than later."

She bit down on her lip and looked at the floor.

"Tourmaline, he's not going to like things happening behind his back. That'll bother him more than if we're honest with him. I can't disrespect him like that."

She gritted her teeth and thought of the woman with the tinkling earrings. How could he demand her honesty when he withheld his own? "Not yet."

"If we tell him, he'll watch out for you."

She blinked, confused. Why would he need to watch out for her? Then slowly it dawned on her—if Dad knew, he would make sure Cash didn't hurt her. Wasn't asked to *betray* her to earn his cut. She swallowed. "That's a risk." Dad might just make it worse.

"I want to kiss you," he whispered and groaned all at once. "I want to . . . ," he murmured the rest in her ear.

She grinned, heart jumping alive. "We don't have to actually figure this out for that to happen."

But his eyes flickered away and he frowned without saying anything. As if she hadn't said what he'd hoped.

After a few seconds, they heard Virginia start downstairs. "Y'all. Did you hear me?" She paused at the door, raising her eyebrow at Tourmaline before going outside.

"Would you ever tell him? If it was up to you?" Cash asked.

"Yes," she said immediately. But as her voice fell away, they both heard a tremor of untruth. Would she tell Dad? She tried to envision it, but she couldn't get a clear image.

This wasn't just about Cash. It was that she didn't feel as if she had a right to say what she wanted—that she didn't just want him, she wanted him with loyalty. She couldn't bring herself to demand it. She couldn't even bring herself to ask for it. All she could do was hope for it. And in that position she'd never planned on being, she had to look at the world, in the face, as it truly was and stop thinking of herself as something different, something special, and join the long line of girls with all the same faces.

"Yeah?" He rubbed his hand over his jaw and looked away. "All right. You tell me when." He straightened off the counter.

He wasn't going to kiss her.

She frowned, following him into the hum of bugs and humidity. She could pretend that Cash was different. That Aubrey and girls like her held no power over him and would never hold sway between them. But she knew too much. Squaring her shoulders, she walked ahead, wishing she could just go home and bury herself under her covers. She'd not thought her life would be this way.

"Hey."

Tourmaline only turned her chin.

"Forgot. The keys to the truck." He tossed them, clinking silver in the dark.

39

TOURMALINE held out her hand for the stamp and waited with the rest of the visitors to go through processing. The air-conditioning was broken, and her back pressed against the sweating concrete wall. She tipped her head to the light, the words she'd rehearsed circling around her mind.

"In an orderly fashion, now," the CO said as the gates unlocked.

Tourmaline roused, pushing off the wall. She passed the guard, standing silent and firm. Then she stood in the empty visitors' room, watching as they brought her mother out, one in a long and shackled line.

"Hot enough for you?" one of the COs said to the other.

"I don't want to hear it," the woman droned, as if he were always trying to talk her up and she was tired of coming up with ways to get him quiet.

The male CO—Roberts—caught Tourmaline watching, and his features tightened.

She smiled prettily and looked away. *Suck up to the bulls.*

Tourmaline's mother sat across from her under the green fluorescents. Scabbed elbows on a bolted-down table. Veined hands dragged themselves through the greenish-blond hair with black roots as she mouthed the precious words to the walls, to the bars, to the guards.

Our fate cannot be taken.

It used to be a thing of power, for Mom to say that. Now it just seemed like words.

Finally, her eyes found Tourmaline. Their expression was flat and sort of lost. But she wasn't high—at least Tourmaline didn't think she was.

Tourmaline smiled. "Want something from the vending machine?"

"Diet Coke. And one of those bear claw thingies."

The vending machines sat across a painted gray line the prisoners weren't allowed to cross. Tourmaline got the last smashed-looking pastry and an already sweating can of pop, suddenly remembering those socks sinking into the trash can liner.

It was good she hadn't made it this far with the socks last time; it only got harder on this side of the gate.

"How did graduation go?" her mother asked, taking the bear claw first.

"Pretty good. I didn't get a chance to order pictures, though. I'll get them next trip, I promise. I'm sorry."

Her mother swallowed a mouthful of pastry and opened the Coke with a loud pop. "How was prom? You and Anna May have fun?"

Prom? It felt like ages ago. Years, even. How had it only been two months? "I didn't go. I went mini-golfing with some friends from youth group."

"Anna May went without you? What happened? Are you two fighting?"

"No. We're fine. She just wanted to go with Dalton and I didn't have anyone I really wanted to do that with."

"You couldn't wrangle anyone up?" her mother asked.

And the truth was that no one had wanted to take the daughter of the Wardens' president to prom. "Dad didn't really want me to go."

"You should have gone anyway. Your dad probably didn't know how important it was to Anna May. I'm sure she missed you." Tourmaline's mother finished off the pastry in one huge mouthful, crumpling the plastic. She snapped the pop-top open and took a long swallow with her eyes closed, smiling when she pulled the can away. "That's the best Diet Coke I've ever had, I think."

Tourmaline smiled, even though she wanted to cry just a little bit.

Her mother took another long, relishing drink.

"I'm . . ." And immediately her words gave out. What was she? Dating? Seeing? Talking to? She swallowed. "I'm in love with a boy."

Margaret blinked over the top of the can. "You are? With who?"

"His name is Cash."

"Oh, thank God it's not that Allen guy. He sounded very nice, just not for you." Her mother's shoulders sagged and she put the Coke down. "Cash? As in, like, Johnny Cash?"

"As in a conscript."

Her mother's eyes widened. "Old Hawk's kid," she said. "Oh, my God, Tourmaline." She reached across the table and gripped Tourmaline's fingers. "And your dad is okay with this? How old is he, again?"

"Dad doesn't know. He's twenty-three."

Margaret nodded. A faint smile on her face. "Okay. Okay, my baby is . . . growing up. Are you waiting for him to patch out to tell your dad?"

Tourmaline nodded. "Yeah."

"Well, at least we know he's vetted pretty well, right?" She laughed and then stopped short. "You're nervous."

"I'm scared out of my mind. This is so much more serious than I expected. It's good, it's just . . . not what I planned."

Her mother smiled softly. "Life hardly ever is. Talk to Shelly, Sauls's wife, if you get a chance; she'll keep it quiet. If you love him, I know he's a good guy and won't jerk around with you. And bring him? Maybe?"

"I will. We'll get that started. I know he wants to come meet you. He's asked about it a few times." Tourmaline swallowed and looked at her hands on the table. "I have something to ask. And it's important you don't react or raise your voice or do anything unnatural."

Margaret stilled.

"Have another drink."

She did, gaze fluttering away from Tourmaline.

"Do you have any idea where your ex-boyfriend would be, if he isn't at the place he used to stay?"

Tourmaline's mother blinked at the ceiling and then put down the drink. "God Almighty, that is better with every swallow." She spun the can on the grated table and traced a finger in the condensation beading on its side. After a long pause, she asked, "Why?"

Tourmaline shook her head and stayed silent.

Her mother sniffed and wiped her nose. She put her chin in her hand and drew more invisible lines on the can. "Is your dad asking?" She looked so hopeful for a moment.

"No, ma'am," Tourmaline said quickly.

Her shoulders sagged. "What for?"

"It's just something I need to know."

Tourmaline's mother looked away and didn't answer.

Tourmaline bit the inside of her cheek. Why wouldn't Mom tell her, if she knew? You'd think she'd want to help her daughter, who'd come asking. "Are you angry at me?" Tourmaline asked finally.

"For what?"

"For putting you here."

Her mother nodded slowly. "I'm mad at you. At Wayne. At the cops. At the judge. I'm mad at your dad. At the doctor who wrote that first prescription. At the doctor who gave me a year's supply of Oxy with no follow-up when I had the surgery. At the doctors for not doing more for my pain. At the first person who sold me that shit. I'm mad at everyone in here. I'm mad at my cellmate. The COs. God." She swallowed and cleared her throat. "But really, honey, I'm mad at myself. Someday, I'll have to forgive myself." She tapped the can and frowned, the sharpness in her eyes pushing toward the unknown. "Someday."

"Not today?" Tourmaline asked through her tight throat. She wanted to be forgiven, but it seemed unfair to ask for forgiveness from her mother when her mother didn't even have it for herself.

Margaret reached out a thin hand and pulled Tourmaline's fingers into her own. "I just wish you'd called your dad first. But I can't blame you for panicking. I know that. You didn't do anything *wrong*."

But she'd not done anything right.

Tourmaline looked away, staring at the blank wall. It was not what she needed to hear. How could she have put someone in hell? Someone she loved and cared for and knew didn't belong there, *not really*. She'd have to live with that night forever, even when Mom got out. She squeezed her eyes tight and wiped the tears off her cheeks.

"What's going on, baby?" her mother murmured.

"Oh. Just . . . stupid stuff," Tourmaline said, horrified it came out in a half-wail.

"It's not stupid."

Tourmaline nodded, keeping her eyes closed until she could stop crying. "It's nothing. Really." It was shards of fragile happiness and of spun-sugar ecstasy with Cash—threatened under the crush of reality she couldn't escape. It was a strange sort of friendship with Virginia— old friends who were new together. Nothing for hell, all things for the living. But she wanted to explain. She wanted to be mothered, instead of having to do the mothering. She wanted everything to be okay. To have the past healed instead of just forgotten.

"Talk to me," Margaret whispered.

Tourmaline opened her eyes and sniffed. She put her elbows on the table and clutched her mother's hand. "I need things from you."

"What?"

"Truth." Her mother held the key. The histories. The fates. The answer was clutched down deep beyond the edge in her mother's eyes.

Tourmaline met her eyes and let go of her fear, diving straight into that tar, slipping through, deep into her mother's soul.

"What truth?" her mother whispered without blinking.

She couldn't say, "The Wardens." She couldn't explain. She and her mother were sitting here with fifteen COs just bored out of their minds, listening while they babysat. Licking her lips, she plucked out the circling words. The only ones she could remember. The club's motto. "Our fate cannot be taken . . ."

"Did someone send you?" her mother snapped.

"Stay calm," Tourmaline said softly. A rush of electricity ran up and down her spine. There was meaning here. Not just coincidence. "No one sent me. I just need to know."

Margaret's jaw set. "There's nothing for you to know. Not even if you were an ol' lady."

Tourmaline lifted her chin. "My life depends on it."

Her mother held very still. Her spiny fingers tightened into a cold sweaty clamp on Tourmaline's hands, and Tourmaline refused to cringe against the skeleton sense of her mother's touch.

"I need the truth," Tourmaline repeated. She pulled away, very near tears. This could not be happening. Her mother had let her down so much; why had she expected that her mother would be there now? "Please, Mom. You don't under—"

"It's not something I can just explain," her mother snapped. "Even if I wanted to."

"Everything in my life depends on it."

She shook her head, lips tight. "It's not what they do, it's who they are."

"Who's Ray?" Tourmaline asked.

Her mother shook her head.

"Is he alive?"

Her mother shook her head.

"Did Dad?"

Margaret's eyes opened wide and she pursed her mouth. "Stop."

"Yes or no. Did he?"

Her mother stayed still. Silent. Slowly she nodded.

Dad had killed Ray. A slow, sinking beat throbbed in Tourmaline's chest. "Who was he? Why?"

"Sometimes the systems we have in place to protect the vulnerable break down. They don't work, for whatever reason. And it's especially tragic when it happens to children. Everyone knew Ray. Everyone knew what Ray did to his baby girl. To his wife, too. The community turned its eyes away, the courts and police couldn't get involved with how the wife protected him . . ." Tourmaline's mother shook her head. "Ray wouldn't leave. He refused to be reasoned with. So . . ." She fell silent, allowing Tourmaline to finish.

So they killed him. Her dad killed Ray.

Virginia's dad.

DESPITE the heavy heat and the smell of people and the murmur of twenty intimate conversations around them, the hair on Tourmaline's arms and neck stood up straight. All she could think of was the wickedly twisted crowned skull with a rattlesnake around its neck, in green and white threads on the black leather of Dad's jacket.

Her whole life, the father who tucked her into bed and smoothed her hair and smelled like wood smoke and beer and leather, walking away with the empty eyes of that skull being the last thing she saw as he turned off the light—her father. Death . . .

Ray.

Virginia's dad?

Tourmaline had to clamp her hands tight to the edge of her seat to keep herself from bolting up and running back through the gates to call Virginia and cry—*I think my dad killed your dad.*

"We are all that can truly stand where justice fails." Tourmaline's mother still clenched her fingers tight. "Everything else breaks down. Justice becomes about other things—about who holds value and what profit will come to the community. We do not falter. The law tried to use me against your father, but I held firm. It's the only good thing I've done. It is the only thing I don't regret."

Tourmaline's chest heaved. She had to get to Virginia. She had to get to Virginia. She had to—

Tourmaline's head snapped up. "Wait. *What?*"

The couple at the table beside them looked over.

"What?" she whispered. Urgent. If only she could speak plainly instead of having to dance around the truth.

"The cops thought if they got me, they'd get him. That he'd be willing to barter for me."

Dad?

"But they did not understand what the stakes were." Her mother smiled a trembling, proud smile. "They do not understand loyalty."

"But I . . . ," Tourmaline trailed off, staring with her mouth open. She couldn't breathe. They'd never been after Mom. They'd *used* Mom to try and get at Dad. Her mother's fate had been decided before she'd done anything. They'd brought it all down around her mother's head, and her father had cried, and Tourmaline was nothing.

Nothing.

No. She was blowback. She was a girl among all the other girls. She was a face in a sea of faces. Words in the middle of more important words. The parts you skim. The nonrelevant part to the story.

She was nothing. Tourmaline took a deep breath. All this time, the act she believed to be the most important mistake she'd ever made, the decision that took away everything she had and took everything after—*it did not matter.*

If she did not find Wayne, it would all continue the same. Things would happen around her, because of her, to her, but they would never be changed by her.

Tourmaline leaned forward, pleading. "Where is he?"

"Hey, you two are up," the guy taking photos called to someone. "Four-oh-four—that's you."

Margaret jerked up.

The guy lifted his Polaroid. "I ain't got all day."

Her mother looked at Tourmaline, cautiously hopeful.

Tourmaline slid out from the table.

They stood together in front of the painted palm-trees-at-sunset background. Margaret's arm slid around Tourmaline's waist, her body nothing but sharp edges and points. Nothing of the softness Tourmaline remembered snuggling against.

It wasn't until the man held out the picture that Tourmaline realized she'd forgotten to smile.

"Oh, you're so beautiful," her mother said, the Polaroid in her hand. Even her smile seemed sharper. More lined. Tourmaline forced herself to freeze the image as her own photo: a deeply detailed memory of her mother right now, with those deep lines in her makeup-less face and the curl in her hair.

Tourmaline handed the photo back. "Tell me where." She did not ask. She did not plead. She simply and softly made the demand.

Margaret bit her lip. "A cabin in the woods off Sheep Creek Road. In the mountains."

THE WARDENS *killed my father?* Virginia blinked at Hazard's office door, phone heavy in her limp hand.

The Wardens killed my father.

The meaning of Tourmaline's veiled questions and halting answers rang in her ears. They *had* intervened, all those years ago. They had stood up for her, when no one else would. And they'd freed her just long enough for her to fall back into the same fate. All the same people. All the same places. It was up to her to change it. No one else could.

Opening the door to the law office, she stepped into the air-conditioning with her head high.

The bodyguard put down his magazine and stood.

Virginia slipped into the hall before he caught her.

Hazard looked startled when she appeared in the door of his office, but he smiled as if nothing out of the ordinary was happening. "Oh, your hair is lovely." He leaned back in the leather office chair and twirled his finger. "Turn. Let me see."

She faced the guard in obedience.

He smirked, resting one hand on his waistband.

While she spun, thinking of her father and the Wardens, it was as if she'd finally hit a secret button and suddenly the whole world unfolded before her. Tourmaline's talk of court runs. The rumors she'd heard, while working for Hazard, of people disappearing or being warned of their own imminent disappearance. The white noise of partying and women and motorcycles, obscuring the high, clear note of truth. They'd done that for her. They'd done it for others.

Hazard had told her, that night when he showed off the heroin, but she hadn't understood what it meant. Hazard needed the Wardens distracted while he built something stronger than they were, something that involved the cops who hunted them, or else he risked his own disappearance. Hazard had let her go when Jason arrived because Jason's very presence was threatening to kill him. Tourmaline didn't need to kill Wayne; the Wardens were already planning to. Or they would be, if they knew Wayne had come after Tourmaline.

Virginia came back to face Hazard.

Jealousy and hope and longing all stabbed deep into her chest, ripping open the anger. She felt as if someone were cutting open a vein, the anger intense and hot and running all over her hands as she tried to stop it. She swallowed, forcing it down into her chest before she killed them all right there and ruined everything.

"It really suits you. Quite saucy," Hazard said, putting a box from his desk onto the floor. "And so are you, apparently, for showing back up here."

She glanced at the stacks of file boxes in the corner behind his desk—at that tiny serial number at the bottom of each one—without moving or answering, hiding the sudden double tap of her heartbeat. The gun was in one of those boxes. With the tiny beige numbers. 7602XF-1842066. It was a good plan—find Hazard's gun, plant it on Wayne, call the cops. A felon on parole couldn't have a gun, much less a stolen one. And when the gun was discovered, with it would be Hazard's dope, all roads trailing back to him.

Find the gun.

"I had to let things cool off a little. You played your part perfect." She smoothed her shirt and plopped into one of the chairs reserved for clients.

Hazard's mouth tightened. Eyes narrowed.

"I did worry for a second that you'd kill him and ruin it all." She plucked a peppermint out of the bowl and unwrapped it. "And I'm still pissed about my hair."

"You did that on purpose? You were playing me?"

"Him. I was playing him. Isn't that what you told me to do?" She popped the mint into her mouth and sucked on it, thankful to hide the twitch of her mouth. "Damn. Do you need notes? How else did you want me to get them to trust me?"

Hazard's jaw flickered. "You didn't think to inform me ahead of time?"

"Ahh. But that would have been so much less realistic. So much easier to sniff out."

Hazard fingered the edge of a folder. "You underestimate me." His gaze held hers tight. That same cold, dead space hidden behind the veneer of pleasantness.

Skeleton fingers climbed up her spine and dug into her hair, holding her by the neck. But she ignored the bones and refused to break eye contact. "No, darlin'. You underestimate me."

The seconds ticked past. Down the hall a phone rang and someone answered it.

Hazard didn't move. "So, Virginia. Why don't you bring me up to speed?"

"Gladly." She moved the mint to her other cheek and leaned on her elbow. "Jason already knew I worked for you. The second I showed up, he knew what was happening. Who I was. But now that he saved me from you, he thinks he's that man, that dark knight I will love forever. That my loyalty is with him. And because of that"—she held up her fist—"he's in the palm of my hand. What do you really want?"

"I told you what I wanted."

"And didn't I deliver a great distraction?"

He frowned. "I notice you've been spending a lot of time with that Harris girl still."

Was he buying this? Virginia felt as if she could almost sell it to herself. He had to be buying it. "I'm part of them now. It just took something big to get that far. These people like to save things." She smiled. "I told you I had it under control. Now, cut the shit with this wild-goose chase you sent me on and tell me what you actually need done."

"Where's the clubhouse?"

She rolled her eyes. "Back in the woods on North Mountain. I mean, if that's all you want." She'd had that before he punished her.

He didn't respond right away. Eyed her up and down. Then he waved his hand and the door clicked shut.

Virginia tried not to cringe as she met his eyes.

"When is church?" he asked.

"Sunday night," she said, head buzzing. "They'll have two guards out."

He nodded. "I need you to take some . . . things over to the clubhouse the night before."

This wasn't what she expected. It was too deep. She needed out of this. *Now.*

"I want you to divide up the heroin. Put it in a few different places in the clubhouse, just in case. Remember each one, because you'll need to tell them."

Them? "No problem, boss." Virginia met Hazard's eyes, her mind racing but her voice calm. "I need to use the bathroom." She pushed out of the chair.

"Before I forget."

She bit her lips together, trying to stay patient.

"When you see that ever-so-helpful friend of yours . . ." He settled back in the chair with his notepad and files. "You know the one. You might think about reminding him even Satan has his revenge in hell."

Jason.

He clicked his pen. "Use the bathroom to the right. Don't scare any clients."

She strutted off, sneakers squeaking on the slick linoleum. Her heart pounded in her head, Jason behind her eyes. What was happening? It felt almost unreal to be here. To still be alive.

She scanned the files in the back room as she passed, only getting one side of the shelves. The smell of perfume mixed with the dry paper. Every breath felt one breath closer to her life closing in on her. She passed another filing room, but also a secretary who looked as if she'd been hired on the basis of her résumé and not the interview, so she only glanced inside before she entered the bathroom and locked the door.

Now what, Virginia Campbell? She stared at herself in the mirror, still surprised to see short hair.

Her chest heaved and her fingers trembled. She thought she was dangerously close to crying, but when she narrowed her eyes and loosened her mouth, what wanted to come out was more like a murderous scream of rage. Or she wanted to vomit, to empty her body of all its contents—her organs, her mind, everything but pain. She had been saved. She lived on. For what?

She shook out the curls. Tucked the hair behind her ears and waited for her chest to stitch itself back over the anger—afraid she might otherwise crumple and burst into flames.

What now, Virginia Campbell?

Tourmaline. Tourmaline needed her to keep going. Jason was waiting for her to return with parts for her truck. And though she was not loved, she hoped. And hope spurred her on.

She took a deep breath and turned on the water. Unrolled a large section of toilet paper and stuffed it into her pockets. Left the lights on and the water running.

On her knees, she peered underneath the door; the hall was empty. She carefully opened the door and looked in the other direction. Voices came from farther up front, but none of them sounded like Hazard. Everything looked clear.

She had one shot. One place to look. One roll of the fucking dice. It was either the room with nothing but files, Hazard's office with the door ajar, or the back room she'd only been able to glance at.

Virginia locked the bathroom door and closed it, then quietly scurried into the small room and scanned the shelves. 7602XF-1842066. Come on, 7602XF-1842066. Down. Across. Back. It had to be here. It had to.

Voices came sharper. Closer. Hazard was coming, somewhere down the labyrinth of halls.

Panic weighted her chest, and her mouth tightened into a firm line. She kept scanning the tiny beige serial numbers printed on the cardboard. The box wasn't here. She'd chosen wrong. *Shit.* She bit her cheek and kept going anyway.

There.

Bottom shelf, far side. She snatched the box out and dug through it. The .38 rested under a stack of aging files.

Hazard's voice echoed down the hall.

Virginia's heart slammed, but she forced herself to dig the toilet paper out of her pocket and carefully wrap it around the gun. *Now what?* One end was covered, but if she slid the gun into her waistband, her skin would be on the barrel. She hadn't thought of that. But she didn't have anywhere else to put it. Staring, she tried to think.

The lights hummed. A coffeepot gurgled.

Hazard.

She hit the wall behind the door just in time.

Hazard's profile passed by the crack in the hinges. Talking with the same guy who'd picked her up.

"Do you think she's playing you?" the man asked Hazard.

"Nah."

Virginia closed her eyes. A small thread of relief mixed in with the panic.

"But I'm done with her anyway. She's unpredictable."

Her eyes sprang open.

"What do you want me to do?" the man asked.

"Make it look like they did it. Dump her at the clubhouse. That's all I want."

She held her breath as they turned in to Hazard's office. Sweat rolled down her back. The toilet-paper-wrapped gun was still in her hands. A distraction. Had this been the plan the entire time? *What now, Virginia Campbell?*

"She still in there?" Hazard asked.

Virginia's pulse raced.

The guy stepped into the hall and looked toward the bathroom. If he glanced a little to the left, he'd see her there, pressed against the wall behind the open door. "Yeah," he said to Hazard, stepping back into the office.

Virginia took a slow, careful breath and tipped her head to the dusty drop ceiling.

If she was going to die anyway, she was going to go on her terms. The back door was dead-bolted, but the front door was open for the law firm's business hours. She closed her eyes and saw herself do it—move out from behind the door, slip into the hall, and run for the door. She'd drop over the guardrail across the road, into the culvert, and run down the creek toward the train tracks. If she ran very fast and had a good amount of luck, he might not catch her.

One. Two. Three. *Go.*

Virginia didn't move. Her legs were weak. Her lungs wouldn't work. She would wither here behind the door until they closed it one day and found a skeleton of dust with a gun at her feet.

Forcing her eyes open, she gathered her resolve. Tourmaline needed her. Jason needed her. There was no giving in until they put her in the grave.

She couldn't see Hazard from behind the door. But the other man stood just inside the doorway, hands in his pockets, listening to Hazard's instructions. In a few seconds, they'd check the bathroom and she'd be out of time. This was her chance. Wiggling out of her shirt, she wrapped it around the gun and stuffed the whole thing in the waistband of her jeans.

Taking one leaping step around the door, she cut into the hall and ran like hell.

"Hey!" someone yelled behind her.

But she was out the door, into the heavy heat and sky. She bolted across the street. Someone laid on the horn. She didn't stop to look. Scrambling up the guardrail, she jumped into the leafy void.

Her feet hit the rocks and she crumpled into the stream. The rocks slipped and splashed out from underneath her, but she ran, ignoring the pain pulsing through her bones.

Something tight and metallic whizzed through the leaves above her head.

She knew then that she was dead.

Doubling her speed, she skittered for the tracks like a rabbit on the run, not stopping until she'd caught a swaying coal train on the Norfolk Southern line, gun still smashed into her stomach.

Tucked into the ladder of the car, she dug her phone out of her jeans pocket and texted Tourmaline.

Got it. Did you?

Tourmaline texted back. *Yep. Tomorrow.*

Tomorrow.

Virginia kept the phone tight in her fist, watching the oaks turn to spruces. The railroad grade fell away into steep rocky banks as the coal train climbed into the mountains—taking her out of Roanoke and northwest toward Lexington. Toward home.

The blue haze that always lay over the ridges turned purple and menacing. The wind whipped her loose curls into a frenzy, and the air tasted of rain and electricity. She took a deep breath. And another. The train rocked and kept on.

Taking her home.

TOURMALINE had always looked up to feel safe. To the ridgeline swept across fathomless blue sky. To the jagged outcroppings and exposed meadows. To the eternal shadows deep in the folds of the mountains.

The sight of the ridges, always on the horizon, did something she never really bothered to explain to herself—as if she'd been formed out of their dirt and it was the gurgling mountain creeks and the muddy James and Cowpasture rivers that flowed in her veins. As if she had crawled out of honeysuckle, bloomed in a humid night, and wandered under the stars before making her way to her crib. She looked to them, as if to her true mother—always there, always watching.

The Appalachians. The Blue Ridges. Those places outsiders drove around and tried not to get lost in had been there the whole time, watching the world give them a wide berth, just as it did her family. Iron Gate was held tight in the still-pulsing umbilical cord of the Great Appalachian Valley. Closed in on all sides, but with plenty of open sky.

Here, she belonged.

But never had she felt so much a child of those hills as when she dropped Virginia off in Roanoke and headed deep into the mountains, turning her truck up Sheep Creek Road to face the sheer gravel switchbacks.

Her parents had lied. The world, with the crib and its toys and those people, was never hers. But the rocks and trees would never deny her. It was as if they'd been waiting this whole time to accept her back into their wild folds.

With her heart pounding in the back of her throat, she stared at the trees climbing up the mountainside, and the stranger kudzu vines tangling pockets of darkness overhead.

The truck skidded around the first turn and kicked up a cloud of gravel; in the rearview, a great swirl of golden dust billowed into the hanging emerald leaves.

Tourmaline smiled.

This place was deceptive. It made you feel alone in the wilderness. Here, on a deeply rutted gravel road that had long been abandoned, the place made you feel that way, and all the while it betrayed you.

Dust whispered to the trees. The trees whispered to one another. And the wind whispered to those faces that remained, warning them that someone had dropped down off that slick, manufactured parkway and entered through the ancient gates.

The ghosts were awakened. They picked up their muskets from the apple orchards and climbed out of moss-covered tombs, watching from deep inside the oak and hickory forests.

Tourmaline pressed on. Slower. Balancing the power needed to climb the mountain and the care needed so she wouldn't kick up traitorous dust along the way.

Her mother's directions were not all that helpful. Tourmaline passed several houses tucked back deep in the hollows. But she kept on, deeper into the mountain, trusting that her mother had told her enough, and the mountain and its ghosts would accept her as one of its own. She fought the ruts and bounced up another twisting pass, trying not to look down the sheer drop-offs. Jason and Cash were still trying to smash Virginia's truck back into drivable shape. She didn't need to add her truck to their list.

The sun streamed in dazzling, white-hot bursts over the valley, and there was a lot of daylight still left for those rolling plains. But here, tucked deep against the mountain's side, a shadow had descended. Some places she passed were always in shadow.

Tourmaline rolled down her window and turned off the air-conditioning. Slowing the truck as much as she dared, she scanned the woods for signs of a cabin. For Wayne's cabin.

The road grew rougher. The trees narrowed overhead. Giant, lichen-covered boulders now marked the hairpin turns.

Finally, something brown and thinly horizontal caught her eye. Pressing the brake, wishing for a gun with a scope or for binoculars, she peered into the leafy shadows and studied the crooked, steep slope.

Slowly, the forest released its secret. The enchantments drew back, and she blinked at Wayne's house, clear as day, hunkered beneath the now groaning and creaking trees.

The breeze poured in the window, lifting her hair off her shoulders and bringing the scent of wild onion and mint—and the trail of something unnatural and poisonous.

She'd been worried that at this moment she would falter. Faced with the reality, what would she do? But she felt no hesitation. If anything, she was assured.

The mucky green cast to the weathered boards hid the cabin well. Rust stains streaked the low-slung metal roof. Shoving the emergency brake to the floor, Tourmaline tucked her hair into her shirt, put on a crushed camo hat from behind the seat, and got out.

Closer, she saw that the windows were covered over with cardboard. Cans of paint thinner and drain cleaner lined the porch and littered the leaves around the house. She didn't see a truck or car, but as she hunkered into the brush, the wind died long enough to let her hear a radio playing inside, and boots scuffing over the floor.

The sun sank far behind the ridge. The shadows deepened to

huckleberry blue and bruised plum. The spiders spun their silver-corded webs. And somewhere far above her, the faint sound of thunder rolled through the ridge.

Shifting her weight on her heels, she memorized the cabin. The road.

The trees began to wail. The wind lashed at their tops and tugged her hair loose from her shirt, playing with it behind her and whipping it across her face.

She'd been here long enough. The mountains were saying it was time to go.

Exhaling, she turned for the truck.

SOMEWHERE on those twisting mountain roads descending into the valley, Tourmaline got a text from her father saying he wouldn't be home that night, as long as she was okay by herself. It only took a minute of staring with all her blood thumping in her ears to decide what to do.

Tourmaline showered and rushed through her room, looking through piles of clothes for one specific dress. Outside her open window the birds were all gone and the summer night darkened early under a blanket of twisting clouds.

A low rumble of thunder reverberated under her bare feet, still damp from the shower. The wind wailed high and dangerous, flattening the hostas and the ferns in the garden below. She rushed in the gray light, the wind chilling the beads of water left on her body as she yanked on underwear and a light cotton dress. Resolving, with fingers trembling, that she could trust herself. And with the hazy vision of Cash yanking the dress over her arms and leaving her sitting there all exposed in just the right way, Tourmaline pulled the door shut firmly behind her and left.

Cash's garage door was open despite the flickering lightning and the thrashing trees. The lights.

Tourmaline slammed the truck door against the rushing wind and ducked inside, flip-flops skidding on the slick concrete.

Cash was bent over the engine block in camo shorts and a grease-stained T-shirt. He glanced up. "Hey."

"Still working on Virginia's truck, huh?"

"Yeah."

"How's it going?" Folding her arms, Tourmaline leaned on the side of the truck.

"Fine."

"Fine?"

He grunted a little, stretching the timing belt over the last pulley. He moved stiffly. Tight.

The wind rattled the roof above them. "I'm surprised I got here before the rain," she said.

He didn't say anything, checking the alignment on the other pulleys. She frowned. "You okay?"

"Yeah. Just a rough couple of days. Good, though." He flashed a tense smile without meeting her eyes, turning to the workbench behind him and picking through a drawer. "What'd you stop by for?"

She shifted. "Just to . . . see you." She'd thought he'd be excited. Eager. Her back stiffened and she looked around, trying to figure out what was off.

Cash frowned, bending back to tighten the pulleys. "Did your dad say something?"

"No. Why?"

He nodded past her.

She looked over her shoulder, but didn't see anything. Then her gaze landed on his vest hanging on his bike's handlebars. "You patched out!" Her heart jumped, out of both sudden fear and excitement, and she didn't move. She gripped the edge of the truck, staring at the new patches on the broken-in leather. What did that mean for them?

Turning back, she watched him finish with the socket. "Are you okay?"

"Yes, ma'am," he drawled. But the tone was very much like Jason and not at all like Cash. Turning his back on her, he dropped the socket back into a drawer.

The world shifted wildly, and she wasn't sure she liked the ride. "What . . . ?" she whispered, trying to catch his eye.

He rubbed the back of his neck and didn't look at her.

"Cash. What's going on?"

"Nothing."

Nothing? What could have changed? And as she raced over what could possibly have changed in a matter of hours, the arrow pierced her heart and she knew. *Knew.*

It was the Wardens. The patch changed things.

She looked at the vest again. Minos changed things. The horned skull with a spiked tail wrapped around its neck stared back at her, hollow eyes blank under the fluorescent light, as if he knew that she knew. *Cash* must not have known what it really meant to be a Warden. The true meaning of what his father had been. He must have just learned what bond of brotherhood he had now been initiated into.

Tourmaline put a hand on his elbow. "Cash," she pleaded softly.

He pulled away, that same stiffness in his body. "I'm pretty busy here."

She seethed.

He turned away as if she weren't even there. As if he could ignore her until she gave up.

Thunder cracked and shook the garage. The lights flickered and buzzed.

This was supposed to be her choice. Her decision. And in the end, the Wardens had taken it from her just as they had everything else.

Fuck this. It was easy to decide now. She shoved off the truck and strode for the outside. Rain washed into the doorway and spattered a slick line between her and the dark; she stopped, staring at it. The wind shifted, lifting the hair off her neck. It reminded her of being back in the woods. Of the sureness in her body as she faced down her fate. The confidence in Virginia's reassurances.

She spun with a tight *schlickt* of her flip-flops.

Cash's eyes flickered to hers.

Now here was the trick, the moment so small and yet so difficult, the moment when she crossed from thinking and feeling to doing. It was a moment that hung entirely on her.

The fluorescent hummed. She took out her ponytail, silent as she ran her fingers through the snarls and watched the flash of silver rain in the dark. Pushing her hair back over her shoulder, she gathered all she had to use and flicked her gaze to lock with his. "I didn't realize you didn't know."

"Know what?" A muscle in the arm that held the wrench twitched.

"About your fate." She met his eyes. Steady. In this moment, she was the experienced one.

She walked with her chin up, the sway of her hips holding him to the concrete.

Something fierce set fire in his eyes, but he turned toward the workbench.

"Oh, no, you don't," she growled, slipping on the concrete as she shoved herself between the workbench and his body.

"What don't I?" he asked sharply.

Tourmaline hefted herself up to sit and didn't answer. Watching that fire flicker in his eyes as she wrapped her legs tight around his waist—pinning him in a vice he could break, if he had the mind.

"You pretty sore?" she asked softly, running her hands down his arms.

He didn't answer. The rain drummed waves on the roof.

She knew he must be. She didn't know much about the year or more he'd spent as a conscript, but she couldn't miss the telltale limp and weak smile of a newly patched member.

Tipping her head, she moved toward him, breathing the sharp scent of grease and laundry detergent that was Cash. She wanted that smell all around her. Wanted to breathe it off his bare skin. But she stopped right before she kissed him. "And then," she whispered, faintly brushing his lips with her mouth as she spoke, "right when you think you're through it . . ."

He swallowed and pushed into her.

She pulled back. This was hers, right now. Not his. Running her hands back up, she brought them to both sides of his jaw, holding the soft push of his full lips just away from hers. "The eternal part of it." Where he would always be a Warden, even if he walked away.

His hands settled lightly on her thighs, smelling of grease and gasoline, and the rough, warm skin of his palms pressed open, pulling her attention in all kinds of directions. The edge of his beard twitched. His lips parted.

"Where will and power are one," Tourmaline whispered onto his lips, reminding him she knew his secrets, that she held power in knowing. Her head throbbed with anticipation.

As she waited, a cool, wet breeze gusted, and she shivered against him.

He rocked her back, mouth opening, hot and needy. His hands slipped under her knees and pulled her to the edge of the bench, thighs snug against his hard stomach.

Relief poured out of her, relief of the pent-up agony that had twisted in her body every night while they talked and that she'd never been quite able to release. Sinking her fingers into the warm skin of his neck, she pushed her chest into him, hardly breathing as he clutched the cotton dress and drew it up her hips and waist.

He pulled away, a set to his jaw that made her heart race.

She lifted her arms, and he slid his hands up the curves of her body, bringing the dress over her head. He dropped it beside them, yanked off his shirt, and came back.

Circling her waist with one thick arm, he brought her tight, erasing all awareness except the feel of her bare skin hitting his.

She pressed tight and slid up to his mouth, relishing each bit of friction between their bodies.

Cash groaned, fingers digging into her waist. He kissed her as if he needed her in order to stay alive. Dripping liquid heat into her bones.

The world could have ended and begun again for the amount of time they spent there, like that. Lost in the pattering rain and the tree frogs croaking under their wet leaves. Content to stay right there while nights fell into years and while ages slipped away.

But then he stepped back.

Her breath came fast. In some faraway part of her brain, she felt the blunt metal edge of the tool chest hit her spine as he eased her back. She was only faintly aware of anything but the way he hooked his fingers into her thong and dragged it down her legs.

Exhaling a shaky breath, Tourmaline flattened her hands on the bench. The moment might have started as hers to lose, hers to start, but now it was all him. This was her world, but, for the moment at least, he ruled it.

Cash caught her eye. "Trust me."

And without his body touching hers, pulling her into complete oblivion, reality stabbed deep into her stomach. But she forgot to think about anything but his mouth when he went to his knees and kissed the inside of her thigh.

She pulled her knee up, feeling exposed and vulnerable.

"Trust me, T." But the way he looked at her made it seem he was asking about everything, not just this moment. This was what she wanted. Him. And here he was, on his knees in front of her.

She curled forward, clutching his face to her chest. Maybe she could not give all her trust, but she could give enough for this moment at least. She kissed the top of his forehead.

He nuzzled deep into her stomach, into her chest, and then laughed, pushing her back to where she'd been. Going back to where he'd started. His hands wrapped around her hips. Breath warm and wet on the shockingly sensitive skin of her inner thighs.

Oh good Lord. She bit her bottom lip tight, as if to clench her teeth would keep her from falling apart. Looking down, she tried to find enough of her body not focused entirely on his mouth to remember the moment. The rain. The scratch of the workbench under her bare skin. Her thighs resting on the broad span of his shoulders. And she might just have to trust him forever, because how the hell would she get over this?

Tipping her head to the light, she closed her eyes. Succumbing to the heavy hum spreading through her whole body.

It wasn't until she was braced and trembling, that he stood and gently hugged her wrecked body to his.

She wanted to weep at his mouth.

He kissed her once more before shifting away. "Don't move."

Not that she could have.

He came back with a condom, chuckling when he caught her watching. But then the smile faded back as he slid his hands into her hair, and widened his legs, keeping his eyes locked to hers.

She slung her arms around his neck and chased after him.

The rain thrashed against the metal sheathing, and the air drifted its sharp earth and wet-grass smell, but she was lost. Lost to the whispery clouds and the ridges of the mountains below her.

His hands moved up her body and she felt herself on his fingertips. She was exactly what he'd said in the kitchen—tight mountain curves that came back in on themselves. This had always been her world, and him in it. Where she was as relentless and lush and inclement as the mountains themselves. And this, right here, was about her. Someday, some other time, it would be about him and about them. But not right now.

VIRGINIA trudged up Jason's driveway in the pouring rain. The gun dug into her waist, her sneakers slipped in the mud, and the trees clashed in the dark overhead. By the time Virginia climbed up the steps and banged her fist on the door, she stood trembling from the cold, drenched, muddy, and exhausted.

The wind shifted, pelting rain in her face. Turning her back, she pounded on the door again.

"Hang the fuck on!" Jason yelled.

She tried the door, found it unlocked, and slid inside.

He was still pulling on his pants. The scarring she'd only ever seen on his arm continued on his chest, on his stomach, running into his waistband. Burns from an explosion, scars of shrapnel, she could see it now.

Virginia leaned against the door, too tired to react.

He started to say something, but his eyes flickered over her—from the wet bra to the T-shirt-wrapped bulge stuck in her skirt—and he clenched his teeth tight and groaned. Turning, he disappeared back down the hall. "Put that somewhere I won't see it," he called before a door shut. "I know nothing about whatever you don't have."

She almost wanted to smile. He knew not to ask and hadn't immediately told her to leave. The hope fluttered alive in her heartbeat until she remembered her father.

Pulling the gun out, she looked around. Where would Jason never go in his own home? She moved into the kitchen area, opening cupboards; when she found an empty one, she put the gun on the shelf.

Voices drifted down the hall. Not just Jason. But a girl.

She wanted to care about that, but there were so many other things to care about—her history, her future—that there was simply no space for it. No wonder he'd been annoyed.

That's something you get to care about. Tourmaline's words echoed in her head. But Tourmaline didn't understand: Virginia knew that people cared about those things. She knew that if she were a whole person, instead of just a shell of one, she would feel more than an easily ignored twitch of jealousy or frustration at discovering that the boy she loved was sleeping with someone else.

"Oh. You," Aubrey said, stopping in the kitchen doorway and smoothing her curls. Her shirt was still twisted, half tucked into jeans. "What are you doing here?"

"Just. Uh . . ." Virginia ruffled her hair and looked out the window, but only her bedraggled reflection stared back at her. The fact that she was standing in Jason's kitchen wearing only dripping jeans and a bra communicated something far more petty and silly than the truth. She shrugged. "Did I interrupt?"

"I have work to do," Jason said to Aubrey. "I told you that."

"So she's staying?" Aubrey asked.

He just stood there, looking wholly unapologetic. "Until I can get her out of my hair."

"Mm-hmm." Aubrey raised an eyebrow and hooked her finger into the back of her sandal.

"I have to take care of this before it becomes bigger trouble than it is right now."

"Yeah, I know the kind of trouble she's in." Aubrey rolled her eyes and picked up her purse. She laughed. "We'll see if you pick up the next time *I'm* in trouble." She opened the door and winked at Virginia. "Have fun."

"Will do," Virginia said, just to drive home the point.

Jason shut the door and glared at her. "What the hell are you doing here?"

"Hmm." She pursed her lips and stared at the floor. "What do you want to hear?"

"You're a mess."

She nodded. "Yep."

"You need a place to stay?"

She kept nodding, looking around the kitchen. Everyplace but at him. Feeling small and vulnerable, and empty—terrified to go looking for feelings about *this man* and what had happened to her father, let alone feelings about what had just happened between him and Aubrey. "Yep."

"I'll put a towel and some clothes in the bathroom for you." He walked away.

Maybe I should just leave. But hope beat against her ribs, and Aubrey was already gone, so she followed him down the hall.

He carried a neatly folded towel and a pile of clothes into the bathroom and dropped them on the sink. Starting the water, he turned and tried to look very stern. "Don't use all the hot water. I still need a shower."

Tucking her chin, Virginia waited until he left, closing and locking the door after him.

Her reflection looked back at her in the mirror.

What now, Virginia Campbell?

The parts of her that looked like her father looked back and told her she was not worth anything at all. His eyes. His chin. His handiwork that had given her the permanent angle of her jaw. She'd been born softer. He'd remade her harder. To see the reminder of violence so clearly written in her features made her stomach plummet. Virginia forced herself to look past it, to ignore it, to remember she'd been worth eighteen hundred—

Hazard echoed back to her. *I'm done with her. Make it look like they did it.* The summation of all she was and all she'd done.

Virginia turned away. She did not ask herself what was next or what she wanted; she simply peeled off her skirt and underwear and ducked into the water before she looked too hard. One day at a time. She'd show up to mow lawns in the sunrise with Tourmaline. She'd help Tourmaline get Wayne back into prison. Hazard would go, too—if Wayne was surrounded by Hazard's drugs and had Hazard's gun, how could Hazard not take a fall?

Then maybe she could care about who Jason fucked, what had happened to her father, and what this had all done to her deep inside. Then maybe she could find something beyond the rusted edge of anger to keep her eyes open.

But not right now.

Quickly, she showered and dressed in the T-shirt and shorts Jason had left for her. They smelled like him, comforting, and her body felt safe inside them, despite the stiffness and aching when she headed down the hall.

Jason sat in the main room, still shirtless, computer open in his lap and the TV on. A blanket and pillow were laid out on the couch. She was glad to see it, but her throat ached with longing to slide into his lap, push her head into his chest, and cry in his arms.

"There should be hot water left," she said.

"Good." He didn't look up from the computer. "There's some food in the kitchen if you're hungry."

Food turned out to be a plate and napkin set on the table with a couple of slices of buttered bread, a can of cheap beer, and a thick hunk of pan-fried venison. She sat down and started eating, gaze flickering to Jason as he stayed focused on the computer. "What are you working on?"

"School."

She startled. "Huh?"

He lifted a heavy book she hadn't seen. The light from the TV reflected on the cover, but she couldn't make out the title.

"Pharmacology," he said.

"For what?"

"I'm in nursing school," he said, putting the book back.

She stared at her plate, head spinning as if she were turning for Hazard. Shoving another bite into her mouth, she forced herself not to look back at Jason. It was hard to tell whether she hated him, or whether this information gave her hope that she'd eventually make it.

"I'm getting a shower." He put down the computer and stood, hiking up his jeans. "Put whatever you want on the TV."

She finished eating in silence, listening to the water hit the shower walls. Putting her plate in the sink, she glanced down the hall, at the light coming out from under the door. The water turned off.

Virginia stared down the hall, mind blank.

NASCAR droned on the TV. Eventually, she forced herself to sit on the couch. It'd look weird if Jason came out of the shower to see her frozen in place. She tucked the pillow under her arm and tried to look as if she belonged, but the night was thin, and deep down she was worth nothing and had no place anywhere, not even on Jason's couch. And here he'd made her bed.

The wind had died down outside, but the rain pattered on the windows and the roof. The only other sounds were the dull drone of racing and commentators.

Jason came back in the room, in shorts and with wet hair, smelling like damp skin and soap. The blue cast of the television reflected off his bare skin. Off the scars and tattoos.

Did he put my old man down? She didn't need to know, but she wanted to know. Needed to know he would tell her. She swallowed and looked away. "Nursing school, huh?"

"Can't just be a drunk forever." He opened a beer and settled back into the chair.

"Oh, but you're so gifted in that area."

He chuckled and opened the computer back up. "You planning on school?"

She looked to the TV. "We'll see."

It was quiet. The TV flickered with a crash replay and engines revved.

"I saw you at the Covington Walmart once," she said, keeping her eyes on the circling cars. "When I was seventeen. You made me feel like I was just like all the other girls."

"What do you mean?" he asked cautiously.

She smiled, still looking at the screen while her stomach tightened with nervousness. "You made me feel seventeen and like I didn't know a thing in the world, not the least of which was my name or anything that had happened to me. And then you made me irritated because you didn't notice me at all." She laughed softly. That memory summed up their entire relationship, still.

"I was probably fucked up. If you think I didn't notice you. What was I doing?"

"Buying Oreos."

He chuckled. "Yeah, I was definitely fucked up."

"I like you that way, Jason." She looked at him now. "I like that it's this front you work hard to make people believe."

He gave a short, bitter laugh.

She raised her eyebrow slightly. "I think I almost love you more for it."

His expression froze, strangled and frightened. He opened his mouth but then closed it and looked back to the computer. "You need to find someone different to love."

"I know . . ." But she couldn't keep going. What if she ruined any life she might have by bringing the dead back? "I know, but then again, maybe you don't have to work so hard with me. Maybe I love you because I don't have to work so hard with you."

He pinched his lips and clicked on something. "I didn't remember you until that day at Tourmaline's, when you ducked like I was about to hit you. I met you a long time ago, and you did the same thing, even though you didn't know me. You just happened to be walking behind me."

"He was a rough and rowdy man," she said, keeping her voice clean of emotion, though her stomach rolled with it.

Jason looked straight at her then, clear understanding on his face. "No, honey," he said softly, his voice low and smooth and *right*. "*I'm* a rough and rowdy man. Your old man was just an evil sumbitch who liked to hit things smaller than him."

She rested her head on the back of the couch and closed her eyes, letting herself sink into the rest that was calling her. "Did you do it?"

"It wasn't like we didn't warn him." He sounded nervous. "He had chances. He was offered grace. He was offered a way out. But he didn't want any of those things. When evil is beyond itself in a person there's nothing left but to put it down."

"That was him," she said. "Did you do it?"

"I didn't. But I knew it was done. And . . ." He shook his head, mouth tightening into a thin line.

"And you've done it since," she finished for him. "That's what you all do. After the court runs and the charity fund-raising rides and past all the girls and the alcohol and shit everyone likes to talk about a lot more than hurt kids or women, there you are. You watch at the edges of everything and intervene when no one else will."

Jason looked at her, something different in his expression—more open, less guarded, something nearing vulnerable. "I always felt like I could do just about anything as long as I knew it was the right thing to do. But I'm afraid, when I close my eyes at night—"

"On the floor?" Virginia interrupted. "Next to your mattress?"

He closed his eyes. Smiled. Tried to stop smiling. Smiled again. "On the floor." He swallowed, eyes still closed in the reflected light. "I'm afraid that instead of putting down abusers, I've only taken fathers. Instead of making places for goodness and grace, I've only made space for a different shade of darkness to slip in. That everything I've done, is just. Nothing."

Never had Virginia wanted to take him in her hands as she did then. But she only swallowed and clutched the pillow. "Y'all couldn't save me."

"I see that now."

"But you gave me a chance. You and Tourmaline. And each time the effort is made, I feel like maybe, someday, I might actually find my way out."

He gave a soft chuckle-sigh, as if he didn't want to be comforted.

"I'm afraid." The words felt clumsy and awful, where the brush of her hand, or her mouth on his, could have said more. "For you."

"About what?"

"That you'll finally find the way to stop breathing."

He rolled his eyes.

"I need you to keep breathing. I need you to make me more venison and . . ." She forced herself to act on what she knew instead of what she felt. "I need you . . ." *To love me back, to not love anyone else.* But she couldn't finish, and she stared at him with all of it unsaid, hoping he could read her mind.

He was silent for a moment. "I'm breathing. I'm here."

Her eyes felt heavy, but she didn't notice she had fallen asleep until Jason gently shook her shoulder. Virginia jolted awake, panicking until she remembered where she was and how she got there.

Jason didn't seem to notice, or he pretended he didn't. "I'm going to bed. Want the blanket?"

After the food and the little bit of sleep, feeling warm and clean inside his soft T-shirt, Virginia was also feeling more like herself. More like she had space in this world instead of being just a wet shadow that showed up on doorsteps when she wasn't wanted. Bringing her arms up, she sleepily pulled on his shoulders.

Even in her sleep, she noticed it didn't take much for him to sigh and drop down beside her. They moved around for a minute, arranging themselves as if they'd done this before. He folded the pillow under his arm and she snuggled into the crook of his shoulder. Until they both came to rest, her body tucked along his. Instantly, something inside her relaxed.

"God almighty this is dumb," he whispered, as if to himself. But he chuckled and shook his head, pulling her tighter. As if it were much easier, for both of them, to breathe, as long as they did it together. "I'm not really a blanket," Jason said, fingers warm and rough as he smoothed the hair away from her temple. "I'll just finish watching the race." He said it as if to himself.

She tucked her face deep into the crook of his arm and breathed the fresh smell of soap on his skin and the hard life of the couch beneath them. She was going to make herself a home here.

45

THE STORMS brought no relief for southern Virginia in late July. And the next day dawned with steam rising off the roads and rocks.

Tourmaline picked Virginia up on time, with the morning thrushes and not many words. They mowed wet grass until it clumped on their sneakers and stuck to their legs. In silence, they loaded the trailers, switched trucks, and parked down below the road, off in the brush.

On foot, the climb took hours.

The day was sizzling—bringing a heavy blanket of cornflower-blue haze over the mountains and under the dappled canopy of trees and thickets. Sweat poured down Tourmaline's back and off her face, until she thought there couldn't be any more sweat left in her body. But she didn't waver, and her steps stayed an even, relaxed pace on the rocky incline.

This had to be done. Even if Wayne caught them (he couldn't), or it didn't work (it would), she had to try. She had to ignore those doubts and at least take a first step.

But the higher they went, the more aware she became of a second step always behind hers and a second breath always between her own.

"Why don't you stay down here?" Tourmaline asked Virginia when they stopped for water. "I can finish this myself. You've brought me far enough."

Virginia just screwed the cap back on the bottle and shook her head. Hauling her backpack over her shoulder, she moved on.

It was one thing for Virginia to help get her to this point, but another thing entirely for her to go any farther when they were so close to Wayne and the risk of getting caught. It would turn ugly instantly if Wayne so much as heard one of their breaths. Tourmaline caught up. "Listen. Virginia . . ."

Virginia shook her head again, put her finger to her mouth, and sped up.

Tourmaline was still trying to figure out how to get Virginia to wait behind, when she sighted the cabin. Pulling Virginia's elbow, she brought them down into the brush.

"Where?" Virginia whispered.

Tourmaline pointed. "You have to let me do this alone."

"Oh, stop. I've got a stake in this, too, don't forget." Virginia hauled off the backpack and dug through it, pulling out two sets of latex gloves they'd taken from Tourmaline's father's stash in the garage.

"You said you would help. You've helped."

Virginia unwrapped the T-shirt and held out the .38.

Tourmaline suddenly panicked as she pulled on the gloves. "Shit. Did we even check if it was loaded?"

Virginia blinked.

Tourmaline's stomach seized tight and she held her breath and opened the cylinder. *Loaded.* Four rounds.

"Oh, thank God," Virginia whispered. "Hopefully Hazard's prints are in there."

"We are dumb," Tourmaline muttered, pushing the cylinder in. She grimaced and then shook it off, trying not to let the momentary panic linger or take a hold in her body as an omen. It didn't mean anything. It'd been fine.

"It's okay. It worked out." Virginia sank back on her heels. "You ready?"

Tourmaline straightened and met her gaze. "I want you to leave."

"No. We agreed to do this together."

"You've done enough. I don't want you to risk getting caught."

"Then just tell yourself I'm here to make sure you don't screw it up."

"I'm not going to screw it up," Tourmaline whispered, eyes narrowed.

"You're going to. Without me. Now, are you ready or are we just going to argue all day?"

Tourmaline gritted her teeth and frowned. "Yes. Fine. I'm ready."

"You sure?"

Tourmaline met her eyes and nodded.

Virginia flinched and took a deep breath. Her gaze flickered from the cabin to Tourmaline and then she frowned and leaned closer. She sighed and frowned at the house. "You should let me do it."

They could not be having this argument right now. "Nope," Tourmaline said firmly. "If I don't take care of this, someone else will. Someone will take my fate."

Virginia crossed her arms. "I get that." She nodded jerkily, lip trembling. "I get that."

"What is there left to do instead?" Tourmaline whispered. "I have nothing. Nothing to do to save myself."

"I'll take this," Virginia whispered smoothly, taking the gun back and sticking it in her shorts. "And you're going to give him something he wants more than revenge."

His freedom. Freedom was what they all wanted. It was far riskier than setting him up, but it was the only thing to do—offer Wayne his freedom. To promise the Wardens wouldn't touch him if he left her alone—something Tourmaline suddenly realized Wayne had no guarantee of. *We will take care of him.* Wayne had known. He'd hidden in the bushes under the bridge at the sound of a *motorcycle*, not because of the cop. He'd been hunted and cornered, and his fear twisted with his desire for revenge. He was a piece of shit, but he was a piece of shit Tourmaline would always have to remember, even if he went back to prison. Especially if she sent him back to prison.

Tourmaline flinched and ducked her chin. She took a deep breath to calm herself, and the air smelled like chemicals and shit and decaying leaves. Her stomach churned and threatened to rise in her throat. She didn't want to offer Wayne safety. It was a risk. It could change. What if he *didn't* want freedom more than he wanted to kill her? What if he came back? Those were risks she didn't want to live with.

But Virginia was right. This history was something she could never be rid of. Wayne would always be part of who she was and who she'd become. Even if she killed him, she wouldn't be freeing herself from that. And that was what she truly wanted.

Not to be free of this place.

But to have never been here to begin with.

Tourmaline nodded.

Virginia squeezed her hand. "Your fate cannot be taken. No one else can change it but you. It's a gift."

Tourmaline rolled her eyes. "You got my six?"

"Like no one ever has."

Carefully, they made their way toward the stick house.

The trees stood still. The bugs droned in the midday heat. Tourmaline's hands were sweaty. The cabin stayed fixed in her sight.

Looking up, she found Virginia standing motionless beside a thick oak tree.

Tourmaline nodded. Her heart thumped so hard she was afraid it was vibrating in her hands, but she carefully stepped up the porch stairs. The cabin door was ajar. Had it been like that the whole time?

Behind her, she heard the soft click of Virginia rechecking the barrel. Her breath quickened. Her heart thumped.

The porch squeaked under her shoes, but nothing in the cabin moved. The door still ajar, a sliver of absolute black.

The hairs on the back of her neck prickled. She swallowed. Gently, she nudged the door open.

The door hit something soft and heavy.

46

TOURMALINE screamed. She bounded off the porch, still screaming. Panicking. She hadn't needed to go farther to know what that weight was. What that sick, soft heaviness was. She shivered a scream again, needing out of the woods, out of this moment.

Virginia was at the door.

And only when Tourmaline realized that Virginia had run inside did she manage to stop screaming, gulp great drafts of air, and run after her.

"V, get out of there," Tourmaline whimpered, sticking her head in and breathing through her mouth. She hadn't noticed a smell, but she wasn't going to take any chances.

"Did you see him?" Virginia said quietly. "Come in. We'll go in a second."

Tourmaline hadn't. She didn't want to. But she knew she should— to know for certain instead of feeling in her gut. She slipped through the narrow opening the body allowed, and looked down, already dizzy from shallow mouth-breathing.

It took her a while.

Seconds of staring. Trying. Blinking. To organize what she was looking at. To realize.

Half his face was gone. The bullet had gone in small, but exploded a massive hole on exit. Tourmaline's stomach turned endlessly, loose and sick at the sight of gray matter and blackened, drying blood and white bone. Only one eye was left, staring unseeing at the dark rafters of the cabin and the circling flies. Instantly she remembered that eye glittering with rage under a streetlight in Roanoke. That eye fixed on her with silent fury under the bathroom lights at putt-putt. That eye as he came for her with intent in the hazy river sunset. She sobbed and squeezed her eyes shut, relieved it was done and relieved she'd not had to watch this happen under her hands: to do this to a person. Her mouth and nose filled with the smell of burned cat inside a burned carpet, a smell that was so familiar—and also something else, that tasted like metallic despair. Turning, she went back out to the porch.

The ridgeline fell the same way as it had before, and the trees remained on guard, and in that golden dazzling underbrush hiding the cabin so well, Tourmaline sat on the steps and cried.

After a minute, Virginia's hand slid up and down her back, soothing her as her shoulder shook. "He was cutting Hazard's dope in there. The heroin. I left the gun, like we planned. Just in case."

Tourmaline nodded. "I want to go home," she said, wiping the tears off her cheeks and trying not to smell—to taste—the inside of the cabin.

"Do you think?"

Tourmaline froze. She hadn't thought. *Hadn't.* Until that very second with the question hanging in Virginia's voice. Did she think one of the Wardens did this? Who else would have? It had just happened—Wayne hadn't begun to bloat, or decay. Her heart pounded and she blinked unseeing at the ground. "I was with Cash."

"I was with Jason." Virginia turned. "And terribly unrelated, inappropriate side note—I want to hear about all *that* later."

Tourmaline glared at her. How could she even care right now?

Virginia met her gaze, eyes clear. "I could have done it. I could do it now. We should have planned for me to do it all along."

A chill ran up Tourmaline's arms.

"He died like my old man."

"Ray," Tourmaline breathed.

Virginia nodded. "It's a mercy. To all he touched. To his own soul.

And I see what they carry for those lives they take. Someone has to pay a price, and they do." She spoke almost reverently. With a firmness that took Tourmaline by surprise. Always, Virginia surprised her.

The truth slithered deep down in her bones. She'd been holding the space left vacant by her mother, waiting. And now she could give it up. "Could it have been someone else?" she pleaded to Virginia.

"You tell me." Virginia glanced back inside and then leaned on her knees. "Do you really think it could be someone else? Where was your dad last night?" She asked the questions gently, prodding Tourmaline toward a truth she already knew.

Won't be home as long as you'll be okay by yourself. Dad's text. She hadn't thought. She'd seen it and thought only of the open night, calling her name. And now.

Tourmaline dropped her chin to her chest.

Her worst fears had come true.

47

AFTER a day that involved a dead body and a lot of mowing, Virginia figured she deserved waffles for dinner. Jason hadn't kicked her out. Wayne's body would be found. They'd pull the thread back to Hazard, and Virginia would be free. And maybe, if she kept on living, she'd become an accountant, and somehow Jason would always be there. Without Aubrey.

She sank her fork into the waffles, thinking of all those things and feeling that shuddering thrum of hope inside her chest, when a middle-aged man in a shirt and tie slid into the empty side of the booth.

"Ms. Campbell." He smiled.

She lifted her head and froze. The cop from Hazard's driveway. The cop who went golfing with Hazard. Whose Impala had caught her and Jason. Who had been parked at the Wardens' open house. "State Detective Alvarez," he said with a friendly smile. "Pleased to meet you." His sunglasses were the wraparound kind, placed on top of his head. His tie had recently been tightened. His shirtsleeves were wrinkled and rolled up. He looked like he'd been in a car for a while. He lifted his finger for the waitress.

"What do you want?" Virginia said through clenched teeth.

"How's your mother?"

"Is she in trouble?"

He shrugged. "Just making conversation."

"I'd rather you get to the point," Virginia said.

The waitress stopped.

"Coffee, please," he said.

Virginia met his eyes and refused to look away.

His jaw tightened. "What do you know about the Wardens?"

"Jack shit," Virginia said, pushing a bite of her waffle into a pool of syrup. "Why?"

"You've been spending a lot of time with them."

"I went to school with one of their daughters. I hang out with her. I'd hardly call that 'spending a lot of time' with the Wardens. Do you hang out with your friends' parents?" She shoved the bite in her mouth and chewed, still staring. "That's a little weird."

He didn't look bothered. Yet.

"You seem like a straight shooter. I know you've got your mom to take care of."

"And?"

"Did the pageant thing for a while. But not much going on anymore." He nodded to the waitress as she set down his coffee. "So it would make sense you're trying to get in with some biker to support you and your mom now."

Years of pageant training enabled her to keep her face perfectly still. "This all sounds like gossip."

He smiled. "Maybe so. Maybe so. I think you have some things you want to tell me," he said.

She snorted. "Yeah? Do people fall for that, much?"

He smiled again and pulled over the container of sugar. "Only people who have something to tell." He ripped open a packet. "We found a body today in the woods and we're certain it's the work of the Wardens. Now, I know you've been hanging around them this summer. And I think you seem like the kind of girl that has something to say. And this isn't anything official right now, you understand. But we can make it official."

Virginia wanted to grab his ears and shove his face into that little coffee cup, but she just raised an eyebrow. "No, thanks."

He ripped another sugar packet. "You're what? Eighteen?" He dumped the sugar and shook his head. "This isn't the kind of life you want to start for yourself. You know that. You can see exactly where you're going, can't you?"

Virginia couldn't think of anything quick enough to say back, so she just kept staring and chewing. It had always seemed to work on Hazard.

"I've seen you so many times y'all look like one girl. Same story. Same look about you." Alvarez dragged his gaze over her as if he might be looking for something different but didn't find anything. "Busted up a little young. Some kind of tragedy hanging over you like a cloud. You attract the same kinds of things. Broken and busted and tragedy. At eighteen, you'll still look alive, you'll still have some youth, something that seems like it could be called potential." He looked out over the diner and picked up the mug as if he weren't even talking to her anymore, but to himself. "By twenty-three you'll be nothing but more busted and more tragic. A few babies and some stretch marks will rub off anything that seems like potential. The only way you can get anywhere is to get out of here. Out of these hills and into some nice city where you can get a nice job. College, even. This is your chance, Virginia. We can figure out a situation that's better than the one you have here."

Virginia dragged in a deep breath through her nose, looking down at her plate. He was a cop. *A cop.* She couldn't lunge across the table and choke a cop. She couldn't stab him with a fork. *A cop.* Everything inside her wanted to scream how wrong he was, but she had nothing to say. Closing her eyes, she heard Hazard talk about moving on to better things and realized how similar Alvarez sounded to Hazard—*you're worth nothing until I can help you.* She spoke calmly. "You want to help me, huh? How much?"

"It's not about the price. It's about what you want." He slurped his coffee and set it down. "I'm not asking you to do anything official. I'm not asking you to testify against the Wardens. I just want to hear what you have to say. About the Wardens. About what you know about their criminal activity. Or their version of heroic activity." He seemed to roll his eyes without actually doing it.

Unbidden, all the things she knew about the death of her father jumped into Virginia's mind. She looked down and stabbed her waffles.

"And then we'll get you out of here. What now, Virginia Campbell?"

Her chin jerked up.

He took another sip of coffee. "Of course, you could always come with me and we can talk about your years of drug dealing instead."

Swallowing the waffles, she looked out the window, at the lights of the mall across the highway. *What now, Virginia Campbell?*

But the thing about knowing you weren't worth anything to anyone: That knowledge made it easy to tell when someone was giving you bullshit. She put her hand in her chin and snarled, "Fuck you."

He shrugged, as if he'd expected as much. Ripping open another sugar packet he dumped it in and glanced at her. "You know they found a weapon."

She gave him a flat look, hoping he didn't have a sixth sense for when someone's heart rate went up.

"The .38." Alvarez said, eyebrow lifting. "You know the one, don't you, Virginia?"

Virginia tried not to panic. Tried and failed.

"That .38 was reported stolen five years ago. It's Calvin Harris's gun." He took another drink of coffee. "I guess they found it, though."

48

TOURMALINE stared down at the Shovelhead, fluorescent lights humming above her and a YouTube video pulled up in her hand. She watched it even though she'd already watched it a hundred times. She just needed to change the oil. Simple. If she could put gas in the Shovelhead, she could change the oil.

She took a deep breath, set everything down, and began looking through her father's tools for a wrench.

The oil was in the middle of draining when the garage door opened; she jumped, kicking the oil pan. Oil sloshed onto her toes, but she grabbed her phone and pretended to be using it as Jason walked in.

He frowned. "What's up, T?"

"Oh." She waved her phone. "Nothing."

"Mm-hm."

Suddenly she realized the phone looked more suspicious than the oil pan. "I needed to call school."

He laughed.

She remembered it was nine at night.

"I'm not . . ." She exhaled and looked around. How much did he know about her and Cash, anyway?

"You changing the oil?"

She nodded, too afraid to say it out loud.

"It probably needs it." He poked through the tool chest. "You see a locknut wrench in here? I can't remember who I lent it to."

What the hell was a locknut wrench? "No." She grabbed a shop towel and wiped off her toes and the little bit of oil that had landed on the floor. "How did you learn to do stuff on bikes?"

"By doing it. And asking for help when I didn't know what I was doing." He met her gaze. "Even when it made me feel like a dipshit."

She smiled and nodded.

"Listen, T." He cleared his throat and went back to searching through the tool chest. "I, um . . ."

She froze and waited, heart beating hard. Was this about Cash? Or Virginia?

"I'm not interested in getting involved between you and anyone else, okay? That's not my realm. But I'm not blind. Your dad is going to find out. And it's not going to go well. I'm supporting Cash, but you both need to be careful and think through all that you're doing, okay? That's my weird speech about that." He shut a drawer, still not looking at her. "God, I'd kill myself if I ever had a daughter."

She thought about that and then laughed. "Karma would probably kill you first."

He looked mortified.

It was strange. Stranger to think she was in a place where she could see Jason looking mortified at something she said.

"It's okay, you know." She waited until his gaze flickered to hers and repeated. "I know. It's fine."

"It's not . . . ," he trailed off, shaking his head.

"If it was any other person, maybe it'd be weirder. But . . ." It was Virginia. And Virginia's eighteen was not Tourmaline's eighteen and it would be silly to believe something different. "She needs someone with power, who won't use it against her. Anything less wouldn't ever hold her respect."

He nodded, back to avoiding looking at her. "I promise I won't . . . I won't use that. I don't want . . ." His mouth tightened and he looked at his feet. "Thanks, T. Let me know if you need any help, all right?"

"Will do."

The oil had finished draining. Pulling out the drain tube, she screwed the cap back on and then began the hunt for the oil filter. Somewhere underneath. By the back tire. On her hands and knees, she carefully eased under the bike and looked around.

Someone came in and slammed the door.

Tourmaline jerked up. God, when had the garage gotten so popular? But it was just Virginia.

"Hey you," Tourmaline said, half frowning, half smiling. Not sure why Virginia was back at this time of night. "Long time no see."

Virginia fumbled with the pack of smokes. "We're fucked."

Tourmaline sank back on her heels. "What?"

The lights hummed above and cast a sickening glow on Virginia's face. Her fingers shook as she lit the smoke and sucked a deep breath in.

Tourmaline knew without asking. Knew without knowing. Something was about to go wrong. Again. Always. She hung her head. Stared at the wrench in her hands. "What is it?"

"Me. I fucked up." Virginia stabbed her fingers into her chest, and then took another long drag on the smoke and passed it to Tourmaline.

Tourmaline shook her head.

Virginia paused, staring at the outstretched cigarette. Suddenly, her expression faltered and collapsed in on itself and she lifted eyes full of tears. "I didn't know the gun was already stolen. He stole it from your dad years ago. That cop—"

The garage did a slow spin.

The smoke twisted with intent.

And Virginia was crying.

We planted Dad's own gun. At the scene Dad—or some Warden—had made.

Tourmaline's stomach dove and all the air left her chest. She sank against the bike and stared.

"I didn't know," Virginia whispered. "I'm sorry. We should have left it. We shouldn't have tried to get it pinned on Hazard. It's my fault. I'm such a fuckup. I am so sorry. You trusted me. And I let you down."

"It's not your fault, V." It was all hers. Only hers. It was her family.

The cigarette drooped in Virginia's fingers; tears left black streaks of makeup on her cheeks. "I just don't understand why I can't keep anything right. It's hopeless."

"It can't be. I won't allow it," Tourmaline said, the words echoing in her hollowed-out chest.

What was there left to do? What could they possibly use? Tourmaline found her own eyes burning and she rubbed them hard. She closed her eyes behind her hands and almost wished she hadn't tried, had just lain on the road and let Wayne run over her that night. But then she remembered Cash's bike in the dark and Virginia in the woods and the sizzle of the sunshine above her as she told Jason why she was friends with Virginia. *When girls stick together in this world, they're harder to pick off.* Tourmaline lifted her chin and waited for Virginia to look at her. "We've got one thing left. But I can't ask you to do this. You have to decide for yourself."

Virginia sniffed. "What is it?"

"It" was the business card with the raised edges of a seal. The man who'd come looking for her in the rain. Tourmaline swallowed. "The FBI."

There was a long pause.

The lights hummed. The bugs droned.

"Yes or no. It's your call. I can't do it without you." Tourmaline's voice cracked. "Without what you know."

Virginia took another long pull on the smoke and exhaled it in a long, hard rush of smoke. She didn't look at Tourmaline.

The crickets sang louder. The quiet itself seemed to move.

Virginia's chin trembled and she glanced to Tourmaline. "Ride or die, bitch."

Tourmaline snorted.

Virginia chuckled over her cigarette, fingers still shaking.

Suddenly, it didn't matter that their throats were too tight and their chests cinched, because they were laughing and crying all at once.

49

TOURMALINE waited at the clubhouse steps with her phone in hand. She had to scroll way down the messages to find Anna May, sadness hitting the back of her throat when she saw how long it'd been since they'd talked. Her Fourth of July text was still unanswered. She flexed her thumbs, took a deep breath, and sighed.

It's been a wild summer. Want to make a plan for brunch the day before I leave for school? I'll buy!

She and Anna May wouldn't be best friends. They might not even be friends. But their friendship wasn't going to end the way it was trying to. It would go quietly and peacefully, with good feelings and great memories and goddamn brunch, if Tourmaline had anything to do with it.

Her dad's bike roared into the clearing. "Tourmaline?" he asked, completely confused. "What are you doing here? How did you get here?"

She tilted her head and frowned. Was he joking? The only vehicle in the lot was the Shovelhead, and she had a helmet between her feet. Had he missed it or ignored it? She gestured to the bike. "Changed the oil."

He looked between her and the bike. "So you've been riding it still?" he asked in a strangled voice. "I was thinking of selling it."

"I'll buy it."

"You don't want—"

"I know what I want," Tourmaline interrupted. "I'll buy it from you."

He didn't respond, sighing and rubbing his face. "What's going on? Why are you here?"

The control was taking over his tone. The assurance. Strange to realize now that it was defensive.

She lifted her chin and forced herself to meet his eyes. "Where were you the other night?"

"What other night?"

"Two nights ago. The storms."

"I told you. I went out. Did something happen?" He looked worried. "Did you see Wayne?"

It stabbed deeply inside Tourmaline's chest to see that flicker of concern cross his expression. That concern not for her, but for maintaining his lies. The breeze stirred the pines, whispering in the space between them.

Her father stood with his shoulders squared and his chin high, the sun behind his shoulder.

"Why didn't you tell me?" she whispered.

"Tell you what?"

She closed her eyes and just sat there, the aching and weakness heavy in her bones. How could he have let her keep the burden of her mother's imprisonment for so long? When all along, the law had only been after him. She dragged in a deep breath and forced her head up. "I thought people who lied to me would look different. I didn't know you could love someone and hurt them as much at the same time. I know the truth. I know all of it."

"All of what?"

She met his eyes then. His challenge. Her spine stilled to think of Wayne's eye, fixed eternally on the darkness of the rafters. "I know what the Wardens are. I know what you do. I know the cops went after Mom when they were trying to get you. I know where you were the other night." She leaned forward, determined. "I found his body when I went to take care of it myself."

He froze. His eyes widened. The control faltered. "What?" he breathed.

"You ruined it," she said. "No one was supposed to go to prison because of me again. I couldn't live with that."

"I told you to tell me," he whisper-yelled, stepping closer. "You were supposed to come to me."

"So you could do exactly what you did, and end up in prison?"

"I'm not going anywhere."

"Bullshit," she snapped, eyes narrowed. "We both know that's bullshit."

He sighed again and rubbed his face. "It's just the risk I take. The risk we all take."

Finally, a truthful answer. Far too late. "Why didn't you tell me?"

"Why *would* I tell you?"

"It bled into everything, Dad. And you let it all fall on my hands and you never once helped me hold it or clean it off. You just let me stand there, with that weight all on me and no idea how to live with it. You could have told me. I would have been relieved. I needed it to understand where I was and what happened."

"I would never lay that burden on a child."

It was as if he were arguing with the paper girl. The daughter he'd drawn in the outline he'd expected her to always remain within. And he couldn't hear that she wasn't that. She stared at him, trying to find a way to reach him. To make him listen. "I never wanted to be protected from the world I live in. I *can't* be shielded from the world I live in—not forever. What I wanted." She shook her head, tightening her fingers on her legs. "What I *needed* was for you to teach me how to live in it. To show me how to see it for what it was and when to bend it to my will instead of always bending to it. You have so much power. You are so sure of your place in this world. Why wasn't I worth teaching that to? Instead you've given it all to this." She looked up at the clubhouse. Gestured to its door whose threshold she was not allowed to cross. "Brotherhood," she spat.

"This isn't about—"

"It is," she interrupted, pointing her finger at him. "It is when you cut me off and gave it to them instead. That's when you made me its enemy. This is my world. And you left me alone inside it."

Her dad didn't respond. His face remained firm. He wasn't listening.

She bit her cheek, head pulsing with anger and helplessness. "They're going to come for you," she said.

He shrugged. "You worry too much."

"I don't worry. I know."

He heard the authority in her voice. The knowledge. His eyes found hers, a flash of alarm running through them. He shrugged again. "I've always known they would. Let them come. You're safe now."

She rolled her eyes in frustration. She'd never been safe. He couldn't protect her from the life she was already living. From the choices she'd already had to make. That was a lie he told himself. "I'm sorry," she said. "For how this turned out. For how it's going to turn out."

"I don't know what I would have done differently." Her father's voice seemed smaller. "I'm not sorry I tried to keep you safe."

She sniffed and nodded, trying not to be hurt that he didn't understand she was talking about something so much bigger. "I'm going to finish this." Her voice caught. "I started this. I'm going to finish it."

"That's not your job," he said. "It's not your job to protect me. It's my job to protect you."

She turned away, staring at the grass. The wind tugged her hair and she lifted her face into it as her chest cracked open and its contents poured out, and she knew she'd keep on going.

Let the world around her keep on as it wished, it could not change what she did, and how she thought, and who she was. And with that knowledge, she could make paths anywhere her feet wanted to go. "I learned this world is mine," she said, picking up her helmet and standing. He had not taught her.

But she *had* learned.

She left him standing by the steps.

The Shovelhead roared underneath her hands.

◆ 50 ◆

VIRGINIA sat beside Tourmaline on a sagging and splintered picnic bench in the shade alongside the James River. Her knee bounced nervously. Her fifth cigarette in twenty minutes was half gone between her fingers. Her stomach clenched tight. The hills rose on all sides, leaves flipping and tossing as a hot wind carved its way through the mountains under a cloudless August sky.

"You're sure?" Tourmaline whispered. "You can still say no."

"Just don't accept anything less than what we want. That's all I'm nervous about," Virginia lied.

Tourmaline sighed and put her chin in her hands.

The grass wavered shaggy and forgotten, tickling Virginia's ankles as they waited.

A car finally pulled into the lot and parked. A man in a suit climbed out. Virginia clamped her fingers to the bench to keep from throwing herself into the river.

"Tourmaline. Good to see you again," the man said, coming through the grass with a white legal pad tucked under one arm.

Tourmaline straightened. "I'd like to deliver a package."

He blinked. "A package?"

"It's all tied up and neatly knotted. But I need to make an exchange."

His mouth dropped ajar and he looked between her and Virginia. "What's in the package?"

"Nope."

Virginia shifted.

"What do you mean, no?"

"No, you do not get to know what the package is before you accept it. That's not how packages work."

"Is this a joke?"

"No. This is what we call a deal."

"A deal?" He straightened. "A deal. Okay. What kind of deal?"

"It turns out, I know something about this heroin problem y'all are having."

"Oh, do you?" He said it smugly. "What is it you want?"

"My mom moved to Alderson. My dad kept out of prison for trumped-up murder charges. And the state detective harassing my family needs to be finished."

He frowned. "I can't do that."

She gritted her teeth. *Don't accept anything less.* "Great. Who can?"

"No. Okay." He sighed in frustration. "Your mom, fine. Your dad— has he been arrested?"

"Not yet. But they already spoke to him. It's my mom's ex. A junkie. With a gun that was stolen from my dad years ago."

He looked up, running his tongue over his teeth as he thought. "Does he have an alibi?"

"He was with me and another club member that night."

"If he hasn't been arrested, how do you know it's going to happen?"

Virginia leaned on the table, boards creaking under her elbows. "The detective spoke to me. Told me. He's working with . . . ," she trailed off and closed her mouth.

"It's complicated," Tourmaline finished.

His eyes narrowed at Virginia. "What is this package worth?"

"More than one man," Tourmaline said.

He sighed. "I don't know. Let me get back to you."

"No."

He frowned again. "No?"

"This is it. You walk away from this, you walk away." Tourmaline stayed firm, her face relaxed. "Your decision."

"Can I make a call?"

"One call. Five minutes."

He rushed off.

"I don't know," Tourmaline said as they watched him put his phone to his ear and talk. "I can't tell."

Virginia didn't respond, texting Jason to focus on something else while she waited. *I need a ride. Whenever you have time.* "We can always kill them all. Last resort."

Tourmaline laughed. "Last resort."

"Watch out." Virginia nodded, heart picking up.

The agent was coming back. Black dress shoes through the tall grass. Tense expression. "All right," he said briskly, sitting down. "Here's the deal. We can't stop an arrest and we can't stop any kind of investigation, but we guarantee manslaughter, tops. If it shakes out the way you say, he'll be home free. If he's charged and tried, the deal is manslaughter. We'll move your mom."

"And immunity," Virginia said. "For anything."

The man flicked to her, eyes narrowed. "What do you mean?"

"I mean. I know this because of what I did in it. Drugs."

"All right, then." He nodded, still staring. "Your testimony is the package, I presume?"

Virginia held out her hand. "Virginia Campbell. Pleased to meet you."

She spent two hours talking into a recorder while the agent took notes. He left them both with cards and appointments to come in to sign the paperwork and start the next step. The next step in a long road of things she would need to do in order to testify against Hazard.

Virginia didn't start breathing again until the agent pulled away.

"Want to get some food?" Tourmaline asked, starting toward the truck.

"No. I'm going to stay here," Virginia said.

Tourmaline frowned. "Huh?"

"Jason's picking me up."

Tourmaline smiled. "See you tomorrow." She pulled out, heading in the opposite direction from the agent.

Virginia dragged her fingers through her hair, relieved to be alone. She lit a new cigarette and took deep breaths. Watching as the sky changed from pale blue to deep gold. Straining to hear the familiar roar on the wind. It was strange—how the world changed along with her. How hope took root and pushed up out of the cracked desert of her life.

Jason pulled up, but she didn't move; she was transfixed by the flow of the river at her side.

He sat beside her and the bench groaned. His arm was snug against hers, his thigh pressed against hers.

"Want me to kill him?" he asked—teasing.

She smiled, still staring at the river. "I want him to know I did it. I want him to hate me in prison. I want to make Hazard suffer."

"Good." He squeezed her thigh. "Let's go get your books before the college bookstore closes."

She smiled deeper and tilted her chin. His eyes were bright, the hazel shimmering with the colors of the sunset. Jason's fingers gently stroked her knee. His expression was open and unguarded and full of things he'd only begun to whisper in the dark, where they were safe beside each other.

After another quiet moment, they left.

IT WAS late August, when the leaves were tired of themselves but dragging on toward September, when Tourmaline got the call. She'd asked for it, worried she'd be gone at college when it happened. They told her with only thirty minutes to spare.

Her father was leaving today.

Virginia helped her load the trailer, leaving the Gaithers' lawn only half mowed. They pulled into Tourmaline's driveway, drenched in sweat, with bits of grass sticking to their skin, to find the Wardens all collected there. "You didn't tell Jason?" Tourmaline asked, breaking the tense silence.

"No," Virginia said, folding her gloves in her palms. "Did you tell Cash the police were coming to arrest your dad?"

"No. Because then he'll have to tell Dad. I told him everything else, though."

"Me too," Virginia said softly.

Tourmaline had to park the truck only halfway up the drive. *Why, oh, why were they all here?* She'd thought it would be dinnertime. Something quiet. Dignified. Not this. Never this.

"You finished already?" her father hollered, untangling himself from the arms of the woman with the silver earrings.

Tourmaline slammed the truck door shut and walked through the mess of bikers and girls. "What are you doing?"

Everything paused for a half second and her father's face tightened.

It was one thing for her to talk like that when they were alone in the house, a totally different sort of thing to take that tone in front of his men. Not one of them would ever talk to him like that. But Tourmaline only clenched her fists, wishing she could somehow tell him to send them all away and take a minute alone. But she couldn't.

Tourmaline met the woman's eyes over her father's shoulder, silently pleading for help.

The woman shifted. "Calvin?" she asked. As if worried.

He ignored her. "Go inside," he said to Tourmaline. "Did you finish all the yards?" he asked Virginia.

"Not quite." Virginia kept her voice even; she was answering her boss.

"Why didn't you finish?" he asked Tourmaline. "Never mind. Get in the house and clean up. The truck is fine where it is." He turned, dismissing her.

Tourmaline had to get him out of here. Somewhere private. "Can I talk to you?"

"I'll talk to you later. Go on."

Tourmaline looked around, looking for help, for someone to understand that her father was about to be arrested, though she knew none of them could.

The woman with the silver earrings met her gaze, forehead creased. But she didn't move.

Virginia looked to Jason.

Tourmaline's stomach tightened further as her gaze swept past Cash, who was standing next to Jason and two women whose clothes left no doubt that they were there to party.

Lifting her chin, she turned for the house.

"I'm down to only one, but sometimes she still makes it feel like I have two women ragging in my house," her father joked as she walked away.

It ripped her heart into shreds, but Tourmaline bit her lip and blinked, trying to ignore the shake in her hands and the burn in her eyes. It didn't matter. It didn't matter because he didn't know he was about to go to jail.

Inside, she got a drink of water, trying to calm down.

Cash walked in, slamming the door behind him. He was in full Warden swagger, no hint of a conscript left in his walk or in the way he looked at her. "You haven't told him yet. You're leaving for school in a few days."

Closing her eyes, Tourmaline took another drink. Oh dear God, why today?

"I'm going to tell him," he said.

Putting down the glass, she pushed back her hair. "No. Don't do that."

"I'm not going to keep going behind your dad's back."

She pinched her lips tight.

He sighed and leaned against the door frame, crossing his arms over his chest. "What's the real problem?"

"I mean, you just . . ." She sighed and straightened. The problem was that part of the deal was she couldn't say anything about the damn deal. And part of the deal was she had to stand by and let it all happen. And part of the deal should have *never* included this moment on this day. She tried to find a real answer for Cash and all she came up with was flat truth. "You'd be the first. He's going to beat the hell out of you."

A flicker of a smile crossed his face, but he gave her a hard look. "Don't be giving me that bullshit." He stepped closer, looking her over as if he were remembering kissing her. Wanting to kiss her again. "That's not the real problem, is it? Between me and you."

"There isn't one."

"Come on, now."

She looked away.

"Tell me, Tour-mah-line," he said in a deepened, joking voice.

"It's not your problem. It's mine."

"I love you," he said softly. "It *is* my problem."

A shudder of pleasure shot through her stomach. It never got old to hear him say it.

"Why are you afraid?"

She pulled back. "I'm not afraid," she huffed.

He laughed, clearly not believing her. "Okay."

"It's just weird." She swallowed, wishing she had better words for him. "I just can't go into a . . . relationship . . . thinking you'll be different, or that you'll change. I can't pretend this world is something different. I can't have expectations." In the face of all she knew about the club and her parents.

"Expectations?"

"Of your loyalty."

"Ahh . . ." He nodded, his body somehow softening. "That's it."

They were silent. She caught his eye.

"That's a good fear. A smart one. That's not a problem you have to work through."

"I'm not a jealous person," she said quietly. "I won't tell you what to do or how to do it, because you're a grown-ass man and that's not my job. I'm not your mother and I'm not God. I'm a coldhearted daughter of the devil; and if you betray me, I'll get my revenge and walk as light by you as you can by me. And if that scares you, you should leave now."

Cash shoved off the wall and walked toward her. "Oh, it scares me." But he just dipped his head, pulling her tight to his chest and kissing her deeply. Breaking away, he met her eyes. "My dad never once messed around on my mom. He raised me with that sense of loyalty and respect for the person I'm with. And that doesn't mean those women won't be around. And that doesn't mean every other guy out there thinks the same way. But I'll never betray you. Ever." He kissed her forehead. "And I'm telling him."

Shit. He wouldn't. He'd wait. Not here, with everyone. Not today of all days.

But he was out the door already.

She scrambled after him.

His back stayed straight, steps at ease as he approached her father.

"Cash," she said, trying not to yell, but trying to get his attention. Deal be damned, she'd tell him. What could it hurt now?

A few of the men who heard her call him by name stopped and turned. There was a split second of absolute silence, with nothing but the breeze stirring the trees and the long, dull song of the cicadas.

Cash had his back to her, but in that split second of stillness, Dad's face turned murderous, and his eyes locked with Tourmaline's.

Shit. No. No. No.

Slowly, he stood.

They all looked at her now. Not Cash. The silence stretching. The world changing.

"This shit true?" Tourmaline's father roared.

Tourmaline lifted her chin and nodded.

Cash didn't budge. He'd known the whole time, how this was going to go. Probably from the first day they'd met. Suddenly, she wished she had trusted him before he had to ask her to.

Her father's fist cracked into Cash's jaw, the sound exploding in the quiet. Cash staggered.

Tourmaline ran.

Cash came right back, shaking it off and meeting her dad with his fists at his side.

Back to finish paying the price.

Someone grabbed her arms and held her. Tourmaline yelled, trying to get her father's attention, but he didn't even blink in her direction.

Virginia stood across the way, watching from behind Jason—her hands on his sides. His hand was wrapped back around her thighs, shielding her. They both watched with silent intensity. Tourmaline blinked at them, stunned for a moment, even though she knew they were together and she'd known Virginia would rule. Things were changing.

Her father's girlfriend pulled her back. "Let them work it out," she whispered in Tourmaline's ear, dragging her out of the way.

Tourmaline didn't fight the woman. The woman . . . *What was her name?* Dad had never said it—or maybe he had and she'd never bothered to listen for it—and yet, she was still here.

The cicadas still sung. The breeze still blew, hot and damp in the late August evening. Their boots scuffed in the gravel, and her father's fist landed into Cash's stomach, pushing his breath out in a tight huff. The women faded behind and the men pressed in tight, gossiping about what was happening like middle-school girls. Their gazes all flickered to Tourmaline, pinned by the woman's arms around her waist.

No one understood. They didn't realize anything bigger was going on.

She tried to kick out, but the woman hugged her tight. "It's okay, honey. He's just getting him down. It'll be over soon."

But Cash wasn't going down. He was taller than her father. Bigger. Younger. Calvin hit hard, and Cash staggered after each blow, shaking it off and coming back, but he wasn't even falling to his knees. He pinched off his bleeding nose and slung blood to the ground, spattering the gravel.

Tourmaline's father landed another solid hit on Cash's jaw.

This time, Cash stumbled back to his ass in the dirt. Slow. His eyes looked spun and lost to his body.

Tourmaline's dad was breathing hard. He bent his knees, catching his breath.

"Don't have a heart attack," the woman muttered. As if she, too, were waiting for this to end.

Cash hauled himself up.

Her father straightened.

It was taking forever. Why couldn't they see what was happening? She was caught in a dream, running in slow motion from impending doom. "You are all *fucking* stupid!" Tourmaline screamed, twisting out of the woman's grasp.

But they were all interrupted by the sudden rush of leaves and branches that moved to reveal boots and fully armored men appearing from all directions.

POLICE. WARRANT.

There was a split second before they touched him. Before they dragged him away from Cash.

Before Virginia caught Jason around the neck and stayed his motion, whispering in his ear as Queen and the ruler of fate.

A moment before the woman with the silver earrings released her hold on Tourmaline's arms and lunged after Tourmaline's dad, brought up short right away by a helmeted and armored man.

A second before Tourmaline scrambled under Cash's arm and held him up as his president was dragged away, while she stared at the dirt so she wouldn't have to watch.

And in the split-second silence and utter stillness among the men, the cicadas kept up their song and the breeze washed eternal, lifting Tourmaline's hair off her neck.

EPILOGUE

THEY came for Hazard the following week. Virginia visited him in the county lockup and didn't say a word, just sat there with a smile until the guard told her to leave because Hazard became so enraged it took three officers and a Taser to subdue him.

Tourmaline was surprised again. Whatever Virginia did, she did with an intense commitment. Even when it meant scheduling her workdays around testifying.

In the first six months of her father's sentence, Alvarez retired. There were whispers it was a forced retirement, but he got a medal anyway. Someone said he was thinking of running for county commissioner.

Virginia took over Tourmaline's role in the landscaping company.

Jason took over her father's.

Tourmaline went to UVA and came home every other weekend.

After her father came home, Tourmaline didn't ask him to visit her mother. She *told* him he would. They went right before Margaret was sent to Alderson, the minimum-security women's prison.

Her father didn't argue, though he did make a rather sullen joke about how serving eighteen months should have been enough, he shouldn't have to visit, too. But then, Tourmaline was halfway done with college, and her best friend reigned as Queen, and she and Cash had made plans for the summer after she graduated, and so her father's complaint simply rolled off her like water off a duck's back.

She'd grown into her life pretty well, after all.

It was only her father's second time visiting—the last time had been when Tourmaline was still seventeen. He was made to take off his vest (no "gang" colors allowed) and his rings. Give up his wallet. His phone. The cross necklace and the chain bracelet that Tourmaline was pretty sure the woman with the earrings—Victoria—had given him. He was made to pull out his pockets and spread his legs wide, arms on the wall. He did it all like a man who had done it many times before.

They patted him down. They corrected his stance against the wall, even though he was standing just the way Tourmaline was. The CO side-eyed him every time he went past. He held out his hand for the stamp you couldn't see but could feel, even though you weren't supposed to be able to.

Tourmaline watched all this, and—while they waited and breathed deep breaths of bleach-scented recycled air—she understood that here he was reduced to the level of everyone else. That he hadn't yet gotten over being angry and being sad and remembering all the spaces her mother used to inhabit in his life that would never be filled again. Not even when she was released.

A wave of sadness crashed over her, and she reached for his hand.

He took her fingers in a firm grip, as if he needed to hang on to her in order to stay found.

Together, they walked through the gates of hell.

"What do you want?" Tourmaline asked, smiling at her mother when she sat down, rubbing her wrists underneath the table.

"A candy bar. And a Diet Coke," her mother said shyly, not looking at her father.

"I'll be back," Tourmaline said, leaving them at the table alone. She lingered at the vending machines, taking her time to get the items and then slowly made her way back to the table. She put the items down for her mother and then sat beside her father.

"What's been going on?" Margaret asked, popping the top on the pop.

"Cash says hi, Mom. He had to work today."

"Nothing much, Maggie."

Tourmaline's mother softened all over, visibly, when her father said her name. Softened so abruptly, with this big smile crossing her face and her shoulders relaxing as if someone had just pulled a knife out of her back, that both Tourmaline and her father sat there, staring. "No one's called me Maggie in so long. I forgot I was her."

"What do they call you?" her father asked.

"Harris."

"You aren't a Harris anymore," he said, which felt cruel to Tourmaline.

But Tourmaline's mother just shrugged, a sly little grin pulling at the corners of her mouth. "I haven't been to the DMV to change my name, but I'll make sure it's my first stop when I get the chance, Calvin." And it felt very much as if Tourmaline could see the person Mom used to be.

They talked. Her father grew comfortable and smiled. All three of them stood in front of the painted tarp and palm tree, and Tourmaline's parents both looked at the Polaroid and handed it to her.

The precious time they had slipped through their fingers, each second felt and treasured. They were nothing, but in the presence of this shadow of their history, this love that was at one time true, and maybe had always been only a shadow of something they would never lose, they ceased to remember their nothingness.

Visiting hours ended.

ACKNOWLEDGMENTS

A **WRITER** is never a solitary being, even if she does do most of her writing alone in a ripped tank top, mismatched Carhartt socks, and men's boxers. (*cough*) I'm so grateful to be surrounded by a host of incredible and smart people.

Endless thanks to my agent Barbara Poelle, who is a ride-or-die, badass MOFO. Thank you for sticking with me, knowing exactly what I needed to write, and giving me the courage to write it. Be my Jack Donaghy forever. And thank you, Brita!!

Anne, thank you for everything—especially for managing to not kill me during edits. Thank you to the entire team at Amulet/Abrams, who have been exceptional at every turn. Alyssa Nassner, for the most gorgeous cover design ever. You made *my book*! Look like my book! Amanda Lanzone for that amazing illustration (Tourmaline's nails!). Caitlin Miller, Nicole Russo, Trish McNamara, and everyone else supporting me at Amulet . . . how many ways can I say thank you, because y'all deserve all of them. To their support staff—I may not know your names, but I know you exist and I appreciate all your work.

To Lee, thank you for the computer I needed to finish this book and the straight up truth telling you've given me along the way. I owe you so many drinks.

To LC, for Thursdays.

Renee, I thank God you're my friend, because you'd be a formidable enemy. Without you, there'd be no Virginia. Thank you for all the important things. Thank you for making it cool for me to learn in your wake. Thank you for reading my shit out loud.

To Ricki, for being the Johnny Cash to my Waylon Jennings and for sticking your fingers in the cake with me. (*drunkenly tips hat*) JJ, for always having the answers, receipts, and a spirit of generosity in sharing all of it. Thank you, Traci, Kerri, Henning, Emily, Nic, & Dhonielle for your texting and emails and reading and commiserating. Thank you, Jeff, for an incredible blurb; and everyone who has/will read and support the shit out of this book.

And listen—*thank you*, authors who have been incredibly kind to me on this long publishing journey, but it would be weird for me to name because you were just being goddamn decent human beings. Your niceness is so appreciated. I want to be you someday.

Thank you, Laura for being the T to my V. Thanks for letting me steal your *Yellow Wallpaper* English paper in college. And everything else.

To my family, for your stories past and future. Especially Mom, for teaching me to read, and Dad, for giving me a love for books.

Thank you to the WC Moms.

Dan and Mo Baker, thank you for reading through this and reassuring me I did right.

Holly, thank you for being so supportive and respectful, you are a dream mother-in-law, and I am so grateful for your role in my life.

To M, E & L—I would not be able to do this without you, even as much as you daily prevent me from getting any writing done.

And to J, for bringing me coffee, riding the ever-living fuck out of a Harley, and having a mind that's like an old curiosity shop where I never know what I'll find.

Finally, dear reader, it's you that brings the magic to being an author. It's because of you that T and V get to come alive. I will never forget that. Thank you.